THE TIGER AND THE DOVE
A TRILOGY

BOOK TWO

SOLOMON'S BRIDE

by
Rebecca Hazell

IM • PRESS

ACKNOWLEDGEMENTS

I would like to thank every historian, alive or deceased, who traced the culture and history of the Mongols, of Iran, and of the Frankish Crusades and Crusader States. I would like to thank Professor Michael J. Fuller of St. Louis Community College, USA, for giving me permission to use his photo of Masyaf Castle on the cover; Professors Trudy Sable, Ruth Whitehead, and Peter Conradi for their encouragement and advice; Jordan Stratford for his timely advice; my many manuscript readers; and my husband Mark, who tirelessly read and re-read my seemingly endless revisions.

ISBN-13: 978-1475289220

Book Cover Design by CreateSpace

DEDICATION

This trilogy is dedicated to Sakyong Mipham Rinpoche.

This novel is dedicated to my beloved children, Elisabeth and Stephan.

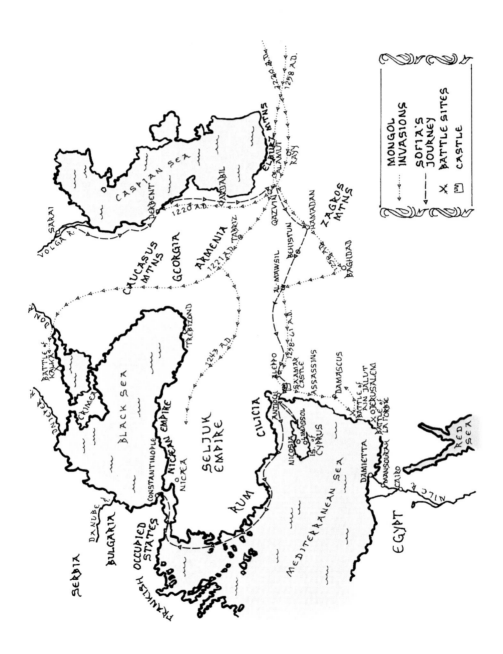

MONGOL
INVASIONS
SOFIA'S
JOURNEY
X BATTLE SITES
CASTLE

SERBIA
BULGARIA
DANUBE
FRANKISH OCCUPIED STATES
DNIEPER
BATTLE OF KALKA
DON
CRIMEA
BLACK SEA
CONSTANTINOPLE
NICAEA
NICEAN EMPIRE
RUM
SELJUK EMPIRE
CILICIA
NICOSIA
LIMASSOL
CYPRUS
ANTIOCH
ALEPPO
SAXAMAR CASTLE
ASSASSINS
DAMASCUS
BATTLE OF AIN JALUT
JERUSALEM
BATTLE OF LA FORBE
DAMIETTA
MANSOURAH
CAIRO
NILE
MEDITERRANEAN SEA
EGYPT
RED SEA

TREBIZOND
1243 A.D.
CAUCASUS MTNS
GEORGIA
ARMENIA
1221 A.D. TABRIZ
1220 A.D.
DERBENT
CASPIAN SEA
VOLGA R.
SARAI
ARDABIL
ELBURZ MTNS
2240 A.D.
1258 A.D.
RAYY
ALAMUT
QAZVIN
BEHISTUN
AL MAWSIL
1258 A.D.
HAMADAN
ZAGROS MTNS
BAGHDAD

"Our cause is a secret within a secret,
the secret of something that remains veiled,
a secret that only another secret can teach:
a secret of a secret that is veiled by a secret."
— *attributed to Ja'far al-Saddiq, sixth Ismai'li Imam*

"Nothing is true, everything is permitted."
— *attributed by his enemies to Hasan–i–Sabbah,
founder of the Nizari, "the Assassins"*

"If it is not possible to chew the stone,
it is necessary to kiss it."
— *old Turkish proverb*

WINTER
ANNO DOMINI 1242-1243

In light of what came later, I sometimes wondered if escaping Batu Khan was such a miracle after all, although it seemed so after that dangerous flight across an unknown wilderness. Thinking I was free from the Mongols forever, I felt such joy that I almost cried my thanks aloud. But how could mere words express my gratitude to this God-beyond-thought, my awe at the wondrous new world of possibilities that lay before me, my hopes for a speedy reunion with my uncle? Everything seemed to have fallen into place, from my having taken my fellow slave Anna with me to our having met up with our guides before they gave up and left without us. Without Anna, I would never have succeeded: it was her trust in me that drove me onward, and without her I'd have been lost forever in the wilderness, for it was she who could light a fire when I could not.

And now here we were, all the way to the Caspian Sea and among friends, or at least trustworthy guides.

How naïve I was. We were plunging into an alien world led by three strange men of a different faith! And I was a little taken aback when we stopped after only a few miles of travel. It was beside a stream flowing into the Caspian, so at first I thought that our guides wanted to water the horses and mules. But after briefly seeing to the animals, they proceeded to their real business: having washed their faces, hands, forearms and feet in icy water, spread out small carpets in the same direction, and placed some kind of packet at one end, they began to chant softly, each before his carpet, and to bow, kneel, prostrate, and touch his head on the packet three times. Anna and I stared in shock.

"Do they worship demons?" She was clutching her amulet tightly.

"No, I understand their words," I said after listening carefully. "They submit, offer thanks, and pray to our shared God."

"But it looks like they're worshiping demons or something."

I smiled. "It's just a different way of praying."

"Well, it's not Christian!"

"Hmm. But you are a Christian and you don't pray to demons when you rely on your amulet, do you?" Her eyes widened and she shook her head no.

Yet I too felt uneasy, for they had entered their world of worship and closed an invisible door behind them without a word to us. I could only assure myself that my good friend Selim al-Din, merchant and fellow-conspirator, had chosen them to take me into Persia and that I already slightly knew Nasr, who had brought Selim's map to me back in Batu's ordu. I had no choice but to trust them now, anyway.

The rest of the day passed mostly in silence, except for two more stops for prayers. I soon recovered my happy mood: a guardian angel was surely watching over us, for the Mongols had not found me! Of course my escape might have pricked Batu Khan's pride, and his warriors might still be searching for me, but he did have so many slave concubines that he might not even care if I disappeared. So when the sun lifted her veil of clouds, tinting the Caspian a deeper blue than the sky itself, my heart soared. I had always wanted to visit a real sea and there it was, vaster and more vivid than I had ever imagined, with waves rippling as gracefully as steppe grasses. Once when a bird glided past us and skimmed over the sea's sparkling surface, the fellow named Ali began a rather flowery poem. But Nasr quickly threw in a silly line that made Ali and me laugh. Our leader Da'ud, however, pointedly did not, and the boys quieted down straightaway.

That evening I studied them while they set up camp in the creeping gloom. Nasr and Ali were clearly bosom friends. Both were perhaps eighteen, dark-eyed and dark-haired. But while Ali's sad eyes and noble profile were beautiful, Nasr's single heavy slash of eyebrow, flat nose, and too-full lips made for mere homeliness. Da'ud was a mountain of a man. Only his gray hair and stern dignity betrayed his age. His nature was like a mountain, too, as I was soon to discover: his surface might change in sunlight or rain, but not his solid core. I was warming my hands at the fire when he sat down near me after their final prayers.

Looking into it, he said, "I am a man of few graces, Lady Sofia, so I speak bluntly. We obey Master Selim al-Din without question. I am your father on this journey, and I protect you with my life. But like all good fathers, I expect you and your servant to obey me without question."

Recalling Captain Oleg and my other lost companions, and how much harm I had caused by insisting on my superior status as his princess, I nodded. Nor could I reasonably take offense that he merely called me 'Lady' since I had not truly been a princess for years. Lady would be a good title for me now.

But when Da'ud would not look toward me, and I had to add, "Yes," my pride was pricked a bit, so I decided to seize the moment. "But may I ask you something?"

He did not look pleased, but he nodded.

"I am unfamiliar with your religion. Will you tell me about your way of praying?"

The question seemed to surprise him. "The Prophet, Allah's Peace upon him, taught us to rely on five great pillars of faith. One of them is to submit body and heart in prayer to Allah the All-Compassionate five times a day when we can. Today we also thanked Him for liberating you from those unclean idol-worshippers. You should offer prayers of gratitude to Him, too."

I tried not to heed the prick of judgment in Da'ud's voice, especially since I had been giving silent thanks all day, and thanked him politely.

"And I have more to say," he added sternly. "We will follow the Caspian shore for many days, since few merchants come this way; remote fishing hamlets do not interest them. But if we do meet anyone, your clothing masks you poorly. You two must behave more like boys and look less like women. In the morning you must wrap your—upper bodies—with lengths of cloth to make you look more boyish. And Master Selim says your servant must act as a mute, as she speaks no Farsi. Go tell her now." He rose and left.

Though I did not like his curtness, I did as I was bidden. Happily,

Anna was only too glad to agree when I explained that her disguise would protect us further. "I have nothing to say to infidel strangers, anyway," she shrugged dismissively.

"Well, speaking of differing faiths," I answered a little tartly, "we are in their world now. You can pray silently, but you must never cross yourself or touch your amulet or you will betray yourself. In fact I think I should tie it around your arm right now."

She gripped her amulet fearfully, but seeing my frown, she nodded. "If I must." And while I was tying it for her, "Mistress, why don't they pray the right way, like we do? They must be mad." I shrugged and said nothing; she was, after all, only thirteen at most and but a simple peasant. Then I had to laugh at myself. I was how old now—fifteen? Well, that made all the difference. I was a woman now, while she was still a girl, at least to me.

That night she and I huddled together for comfort in a small tent. At one point I started awake from a deep sleep. Anna was sitting up and coughing. She assured me it was nothing and I fell back to sleep, waking early the next morning to what I thought at first was the whistling of a Mongol arrow. I sat up, terrified, and realized it was only the wind shrilling through the tent ropes. A storm was blowing in from the sea, and by the time we broke camp, fat dark clouds were dumping sleet on us. But I was determined to believe in my happy fate, and surely bad weather was a blessing sent to cover any trace of our flight.

Over the next two days, we pushed south against rain, sleet, and fog. Once we had to ride inland to avoid a fishing village, but mostly we simply followed the shore so that our tracks would wash away. Our guides were courteous enough, but they clearly thought of us less as people than as valuable merchandise to be handled carefully and delivered in good condition. I think they knew no more how to act toward us than we did toward them. It was partly because we dressed as men. That was also why Nasr and Ali thought we were practicing taqqiya, which I later learned means to avoid religious persecution by dissembling in some way. Since I was somehow serving their cause, wearing men's attire was permitted.

Yet—I pieced all this together later—many Muslims welcome what they call martyrdom when they choose the time and place.

Over the next day or so, the men rarely talked with Anna and me, though Nasr was full of jests that Ali and I delighted in, but which Da'ud seemed to scorn and Anna could not understand. At night with the weather so bad, we ate quickly in silence before she and I curled up together in our tent and they went into theirs.

Her cough was no better, but she was as warming as a little fire. I often awoke during the night, partly from her coughing and partly from unease, and cradling her in my arms kept me from falling into some pit of anxiety. I must keep up my spirit in order to keep up hers. She deserved that.

We'd have maintained our rapid pace, but one morning Anna coughed so hard that she almost fell from her saddle. We reined in at once, the two boys awkwardly helped her off her horse and laid her on a saddle blanket on the ground, and I hastily wrapped her in my own cape. Her eyes were too bright and her skin too pale, and when I felt her forehead it was on fire. With none of my familiar remedies at hand, panic stole my very breath.

But Da'ud was already sending Nasr to find wormwood among the bracken and Ali to bring him water from a nearby stream. After giving me some more blankets and saying, "Put your cloak back on or you will freeze," he built a small fire and pulled his cooking pot out, as well as a piece of dried willow bark from a bag in his pack. When the boys returned with water and wormwood, he boiled the water and made a tea.

Meanwhile, all I could think to do was to chafe Anna's hands. At one point, I cried, "I should have seen … we should have stopped for you…"

"No, no, I didn't want to slow you down, Mistress. I thought I would get better. But now I hurt everywhere—oh, please don't let me die!" She burst into tears.

"You'll not die, Anna. I will take care of you," I said. But it took almost all my powers of command even to coax her into slowly drinking Da'ud's bitter brew. And in truth, I was afraid for us all.

Da'ud and the boys, meanwhile, had been standing apart and speaking in low tones. Now he came and knelt beside me. "Come aside; I must talk to you." He led me away from Anna and spoke softly, "There is a fishing village a little further on from here. I meant to pass it by, but your servant will die if we do not take shelter. I know someone there who will take us in. He is one of us. Nasr, if you permit him, can carry her before him while Ali takes her mule."

"Yes, please!" I could not hold back my tears. I turned away so no one would see.

We were soon on our way again, Anna so wrapped in blankets that only her face showed, her head bobbing against Nasr's chest. He had wrapped a white scarf around his nose and mouth, making him look like some ghost carrying her off into death. And having been without my cloak, even for that short time, I was chilled to my bones. After an endless struggle against walls of sleet, we finally came upon a huddle of tiny dwellings, a pile of fishing tackle that looked past redemption, and a few boats turned upside down on the shore.

Da'ud stopped at one of the hovels and pounded on its door; when it did not open at once, he beat on it again. Finally a man as worn and gray as old wood opened it. Scarcely raising his eyebrows, he motioned us into a small, dark, bare room. A fire in a round central hearth provided warmth and smoke in equal amounts; a few threadbare carpets on the dirt floor kept it from total desolation. Two boys sat together on one side of the fire mending fishing nets. A woman on the other side quickly drew a veil before her face. She looked far too old to be bearing children, yet a thin-cheeked baby pulled from her nipple to stare at us with hollow eyes. A girl of perhaps ten was spinning beside her, and a loom in one corner held a partly-finished carpet.

Da'ud spoke in an unfamiliar language, perhaps explaining our needs, for when Nasr set Anna down near the young-old mother, she signed to her daughter, who dropped her spindle and distaff and took the tiny burden from her mother. It began to cry feebly. Da'ud vanished outside with the boys, saying they would tend our animals. When I sat down beside Anna and began removing her dulband and cloak, the woman gently motioned me aside, felt my servant's forehead, and shook her head in dismay. After handing me a bowl of cold water and a worn rag for bathing Anna's face, she silently prepared a meager repast of hot water, flat bread, and dried salted fish. The girl stared at us and bounced the fretful baby.

When the men returned, Nasr and Ali brought in not only Da'ud's medicines but also, to my relief, some of our food; I'd have felt like a thief taking bread from the mouths of such poor people! While Da'ud sat near the fire and talked, the old man went back to mending his fishing net. It seemed to hold all his interest. Indeed none of these weather-beaten folk seemed to feel much curiosity. If the man now knew we were fleeing the Mongols, then I hoped he truly was "one of us" and could hold his tongue this well if they came looking for us.

We spent the rest of the day in semi-darkness and silence but for the nets rustling or fire crackling, or the baby crying. Though I kept bathing Anna's face and hands and feeding her the broth, she seemed on fire. I held her hand when she would let me. When dark came, the men set up a dividing curtain—so like the Mongols!—and those who could went to sleep. I stayed up with Anna, dozing in fits.

I awoke the next morning with a huge sneeze, feeling as if a cat had scratched my throat. But Anna needed me: she groaned and tossed endlessly, thrusting off the blankets crying she was too hot or wailing that she was freezing and wanting them back. The fisher family had gone back to their silent tasks as if we were not there. Da'ud and his boys came in and out but mostly sat staring at the fire. Only prayers and meals broke the tedium.

By nightfall Anna no longer knew who I was. When I tried to help, she pushed me away. Again and again she croaked, "No, no! Please stop! Let go! It hurts so!"

Another night passed. Anna thrashed about and wept, and I prayed. I began to cough, too. My throat felt as raw as if scraped by a file, while some invisible brute had crept inside my skull and was battering it with an iron bar. My whole body began to ache. When I tried to stand the next morning and nearly fell, I finally had to admit that I was ill, too. Da'ud and his boys started up in alarm. He spoke and the old-young mother came over, almost pushed me down next to Anna, felt my forehead, and gave me some willow and wormwood broth.

"Don't come near," I cried, "the fever might spread to you or your baby!" But she simply covered me with my camping blankets.

"Lady, you must rest," Da'ud ordered me. "Stop fighting her." I gave up and drifted off to sleep, but coughing fits kept waking me. By the next morning I was unable to rise, and by afternoon I had fallen into a nightmare that repeated itself endlessly: howling Mongol wolf-demons pursued me through icy rivers, between fiery piles of beheaded bodies, thrusting spears into my throat or beating my head with clubs while the cries of living corpses rang in my ears. I looked back and there was Batu Khan, a wolf grin on his face and fiery rage crackling in his eyes.

Once I thought I heard Da'ud say, "She is dead. There was nothing anyone could do. May All-Merciful Allah take her to his bosom and grant her eternal peace."

"Who died? Anna? The mother? Me?" I thought I spoke aloud, but no one answered and I sank back into painful dreams.

When I finally truly awoke, it still seemed to be dusk. Anna was sitting next to me, drinking a fishy smelling broth and looking wan and afraid, but when she saw me open my eyes, she smiled in delight. I was so happy to see her alive!

"Praise God," she said. "I thought you lost." And she burst into tears.

That seemed strange; I surely hadn't been asleep for long if it was still afternoon. Da'ud rose from beside the fire and came to my side, the usual looking ban forgotten in his joy. "Praise Allah's unfailing Mercy! Fever stole your mind for three days!"

"I thought it was still the same day," I croaked. I tried to sit up but could not. The mother appeared by my side, looking even older than I remembered, with a steaming bowl of fish broth. She helped me drink it. My throat still hurt, but I could swallow.

Anna said, "I was ill, too. I fell into a dark pit of dreams. Dogs were howling and trying to bite me, sure signs of bad luck and death. I awoke last night, and you were out of your head. Where are we, Mistress? And who are these people? I don't understand their speech."

"We're in a fishing village, and they are friends. You were very ill and they took care of you. I'm glad you're alive, too." I was too weary to say more.

Da'ud spoke from far away. "You both must rest now. You'll be better soon."

I fell back into uneasy dreams. The next morning, I awoke to sunshine and bitter cold—someone had opened the door—but I felt much better. Blinding bright snow blanketed the world outside, and the sky was brilliant blue. The door shut again and Da'ud was crouched next to me on one side, Anna on the other; the daughter was sweeping the room while her mother sat at the loom. The other men and the little boys were gone.

"How do you feel?" he asked. "Can you sit?"

"I think so. I feel much better," I smiled.

Anna helped me up, her face lit with joy. How thin she was! "I am so glad, Mistress! Here is some bread and tea. They help."

As I slowly ate, I looked around the room. "Where is the baby?"

"Da'ud said, "With Merciful Allah. She was already sickly, and she caught the fever."

"Dear God, we killed her baby!" Tears sprang to my eyes.

Da'ud spoke sternly. "Lady, we were only fulfilling the plans of Allah the All-seeing. Our fates are subject to His will. Death took the child quickly."

That was no comfort whatever.

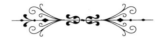

We left as soon as I was well enough. The snow was melting fast, and the sun stroked my cheeks gently as we took horse. I looked back at the village with regret. I had tried to offer sympathy to that poor woman, but she had seemed to bear her loss better than I did.

"She says Allah has taken others," Da'ud had told me. "She knows they all rest in His bosom, and she will see them in Paradise. They are happiest where they are now, for they had no time to commit sins."

Father Kliment had said the same thing back in Rus' when my Mama and baby brother had died. Perhaps it is true, for wherever I go, people say this life is a vale of tears and corrupted by sin. But something in me wanted to argue that it must be more.

Once away, Anna seemed to lift her head higher with with every step her horse took. "You seem to be feeling much better," I said.

"Yes, inside and out. I awoke from my fever with a strange woman beside me and you raving about wolves. And the baby was dead, so my evil dream had come true. You cannot know how lonely it is to be alone among strangers who don't share your speech."

I did know, but what was there to say? I just leaned over and pressed her hand.

Days passed; the sunshine hid behind a barricade of clouds; rain, sleet, and snow took turns pursuing us south. The restless sea seemed to thrust waves at us like grasping hands, while to our right another sort of sea, of endless dull marshy plains, was sinking into winter's bitter embrace. Now and then, just as on the escape from Batu's camp, we had to circle around boggy river mouths where reeds stood taller than our heads. But usually we stayed our course along the ever-changing shore: rocky or marshy or sandy, sometimes edged with spiny clumped grasses. A few times we skirted great stinking pools of a black liquid that sat on the water like pond scum. It smelled like the stuff Selim had sold to Argamon for his fire missiles. I saw no more settlements, for we avoided them. Only when we needed more supplies did one or two of the men go alone to barter for fish and bread.

An odd thing happened one night. I woke up and heard Nasr and Ali huddled together for more than warmth, or so it sounded to me. I had never dreamt of such a thing! I peeked out of my tent, but Da'ud's eyes were gleaming from the other side of the small campfire, and I shied back inside.

As we broke camp the next morning, I cast several sidelong glances at the two youths. Da'ud must have noticed, for when we stopped for prayers and a midday meal, he came up and spoke to me stiffly. "Last night: in Iran, men mostly live separate from women, a good thing for both. Manly friendship is natural and good, but acts of perversion are clearly forbidden by the Quran. Ali and Nasr are good Muslims—unlike certain Christian monks and soldiers, who do sin—and their close bond keeps their thoughts from straying to you two!" The boys looked over in alarm at this speech and shared a secret glance that only I caught. Between that and Da'ud hard tone, I felt both affronted and afraid, and I vowed to keep my ears and eyes shut tight at night.

As the steppes swelled into rolling, well-wooded hills, both my body and spirit slowly revived and I sometimes forgot to be afraid. For an entire day I could pretend we were merely on some wondrous journey of discovery: we might be edging along narrow cliffs where waves boiled into creamy foam below us or come upon a wide river rushing into the sea. If we were then forced to ride inland, sheltered under shady trees and serenaded by the river's song, to find a decaying bridge or shallow ford where we could cross, that was only part of a delightful adventure, nothing more. I ignored the grim watch Da'ud kept as we traveled, how he guarded my every move.

Perhaps I could do that because he also relented and allowed more speech among us. Ali always found an apt verse for the wonders we passed, which lightened any sense of possible trouble. He was also given to reciting parts of a wonderful epic poem, the Shanameh, which tells about great shahs and heroes of Persia's past. And Nasr often added some silly twist to Ali's elegant words that added to my delight.

Although this land was fertile and well-watered, there were surprisingly few settlements to avoid, especially inland. Sometimes I would glimpse a tiny walled village perched on a steep hill above us, but we never approached it. A necessary precaution, Da'ud said when I asked why we never stopped at any of them. "Once we would have had to take far greater care. Half the towns were bandit lairs—those and the caves hereabout. But few people live here now."

"Why is that?" I asked.

"The Mongols, years ago. They wanted no one at their backs when they attacked the infidel Georgians, so scouts destroyed every village they found and killed all the people."

I suddenly realized: this would have been part of the great sweep Noyan Subodai's armies had made around the Caspian, which led to the terrible battle at River Kalka where my grandfather and several uncles had died. From then on I saw that land in a new way—not just desolate but desolated.

One late afternoon soon after, we passed the remnants of a ravaged fishing village. Da'ud considered sheltering overnight inside its ruined walls, as the weather was wicked, but even the rain clouting our faces could not drive him to camp in that haunted place. A spirit of evil still clung to the charred remains, littered with skulls and bits of bone.

The hills that rose from the shore slowly gave way to a series of mountain ranges rearing ever higher above us: the craggy, snow-topped Caucasus. Back when Argamon had carried me to his war camp and I had first glimpsed them, I'd had no idea of their size. Now they felt like lines of monstrous jagged fists thrust up from the earth, threatening anyone who dared pass. They seemed much more threatening than the mountains leading into Hungary. I was glad we did not have to climb them.

For most of the journey, there had scarcely been a track to follow, but now we joined a clear path—it could not be called a road—linking a series of fishing villages. A few times we stopped in some isolated spot while Da'ud or Ali went off, returning later with a rolled-up carpet or a bag of salt or dried fish and a pleased look on his face.

One chill morning, the sun having finally come out and lit every tree and rock with glory, we stopped in a clearing well-hidden from the track. Ali was mounting his mule when Nasr asked if he might go instead. Da'ud sternly replied, "You are too childish. You would give us away. Water the other animals at the stream, and then fill our water bags."

Nasr said nothing, but he flushed bright red and his eyes grew bright with unshed tears. After his tasks were done, he sat sullenly at the edge of our clearing for the rest of the morning, as far from us as he could get. Da'ud, busy repairing a harness, ignored him, while Anna and I tended a small campfire.

Finally, when Da'ud had told Nasr to bring out a bag of dried meat for our midday meal and he dropped it in careless anger, almost spilling its contents, I whispered to him as he passed it to me, "If you behave thus, you give weight to Da'ud's judgment. Do not reveal every little feeling and he will respect you more!" He looked startled, angrily turned away, and stamped back to his self-inflicted exile.

But after most of the afternoon was gone, he came up to the fire, squatted down, and began warming his hands at it. "You are right, Lady. What have I done today but gotten a chill? I will remember your advice. I must live up to my great mission." And from then on, while he did not lose his laughing ways, he also took more command of himself, to Da'ud's clear approval.

We came to a wide road and began to cross paths with a few caravans, camel bells tinkling in the frosty air, the beasts' handlers walking indifferently beside them. A day or two later, Da'ud beckoned to me to ride beside him. "Soon we enter Derbent." A thrill passed over me, for it is an exceedingly ancient city, the very citadel that Alexander the Great had built to hold back Gog and his armies of Magog! We Rus' always called it the Iron Gate.

"It is my birthplace," he added. "For over two thousand years, it has been the gateway between Iran and the lands north of the Caucasus, for caravans—and for armies. It lies between a great mountain spur and the Caspian. A fortress guards it from above, and battlements reach into the sea to the north. It cannot be taken easily because there is fresh water inside its walls. Indeed, the citadel is invincible. Men have always fought over Derbent. By rights it was always Persian, but sometimes Georgian unbelievers held it, and sometimes renegade Muslim princes who cared only for their own gain!" He spat on the ground, and I silently begged

Mother Earth to forgive his insult.

"Years ago the Mongols seized Derbent. They wasted no time trying to take the citadel. Instead, they parleyed with the city's mayor and agreed not to destroy the city in exchange for tribute and ten expert mountain guides to lead them through Georgia and into Kipchak and Alan lands. But only nine returned—and it was only by the merciful will of Allah the All-Mighty that any were freed, given what happened to the tenth."

"What happened?"

"When the guides entered the Mongol camps, soldiers seized one man and beheaded him in front of all the others as a warning not to mislead their army. That man was my father. Because of him I made a vow …."

He fell silent and looked up at the sky before adding, "The brutes rarely bother with Derbent these days—too busy destroying the rest of northern Iran. At times the basqaq and his army appear and demand what he calls taxes, and then they vanish. There is no true rule, only the holy words of the Quran to guide us. If Infinite Allah smiles on us, there will be only a few Mongol soldiers in the city."

Mongol soldiers in Derbent? I was too shocked to ask him to say more.

After we had ridden awhile, each with our own thoughts, Da'ud spoke again. "Now, when we reach the city, follow my lead. Keep your eyes down and look humble, as if you are beaten often." I knew what he meant: some of my own servitors had looked that way. Indeed, Papa had once taken the head groom to task for beating a stable boy senseless. I had thought I was behaving like a lowly menial when escaping Batu Khan's camp, but when I tried it now, Da'ud said, "No! You look not at all humble. Stoop even more, as if not only your body but your heart is battered: like your servant. Yes, that is better. And when we arrive, do not speak or look up. If anyone still pursues you, your green eyes will betray you! Thank All-Merciful Allah that your brows are dark, at least. Now, go tell her."

I hastily obeyed. When Anna understood what she must do and why, her whole body went stiff with fright. For the rest of the afternoon I brooded, while the snowy mountains glowered down at us as if to say, 'We can crush you like bugs if we wish.'

The sun was lowering when Da'ud suddenly stopped. After a moment's thought, he drew us away from the road into a protected dell. "Ali, Nasr, we are almost in sight of the gate. I want you both to go ahead. Ali, you will be the master and Nasr will be your servant." Nasr grinned with delight, but Ali listened attentively. "Go find your best vest and put it on, and wind on a clean dulband. Nasr, take one of the mules and load most of the carpets and salt on it. Ali, you will ride the lady's horse. You are a young merchant coming from a small mountain village with wares collected from the nearby area. If you are asked for more, say your father is the village headman and you are hoping to meet up with a caravan to take you south. Feign eagerness to have a great adventure. If they want a name for the village, say that everyone in the area simply calls it the village.

"Once you get into the city, go to the first cross street and turn left out of sight of the city guards. Await us there—I don't want Lady Sofia to have to walk through the city farther than she needs to.

"Lady, you and your servant must also arrive in disguise. I will be your master and I will ride, but you must walk from here, as befits my servants. Can you lead the mules easily?" We both nodded yes, though if I looked like Anna, fear was proclaimed on my face for all to see. "There will be little for the mules to carry, but that is good—it fits in with my plan."

He looked us over after we had dismounted. "Yes, you will pass. But Lady, keep in mind what I said about looking humble!" As if I could forget!

After the boys were ready, Da'ud gave them time to get far ahead of us before we moved on. Though all this play acting seemed a little silly to me, the farther we went, the more uneasy I became. With sure danger ahead, my legs began threatening to go no farther. Just then we turned a bend in the road, and there they were: the famous Iron Gates of the city.

Da'ud grunted in surprise to see such a long line of people waiting to be admitted so late in the day. I glimpsed Ali and Nasr in the crowd ahead of us, Nasr looking dusty and weary. But Ali was seated grandly on my horse, his head held high, as if to say he knew he was gentry.

While we awaited our turn, I looked timidly around. The thick, iron-plated, spike-studded—but rusting—gates guarded an arched entrance. The even thicker city walls stretched away from the gates up to the mountain top to meet the citadel, and down past the town to join the sea and disappear into it far from land. It reminded me of some ancient crenellated serpent encrusted with battlements. Its indifferent, unyielding massiveness must surely cast dismay into any attacker's heart, especially with that great squat citadel brooding above everything. When we reached the gateway, I felt like I was entering jaws that might snap shut on me.

Anna and I followed Da'ud, trying to look as humble and boy-like as we could. I am certain our fear helped; she looked close to tears. I furtively touched my modest dulband to make sure it was in place. The city guards waved us past with little more than a glance at the coins Da'ud slipped into their palms, but I almost froze when I saw scowling Mongol soldiers standing behind them eyeing us with suspicion. They were Berke Khan's men: I saw his symbol engraved on the leader's pectoral disc. I had sometimes seen Berke with his brother Batu Khan, and I only recalled his one ruby earring, red boots, and a bejeweled green belt, all as filthy as they had once been fine. Now I remembered something more important: Batu had confirmed Berke's rule to the south, though how could it extend all the way to Derbent? The thought of being seized and brought back to Sarai made me tremble so much, I feared I would faint.

One of the guards thrust himself in Da'ud's path. A sentry, local from the looks of him, hurried up. What a change came over our leader: he suddenly seemed old and small and bent over with age—now he was the mountain in rain. He bowed respectfully, hands cupped, and we did the same. I tried to disappear behind Da'ud, my gaze on the ground, and Anna tried to disappear behind me. "I will translate for you," said the city guard. "He wants to know who you are and where you are from. Speak quickly; the brute has a nasty temper."

Da'ud's usual commanding voice came out sounding scratchy and terrified. "I come from here, sir. My master is a rich merchant, and my boys and I are but humble worms, returning to him almost empty-handed. He sent us north to trade for carpets and salt, but we turned back when we heard about the bandits. I fear his anger—"

"Bandits? What do you mean? The trade routes are safe!"

"We thought so, too. But at every village people barred their gates in terror until they made out who we were. They said that brigands come out of the hills again. All-Merciful Allah blessed us with good fortune, for we were not attacked—"

"Who? Kipchak? Alan? Georgian?"

Da'ud shrugged. "No one seemed to know, sir."

The Derbent guard, who barely knew Mongol speech, translated this as best he could. It was enough. The Mongol leader barked an order to one of his men, who hastened off to form a party to search for Da'ud's imaginary bandits, and then turned back to the guard, looking impatient. The fellow nodded dutifully and spoke again. "Did you hear about or cross paths with anyone heading south escorting a maiden with green eyes and red hair? Or she might be hidden in haram. She would be heavily guarded, but unless they are madmen, there would be fear in every move her guides make—no one with sense willingly crosses a Mongol." So my ger had not burned down, and Batu had gotten my insulting message. How utterly foolish I had been, a slave who had in word and deed thrown dung on the pride of a mighty khan: of course he would pursue me. Men had killed each other, even started wars for less. If I were caught, I would be tortured and killed, and I knew what fiendish delight the Mongols took in creating new tortures. It took all my willpower not to turn and run.

Da'ud answered humbly, "No, I heard of no one but bandits."

The guard relayed this to the soldier, who scowled, scratched his scarred chin, and said, "Well, it's a fool's battue we're on, anyway." Though I kept my gaze locked on the ground, I felt his eyes boring into my disguise as if he could sense that I understood his every word. "What is his master's name? Where does he live?"

The guard translated for Da'ud, who answered, "Musa ad-Din, lord, in the merchant's quarter, third from the end in the street of the carpet sellers."

"The old man better be telling the truth about these brigands. We have enough trouble already! If he lies, we know where to find him," the soldier growled. But he waved a dismissal to us.

The Derbent guard turned on Da'ud. "Well, get on with you!"

Da'ud hastily remounted and we left. When we were out of earshot, he gave a deep sigh and straightened up. "Thanks to Infinite Allah that I thought to bring you in without any guards at all! Accursed Mongol pigs—but that insults pigs!" And he laughed. "These last few days, we have given out that story of bandits to every village we passed. Everyone has a different notion of who the villains are. And since there are always a few brigands in the hills around here, those Mongol butchers can do some good for a change! My master will be glad. He tires of buying off every little band of robbers from here to Sarai."

Spreading stories: no wonder he and Ali had looked so pleased after every visit to a village. Selim must have smoothed our way with bribes, too—no wonder our passage was so easy! At least Batu Khan must never have learned about Anna, since they were looking only for one woman and perhaps a large party. How grateful I felt for Da'ud's foresight.

Though the Mongol soldiers' interest in finding me was clearly nil, I felt I should warn Da'ud about what the leader had really said. He shrugged. "Not to worry. Allah watches over you."

He led us to the nearest cross street, and there were Ali and Nasr watching people pass by as if they had no other purpose in life. We moved on together into the city, us women wedged between him and the boys. We dared not trade mounts for fear of bringing attention to ourselves, so Anna and I rode on the mules. The citadel loomed over us, a stone giant, while houses and streets clung to the steep mountainside like children afraid of falling into the sea.

The thoroughfare we followed was awash in half-frozen mud and jammed with men on foot or mounted on beasts of various types. I saw a few figures covered by long veils with only their eyes showing, all walking with guards; perhaps they were women. But there were no more Mongol soldiers, thank God. We wove past lines of camels and a few vendors' stalls, past tumble-down buildings and windowless walls broken here and there by closed gates or steep cross-streets. Much was newly built, though many shells of buildings remained. I saw a worn inscription in an unfamiliar language on one ruined wall and, to my surprise, a battered church—or so I thought at first, for it was shaped like one and crowned with a dome. But Arabic writing was carved over the entrance, and a tall, slender brick tower stood beside it, so I was not sure. The clean scent wafting from its doors was almost overcome by the reek of urine and rotting garbage.

We also passed starving cats, mangy dogs, and starving, mangy beggars rooting through refuse or crying out for alms—just like the refugees from Mongol-wrecked northern Rus' who had once fled to Kyiv.

The children broke my heart. At one point several crowded around Da'ud's horse, some half-blind or halt, and thrust up their scarred, pinched, closed-off faces at him, their hands outstretched—those who still had hands! A few even clung to his boots. Poor lost dregs of war and famine; I could so easily have been one of them. Had I had any money about my person, I might have given it all to them. Da'ud and his boys gave some coins to a few, but when the children went for Anna and me, calling to us and plucking at our garments with their bony, scabby hands, he turned on them with blows and curses. And I was torn between pity and gladness to get away, for now they frightened me.

We turned onto a narrow street and wound uphill along twisting alleys until we were in a part of the city that must have been destroyed and rebuilt for the wealthy, if the sturdy new walls and prosperous-looking men we passed were any clue. How inward-looking the buildings were, like guards lined up tightly side by side, backs to us. By the time we stopped before a double-gated building near the end of a steep alleyway, I was hopelessly turned around. Da'ud spoke in low tones to someone on the other side of the gate, it swung open, and we rode into a large square courtyard.

It was like stepping from a dreary purgatory into a piece of heaven. On two sides of the yard stood the main building, built almost into the mountainside; on a third, screened by a row of cypress trees, sat the stable; behind us, the fourth side was the thick, gated wall. An arched colonnade ran along the two sides of the main building, unlike anything I had ever seen before. In the middle of the yard was a stone-lined pool, and around it sat a geometrically laid-out garden containing a pair of young fruit trees wrapped like children to protect them from the cold. Benches stood here and there, clumps of snow resting on them like ghostly guests. The house walls were brick, banded in decorative rows of triangles, squares, herring-bones, and square crosses.

A large carved door opened, revealing a thin bearded man dressed in a long, fur-trimmed, quilted garment. Da'ud dismounted and greeted him with a deep salaam and respectful words. Selim had taught me that bow, which means "peace upon you." They spoke together in low tones while the rest of us dismounted and waited. Finally Da'ud waved Anna and me forward. "This is Lady Sofia, sir, and this is her servant Anna. This is Musa ad-Din."

The man was frowning. Looking at my feet as though they carried plague on them, he said, "Please, enter. My home is yours to command." He led us inside, to a lovely whitewashed room where brilliant carpets lay over the floor and on divans built out from the walls. Niches built into the walls here and there held pots or brass items. Musa ad-Din continued speaking to Da'ud as though Anna and I were not there.

"So you told them bandits are raiding along the northern route." He laughed without mirth. "Arrogant scavengers: far worse than bandits themselves, but they want no one rooting through their leavings." Da'ud nodded respectfully.

After an awkward silence with no invitation to sit, Musa ad-Din finally said to the air between Anna and me, "I was to host you for some days, young woman, but it is not to be. We never expected Berke Khan's troops to come to Derbent; they mostly keep to the plains to our north. We think Batu Khan asked his brother to send them after you. They have been here for days, questioning all the merchants coming from the north. In fact, before Master Selim al-Din even reached Derbent, they stopped his caravan and threatened him. You must be quite valuable to Batu Khan.

"Now you are in the territory of Baiju Khan, the swine's offal who crushes us under his thumb. For years he has done naught but spread more fear and hatred, which is good for our cause, at least. All-Merciful Allah blesses your journey with good fortune: with the Great Khan Ogedai dead and no successor yet named, there is much confusion. Someone called Kuyuk Khan, an enemy to Batu, is likely to succeed, they say, and he already claims all conquered territories as his. Berke cannot send his men further into Iran without offending this Kuyuk, but until you are far to the south your guides must be most careful how they proceed. As well, there are rumors that Baiju Khan will be replaced if this Kuyuk ascends as Great Khan, so that lends more uncertainty to our plans for you."

Da'ud asked, ducking his head meekly, "Meanwhile, sir, what should we do about the soldiers here in Derbent? It is unlikely, but they may come here looking for me and two boys."

"Well, if the soldiers did not look at the females closely, two fellows in my service could pass for them. But we must get them away quickly." They talked on and on. After our hard travel and that terrible fright at the gates, those glorious carpets seemed like a field of summer flowers to my weary eyes. How I longed to lie down on one and rest instead of listen to men plan my life for me. Finally our host summoned a servant and sent him off, not for refreshments but for someone else!

As the man disappeared, Musa ad-Din spoke to the air beside me in a stiff, formal way. "Until we know what to do, please consider my home as yours. We have prepared special lodging for you, and perhaps you would like to refresh yourselves and then rest."

"Yes, please," and I bowed politely, all the while fuming at the man's rudeness, so unlike Selim or even Da'ud! The servant reappeared, behind him a veiled woman who beckoned to us. As she led us away down a corridor, Musa ad-Din's voice trailed after us. He seemed not to know or care that we could hear him. "They're covered in filth! Could you not have cleaned them up somewhat? And this men's clothing is unnatural!" I had not thought about our appearance! Shame flared, followed by anger, for what choice did I have?

"Sir, please forgive me. All of us are travel-stained, but as to the clothing, our master himself ordered ..." Da'ud's voice faded as we turned one corner and then another onto a corridor leading to the back of the house. The maid opened a door into a delightfully warm, beautifully tiled room, where two more women smilingly took our hands and led us inside. As soon as the door was closed, they removed their veils to reveal no clothing but bright patterned payjamas. Before us lay a steaming pool; water ran into it after passing under a stove that also heated the room. Anna turned to me with eyes as round as an owl's, which made both women laugh. Quickly they set our bundles aside, stripped us of our soiled garb, thrust it all into the stove, and motioned us onto stools by the warm pool. One of them poured steamy water over each of us in turn while the other silently scrubbed us from head to toe with a fine, spicy-smelling soap. It brought back such sweet memories of my bathhouse at home. The heat felt so glorious, I could have stayed there forever—and we almost had to! Before they could get all the grime out of our skin, they needed to patiently wash and rinse us again and again. They even picked out the nits in our hair, which at least only reached our shoulders in ragged strands.

The veiled maid appeared with clean garments—men's again, so our host must have bowed to Selim's wishes. When we put them on, the women covered their mouths, half laughing and half horrified at our daring, but we had gotten over our own misgivings long ago. The maid then led us along the corridor to a carpeted, white-washed room furnished with divans, silken quilts, and a glowing brazier. And soon thereafter she brought us food, which she spread out on a clean cloth on the floor and described to me in Farsi: mutton brochettes, which she called kebabs; rice with raisins in it, which she called pulau; and mint tea. Musa ad-Din's home was a world I had thought entirely lost: of cleanliness, order, and beauty.

After she had cleared the meal, I sighed. "How wonderful it feels to be clean and well fed, not to mention warm—"

But to my surprise Anna intruded, "This is the lair of infidels, Mistress. Beware the trap of seeming goodness! Besides, we're locked in." She uttered a protective charm and crossed herself, looking at the windows with meaning.

It was true: there were decoratively twisted iron bars on them and the beautifully carved door was locked, but I only said, "Yes, we are locked in, but for our protection. We are entirely in these strangers' hands, yet they don't harm us. Instead, they feed and clothe and shelter us. Indeed, from from what our host said, we put him in danger. You must learn to accept the good in small moments, Anna. Let us simply enjoy Musa ad-Din's hospitality. You look as weary as I feel!" She unwillingly lay down on her pallet. I shut my eyes and remembered nothing more until one of the women wakened us the next morning with warm flat bread, dried fruit, and more tea. Neither Anna nor I had even turned over in our sleep.

We spent a dull day, though. At first we talked together about the next step of our journey, wondering what it would be like and how long it would take before we arrived, met Selim's master, and started our real journey. I regaled her with what stories I knew about Constantinople, trying to tread lightly on her Catholic prejudices just as my guide in the Mongol camps, Dorje, had once tread lightly with me about my Orthodox certainties. At least he knew what he was talking about; other than knowing it was occupied by Catholic Franks, I was merely guessing about Constantinople.

After the midday meal, Anna paced restlessly around the room, stopping to look out the window every once in a while as if something might have suddenly changed, and gustily sighing. I tried practicing peace for part of the morning, but Dorje's instructions were fading in my memory, and Anna's pacing was less than peaceful. Finally, weary of sitting, I too began to pace. We must have been a sight.

Musa ad-Din did not summon us back to his public room until that afternoon. Da'ud was there, too. Our host still seemed ill at ease. "I have found a way out of the city for you and your servant," he began after the barest exchange of civilities. "You can travel with a caravan leaving tomorrow that already has a guarantee of safe passage from the local basqaq." He laughed without humor. "Berke Khan's soldiers will never think to look for you there, since a bride for another basqaq will be among its passengers. A highborn Persian maiden marrying such a brute, another sign of these corrupt times—that and the way her father extorts taxes from us, his own people, and hands them over to our destroyers!"

Back in our room, we waited with nothing to do until late afternoon when, after politely thanking and bidding farewell to our dour host, we followed Da'ud back out of the maze of alleys to a small caravansary for

Muslims only—another sign, I believe, of how important I was to Selim. Da'ud took us upstairs to a noisy, crowded common room overlooking the street and close to the stinks and bawls of the animals penned up in the front courtyard. Well-dressed merchants passed along the gallery at the back where the rooms were surely quieter and more private. Inside our lodgings for the night, we met our new guide and protector, a bony, smiling petty merchant named Habib, who was missing a front tooth. His shyness with us reminded me of our peasants at home. But his bearing was friendlier than either Da'ud's or Musa ad-Din's.

"I am like your mother," he said, looking at my feet. "I vow on my father's grave to care for you as I would my own children." He turned searching, almost pleading eyes to Da'ud, who nodded with stern approval.

Before parting I thanked Da'ud for safely guiding us. "Will we meet again?" I had asked Selim that once, and Da'ud gave almost the same answer.

"If Merciful Allah wills it, yes. I would go with you myself, but I must stay here for a few more days in case those soldiers come looking for us. Two of Musa ad-din's boys will stand in for you. You will be safe with Habib. He is one of us. And my boys will be in your caravan, too, looking out for your well-being." Da'ud bowed and was gone.

Habib and his porters shared a meal with us, while other men came and went amidst chatter and laughter. We spoke little and looked at each other even less, but when his servants were finished and had moved away to play a game of backgammon with each other, I quietly pointed out to him that he must treat us more like males. From then on he stopped averting his gaze, although he blushed terribly at first and nearly made me laugh!

However, when he and his men went off to see to his animals, my unease returned. Every noise outside sounded unfamiliar and menacing. Once I thought I heard the tramp of Mongol soldiers' boots and grew faint with panic. But the sound faded, and after an eternity the men returned just as we heard the call to evening prayer. Habib whispered, "You must join us or be exposed as an infidel. Here, take these rugs and spread them next to mine. Here's a jug of water; you must wash before we pray."

Thus did both Anna I truly practice taqqiya that night. Although she could remain silent, I must not only prostrate but also try to behave like a true Muslim, all the time secretly praying that my clumsiness not be my undoing. At least I could wholeheartedly join in offering praise and thanks for our deliverance. At last it was over, and Habib gave us bedrolls to spread on the floor next to a wall while he and his men settled around us as a human fence. He had extra blankets, and our bundles became pillows. Anna and I both slept fitfully; I started awake at every sound, certain that Mongol guards were about to rush into the room and seize me.

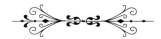

After prayers the next morning, we left through the southern wall, which was almost a mirror to the one in the north. My trust that I would fly to Constantinople like some escaped songbird had vanished with the realization that even hidden among some two hundred men and beasts, I would be surrounded by Mongol soldiers for most of my journey. Though Musa ad-Din was probably right in placing us there, I only felt danger. What if Anna ever forgot herself and spoke? What if either of us did something else to expose ourselves? And especially, how were we to maintain our deception as boys for days on end?

Fortunately, over the next few days I also realized that none of those fears would come to pass. First, a Muslim can be at home anywhere in Dar al-Islam, the community of Islam, so no one saw us as foreigners. And from the first day, whenever anyone asked me a question I wove a history for us from it, created thread by thread. Soon Habib began embroidering it with details of his own. He had already told his men that we were under his special care. They all thought we were orphaned Alan youths who had recently converted to Islam from Christianity and had escaped our uncle, who disapproved. Although our deception gave me an excuse if I made some foolish mistake, Habib took too much delight in adding silly details: in his story, our uncle became a bad man who had no use for us, while he had heroically helped us get away.

Also, at first I was uneasy prostrating and worshiping when I was not truly a Muslim. Anna needed only to go through the motions, but I had to repeat the prayers with faith in my voice. However, not only were they beautiful but also I could silently include my own devotions, just as I had done among the Mongols—my own taqqiya within taqqiya. Besides, I was praying to the same God. Anna, so fearful of infidels, was glad never to speak, and if she ever started to cross herself it actually fit in with our disguise. Our third problem, bodily matters, did present a challenge at first, but Habib quickly came up with some story to explain our peculiar modesty, for we were the objects of crude jokes whenever we disappeared together. I did not want to know what he told them, but it had something to do with the same kind of friendship that Nasr and Ali shared. I bore it as best I could, and Anna, speaking no Farsi, knew nothing.

Despite their jests, not only Habib's men but all our fellow travelers included Anna and me in endless generosity. No day passed without someone sharing something: a handful of walnuts or raisins or dates, or a pickled egg, or an item of clothing. At first it felt strange being unable to repay their kindness in some way, but when I said this to Habib, he only laughed. "We don't share expecting anything in return. Generosity is not a bargain; it must come from the heart or what good is it? It is a pillar of our faith."

With this answer I had be content. There was nothing I could do, anyway. I even thought of cutting some jewels from the lining of Papa's coat to buy goods to share, but how would I explain the cloak, much less such wealth? In the end it seemed better to leave things as they were and to be grateful.

I caught glimpses of Ali and Nasr from time to time. They never approached me, but it felt good to know they were there.

On that journey I learned much from my companions about Iran and its woes. The first surprise was that the Mongols had never left. Indeed, they occupy Iran to this day, and they are even more brutal there than they were in Rus' or Hungary. Had I known that, I might never have tried to escape from Batu Khan, so it was lucky that I had been in the dark. No one is safe. The noble landowners do their overlords' bidding—and earn their countrymen's hatred—but they can easily lose favor with their masters, who will seize their holdings and put them to death; merchants pay bribes and their caravans are mostly left alone, but some Mongol captain might still follow a whim and set his men on them; and towns and villages are totally helpless. A single lowly soldier can ride into a peasant village, strut into any home, rape some poor woman or girl, kill her and her family—indeed, kill everyone in the village if he wishes—take what he wants, and ride away, and no one will dare stop him.

It was whispered amongst my fellows that an unarmed Mongol soldier had once wanted to kill a man, so he ordered him to lie down and wait until he returned with his sword. Instead of running away, the man lay there until the soldier returned and beheaded him! I could hardly credit such a tale, but certainly everyone was terrified of the Mongols.

What a strange journey it was. Jostled between men and camels and donkeys and baggage, and burdened with fears for Anna and myself, at first I felt little interest in my surroundings. And because the bride's guards made a habit of strolling among us and poking into our baggage—and taking what they wanted—I kept my head down much of the time. I did learn to ride a camel with Anna perched behind me; I soon vowed never to make a long trip on one again. One camel in particular tried to spit at me every time it saw me!

We traveled south along the stormy shores of the Caspian until we could no longer avoid climbing into the snowy mountains. Often, trudging up some twisting mountain path just as I had in Hungary, breathing the cold, clean air and struck by the beauty of the huge snow-laden evergreen trees about me, I would be confronted with some fantastic stone outcrop—rounded and lumpish as if rock could get soft and melt. Once we passed a wide cleft in a mountainside where a strange red-gold light flickered deep inside. I nearly crossed myself, for surely demons dwelt there. But one of my companions just laughed at me when I fearfully pointed it out.

"No, inside that cave is a fire that never dies—all over Azerbaijan you can see flames endlessly rising from the ground. The Zoroastrian infidels think it a sign from God, so they worship fire and the sun. Idolaters!" He spat. "Most of them fled to India rather than convert to the True Faith."

Finally past the mountains, we descended into the great plain of Azerbaijan, stretching like a vast wrinkled carpet of dull yellow-green and blessed with a soft winter that has, alas, been its undoing. Once I was walking beside Habib. He looked around and said sadly, "You should have seen this land when I was young, before the invasions. No one could be poor in such a place, not only because of good soil but because it was so beautiful. Mongol armies have come here again and again—over twenty years of looting and killing—and now it is a wasteland. This is how they like it! Baiju's ordus spend each winter on these plains. Thank Merciful Allah we have not crossed paths with them!"

I agreed! Ironically, I understood why Mongols would like it here. Such rich grasslands are ideal for their herds. Alas, they are being claimed in the same way Chinggis Khan had thought to do in China—by destroying all settlements and converting the land to boundless pastures. After that day, Habib often pointed out where towns or villages or farms had once stood. Mongol blows lay on the land like festering wounds that would never heal. We passed so many fields of bleached bones, so many piles of rubble.

Another irony: he once commented that even before Mongol boot heels landed on them, those lands had seen centuries of wars between pagan and pagan, Muslim and Christian, even Muslim and Muslim!

"So many men fighting and killing each other," I mused, "only to die in their turn; so many people passing their mutual hatred down to their children. Can this never stop?"

He shrugged. "It is that way everywhere."

After a few days, we left Azerbaijan for more mountains and high valleys. Though we were sometimes delayed by snowstorms, we slowly made our way south, staying at caravansaries in what few towns were left: an endlessly gray, chill journey. Although we passed Mongol troops now and again, no one seemed to be looking for me and I dropped my guard a little and began to notice more.

I'd had no idea Iran was so immense and so beautiful. I remember one city, Ardabil, whose pitiful remains stood in a beautiful high mountain valley near a river. As was often the case, a handful of people had returned and were scratching out a livelihood among its ruins. Despite the destruction, I wished we could have stopped longer because the area boasts many hot springs. At last I could have bathed in one without punishment! We left the Persian bride at an ordu near there. I saw her led away weeping and prayed for her happiness, or at least for God to give her strength.

A few days south of Ardabil, our diminished caravan arrived at a half-destroyed city called Qazvin, passing a Mongol garrison with little trouble beyond some "taxes" and a few more choice items seized. The city might once have been as lovely as its setting, a plain near a river with two ranges of mountains in the distance, one to the west and one to the northeast. "Those are the Zagros and the Elburz ranges," Habib said when I asked him. He added, "Qazvin is exceedingly old, but it was mostly destroyed by some Mongol khans a generation ago. To this day the Mongols allow us no city walls. They killed almost everyone, but the city itself did not die." I knew who he meant: Subodai and some son of Chinggis Khan! This too would be part of their trail of ruin, which led all the way north to Kalka River where my grandfather had died so horribly.

Qazvin's walls were indeed missing, and much of the city scarcely deserved the name, being only clusters of half-wrecked villages and ruined fields. But around its hub where the central square and mosque and bazaar stand, many hands were busy at rebuilding. Of course these people were mostly newcomers. Nonetheless, something in me eased: Kyiv too may rise from its ashes.

After all the confusion of camels, mules, and merchants gathering themselves and their merchandise, and of good-byes and blessings and vows of eternal friendship from our companions, Habib led Anna and me toward the bazaar. Most of his men went on with the camels and many of the goods, but two followed us with a pair of mules laden with merchandise. Delicate flakes of snow were drifting down—such a contrast to the harsh storms of the steppes. We passed through some streets lined with ruins, but with so much rebuilding going on, the city felt much livelier and newer than Derbent.

And amazingly, a few fine buildings had even survived the Mongols' destructive frenzy. Habib pointed out some of them when we reached the inner city, all very foreign to my eyes. "Here is the Friday Mosque," he said, waving a hand toward a great temple with lovely pointed archways. "And there is the madrassa."

"What is a madrassa?"

"You don't know? It is a school for philosophy and the sciences," he answered proudly. "It is open to any man with a desire to learn." It was a huge square building set within a walled courtyard, with a cupola on the roof and beautiful decorative brickwork. When we went by the courtyard gates, I saw several young men robed in gray hovering around some long-bearded, black-clad sage, all of them looking most serious. A public place for study that still thrived despite decades of Mongol deviltry: how highly these Muslims valued learning. Well, we Rus' had had monasteries where one went to study. Were there monasteries here, too? Perhaps those would be set somewhere away from the distractions of city life.

We turned onto another thoroughfare. "Here is another mosque that contains the tomb of a famous traveler, I forget his name. The Mongols spared it because of its great beauty," Habib said. He also led us past the broken remains of a palace of some long-ago shah, as they call their emperors; this time it is I who cannot remember whose. There were so many shahs with names like Shapur and Khosrau. Iran is such an ancient land, and its history overflows with emperors like Cyrus and Darius and Xerxes whose empires stretched across much of Asia, and whose names anyone who has read Herodotus already knows.

We wound through the central bazaar, a place that utterly delighted me. It was so like home. Just as in Kyiv, it was half-indoors and half-outdoors, with little booths lining the alleys. Despite the bazaar's partly-wrecked state, I saw a wealth of goods: saddles and fine swords, carpets, jewelry and brass items, precious stones, bright turquoise or golden brown ceramics, spices, winter vegetables, and meat animals. And as at home, men called out the merits of their goods, customers jostled one other, boys played chase among the booths, and stray dogs ran underfoot.

Finally we stopped at a booth, and while Habib delivered his goods to its merchant, Anna and I wandered over to listen to a man dressed in a ragged striped robe and equally ragged dulband. He was singing a peculiar lament about a nightingale longing for a rose, but the flowery phrases somehow felt incomplete. After Habib was done, he ambled over to speak with the fellow in low tones. Had I not been close to them, I might have missed him stealthily exchanging a gold piece for a small leather-wrapped packet.

"Who was that?" I asked him as we left the bazaar.

Habib gave me a sharp look. "A mendicant whose holy songs carry both outer and inner meanings. Those with ears to hear can understand both. He is one of our brethren." I made to ask more questions, but Habib raised both hands. "That is all you need to know."

Having been a secretary for Batu Khan and worked out his war codes for myself, I felt a little insulted. I was not some dumb creature that could understand nothing. But I held my tongue. Soon I could ask Selim to explain all these sly hints about brethren, causes, missions!

Now we followed another series of narrow streets, confined by recently built blank walls and broken only by heavy gates. Trenches ran down the centers of many streets, carrying water and sometimes waste. The buildings thinned out, and large compounds began to appear, sometimes enclosing open fields and newly planted orchards. We came to one that stood close to the city's southeastern edge. Habib greeted the guards at the gate, and they let us into a huge, busy courtyard with a stable and storerooms and other outbuildings, a stone-edged well, and a small, enclosed orchard of young trees. Several camels sat along one wall while men heaped bundles on their backs. There were Nasr and Ali, smiling and nodding at the air near us as we came farther in.

And then, to my great joy, up hastened my old friend Selim al-Din! We kept up our pretense, salaaming to each other and pronouncing the greeting of peace. Selim thanked Habib extravagantly and offered him a jingling bag, probably containing some coins. After the usual refusals and insistences, Habib accepted it; I noticed that small packet changing hands at the same time.

I too thanked our guide as we bade farewell. "It was nothing." Habib smiled, closing his eyes and pressing his hand over his heart. "I enjoyed our journey. I pray that one day you will submit to the one true religion in more than outward form." With another bow he was gone. I shrugged inwardly and turned eagerly to Selim.

"Please come this way," said my old friend, waving us toward an arched gateway that led into an inner walled compound. An armed guard bowed and opened it for us. On the other side lay not one but two inner court-yards. Before us a geometrical garden lay like a magical carpet leading to a newly built, colonnaded, two-storied house with elaborate brick trim running along its upper façade. It looked south, with an outdoor staircase that led to a flat roof. Musa ad-Din's yard now seemed a pallid reflection of this perfection! And in the next courtyard, bounded by the farther wall, I saw the tops of trees and another group of buildings, including a house that seemed almost a twin to the one that sat in this yard. Selim might serve a master, but he was clearly a wealthy man.

"Oh, it's all so lovely," I cried.

"Welcome to my unworthy home." His delight belied his words.

"Why, Selim, it's perfect! I never saw anything like it: at home we mostly just grew vegetables, and our country palace was never carefully arranged like this."

As he led us across the garden, Selim spoke what he truly felt. "Did I not once tell you that our gardens would melt the heart of a stone? They remind us of the glories of the Hereafter that await the faithful. Of course, in spring it is at its best, if such a humble one as I can speak its praises. I love it only less than my wife and children." Another surprise: Selim was a husband and father. We passed a long, narrow pond, pale with a thin mantle of ice, and a bench that overlooked it. "A reflecting pool," said Selim as we passed. "Very calming and cooling on hot summer days."

"I never heard of such a thing before." All we'd had at home was a weedy duck pond. I suddenly felt like some ignorant country peasant. Indeed, my Papa's entire country palace shrank into nothing beside this glorious property. Even his city palace was never this beautifully laid out. Around the pool were straight paths that crossed one another and led to every corner of the garden. If you were a bird and flew over it, you would see that the paths formed a great six-armed star. Within the spaces they made were flowerbeds, cedars, poplars, and fruit trees—all lovingly protected against cold—and stone benches placed about in the most inviting way. Even lightly veiled in snow, it was both beautiful and serene.

Nonetheless its glories could not distract me from my many questions, although when I started to ask Selim about his journey home, he put his finger to his lips and ushered us toward the house. We reached the shelter of the colonnade. Another armed guard warming his hands at a glowing brazier bowed respectfully and opened a richly carved wooden door with a pointed arch. Around the door, the wall was adorned with a border of turquoise tiles painted in a pattern of flowers and birds. We passed a large room on the left that resembled the public room in Musa ad-Din's home. But instead of leading us into it, Selim took us along a hall that opened to our right, through another door, and straight out of the house! A short walled passageway open to the sky led us to another guarded gate, which opened to reveal the other large house—and yet another guard!

"My own design," Selim announced with pride. We followed him along a gravel path, passing another lovely garden. A guard opened a door surrounded by the same lovely tile work, and we went inside and up a flight of stairs, past windows with small panes of glass that were shielded by half-open, lacy-looking beaded shutters. Real glass: this alone proclaimed Selim's wealth! I glanced through them and got a hazy view of the garden from above, which was a mirror to the first one, though smaller.

It felt as if we had wandered into a world of secrets nesting one inside another, like a story my Baba Liubyna had once told me about a great hollow golden statue of the Mother Goddess worshipped by certain tribes of the northernmost forestlands, far past the bounds of Rus'. Another, smaller golden Mother Goddess sat inside her, and inside it sat another, and another, and another.

At the top of the stairs, we turned at a landing; to our right another glass-paned window revealed distant mountain peaks made hazy both by the thick glass and the falling snow, and before us stood a beautifully carved door. Selim opened it and with a flourish motioned us into a large room whose floor was entirely covered with overlapping carpets. Divans were built against the walls, also covered with carpets, various boxes and vases rested inside arched niches set into the walls, and brilliant silken pillows and bolsters were scattered on bench and floor. A few low tables sat here and there, some carved and inlaid with mother-of-pearl, others of bright glazed ceramic. A pear-shaped stringed musical instrument leaning against the wall reminded me a little of one of our kobzas in Rus'. Although a round, low-walled hearth sat in the center of the floor and several glowing braziers stood in its corners, the room was barely warm. Two birds sat in a cage near a brazier, golden trills pouring from their throats. The room smelled of musk, roses, and of beeswax from tapers burning in tall candelabra set about the room.

A handsome, wide-hipped older woman and five other females, ranging in age from perhaps twenty down to ten, had been sitting on divan or floor engaged in various tasks, but they jumped up. All but the youngest girl hastily pulled their short, colorful veils over the embroidered caps on their heads, drawing them close over their faces and leaving only their dark eyes showing. Before the eldest girl drew her veil, she tossed back her elaborately plaited hair, which was secured with golden baubles. A pair of little boys, perhaps four and five years old, jumped up with cries of joy and eagerly ran to Selim. The younger of them had fair hair, the elder's was dark. Just as I had often done with Papa, they stopped short of throwing themselves on him and merely kissed his outstretched hands, the eldest boy first. Then the women all did the same, first the eldest and on down to the youngest.

"I am honored to present you to those of my family who are home— my grown sons are away at present," Selim said to me. He smiled at the older woman. "Please welcome our long-awaited guest, Lady Sofia, and her companion, Anna."

To me he said, "This is my youngest son, Akbar," he gestured to the boy with light hair, "and this is my grandson, Ali. Please meet my wife, Layla, and my two daughters-in-law: Effat is wife of my eldest son and mother of Ali, and Perijam is wife of my next eldest. And these are my daughters: Banu, Aftab, and Sarah." His love for them all lit his face.

The women released their veils, and we all bowed to each other rather awkwardly. Not knowing whether it was proper, I salaamed, which made the youngest girls laugh timidly. But Layla only smiled slightly. My heart sank, for how could she welcome us if I had caused her husband trouble with the Mongols?

Yet her greetings were warm and graceful. "Welcome to our home, pitiful though it is." And she seemed to mean it. The Persians are the politest people on earth, I think. Selim's courtesies had struck me as absurdly flowery when I first met him in the Mongol camps; but on my journey to Qazvin, I had learned that this was the Persian way, not some attempt to mock me. "Please use our home as your own. We are your slaves," she added. Of course, just like Selim. Layla meant it only as a pleasant greeting; but having just escaped real slavery, it carried a certain irony for me.

"Please accept my deepest gratitude. You graciously make me welcome when you have every reason to dislike me," I answered in kind. She smiled a little more fully. Selim, meanwhile, was hovering at the center of the group like a mother hen. I turned to him.

"Please forgive all the trouble I brought on you. It is entirely my fault."

"Taking on more blame, are you? Well, you may atone for whatever you think you did by getting to know my family, especially Perijam, who I think is your age. She will teach you our ways while you are our guest. Oh, and your servant, too, if you wish."

I translated for Anna. It had been so long since she had spoken aloud that she almost croaked like a jackdaw. "Only if you wish, Lady, for my trust is in you, not in any of these accursed unbelievers." Luckily, we spoke Hungarian, or she'd have caused deep offense—and after all the kindness we had received from our fellow travelers, too!

"Anna, it's important to know how to conduct ourselves properly in Iran. It's lucky they don't understand you." She looked so chastened that

I added, "You and I will learn together."

A veiled maidservant appeared with refreshments, and we sat down on benches or cushions, all a little shy and uneasy except for the boys. They sat proudly at Selim's feet.

"And how was your journey? Your disguise once would have seemed strange to me, but in these terrible times we must all do what we can to survive," Layla began.

"Yes, I look forward to a time when such pretenses are no longer needed. And as it turns out, it was necessary in Derbent—"

"Here, have some dried apricots," Selim broke in, waving the serving woman toward me. I looked at my old friend in surprise; it was unlike him to interrupt. He gave me a queer look and shook his head slightly. "—but otherwise nothing happened of note, other than learning to ride a camel," I finished, trying to imagine why he did not want me to say more. "If I ever travel in a caravan again, I hope to travel as a woman and be allowed to ride in a howdah. It looks much more comfortable to me." The youngest girls smiled.

After a little more stiffly polite conversation, Layla said, "You must be weary after your long journey. Would you care to wash away the dust of travel and then perhaps rest?"

"Yes, please. I fear we have carried said dust into your beautiful home."

Layla turned to Perijam. "Daughter, will you see to our guests? The young woman nodded graciously and led Anna and me away. She was quite a beauty, with a plump waistline that made her resemble a little pigeon, huge brown eyes, full lips, and abundant dark curly hair that she wore pulled severely back, although little mischievous curls had escaped around her face in a most charming fashion. She was much like her hair when I think on it now. When we met she had been married only a year and was trying her utmost to be a proper matron, but at heart she was still full of childlike fun.

She first took us downstairs to a room where maidservants were already heating water. Once again we were treated to a wonderful bath—another sign of Selim's wealth, I was to discover later, for most people go to public baths. In Iran everyone bathes, a custom I still wholeheartedly approve, having gone for three years among the Mongols without one. I must add that Muslims seek not only outer cleanliness but purity of heart before

God. I admire that.

And how good it felt to put off rough payjamas and don soft women's attire, all of silk. My gown was deep yellow, patterned with red birds and vines. A fitted quilted robe went over it, of rich peacock-colored samite shot through with silver threads. At first we had all been a little shy with each other; but by the time Anna and I were dressed, that had passed, at least for Perijam and me. The servants having removed every single nit from our hair, she herself trimmed our wild manes into something resembling women's styles, though Anna was loath to be touched by an infidel until I sharply insisted. Last, Perijam gave us little silk caps and veils that harmonized with our robes—mine was of shimmering turquoise—before leading us back upstairs and through the main room where Selim, surrounded by family, paused mid-sentence and smiled at us in admiration.

One of the girls exclaimed, "Why, they're so beautiful," before Layla hushed her.

"Father Selim cares for us all so well," Perijam said after we had left the family behind. She was leading us along a corridor and opening a door to two small, beautifully appointed adjoining rooms; other doors lay farther along. "He built this entire house for our andarun and made it almost as large as the biruni—oh, you don't know? The biruni is just for men except for nights with our husbands. We rarely sleep in our rooms in the winter, but we thought you might like to have your own rooms since you are … our guests." She blushed and smiled and turned away to light some tapers in a candle stand, making me wonder what she had truly meant to say. "There is your baggage in the corner, and you can store things over here." She pointed to a finely inlaid chest near my divan.

Perijam led us into the second room. "For your servant."

Anna had never had her own room and was not certain she wanted it. "It's so big," she cried, clutching my arm. "Can't I stay with you?" Ironically, having a room alone after life in a crowded Mongol ger seemed heavenly to me. Only when I assured her I wasn't leaving would she release her grip and even enter hers to timidly explore it.

Meanwhile, Perijam lingered on in my room, and the more we talked, the friendlier we became. Indeed, she took my hand and held it in the most natural way as though we had been bosom friends all our lives. "I am glad Father Selim wishes us to become friends and for me to teach you our ways," she said at one point. "You already speak Farsi so well, though!

How did you learn it and where?"

"From Selim. We studied Mongol speech together."

"Oh yes, you were a slave in the Mongol camps! And after he bought you, Father Selim sent you to Derbent because you could not come with him right away; he had other business to attend to. But he told us he did not buy you for himself but to set you free. Another example of his great kindness."

I was rendered almost speechless. "Yes, something like that," was all I could muster. "And when might I be allowed to speak with your father-in-law again, to thank him for his generosity?"

"I cannot say. I think, with you safely here, he has left to see to business. It takes him from us so often that we are happy when he can be here. He is very kind to me, a pitiful and useless daughter-in-law." She flushed prettily.

I had to smile, but this seemed to be the Persian way. "Well, surely he will be back tonight. And what is your husband like? Where is he, if I may ask?"

"Kerim is my second cousin, and he too is very kind to me. I hope by next spring to reward his kindness with a son," she beamed, placing a hand on her belly. "I will tell him when he returns from his latest trading mission. He and his older brother Umar—Effat's husband—have gone west, all the way to the lands held by infidels. He is very brave, for he must cross over mountains and deserts and fight off bandits as well as nonbelievers. I pray every day for his safe return, and I know that Allah is always merciful. Meanwhile, though, I protect his unborn child with these," and she pointed to the many charms and beads she wore on cords around her neck. She touched one that was shaped like a hand but decorated with swirls and lacy shapes. "This one is my favorite: the hand of Fatima, the Prophet Mohammed's daughter and queen of blessings. She makes me feel so safe."

My amulets had failed to protect me, but I held my tongue; she would likely say that hers would, as they were Islamic. "Your husband sounds very brave indeed. Is he your age? What does he look like?"

"Oh, Kerim is not much older than I am: only twenty-six years to my fifteen. And he is very handsome. But you will see for yourself when he comes home next year."

"Oh, will I be here that long?"

I must have betrayed disappointment, for she looked at me queerly. "I think Father Selim does plan to take you somewhere next spring." Next spring? I had hoped to leave much sooner than that, right after meeting his "master"! But since winter was setting in fast, that must explain the wait. At least Selim was already planning my journey home. I would probably join one of his sons' caravans, reach Constantinople by next summer, and leave my bad memories behind forever, a cheering prospect after the shock of plunging so deep into Mongol-held territory.

Perijam took her leave, saying she would come for us when the evening meal was ready. "Meantime, you and your silent servant may rest." She squeezed my hand and left, softly closing the door behind her.

"What did she say?" asked Anna, who had crept back into the room and was standing forlornly by the connecting door. "She seems very friendly." But she did not look or sound at all pleased.

"She says to rest and she'll come for us when it's time to eat. You go lie down in your room and enjoy being safe. I'll be right here, doing the same." Anna sighed and stumped off.

I opened the window's inner shutters and stared out at the snowy garden. Although I could open the glass-paned window inward, iron bars stood outside it. Even fashioned into ornate twists and elegant curves, they could not be mistaken for anything else. Only for protection, I assured myself as I closed the window and settled onto my divan. After piling on several thick silk quilts, I dozed off planning the thanks and apologies I would shower on Selim when I finally saw him alone. And the questions I would ask.

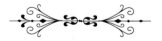

Selim was not there for the evening meal, though Layla and the girls politely hosted us. The food was abundant and delicious: a pulau with lamb, rice, carrots, almonds, and spices. Oddly, though, while we were served the same food, it came from different platters. It felt strange to be with a real family again—at first I had an impulse to serve the boys as I had once served my Mongol master, Argamon, but a maid tended us all. Anna clearly felt overwhelmed. But after our first courteous exchanges, we ate in shy silence. Afterwards I praised Selim's beautiful home and garden, which drew forth more open replies.

"He is so proud of his new houses and his gardens, though he is unable to spend much time here," said Layla. "We lost everything after the first Mongol invasion, but we were lucky and escaped far into the mountains before they reached us. When we returned after they had moved on, the destruction was past belief! Almost all our relatives and loved ones missing; we never heard from them again.

"Many lost heart, but my husband turned hardship into opportunity. We fear and hate them, but the Mongols bring us our great prosperity: he uses their blind greed against them." Once I had scolded Selim for doing that very thing, but now I understood.

"And will he return tonight?"

"Perhaps," Layla answered, but there was no promise in her voice and possibly a hint of displeasure. "He often leaves with no warning, and we never know if it will be for days or months. He tells us only what we need to know. As he puts it, his is the public world where men must struggle against each other to survive and protect what is theirs. But ours is the inner world of haram, a sacred space where strife is forbidden entry, where peace and beauty can reign freely. And he says we are safer if we know nothing about what he does in case he is ever discovered. Although he doesn't say it, I think he means discovered by the Mongols, for doubtless when he visits them, he spies out their weaknesses and uses them to his benefit. But I am only guessing. And best so, for then we have neither lies to tell nor slips of the tongue to fear."

I couldn't understand why Selim would fear discovery. Long ago I had warned him that the Mongols knew he was a spy, and they had never harmed him; so why would any Mongol in Qazvin care? And this sudden departure: was the packet that Habib had slipped to him connected to it? And why his wife's hesitant manner with me? And what did she mean by months? Surely he would return tomorrow!

The next day dawned cold and clear, the muezzin from a nearby mosque calling me to waken and pray. Although I did offer deepest thanks, I lay warmly abed since the braziers had gone out in the night. I finally stretched luxuriously under my quilts and hit something heavy. Anna had crept back into my room and was sleeping in a pitiful huddle at my feet.

"Anna, you're half-frozen! Why didn't you stay warm under your covers or at least bring your mattress and quilts in here with you?"

She hung her head. "I don't know, Mistress. I—I just was lonely and afraid. I didn't think about covers when I came in. Then I was afraid to go back."

I had to pity her. "You may sleep in here, then. But I do want some time alone."

Tears welled up in her eyes. "You wish me away. I am sorry."

What was the matter with the girl? "Anna, listen. I care deeply about you. But before Argamon enslaved me, I had so much time alone to feel the heartbeat of the world. I learned not to miss that when I was his slave, but I'm free now and I want back some of what I lost. Can you see what I am saying?" Anna wiped away her tears and nodded, but I could see she did not.

Perijam escorted us back to the common room where we all enjoyed a breakfast of dried apricots, figs, goat cheese, tasty—and clean—flat bread, and sweet mint tea. Everyone felt more at ease, and Perijam and I chattered away with each other about little nothings. I glanced over at Anna once and saw her glaring sideways at my new friend.

At one point a maidservant entered and whispered to Layla, who turned to me, her face a mask. "Noor brings word from my husband. He is eager to come home. Tonight," she added in a strained voice that communicated alarm to me without there being any reason I could see. I was just glad to know I had been right.

After breakfast, Perijam invited me to sit by her. "In good weather we mostly live outdoors, but winters we spend here in the main room where it is easy for Mother Layla to direct the household. We even sleep here. You will like it."

"Oh? Why does she not go about her house and see to tasks directly?"

Perijam looked surprised and almost affronted by my question. "Is it not that way everywhere? Why would a queen bee leave her hive?"

"Why indeed?" I smiled, realizing that I must be more cautious with my questions.

I looked around the room. The two youngest girls, Aftab and Sarah, had settled behind the boys in one corner, where the woman named Effat began to give them all lessons. I had never seen anything like it before. She would copy something from a book onto a board with a handle and then hold the board upright for the children to see. The sisters took turns reading aloud from it while the boys tried to do the same. I recognized the language as Arabic; it sounded like a sermon or discourse from a holy book. Then she would wipe off the words and write another phrase, and so forth.

The other women set to work. Banu, the girl with ornamented braids, helped Layla card wool for spinning, while Perijam took out a basket containing rolled silk threads and a half-finished garment. At least I understood those activities. How content everyone seemed. Such love seemed to fill the room that I could almost touch it. Heady gladness to be there rushed over me. Here I was finally safe!

"I can help you, Perijam, if you like," I offered. "I sew a neat seam." Layla looked over in surprise and then smiled her approval. "And if you show me the stitches you use," I pointed at her embroidery, "I can help with that, too." Perijam nodded eagerly. I suddenly realized that Anna was hovering at my elbow, looking lost. "But we must give Anna something to do as well. Mother Layla—may I call you that? Could Anna help you?" She assented to both questions and motioned to Anna to join her.

"Go help her card wool, Anna. And don't be so gloomy," I said in Hungarian. "These women are our friends. You're safe here." Anna looked disbelieving.

"What is the matter?"

"I just don't like it here. I liked it better when we were running away and you held me and talked with me alone. I don't like how Perijam takes your hand and holds it."

"Oh, Anna, that's just a polite custom here. Listen. Since we met, when have I not cared for you? Do you think I would desert you now? You must accept these women's hospitality with grace, or they'll be hurt. Now, go help Mother Layla. You seem to be about the same age as Banu, so perhaps you can become friends." Scowling deeply, Anna dragged her feet across the room as if going to her execution. Layla looked a little surprised but wordlessly handed her an extra set of carding combs and a hunk of wool. I smiled encouragingly, and Anna sighed and set to work. She was actually much better at carding wool than I had ever been and seemed to settle into her task. I sighed a little with relief and turned to my own work. Sewing was such a pleasant occupation.

Indeed, I felt so glad to be there that it was easy to enter into the morning's quiet rhythm. Lessons over, the boys played with one another or wandered about, always finding a friendly lap and a kiss on the cheek. They even adopted me, as they would have Anna had she given any hint of welcome. Noor came and went with Layla's orders about various household activities. I truly did not understand this way of managing a household, since how did Layla know that her servants obeyed her? But I dared not ask.

Now that she was free, Effat performed for us on that kobza-like instrument while Perijam sang and sewed. Effat called it al'oud, the oud; years later among the Franks, I heard it called a lute. Once the carding was done, Layla turned to spinning. She used a device I had never seen before: the distaff was embedded in an attached board, while a foot treadle turned a spindle. What a miracle: it spun the finest thread I had ever seen. Again I felt more like a peasant than a former princess.

After a whole morning of sitting, though, my body grew stiff. "Mother Layla, may Anna and I walk in the garden, perhaps with Perijam?" I asked.

Perijam seemed startled, but Layla merely stopped spinning for a moment and said, "I will have Aftab arrange it. Go, my little flower, and tell Noor to send away any guards who might disturb us in our garden." Aftab hopped up and left the room.

"Oh, dear, I do not want to put you to trouble. I can walk around the room."

"No trouble at all. We should take walks more often. In winter I often get lazy. Indeed, I think a turn around the garden will suit all of us." So instead of the brisk walk I had wanted, I was forced to move at the stately pace of a Persian matron, and not in Selim's large garden but in the smaller one in back. When I asked about it, Perijam explained that his garden was part of the biruni and was for men, so women rarely went there and then only heavily veiled. All the girls seemed glad for the change of air, although they were ready to return indoors far too soon. They said it was too cold. I bit my tongue. Compared with the stormy steppes, it was scarcely cold at all.

For the rest of the afternoon, we worked and ate or, whenever the muezzin's call sounded, stopped and prayed. Anna and I sat to one side, free to pray in our own way if we wished. Alas that when she no longer needed to conceal her feelings, she made her aversion to their customs plain. She turned her back on them and prayed aloud. "Lord God, I beg you to free Mistress and me from all infidel wickedness." I had to stop my own prayers and order her to pray silently.

As the day grew to a close, I began to await Selim's arrival with increasing eagerness, but he did not appear until after the evening meal. His wife and family stood and kissed his hands as before, after which he greeted us with a smile. "You and your Anna are transformed, Sofia. Lovely. I know you must wonder what happened to me, and we have so many questions for each other. Once I eat, I will speak with you." Courtesy demanded that I submit graciously, but had it not been for another peculiar look from Layla I might have hidden my impatience less well, for it suddenly came to me: she thought Selim had brought me there as his concubine! She had been so carefully hospitable that I had not understood that her reserve came from jealousy. I must find a way to reassure her.

The meal over at last, Selim stood up and said, "Come, Sofia, let us talk."

I caught sight of Anna's stricken face as I rose. "Selim, may Anna come with us?" Selim nodded and I beckoned to her. Heaven knows what Layla made of that!

"Here are your veils," called Effat. We hastily draped them over our caps.

Selim led us out of the andarun and into a small downstairs room in his house. A low desk and shelves piled with scrolls marked it as an office, and a brazier offered heat and some light, though there were also more costly beeswax candles set in a wall sconce. He waved us to cushions on the carpeted floor. I was bursting with questions, but first a manservant brought in tea and sweets, and we all had to wait in silence while he set everything out. When the man stood, he gaped at us as if we were the first women he had ever seen. I hastily pulled my veil over my face; Anna followed my lead.

At last Selim's man departed. "Here, please have some tea." Selim poured and served it with the same flourishes I remembered from another time we'd taken tea together, in Batu Khan's encampment. Anna huddled as near to me as possible and nibbled on a piece of halvah.

"Are you settling into my humble home? And are you making friends with everyone?"

"Indeed yes, Selim. Perijam is a jewel. We are already friends. Your wife is a paragon of hospitality, your daughters are perfection, and your home is lovely."

Selim laughed. "You are quickly learning Persian ways!" And then, looking most serious, he put his hand over his heart. "Sofia, please accept my deepest regrets for departing yesterday without speaking with you first. My business often calls me away without warning, and it never promises me a speedy return."

"Yes, your wife told me," I answered, feeling awkward. "Please tell me about your journey home. Da'ud told me you had trouble with the Mongols, that they threatened you. I fear it is entirely my fault."

"A few days after we left Sarai, a troop caught up with us, demanded I surrender you, and searched my caravan inside and out. Had you been there, not even my paize—a gift from Batu Khan himself—would have saved us! Happily, Da'ud and his boys had not yet left us, either, so there was no way for any of my men to accidentally betray me."

"But it truly is my fault that they were pursuing me—had I not written the khan an insulting farewell letter and … done some other foolish things, he might never have known what became of me, nor would he have cared that much, either. I am so sorry I caused you any trouble."

"Enough, Sofia," Selim said, looking amused. "I accept your apology, but it is not necessary. Why, knowing you twisted the tiger's tail like that makes it entirely worth the small trouble they gave me. Well done! And with no trace of you in my caravan, I will still be welcome in Sarai every year. Batu Khan plans to establish it as a year-round city where merchants can gather—a giant 'caravan-Sarai.'"

We both laughed, and my guilt vanished like smoke in the wind! It was short work for each of us to finish our tales. The rest of Selim's journey had been uneventful. He had indeed spread a little extra baksheesh along the road to smooth my way, and unseen guardians might well have been marking our progress to Derbent.

At the end of my account I added, "But this I do not understand, Selim: why did you tell your family you bought us? Mother Layla seems to think you've brought home a new concubine—absurd as such an idea is," a little unease creeping unbidden into my voice.

"Ah, my beloved Layla, ever finding new worries. But I told her less than the truth for a good reason: to hide your tracks, so to speak. And be assured that I have only the greatest respect and affection for you. You can trust my good intentions."

I smiled with relief. "So until I leave, how can we assure her that she is mistaken?"

Selim gave my question some thought. "It might be best not to say anything at all. Even your being here puts my family in some danger, so the less my women know, the better. In fact had I been thinking more clearly, I probably should have renamed you."

He looked at me hopefully. "All right, I agree," I finally said, "but I am not happy about it."

"Thank you from my inmost heart. As to leaving: alas, we cannot, since snow makes the mountains impassable until next spring. I fear you must stay here until the Elburz passes are clear. Then I can take you to meet my master."

That was a shock. I had just gotten used to the idea of not leaving until spring, and now I must wait until then just to meet his master? And there were mountains to cross first?

"Just where are we going?"

"Deep into the mountains to a very holy place."

"Are we going to a monastery? Is he a priest or a monk or an abbot?"

"Priest? No, in Islam no one stands between a man and Allah, the All-seeing, although our mullahs teach righteousness and lead Friday prayers in the mosque. And certainly not a monk; God abominates your Christian monks—flesh-hating and filthy! I have met a few of them in my travels. I do not know what an abbot is, but my master is certainly a man so holy that I do not speak of him lightly. Even my wife knows little about him, though it was he who gave us refuge from the Mongols. We stayed in one of his many castles."

"So I must wait until spring. I must admit I am deeply disappointed."

"Well, I hope that you will not be too disappointed, as we all will try to offer you the best hospitality we can until it is time to leave. Please do not be discouraged; Allah the Compassionate has a plan for you, I am certain, and we are honored to be part of it."

How could I complain in the face of such relentless kindness? Soon thereafter, Anna and I returned to the andarun. Layla tried not to look surprised and relieved at our speedy return.

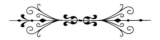

The next morning, Selim was gone again with no word. I idly wondered when I would see him next; probably at supper. Luckily his family made every attempt to welcome us and put us at our ease. After all, they might have shunned us as unbelievers.

However, he did not return that night or the next or the next, until I realized he might be gone a very long time. Nonetheless, each day I looked forward to his return, ready to ask him my other questions. Surely the mysterious remarks that Habib and Da'ud and others had dropped had something to do with his master—that would explain these words like brethren and missions. But why all the secrecy around the holy man?

The women and girls seemed to find nothing amiss with Selim's absence, though they knew nothing of his whereabouts. I might feel impatient to move on—having to wait until next spring was not my idea of how things should go—but I saw no other way of getting to Constantinople. Indeed, just getting out of his heavily guarded home would be impossible! So I applied myself to fitting into the household and waiting as patiently as I could.

Within a week Mother Layla had begun to abandon her fears about me with no word spoken. She was a kind-faced and kind-hearted woman with graying hair who governed both haram and household with quiet dignity. If Selim was right that she tended to worry, I did not see it.

Her senior daughter-in-law, Effat, was a long-faced young woman, a little older than Perijam and me. She was mostly reserved and courteous, though not always. Once in awhile when Perijam had done something too playful, she would burst out with stern advice on how to behave with more dignity. At which point Layla would correct Effat for presuming on her status, and Effat would draw back into herself.

The dark haired boy, Ali, was Effat's son, a charming child who loved his mother dearly. Not taking into account Akbar's light hair, I thought that he, who was just as charming, was Layla's youngest son. And there was affection between him and Layla, though not like the love Effat showered on Ali.

The girls—Banu, Aftab, and Sarah—were each a perfect blend of their parents. All three had such beautiful eyes and glossy dark hair. Banu was almost thirteen and already betrothed to a man of good family, so she tried to act like a woman whenever she remembered. She had a habit of tossing her head so her braids flew about and then of stiffening into dignity when she realized what she had done. But Aftab and Sarah, being only eleven and nine, were still silly girls looking for reasons to laugh when they were not quarreling over some minor thing.

And Perijam became my lovely new friend and, in many ways, the first partner in play I'd had since I was small. It saddened me that Anna felt so jealous of her. Under Perijam's gentle questioning, within days I found myself sharing a little of my story with her, always careful not to say too much. But how could it matter to Selim's plans for me that I had once been a princess of Rus', captured and enslaved by Mongols; or that Anna had been a Hungarian peasant also enslaved, whom I had protected from our master and who had helped me in so many ways? Our escape I did not mention, as that seemed to be part of his plan to cover my tracks.

And for the first week or so, everything seemed so new, interesting, and wondrous. Mornings always began with family prayer in the main room. Often Anna and I arrived while they were still at their devotions. Just listening to them touched something in my heart, for these prayers always began with submission and adoration. Throughout the day, whenever they stopped to worship, Anna and I would sit quietly and pray together. Only once more did she try that trick of crossing herself and loudly begging to be released from "this accursed infidel prison." I angrily commanded her to pray silently from then on, and she never did it again. As for me, I found that after praying, if I did that little practice of peace as well as I remembered it, I could avoid comparing my Christianity with their Islam and not be swept into rivalry.

After breakfast Effat usually gave the children lessons from the Muslim holy book, the Quran. Muslims say it is even more sacred than our Holy Scriptures, although I was surprised to learn that they revere them, too. As People of The Book, both Christians and Jews are more or less protected, or at least tolerated, in Muslim lands. I was also surprised to learn from Effat that because of me the girls had only recently learned to read!

"Father Selim, unlike my own father, Allah's peace on his memory, never thought to teach his women to read until he met you," she said a few days after we had arrived. She had been reading the Quran aloud while we sewed.

"Yes, and we were content." Mother Layla spoke with a little edge to her voice. "After all, if my husband or the mullah reads the Quran to me, then I have no need for letters."

"Now Father makes us learn too," added Aftab sourly, "except for Banu because she will be married soon."

"And what of you, Perijam?" I asked. "Do you know your letters?"

"No, Father Selim offered to let me learn, but like Mother Layla I am happy to listen to Effat and the mullah. I never asked for more than to be married into a loving family. I already have everything I want." She looked pointedly at Effat.

I was a little taken aback. I had been raised to treasure knowledge, but then Papa had been swimming against the current of tradition in offering me such a thorough education. It made me wonder. Given the choice, would I have preferred to be ignorant and dependent but content, or as I was now, learned and with a broad understanding but having to decide so many things for myself?

Later on Effat found an opportunity to whisper in my ear. "There is another reason why my father-in-law never thought to educate his women. He is only a merchant. He thinks knowing a few lines of poetry makes him cultured and that an education means basic letters and sums. He thought women were too simple even for that, so I never dared to read the Quran in their presence except when he was gone." The bitterness in her voice took me aback. "But," she added in a happier tone, "you showed him otherwise, and I thank you with all my heart. Now I can read Allah's Holy Book aloud to everyone every day! I can even teach the boys until they go to the mullah for instruction." Wanting no part of her fault-finding, I smiled and said nothing.

For the next few days I rested in a new contentment. We would all work in leisurely fashion until it was time for another delicious meal—one of Layla's great pleasures was to introduce Anna and me to the delights of Persian food. After the dismal fare in the Mongol camps, at first I could not resist all the pulaos, spicy lamb dishes, and sweet sherbets and pastries that Layla pressed on us, most of the sweets made from costly white sugar instead of homely honey.

All these kinds of food were what she called "halal", which means permitted, but there were other dishes I never saw, especially anything with pork in it. My Mongol captors had never been particular about their diet; indeed, they would eat almost any animal, including parts of it that I had found disgusting. Now I learned that there was another meaning to haram: some things, like pork, were haram, not because they were sacred but because they were thought to be polluted. Such ways of looking at the world left me puzzled, but I tried to respect my hosts' ways of doing things.

We at least found mutual delight in Effat's music and Perijam's singing. And at any time we could play with the boys, nibble a few sweets, challenge someone to a game of backgammon, or talk with each other. The women often gossiped or conjectured about their friends' and relatives' doings, though it was months before we actually saw any of them. Perijam and I sometimes told riddles or played guessing games with the younger girls, while Effat smiled at our childishness with poorly concealed scorn.

We also shared fanciful folk tales and fables with each other, which thrilled the little boys, especially stories with mighty warriors in them. Some Persian tales were just like mine from Rus', and we had to marvel that, though we were so different, we shared so much.

I particularly remember the Simurgh, a magical bird with a dog's head and a lion's body that has seen the world created and destroyed three times and is unutterably wise. It reminded me both of our pagan protector of plants and crops, Simargl, which is also a winged lion with a dog's head, and of our Firebird, who is as brilliant as the sun—just like the Simurgh! I think these stories must have come from the earliest times, before the Tower of Babel fell.

Regular baths were another luxury I melted into. They were among the many small ways of doing things that invited me to feel at ease, safe and cared for.

But Selim did not return. A month passed with no word, and though no one in his family seemed to find anything strange about his long absence, my sense of comfort and safety began to slowly dwindle away. Other than Anna, who never let down her guard, only I seemed uneasy. My limited life began to chafe.

I learned that Anna and I were thought rather odd, both for keeping the hours we did and for staying in our rooms at night. Day and night meant little in haram; everyone took naps at odd moments, and the boys often stayed up late and fell asleep on the carpets. Someone would pick them up, lay them on cushions, and cover them with quilts. After living on a farm and on the steppes, where waking and sleeping were ordered by sunrise and sunset, I found that strange at first. But it was too easy to doze off and get no real, refreshing rest. When I finally saw how I was falling into the same habits, I determinedly asserted my way of doing things and went to bed in my own room with Anna trailing sleepily behind me. Everyone else might be content to float in a dreamlike now, but my urge to move on was growing daily.

Still, I tried to keep occupied. There was always useful work to be done: the entire household was preparing for Banu's wedding since she had recently become a woman, and I enjoyed helping with the sewing and so forth. Indeed, from something Effat let drop, hers was not a particularly early wedding, for nine is the age of marriageable womanhood, a custom dating back at least to when their Prophet married a girl that age. Remembering myself at nine, I would say it is too young, but in Rus' eight was considered old enough, though such marriages were rare.

Even without the upcoming wedding, Mother Layla would have found useful tasks for us all. "Otherwise, we are mere baubles," she told me. "When I sew a shirt for my beloved Selim, I whisper prayers and charms over every stitch to protect him on his travels." How touched I was by her loving tenderness! How I envied Banu, who soon be mistress of a home of her own.

As the days passed, however, I came to wonder how they bore the sameness of their lives. We only knew one week had ended and another had begun when Fridays came. From midday on, the women prayed and Effat read from the Quran, or a gray-bearded mullah visited and read to us or retold stories of early Islam while we sat behind a screen. Beyond preparing for the wedding, it was probably the most excitement they had, especially when he told one story in particular: about Hussein, a saint who with his people was ambushed and killed by the army of an evil usurper of the throne who was a defiler of Islam. The women always broke into moans and sobs, especially Banu.

After the first time I saw this outpouring of grief, I politely asked what it was about. Effat said, "We mourn the holy martyr Hussein, peace upon him, who suffered torments in the desert and was foully murdered by heretics. But we also weep for our own martyrs who died at Mongol hands. Each of us remembers loved ones slain or missing."

The next time I heard that story, I was reminded of all the people I had lost. The same sorrow welled up from my heart, too, and I joined in their tears. No one thought the worse of me for it—quite the contrary.

But I grew to hate being so confined. I could wander about in the garden for a short time each day, but it was not like striding across steppes, so I began jumping up and pacing around the room once in awhile. No one said a word, but they must have thought me mad.

I took to writing again. As I had long ago filled the book my Papa had given me, I was now using the one Batu Khan had given me, the only gift I truly treasured. Writing was not something I'd had time for or interest in since escaping him. It did help me pass the time away, and I found the passage that described my little practice of peace, so that helped me remember to do it more.

Still, sometimes, though in fact they were growing shorter, the days seemed so long that time seemed to stand still. I wanted to scream with impatience. Where was Selim? When would he come for me? Was I to be imprisoned here forever? I grew ever more desperate.

One day I even fled to my room, kicked the pillows, and threw open the shutters and window to get at the iron grillwork. I shook them so hard, cold streaming into the room and down my arms, that one shifted a little in its socket. I felt both guilty and fascinated by the damage I'd caused. I didn't want to do more, but what if I could escape out the window? I looked out: snow, dreary sky, no food or other supplies, and no idea how to get anywhere in Qazvin, much less to Constantinople. I had tried escaping on my own once before, and had I succeeded, I'd have died of the cold. I closed the window and put my room back in order.

I began eating too many sweets, but they made my teeth hurt. Perijam gave me a round, dark, strong-smelling pill to chew for the pain, but it gave me strange dreams. When I asked her what the pill was, she said, "It's just opium. It's good for many ailments. I chew it or drink it as tea when I cannot sleep or I miss my Kerim's embrace, and it puts me into a lovely, misty state." I decided that a better plan was to avoid sugary treats. Opium offered me no real escape, anyway.

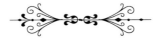

As winter dragged on, the main room sometimes grew so cold that work and lessons and writing and even pacing came to a halt, and all of us would huddle together under warm quilts draped over a ceramic table set in the hearth. There was no retreating to my room then, at least most of the time. The warmth from the hearth was all that kept us from freezing into statues, though it was too easy to sleep much of the day away.

But when night came and sleep did not, or when I was wakened by a nightmare of being chased by shadowy Mongols, I would sometimes give up, defy the cold, and return to my own room to try to pray, shivering, though I was wrapped in all my quilts. I always hoped that in the night's stillness I might recapture something of the peace and confidence that had borne me up in Batu Khan's war camp. And a few times I felt a whisper of trust, even if it too often failed to follow me into the next day. Oddly, at such moments, I was no longer praying as such but following my breath out, emptying out into simplicity and calm.

But often I could not pray. Sometimes I simply wept. I felt so alone and small, halfway around the world from anything familiar, poised over an abyss of the unknown. Over two months had passed with no news of Selim. What if something bad had befallen him? How would these helpless women survive without him? And even if someone took them in, what would happen to Anna and me? At best we might be held in luxurious captivity forever, at worst cast out into an unknown land. I had once thought I could choose who I would become, but how few choices I really had. And at heart all I wanted was to find my own family again, to be with my own people where I understood what things meant.

Like little Akbar's nightmares: in the darkest hours he would often awaken and call for his mother, and Perijam would always be the one to comfort him, never Layla or Effat. Was it some Persian tradition for the youngest daughter-in-law to tend to crying children in the night? Layla never seemed to reach out for him. And the next day Akbar would be listless and easily upset, but no one spoke of his bad night.

With little events looming so large, I was as excited as Selim's family was when Perijam's mother and sisters sent word that the entire family was coming to visit for a few days. They lived just across town, but they rarely braved the larger world. Indeed, to avoid attracting unwanted attention, they arrived at night surrounded by family guards.

Watching their torches march along Selim's garden, Perijam explained, "They must come to me because I should not go outside Father Selim's walls while expecting a baby. I don't want to attract the evil eye or malicious djinn—oh, have you never heard of them? They are fickle spirits and we must beware of them— And here come my Mama and Papa!"

Most of us hastily pulled our veils across our faces when "Papa" came to the door, but Perijam ran to kiss his hands. He was only there to escort his family to the andarun, and after offering a few loving words to his daughter, he left for his home again. He seemed a kindly man, a little stooped, but both dignified and warm. After Perijam's mother and sisters had exchanged tearful kisses and embraces with her, they looked over at Anna and me curiously. Layla had a story at the ready: I was an orphaned distant relative from some city in Azerbaijan called Tabriz, and Anna was my servant. Despite my red hair, no one questioned her further.

Along with two younger sisters who straightaway settled down to play with Aftab and Sarah, Perijam's older sister Rabia had also come to visit. She was recently widowed, and her little son Khorshid was the cornerstone of her life. She thought everything he did was delightful, and he teased his milder cousins until they began to behave as wildly as he did. But their mothers only needed to say that Selim would hear of it and the boys dropped their mischief. Rabia did nothing to stop her son, despite her mother's clear disapproval. At one point he was hopping about the room like a crazed grasshopper and crashing into things when he almost overturned one of the braziers. That alarmed his grandmother into exclaiming, "Khorshid, stop your wildness or Eskander the Accursed will get you!"

With a cry of terror, he rushed to his mother's side and buried his head in her lap. For the rest of the day, he kept a wary eye on the corners of the room. Rabia looked both angry and ashamed, but she held her tongue. After that she restrained her son better, too.

A week later with the visit over and the women collected by "Papa", I asked Perijam who or what Eskander the Accursed was. I expected to hear about some djinn.

"Oh, surely you've heard the story of the barbarian world conqueror who came from the west and overthrew the greatest empire in history: the Persian Empire! He cast an iron mantle of conquest over many lands, from the shores of the great sea to our west—I cannot recall its name—almost to India. They say he would have conquered it, too, had he not died young," said Perijam eagerly.

"It's called The Great Green Sea, or the Mediterranean," Effat added impatiently.

"Yes, yes, but what's important is that Eskander was a monster! This I know for certain: he ordered his troops to kill all the young men in our great capital, Persepolis, and then he burned down the city. And he forced girls of highest birth to marry his own generals, shaming and defiling them!" I suddenly realized they were speaking of Alexander the Great. "He spared us nothing—stripped our glorious monuments and palaces of their beautiful gold and silver coverings, stole our emperor's many treasures. My father says we should still hate him like it was yesterday! He was worse than the Mongols!"

All the women around me nodded, even Effat, who seemed annoyed that Perijam and not she was telling me all this. So when she cried fiercely, "Were he in this room today, I would take these scissors and kill him myself for what he did," I thought she was just venting her feelings. But then everyone, even the little boys, cried out in agreement. My tutor had taught me that Alexander was a great man, but the Persians believe Alexander was the worst of all the conquerors who have trampled Persia under their iron heels. How amazing that people see the same thing so differently—and that they pass on their rancor to new generations! After all, Alexander has been dead for a thousand years and more.

Life grew both duller and yet more tense. Of course living in close quarters with anyone is difficult, although Persian courtesy forestalled most outright quarreling. But after that family visit, Effat seemed to find Perijam even more annoying than usual. And Banu was forever either giddy or gloomy, one moment striving to behave like an adult, the next moment bursting into tears over a misplaced bracelet. I thought it trying, but now I think this must be the way all girls behave as they approach womanhood—even I, who had been forced to become an adult almost overnight, had been subject to fickle moods. And Banu was about to be married, so that might account for part of it. As for the rest of the family, I blamed the cold weather for making them stale and sullen.

To keep my mind from turning into a pudding, I asked if I might study Arabic with Effat and the girls. Now Perijam became jealous! I had to explain to her that I wanted to understand the Prophet Muhammad's revelations—the Quran—and then her eyes lit up with hope. "Perhaps you will feel the power of its holy words and accept the one true religion."

"Perhaps." I was not prepared to discuss my faith with anyone.

Of course Effat was thrilled, and she fairly leapt into her role as teacher. At our first lesson she stated, "Islam means submission to Allah, the One True God, Omnipotent, Just, and Merciful. From surrender comes true peace. The Prophet Mohammed, blessings upon him, brought the world the final truth; he was the Seal of the Prophets. Those who came before him, holy seers such as Jesus and his saintly mother, whom you worship as God and the mother of God; and Moses, who brought us the Ten Commandments; and Elijah and all the other prophets of your holy books brought mankind part of the truth. But there was more. Mohammed, blessings on his name, showed us how to mingle the streams of truth and love and mercy and justice into one mighty river."

She handed me her own prized copy of the Quran and would have given it to me had I not insisted on saying I would return it. The polite little quarrel that followed allowed me to keep my own counsel. I had been raised to regard Islam as the great enemy of Christendom. But to my surprise upon reading it, I found that this Quran, which means recitation, has much wisdom and good sense in it. I straightaway felt I understood the heart if not the form of three of its Five Pillars: faith, prayer, and charity, although I did not see why other forms of prayer besides prostration counted for nothing. Nor did I understand the fourth, which is fasting—it had something to do with an occasion called Ramadan. I had once fasted as a way to atone for my sins, and it had only made me faint. And I knew little about pilgrimage, to Mecca or anywhere else, since we had never gone farther than the Monastery of the Caves near Kyiv when I had been a child. Effat spent quite some time explaining to me why one went, how one behaved, and what the spiritual benefits were, but I could get no feeling for it all. And in truth, some of the Quran's revelations were so mystical that I never understood them. They seemed to spring straight from some strange, distant desert world.

On the other hand, Islam certainly has surprising views on things we Christians take as given. For instance they do not blame Eve for the Fall of Mankind.

Poor Anna was endlessly miserable that entire winter, first over Perijam and then over Effat. I once asked her why, and her answer was like a needle thrust into my heart. "Of course I was friends with other slaves. We were the same. But I can never fit in here, and I never wish to! I hate how they drop everything and fall on their faces before their false god when that wailing starts outside. My only reason to live is to serve you, and you don't need me anymore!"

"Oh, Anna, no," I protested. "We share a bond that none can break, nor can anyone else take your place in my life. But surely you can find friendship here as well as I can."

"No, you don't understand. You are nobly born. I am but a peasant."

I was taken aback by her outlook. Anna had endured such suffering, had fled with me into danger—indeed, had saved both our lives. She had survived so much and with a will that had never flagged, yet she could not see her own strength. And with the eyes of her understanding shut fast, she was utterly trapped in that household. I prayed especially for her from then on.

As winter dragged on, there were other sources of dissatisfaction that had nothing to do with Selim's family. I often missed my old friend and teacher Dorje: his cheerful countenance and magpie curiosity, his kindness and gentle advice. Surprisingly I also missed Argamon's embrace. He might have enslaved me and stolen my life from me, but he had also awakened my lust. While there were ways to satisfy it that I could use if I chose, lust was only part of my problem; I wanted not only a man's touch but a good and brave and caring mate, someone I could truly love, someone who would protect me and not vanish for months at a time as Selim did! It was a wish I believed to be hopeless.

WINTER INTO SPRING
ANNO DOMINI 1243

I finally learned the reason for Akbar's nighttime tears. He had had one of his bad nights, and the next day he quarreled with little Ali over a wooden toy they both wanted. When Effat was short with him and Perijam rushed to his defense, Effat exclaimed, "He's just like his mother, always wanting more than his portion!"

Perijam snapped back, "He misses her. He shouldn't be blamed for her sins!"

"He is lucky to be alive and not stained with the same brush that she was—"

"Enough, both of you!" snapped Layla. The whole room fell silent. No one spoke for the rest of the day, so after supper I went to my room, trailed by Anna. Perijam followed us soon after and closed the door.

Words tumbled from her mouth. "I am sorry our quarrel ruined your day, but at least it firmed my resolve to tell you about this. I have had enough of pretending that nothing bad happens in this family, that we all share the same mind, especially when Effat treats me like a fool! I've often seen you look at poor little Akbar with a question in your eyes, and now I will explain everything!"

Anna, not knowing Farsi, merely glared at her rival behind her back, knelt in prayer, curled into her quilts and went to sleep, but I listened with growing unease.

"Before I married into the family, Father Selim bought a young concubine with blue eyes and fair-hair, a Christian from the Caucasus. He was mad with passion for her. Mother Layla could have been jealous and cruel, but she treated her kindly out of pity. This girl and Effat even became friends. When she produced Akbar, they welcomed him into the family. Kerim married me when Akbar was two, so I knew her for a little while.

But she committed a terrible crime: she and one of the andarun guards fell in love. No one knows if there truly was a love affair—it would have been extremely hard, the way we live—but Selim discovered their secret. Rightly, he felt his honor had been stained. That was a terrible day. He beat his guard and threw him out. Her he dragged screaming into the biruni, where he meant to strangle both her and Akbar because he suspected the boy was not his. But then Selim returned carrying little Akbar. He said she had fallen at his feet and begged for mercy, not for herself, but for her son.

"She swore on the memory of all the saints, Christian and Muslim, that Akbar was his. Father Selim is a kind man, and he relented toward them both; he said that instead of killing her, he had sent her off to an old leper who begged in the market. What happened to her no one knows, and we dare not ask Selim. If she was lucky, the leper sold her to a rich man for much money. If not, by now she is probably a leprous beggar, too. But to this day, Akbar understands nothing of what happened. Of us all, I think Effat most regrets befriending her. And she looks down on me for taking Akbar's part."

I was deeply shocked, though probably not for the usual reasons. Though I pitied that girl for losing her son and falling into the worst sort of slavery, I thought her utterly foolish to have taken any risk that would endanger him. When I was Argamon's slave, I had nearly been compromised by a man who had terrorized me! When your life is not your own, how much more shameful it is to betray your owner with someone you love, to put both your lover and your child at risk. Now poor Akbar was orphaned, missing his mother, and had no one loyal to him but Perijam.

Worst of all, what did this story say about Selim? I had seen men be jealous and possessive and violent, but I could hardly imagine him strangling someone he loved. It made me realize how little I knew the man to whom I had entrusted my fate, and it both clouded my present and further darkened my future.

At last the days began growing longer, the snows gave way to occasional cloudbursts, and spring hovered in the air waiting to arrive in full bloom. But still there was no sign of Selim.

One morning Perijam approached me and said, "Ramadan arrives soon. It's the holiest time of year for a true believer. But since you are Christian, we must decide what you will do."

"Well, since we're your guests, perhaps we should follow your customs," I replied.

"Oh, that would be wonderful!" Then Perijam hesitated. "But are you ready for the demands it will make upon you?"

"I understand little about your Ramadan beyond the fact that you fast."

"Ramadan is the month when the Prophet Muhammad, peace upon him, received his first revelations from Allah the Almighty. We pray and contemplate all day, and all who are able-bodied neither eat nor drink while a black thread can be told apart from a white thread—from well before dawn to long after sunset. Thus we remember to be humble before Allah the All-Merciful, recall that all blessings come from Him, and remind ourselves how it feels to go hungry just as the poor do all year long." All this Perijam recited as if from a lesson.

But then she added, dimpling charmingly, "Of course, when it's dark, we can eat and drink, so that time is quite festive! I won't join the fasting this year, as it might harm my baby, but after he's born I'll fast to make up for it. But for you, Sofia, will not such abstinence prove a burden?"

"Oh, I think I can manage a day without food or drink easily enough," I smiled, thinking that this Muslim fasting was shockingly simple after what I had once done to myself.

Perijam looked grave. "Well, it's actually for thirty days, the whole month."

"I see." This was no mean obligation after all. I wanted to respect their customs, and surely it would be rude to eat when others must not, so I must stand by my word. But I did not feel right about making Anna do the same. "Perijam, I think I will fast with the family, but perhaps since you'll be eating during the day, Anna can join you."

"Oh, yes. We can do that."

So during their Ramadan, I joined in the fasting and learned that doing without food may be a little hard, but that doing without drink can be most painful—and that knowing what it feels like to go hungry and thirsty can indeed make you aware of what true poverty might feel like. Selim's family spent each day in prayer and reflection, while Anna and I did very little. I have to admit I often dozed off, as did the little boys and the girls, which did make the days pass faster. I was glad they were still shorter than the nights! And we both joined in the late-night feasting and pre-dawn breakfasts. But it seemed like the longest month in my entire stay.

Even before Ramadan was over, the women began preparing for another holiday. Early one morning Noor brought Mother Layla a dish containing grains of wheat and lentils, to which Layla added water before setting the dish on a sunny windowsill. Her family watched gravely. As I stood beside Perijam trying not to think about another day without food or water, Effat announced, "Sofia, this is the first step in preparing for the Persian new year, which we celebrate when day and night are in perfect balance."

I must have shown my surprise. "When do you celebrate the new year?" she asked.

"In midwinter," I answered. "Just after the days begin to grow longer. We Rus' learned it from the Romans when we became Christian."

Effat looked thoughtful. "Yes, I can see reason behind your custom. But we Persians feel that spring marks a year's true beginning. We call it Now Ruz, New Day, and its roots go back to the beginning of time. What a joyful occasion it is! You will see."

"Yes," Perijam added, squeezing my hand. "It is most auspicious that Ramadan and Now Ruz will fall so close together." I mistakenly thought that the one always led into the other and did not discover my error until another year had gone by.

The next day the grains began to sprout, a good omen, everyone eagerly assured me.

And so it seemed, because the day after that Selim finally came home! It was a joyous occasion for us all, for I had almost given up hope. After gravely greeting us, he asked after our health, gave us all gifts, and settled into enjoying being with his loved ones—Layla disappeared into the biruni for several nights running. But after a day or two, though I understood his delight at being home, I grew impatient. I tried to justify his silence and seeming indifference to Anna and me, thinking he must be waiting until Ramadan and Now Ruz were over before sharing his plans. Seeing Akbar sitting happily at his feet, it was hard to imagine he had nearly strangled the boy's mother.

Ramadan finally ended with a huge three-day feast called Eid al-Fitr—talk, laughter, too much food, and even a mild wine! I had always thought from what my friend Toramun had said, back in Batu's camp, that wine was forbidden to Muslims, but Persian wines are so good that the Prophet himself could not keep them from drinking it.

Now all the talk was of Now Ruz. As if eager for it to come, the weather grew mild. Layla's songbirds competed with the birdsong outside. The garden shrubs put out new green almost overnight, the fruit and almond trees burst into blossom, and little crocuses suddenly dotted the ground. The andarun garden drew us outside on most days, always to discover some new delight: trailing branches of a willow tree swelling with bright leaves, and the junipers and cedars growing tender new tips. A pomegranate tree near the center of the garden unfurled new leaves, and it seemed as if more flowers were blooming every day, many of which I had never seen before: first yellow cup-like ones that reminded me of upside-down dulbands; then lilacs and violets; red and pink roses; a flowering vine called jasmine; and bright pink ruffled flowers with jagged edges, which they called pinks. Most made me giddy from their perfume. Perijam and I often sat beside the small reflecting pool telling the boys and each other some fanciful story, and hope swelled unbidden in my heart.

Now that the sewing for Banu's wedding was done, the women turned to stitching garments for the Now Ruz celebrations. Servants cleaned both houses from top to bottom and set out offerings for all the ancestors and loved ones who had departed this life and whose souls were expected to return for the occasion—all this Perijam or Effat explained to me a little at a time.

A few days before this Now Ruz began, a group of entertainers arrived at Selim's compound. He invited them into the outermost courtyard to perform for the entire household. We gathered before the outer gate of the biruni where we women, heavily veiled, watched the revels through its cracks. The boys, however, were allowed to stand outside with Selim, to their unutterable joy. What a motley group the entertainers were! Most of the men wore tall hats and cloaks that were patched together with bright scraps of fabric, all covered with tiny tinkling bells. They also had a furry monkey and a chained bear. I was sorry for that: to me bears will always be sacred.

Perijam was almost dancing with delight. "This is a most ancient custom. When I was little, a company like this came to our home every year, and our whole family watched them together. My father was never as strict as Father Selim is about women keeping to the andarun, but then he is not as pious. Now, see that man there with a sooty face, dressed in red? He is the leader, The Man Who Burns Fire. And that one strikes those two boards together while The Man Who Burns Fire speaks the old, old words. Now you shall see all sorts of marvels."

I certainly had to marvel at the old, old words, for they made little sense to me. It sounded as if he was saying: "Once a year I appearing, being orphan and poor. Once a year, something comes," but what it was that came, I could not make out.

A stage had been set up with a pole standing at each end and a rope strung between them. Suddenly one of the performers leapt upon the rope as lightly as a bird and balanced, hopped, and pranced along it, never once falling off. The little grinning monkey danced until we laughed, and I wondered how I could have been so afraid of Batu Khan's. The poor shackled bear was forced by prodding to stand on its legs and dance, too. Luckily, not for long; it was replaced by a pair of wrestlers who rolled and twisted about amidst cheers from the onlookers. And at the end, all the performers balanced on each other's shoulders to make a pyramid, most amazing. Perijam, who clearly would have loved to join the audience outside the gates, clapped her hands like a child.

At the end Selim came forward and spoke briefly to the Man who Burns Fire while handing him some coins, and the man whispered a response. Selim's smile turned wooden. He walked away, head bent in thought, and opened the biruni gate, where we had to retreat in a great rush to make way for him. He hastened through his ccourtyard and vanished into his house. I looked at the other women in surprise. They seemed not to know what had happened, either, and we all returned to the andarun feeling less cheerful. Indeed, we saw no sign of Selim for several days after that, but as always, no one said a word. And I still had had no private conversation with him. I was turning into the Woman Who Burns as if on Fire!

On one of the last days of the old year, called Chahr Shambeh Suri, the menservants built a great bonfire in the outermost courtyard. Mother Layla allowed us to go look through the gate again. What a sight! All the men and even some of the women servants took turns leaping over the fire and singing to it:

> *"You take winter's pallor from me*
> *I take your ruddy glow,*
> *You take winter's chill from me*
> *I take your kindly warmth."*

At one point, Perijam leaned over and whispered in my ear, "They are burning up any defilement that clings to them from last year and inviting in good luck. No one must breathe on the fire while they leap over it, or it will bring bad luck."

While I did not understand this custom, it struck me as most entertaining for the people doing the leaping. It reminded me of the way our peasants had honored Kupala, goddess of living water and healing plants every year on midsummer's eve—Saint Ivan's eve. They too had cleansed themselves by leaping over a bonfire, and held hands and danced in a ring around the fire to symbolize that our earth is one. I would go outside our palace with Baba Liubyna to watch. Herbs gathered on that night held special power, and it was said that trees could move and speak. When I was old enough, Liubyna even let me join their late-night search for the fire flower that would gift its finder with the power to understand the trees' speech—I had always thought I understood it, anyway, but I had wanted to see the flower.

"Oh," whispered Perijam after the bonfire had finally burned down and we were returning to the andarun, "I forgot to tell you. The ashes must be scattered at a crossroads. But I cannot remember why. Don't tell Effat or she will look down her long nose at me."

Now Ruz arrived. After we had eaten a festive breakfast, servants brought a new table into the room and set it in the corner. Noor carried in a bowl of pudding, looking most pleased with herself, and handed it to Mother Layla. "Now we can begin," said our hostess.

Perijam turned to me. "Everyone will gather this evening to welcome Now Ruz, so this morning, we prepare the table... But I think I will tell you no more, so you'll have a pleasant surprise when it all happens."

So Anna and I stood out of the way, both of us confused by all the goings-on. No one spoke much—even Effat seemed too wrapped up in her work to tell us what was happening when Perijam failed to do so. Everything seemed to center on that table. It was not quite a shrine, but their reverent manner made it seem as if the women were preparing for a religious ceremony. In the center of the table, Layla placed a large polished steel mirror and set several candles to either side. Around these she placed other items—or they might have been devotional offerings. Certainly the Quran was an object of devotion; but there were also a large sheet of flat bread, a bowl of water on which floated a green leaf, a glass of fragrant rosewater, nuts, fruits, sweets, beet-dyed eggs, some cooked chicken and fish, and even a few coins. Then Layla set up a brazier with a bowl of herbs nearby, and Effat set out a largish tray full of the oddest items.

I could contain my curiosity no longer. "Please, what are all these for?"

All three women turned and laughed, but Effat spoke first, which seemed to displease Perijam. "You look so puzzled. Since Perijam hasn't told you, I will explain. This is our offering table. The mirror on it reflects Allah's great Creation, and there is one candle on the table for each child in the family, to invite wisdom and happiness in the coming year. The coins are for prosperity, the eggs are for fertility, the leaf in the water is for the earth floating in space, and the rose water has magical cleansing power. We'll burn wild rue in the brazier, because it's a sacred herb. Its smoke wards off evil spirits."

Perijam spoke tartly, "Well, I was going to wait until tonight so she'd be surprised! Anyway, the tray here is for haft sin. The name for everything on it starts with 's'. See, senjed," she pointed to dried jujubes, "sib," she indicated apples, "sir," she touched a head of garlic, "serkeh," she pointed to a bowl of vinegar, "samanu," Noor's special pudding, "sabzeh," which were green sprouts, "and a twig of sumaq."

"The number seven has been sacred in Iran since ancient times," Effat added, looking slightly annoyed in her turn. "Each dish stands for a different angel of life: senjed is for love, sib is for health and beauty, sir is for medicine and health, samanu is for transformation, sabzeh are for rebirth, serkeh is for patience and maturity, and sumaq is for good conquering evil."

"Thank you both," I said, smiling and secretly wishing Perijam had not waited. Even if I could not share their joy, the custom at least made some sense now that I knew what it meant.

The rest of that day was spent preparing for the evening. Anna and I were each given a candle to put in our rooms; every room in the house got one. She was loath to do anything with hers, so I took it her from her and put it up myself, feeling a little impatient with her relentless refusals. Late that afternoon, having dressed in our new finery and lit all the candles so that every room glowed, we gathered around the special table. Mother Layla took one of the colored eggs and formally placed it upon the center of the mirror. Then we stood and waited.

Since I had no special feeling for Now Ruz, I found this part of the celebration rather tiresome; but there was certainly an air of great expectancy among the women, so something important must be about to happen. I tried to ask Perijam, but she put a finger to her lips and signed for me to watch. Just before dark, Selim reappeared, to be greeted quietly but with great delight. At first, I thought it was his appearance that the women had awaited with such hope, but his homecoming seemed only to heighten their feelings.

We waited and waited, and my thoughts had wandered far off to the jolly spring celebrations of my childhood, when a great sigh escaped from everyone's lips at once.

"Did you see? The egg moved, I saw it!"

"No, no, the leaf stirred! The egg never moved!"

And while the air filled with aromatic smoke from the wild rue, all the family cheerfully debated egg versus leaf. Selim and his wife smiled as if they might never stop, the girls clapped their hands, the little boys capered about, and Anna and I looked on in puzzlement. Perijam finally joined us, standing outside the happy group.

"What do you think, Sofia? They both must have moved! Surely an auspicious sign!"

"What was I supposed to see? I didn't know where to look!" I felt cheated.

"The egg on the mirror and the leaf on the water! One or the other moves, and tonight both did! That's how we know when Now Ruz has arrived! But you missed it; what a shame."

Effat overheard us and cut in, "Our oldest legends say that the earth spins on one horn of a great bull. At the instant when day and night are equal in length, he tosses the earth from one horn to the other; but he does it so smoothly that only the egg rocking or the leaf moving on the water can measure when that happens! Well, perhaps next year you'll get to see it."

"Perhaps," I said, thinking sadly that there would be no next year with my friends. I would be celebrating it at the familiar time of year with my uncle.

Afterwards we feasted upon rice, the chicken, a special fish called bass brought all the way from the Caspian Sea packed in ice, various other tasty dishes, and many toothsome sweets, served separately for Anna and me. I now knew why: we might be People of the Book but we were still unbelievers. I think the dishes were even washed separately.

Well, that was not the end but the beginning of Now Ruz! For several days the entire family celebrated—indeed all Qazvin did—and every servant in Selim's household received gifts and coins. There was constant feasting, and Selim welcomed a stream of men friends—or so I gathered from the number of their wives and daughters who arrived in the andarun, to sing and dance and down endless sweets and tea amidst jesting and laughter.

Selim also took Mother Layla, Effat, and the girls on some visiting of their own, but Perijam stayed home with Anna and me. It could have been lonely for her, but her sister and mother came to visit, along with a few of her childhood friends. It reminded me of the good times I had once enjoyed with my own cousins and friends, when we all gathered together to celebrate some special occasion—the laughter, the gossip, the songs … all those lovely girls, probably now dead.

I had thought the New Year well-enough established after all that, but I was wrong. It seems that the thirteenth day after Now Ruz is unlucky. Not to me, though, because for the first time since arriving, I was allowed to leave Selim's home! We all got up early and fluttered out in our best finery to waiting litters in the outer courtyard. Even Perijam came. "I am so happy to get out! We'll spend the entire day in the country, to trick away all this day's bad luck from our homes."

I probably felt even happier than she did! Anna and I rode in a litter together, and she was just as excited. Although it was covered on all sides so we could not see out, I enjoyed the ride. I believe menservants bore the litters on their shoulders, but I never saw them, nor they us. From the noise and chatter that accompanied us, everyone in Qazvin was there and in a festive mood. Who knows, perhaps even any Mongols encamped outside the city were celebrating.

We climbed into low hills, stopping at last in a level area. Borne on the wind, laughter and happy song reached our ears from other Qazvinis all around us. We women had to wait for something to be set up. When allowed out, we were in a sheltered area under a willow tree, surrounded by a tall fence made of lengths of cloth stretched between poles. That was disappointing! I saw nothing except for flower-spangled green hills and blue sky above us. It would seem that even here, the andarun was still maintained, for we stayed inside the fence until it was time to leave late that afternoon. At least it covered a large area of bright green grasses adorned with little jewel-like wildflowers.

And a sweet stream flowed through our makeshift room, although that was necessary. Mother Layla had carefully carried her bowl of lentil shoots all this way, and the first thing she did was to drop them into the stream! Selim's family breathed a shared sigh of relief, and Perijam whispered, "There, that's done. Bad luck is banished and good luck is invited in."

While we rested upon carpets as beautiful as the meadow itself, women servants set out a huge feast of cold foods and the little boys played a game of chase. Aftab and Sarah began singing together, little prayers to find good husbands and have many sons. Selim and Layla smiled and nodded, and even Effat hummed the tune. Again I marveled at how meaningful their customs were to them. To me they were interesting, even delightful, but that was all.

We idled the day away under the shade of the willow tree, enjoying the sweet spring sunshine. Even with my disappointment, I was so glad to be outdoors and away from the familiar. I could still take pleasure in the way sunbeams danced among the tree's slender branches and leaves, as though playing at hiding and being found. I even sat down by the stream and let the cool water curl over my hands, where Anna joined me.

"For some reason, Mistress, I feel happy today. I think a change is coming."

Altogether it was a lovely day and, I hope, a lovely year for all of Selim's family.

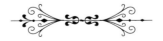

After Now Ruz, Banu's wedding loomed large. Selim was often in the andarun, but I still had no idea who his master was or when we would leave. Although one part of me understood his distraction, for there was much for us all to do, I was sorely tempted to complain. Having faced such dangers to find freedom, it was hard to be locked up like a piece of jewelry until I was to be used!

Beyond that, I had never been able to completely dismiss my unease about him since hearing the story of little Akbar's mother. Not that I was afraid Selim would strangle or sell me, but I was painfully aware that he had too much power over me and that I was not being allowed to ask my growing number of questions. But whenever I got so impatient that I was ready to burst, Selim would look at me and smile and say something kind or comforting. He surely knew I was restless, but he seemed to have such a different sense of time.

Three days before her wedding, Banu underwent a traditional plucking of hair in private that left her looking less than happy when she and Layla returned to the main room. It was not clear to me what had been plucked. As all was in chaos, there was no one to ask. Effat and Perijam had been pulling beautiful wall hangings from chests, telling the servants where to hang them, sorting through sweet-scented flowers, weaving garlands and hanging them, and they had no time for me.

The next afternoon with a great din of drums, the groom and his family, servants, and guards arrived. At first they set my heart racing with fear, they sounded so like Mongol war drums. We younger women took turns looking through a window facing the andarun garden; it was set at an angle where we could see part of the biruni entrance and garden. Out of courtesy the girls insisted I go first. "I see a line of finely dressed men carrying large flat boxes on their heads. They're crossing the garden."

"Now it's my turn," said Aftab, and I stood aside. "I see two well-dressed men helping an elderly woman who leans upon a walking stick. Behind them are menservants carrying their baggage—or maybe presents for you, Banu."

"Let me see," cried Sarah. "Oh, Banu, one of those men may be your future husband! I hope it's the younger one. Even he looks old, but at least you're marrying a rich man! And brave, too, to bring so many wedding gifts without fear of being robbed."

Banu, torn between excitement and fear, pushed her sisters aside to peek, too. "I don't see how you can tell anything from here."

"Well, all those presents mean he's rich, anyway, and brave!" countered Sarah.

Banu replied with her idea of womanly dignity. "Yes, yes, but most of all Father says he's a devout Muslim, and that's what counts."

She failed to humble her sisters. "Yes, yes," Aftab mimicked her, "a devout, rich, brave Muslim!" And she and Sarah fell to laughing and prancing about in glee.

Soon the elderly lame woman was in our midst, welcomed by Layla and presented to everyone: a soft-faced, white-haired lady named Fatima. She and Selim's family had never met before, which was most unusual, I gathered from the conversation, as was coming to stay with us. The groom was the younger brother of a merchant friend of Selim's who lived in another city, and he and Selim had arranged the marriage and signed the marriage contract a year earlier. So the two families had only days to become friendly—not that they had trouble with that. It soon seemed as if Fatima and Layla had been friends forever.

On the day of the wedding, the handful of relatives who were left in Qazvin arrived, and all the women crowded into the main room, laughing and calling to each other, singing songs, and nibbling treats. They treated Anna and me like family, and I thoroughly enjoyed myself. But Anna pretended to be mute, sat in the corner, and spoiled her appetite with sweets. At least she smiled politely whenever anyone spoke to her—due to my warning her in advance that she must!

Layla had given us new garments, and we sat in an uneven circle, elbow to elbow and knee to knee, admiring Banu in her wedding finery: a white silk gown for purity, plus a matching embroidered cap, heavy white veil, and a garland of white flowers around her neck. She was ashen-faced under the kohl and rouge on her eyes and cheeks. Still, she looked so pretty with her little hands and feet all painted with henna designs—just as I once had been for a completely different occasion. Several of the women began teasing her about the great change she would experience once she was introduced to the mystery between man and woman. Some hinted darkly, while others insisted she would find great revelations. But I remembered my first time and silently prayed that she would find a gentle awakening in her husband's arms.

Layla and Fatima sat on either side of the trembling girl. At one point

I overheard Layla speak apologetically across Banu, "This is not a lavish wedding in the old style. The Mongols even rob us of that. My husband had to bribe the basqaq to allow us this much."

Fatima nodded her agreement. "Yes, my elder son Farhad had to do the same. Even so, we'd have had more gifts for our little bride had those Mongol guards not stopped us at the city's edge and taken so much." Fatima patted Banu's hand while she and Layla clicked their tongues over the cruelty of their conquerors. "But Allah wills it," she added.

"And tomorrow, the feasting and revelry will make up for it all," Layla smiled.

Perijam leaned over to me. "In the old days, I'm told, weddings were much grander, and the celebrations lasted for days afterwards. No one dares display such wealth in these times. We'd be marks for the Mongols to come seize whatever they want! Oh well, today is simpler, anyway. The mullah reads out the marriage contract that binds Banu and her husband together. She gives her consent, and he agrees to her portion should he divorce her.

"It is a little strange for Banu to be marrying outside the family. But too few kin are still alive, so we must believe that Farhad's family is trust-worthy, as this marriage binds his to ours. Hopefully, it will give strength to each."

Sarah was sitting near the door and, hearing a soft knock on it, cried over the laughter and song, "He is ready!" I thought she meant the groom, but I was wrong—the mullah who was to perform the ceremony had arrived.

In a strained voice, Mother Layla said, "Go, go all of you, to await the bride! Fatima and Banu and I will follow you." I hoped they might give the poor girl some truly useful advice first. She looked terrified after all the teasing. I suddenly recalled my cousin Irina, who had found joy in her hus-band's embrace but an early grave in childbirth. I thrust that thought away and prayed for Banu: not only happiness in marriage but also a long life.

Following the others' lead, Anna and I donned heavy veils and trooped down the stairs. What excitement at being allowed out of the andarun! I had hoped we might go to a mosque, but it seemed that Muslim wed-dings were not held there. Instead, we all trooped across to Selim's house and into his large, handsome public room. Everything was beautified with wall hangings, burning candles, oil lamps, lush carpets, and many cushions for the guests.

But to my surprise, the only two men in the room were the mullah, dressed in long white robes and black dulband and seated facing the door, and the groom, also wearing white and with a garland of white flowers around his neck. His name was Salman, I had learned, and he was sitting on a large pillow facing the mullah, so I could not see his face. From the rumble of voices outside, I gathered that the other men were waiting in Selim's garden.

As Anna and I were led to a back corner of the room, I glanced about. A second embroidered pillow sat next to the groom's, both resting upon a large square of green silk. The large mirror used on Now Ruz was now set up before the mullah facing the bridegroom, and to either side of it stood a lighted candle. Bountifully filled dishes were lined up before it, as well as various items made of gold. Whether those were part of Banu's dowry or gifts from the groom I did not know, but it all looked beautiful. We sat down, crowded knee to knee with the others, and I could see little more. There was much jesting and laughter—not at all solemn as in a Rus' church ceremony.

A hush fell over the group. Banu came in, led by her mother and followed by Fatima. She was so heavily veiled that I wondered if she could see anything at all, but Layla drew her to the front and settled her on her cushion. The mothers both stood, Fatima leaning heavily on her cane. Banu lifted her heavy veil. The groom turned slightly toward Banu, and my heart sank a little for the bride. Though he was the younger brother, he seemed well over thirty and was plain and unsmiling. I could scarcely hear the ceremony, but I know Banu gave an almost whispered consent to the marriage after the mullah asked her three times, and that each time he asked her, Fatima pressed a gold coin into her hand.

Then the mothers held another square of green cloth over the couple while Effat scraped two sugar cones together above it, showering "sweetness" on the couple, as I learned later. Meanwhile Perijam took the couples' white belts and sewed them together with red thread, to join them for life, I think. The mullah also read several lines from the Quran about leading an upright life.

At last Banu faced her husband for the first time. She looked white with fear and scarcely raised her eyes to his. Presumably she and her husband could have already seen each other in the mirror, but their first true glimpse of one other came after they were married. Banu rose and turned to leave, and—I do not know if this was part of the ceremony—her husband caught her sleeve and offered her a pomegranate he had been carrying in the folds of his clothing. They smiled at each other shyly, and she left the room, the rest of us following her back to the women's quarters. Salman's gesture seemed to offer some promise for the future.

We celebrated late into the night with boisterous song and dance and more bawdy jests about the wedding bed. We all ate too much, and I drank too much wine! It did me little good, however, for a dull ache of regret for my own lost ambitions weighed down my heart: a princess destined for greatness at the side of a handsome and valiant prince—and now, no one at all, estranged from home and family and, so it seemed, even a future.

At some point Layla and Effat pulled Banu to her feet and escorted her away to the biruni's bridal chamber among laughter and lewd remarks. I was sitting near the door, thick-headed with wine and half-dreaming of lost hopes, when I heard, from the other house, a shriek followed by wild weeping. It made my hair stand on end! I jumped up in fear—surely a Mongol attack!—but my neighbors laughingly pulled me back down.

Perijam pushed her way to my side and whispered, "He has just taken her maidenhead, that's all. Don't worry; you know how Banu is." But that weeping had awakened such harsh memories of my own introduction to womanhood that it took some time before I could stop trembling.

Meanwhile one of the older women guests had left the room to stand at the top of the stairs. She soon returned, waving a white silk scarf at all the women. It was smeared with a little streak of fresh blood: Banu's, apparently. "Honor is satisfied," she cried, and both mothers smiled broadly.

I heard Perijam's voice near my ear. "Salman's elder brother Farhad has sent it to us as proof of Banu's purity and to show that Salman has taken possession of her. Don't be so shocked, Sofia! Banu always goes to extremes. Besides it was over quickly, and every married woman in this room went through much the same thing. The wedding bed isn't the same as the marriage bed, you know. Banu can hope for much tenderness from her husband in the future. It was thus for me. And if she doesn't find love with him ... well, at least she'll be well cared for and protected from danger in these evil times. Father Selim assures us that Salman ibn

Hussein is a powerful man as well as good—he is his brother Farhad's partner—and since he has two other wives, she can make friends with them. Plus he already knows how to please a woman."

I nodded, but a terrible image had thrust its way into my mind: so many girls like Banu, so young and small compared with her husband, undergoing just the same sort of wedding night. How often are we married off to men more than twice our age so that they can "mold" us properly? My father had promised to wait for the right man, but he could have married me off at any time—"Uncle" Dmitri had at least been right about that when we had quarreled in Batu's camp!

It was then that I finally realized that my dream of marriage to a handsome and kind prince had always been a delusion. What kind of husband might Papa have really found for me? Perhaps a man much older than Salman ibn Hussein and far less kind.

The next three days overflowed with pleasures: roast lamb, special rice dishes, many sweets, song, music, and dance. Everyone but Banu seemed to enjoy themselves to the fullest. But I watched her and saw a frightened, miserable child.

On the fourth morning, sobbing under her heavy veil, she was borne away with her dowry from her father's house toward her new home, probably to live much the same life she had always known. Layla wept, too, and for days she seemed utterly bereft.

The house emptied of guests, and we were alone with each other once again. The house seemed so vacant and quiet. It seemed strange to have no special task to turn to that day, and there were so few laps for the little boys to climb into. For many days thereafter, my thoughts would suddenly turn to Banu and I would repeat my prayer that hers would be, if not a happy life, at least a tolerable one. And Fatima seemed a good woman. Perhaps she would act as a mother in Layla's stead.

SUMMER
ANNO DOMINI 1243

Selim finally summoned me to his room of business. "The weather has turned warm enough to melt the mountain snows, Sofia, and I can soon take you on the next leg of your journey. I imagine you will be glad to move one step closer to—was it your uncle's home?"

"Yes, in Constantinople," I exclaimed, joy flooding my entire body.

"I trust you've enjoyed yourself now and then despite your unflagging eagerness to continue your journey," he added, a twinkle in his eye.

I almost blushed. Doubtless, Mother Layla had told him of my restless walking fits, and a few times over the past few weeks he had at least hinted that he knew, too.

"Selim, I cannot find enough words to thank you properly for all your kindness. Everyone has treated me like family, and our friendship is unbreakable. And I may even have mastered some Persian customs, like the womanly virtue of patience." And I smiled demurely.

Selim laughed. "I always thought that, freed of the burdens laid upon you by slavery, your true nature would arise again. And so it has. Well, your patience shall be rewarded very soon, and it will be time to say goodbye." I suddenly realized that, once on my way home, I would never see Selim's family again. Tears misted my eyes without warning.

"Ah, don't be sad yet, my young friend. When your stay in the Elburz is over, we return here. And even after you reach Constantinople, we may still meet again. Perhaps I will bring my whole family to your fabled city. Stranger things have happened. Or perhaps, once you meet my master, you will not want to leave us. I hear you've been studying our Quran."

Perhaps he meant to comfort, but Selim's words fell between us like stones rattling down the narrow but deep crevice that separated his world from mine. I would never feel safe in Mongol-held lands, nor did I want to stay cloistered in an andarun for the rest of my days. All I could say was, "And if I cannot stay longer with your wonderful family, I will still be traveling with you or your sons, perhaps on your next journey west. I am deeply grateful."

"Yes, my sons will return soon; they will accompany us into the mountains." Selim hesitated. "Alas, when they arrive we will be faced with … a delicate problem."

"Yes?"

"You see, they will not be free to join their families in the andarun unless you and Anna remain veiled at all times. It would be most improper for them to see unveiled women who are not their relatives. I would not violate our holy law if I could avoid it."

"I see." The thought of draping my face while trying to do anything else did seem a little daunting. "Well, I suppose there is no hope for it. I will tell Anna."

"There is another solution, but I waver about mentioning it in case you mistrust my motives. The adage tells us, 'Be suspicious, the better to avoid another's tricks.' But I mean no trickery toward you, and it actually might be a good idea once we are traveling together."

"Selim, I trust you. What is this solution?"

"Well, we of the True Faith, we Shi'a, have a custom dating back to the time of the Prophet, peace on his name, wherein a man and woman marry for an agreed-upon length of time. There are many good reasons for this custom: one, which is not my reason, is so that a woman, perhaps a widow, can fulfill her natural desires, even if she is not Muslim. Another is so that a woman can appear unveiled before her husband's male relatives. It would be for this second reason that I mention the custom and for no other, I assure you!" Selim closed his eyes and put his hand over his heart.

I drew back in shock at first, but after some thought, I asked, "Does this mean you would marry Anna as well?"

Selim looked surprised in turn. "Yes, I suppose that would have to be the way of it. I assure you that I have no designs on her honor, either."

"Let me think on it and speak with Anna. It would not be until your sons return?"

Selim looked relieved that I had not taken deep offense. "Of course."

"And Mother Layla? I owe her such a debt of gratitude—will she not find it strange?"

Selim smiled in his self-secret way. "You need not worry about my beloved wife. I will protect her. But while you are deciding, it would be best to say nothing."

Back in the women's quarters, when I told the other women that we would be leaving once Selim's sons returned, everyone cried out their dismay, especially Perijam.

"I'll only be gone briefly," I assured her. "I'll be back for another visit before we leave for Constantinople. And who knows? Perhaps you can travel with us and see the world!"

Perijam shook her head. "Women rarely travel unless they are fleeing danger or are on pilgrimage to the holy places. I have no desire for more danger and little hope of being a pilgrim now that I'm to be a mother. No, Sofia, it will be farewell forever, I fear."

To prevent trickling sadness from turning into a flood, I only said, "We'll see, my friend. Father Selim first suggested it. Meanwhile we can enjoy our time together now and let tomorrow take care of itself. Come; let's see what new blooms the garden has produced."

The next few days with Selim's family were sweet mixed with sour, though Anna could not contain her happy outpourings to me. I often had to bite back a harsh retort. I showered gratitude and affection on everyone, but above all on Perijam. At night I worked in secret on little keepsakes for them all, embroidered in the style of Rus'.

Late one afternoon, Selim's sons Umar and Kerim arrived from the Holy Land. Effat greeted her husband with quiet dignity, but Perijam, who was now as plump as a sweet Persian melon, was almost beside herself with joy. My face carefully veiled, I watched and decided that my own dreams of happiness within an arranged marriage had not been so far-fetched after all. Perhaps my Uncle Vasily would find me a husband…

But who would want to take an ex-slave, a tainted concubine, a sinner, to wife? This proposed "marriage" with Selim scarcely counted. And truly, did I want to be at the mercy of any man again? No, once home and free I would try again to make a new life for myself and put my past firmly behind me. I would even dissemble about it if necessary.

Before dinner, Selim's sons passed out gifts and regaled their loved ones with tales of hardship and adventure while Anna and I stayed in the background. Alas, when it came time to eat and we must join the family, keeping my veil in place proved quite a trial. Selim's offer clearly held merit, but I was still not ready to try it.

All the wives spent the night in the biruni with their husbands, while we were left with two silly girls and two lonely little boys.

The very next morning on returning to the andarun, Layla said, "Sofia, I wish to propose something to you and Anna. Please know that this is only out of love, and with no other thought than your well-being." And she spelled out almost word for word what Selim had said to me. He had clearly worked on her mind the night before. In turn I had to explain Layla's offer to Anna and how this sort of marriage worked, assuring her that she was in no danger of Selim even touching her. She responded with storms and tears, but by the next morning, having spilled food on her lovely veil at breakfast, she too saw value in the idea.

So we agreed. Selim married us both in the simplest of ceremonies: after he wrote up a document that we all signed—Anna put an X by her name, which I had written for her—he took it away to show a mullah, and that was that! We were married, not for a length of time and not for money, which was the usual arrangement, but until he had delivered us to Constantinople. Until then we were under his undying care and protection. He even added a commitment that should anything happen to him, he would entrust our safety to our former guide Da'ud. In return, we would visit his master and I would share what had happened to us in the Mongol camps. I could see no reason why anyone would be interested, but if it was what Selim wanted, I would tell about every nit I had ever picked out of my hair!

For the next few days, Anna and I were truly one of the family, and no one seemed to find our temporary marriage at all strange, although Umar and Kerim stared at us when we were not looking—I know because my eyes met theirs by accident a few times. Umar averted his gaze, but Kerim always smiled in the friendliest fashion. I felt I had gained a brother. The other oddity was that Selim actually touched me for the first time since we had known each other. It came as a shock when he did—he was merely passing me—but Kerim was watching. He smiled in a knowing way that I did not like, and I hastily stepped aside.

One morning Selim announced that we would leave in two days. Perijam burst into tears, which made Aftab and Sarah and the boys cry, and even Effat's eyes grew red. Mine did, too, glad though I was to be on my way.

The next day was filled with preparations for the journey. Mother Layla ordered a special farewell supper, and afterwards I gave out my little embroidered gifts and returned Effat's Quran to her with many thanks. She might have argued with me politely, but luckily there was no time. To my surprise, she and Layla and Perijam produced gifts for Anna and me, as well: glass bangles, filigreed earrings, and little bottles of rosewater and orange blossom water. Even Anna wept—it was the first time anyone had ever given her a gift.

We arose well before sunrise. Selim had decided it would be safest for Anna and me to return to our disguises, so both of us put on loose white shirts, cotton payjamas, and light coats called kaftans, which we could bind with sashes if we chose. Donning them spoke to me of new adventure, and part of my heart soared like a lark at the thought of leaving the andarun.

Just before we left, Layla brought out a tray on which sat a small mirror, two lumps of sugar, and the Quran. "This is the way we bid loved ones farewell, and I hope you will consent to our little ceremony. I know it contains the Quran, but …."

"Of course we do."

So Layla held up the tray and directed Anna and me to pass under it three times. Then she showed us our faces in the little mirror. "For light. And were you Muslim, you would kiss the Quran for guidance from the One God we share," she explained. "But as you are not, I will do that for you." To finish, she gave Anna and me the lumps of sugar for happiness. After that, more little gifts and promises of eternal friendship were offered, but in the end Noor came up to fetch us and we had to go. Anna was included in their embraces, and she even returned them.

I looked around the room one last time. A songbird chirped sleepily as if in farewell. With Noor bearing a torch before us, we all hastened out of the andarun, through Selim's house, and along his elaborate garden paths. I smelled the heavy perfume of flowers, glimpsed the last stars of night in the reflecting pool. Each step was filled with sadness and joy, with precious memories mixed with hopes for the future.

At the gate leading to the outer courtyard, we each embraced for the last time, our faces illumined by torchlight.

"Have a green year," each woman told me as we kissed each other's cheeks. Thus will I always remember them: a timeless moment that death itself cannot destroy. Looking back, despite all my petty complaints, my time with them had been a respite from sorrow and a source of deep joys. I still wish I had spent it more wisely, or at least more gratefully.

Chaos greeted us on the other side of the gate: the clamor and bustle of men, animals jostling, whinnying, braying, bells jingling in the fading indigo of pre-dawn. Selim and his sons seemed to be everywhere at once, giving orders or seeing to some detail of loading the mules. After the quiet life of the andarun, I felt like I was drowning in a sea of commotion. Perhaps it was because I had been so cloistered for so long, but everything—people, noise, animals, even the buildings—appeared louder, brighter, more vivid, and growing more so by the swell of predawn light. Da'ud appeared from nowhere and saluted me gravely, and Nasr and Ali and I salaamed in passing. Selim led us to our mounts, a pair of stout mules, and we were off. I looked back and waved at my friends, though the gate hid them from my sight.

Selim led the procession, followed by his sons, my former guides, a few other guards, and Anna and me. Several dozen armed servants strode behind us leading more mules loaded with assorted bundles. His house sat so near the city's edge that leaving Qazvin took scarcely any time at all. Selim seemed well-known among the small detachment of Mongol guards we passed. They were encamped where the southern caravan road began, and they let him pass with an exchange of bawdy witticisms, his paize, and a bag of baksheesh. Though Berke's soldiers would surely have long ago given up any search for me, I held my breath as we passed by them.

To my surprise, some time after we were out of the Mongols' sight our procession turned east along a faint cross-trail that took us north in a great arc around Qazvin. As the sun rose, we stopped briefly for prayers, the snowcapped Elburz mountain range at the edge of our sight. What a beautiful morning it was, the brightening sky turning ever bluer, not a cloud in sight. The sun almost leapt up from behind the mountains, dazzling my eyes and casting a golden veil of beauty upon the earth. I had not greeted the rising sun or the morning goddess in so long that I almost burst with joy. And I cared not one whit that the morning goddess was pagan!

Yet, strangely, my eyes seemed to have weakened so that I could only clearly see the things that were closest. Indeed, a few days passed before distances came sharp to sight again. Not that this stopped me from feeling how beautiful it all was. That morning we rode uphill, passing over a rolling, mostly treeless land blanketed in spring's soft gold-greens and swathes of wildflowers: red, yellow, and blue. Beyond us, clothed in purple veils of haze, the Elburz range jutted up behind a straight ridge of nearer mountains. The stillness of the day was broken only by flocks of birds soaring above us, crying out delight, or the mournful singing of one or two of Selim's men. Other than stopping for prayers and a midday meal by a stream overhung with willows, we moved steadily onward until toward evening when we reached a small village.

It reminded me, at least in spirit, of Papa's smerdi village huddled outside the walls of our country palace, only here there was no palace or prince to turn to for refuge. Instead, high walls surrounded the little settlement. An arched gate led into a narrow street lined with blank-fronted homes all built of stone or mud brick. I saw not only men but a few women hurrying home from their gardens or chasing a wayward chicken back into a tiny compound. Goats or sheep bleated invisibly. Once or twice doors swung slightly open and eyes followed our progress to the headman's home that also served as a guesthouse.

After sunset prayers and the evening meal, Anna and I were sent up to the flat roof. We lay talking quietly in the mild twilight, wondering to one another what lay ahead and looking up as golden stars glowed overhead until our eyes closed in sleep. I dreamt of a happy land.

The next day passed pleasantly. Everywhere, spring had laid her gentle hand on the land: trees greening, boys driving their flocks up toward higher pastures, women hoeing their little gardens or tending the orchards around their villages. Where the land was flat enough, men were furrowing their fields, crying out to their oxen to turn as they reached the end of a row. Beyond the fields rose a rock-strewn wilderness that not even a few hardy wildflowers could soften. How hard those men must work to nurture their lands!

I saw little of Selim, although his younger son Kerim often rode nearby and Da'ud was always right behind us. Kerim seemed to know the reason for our disguise, and it must have filled him with wonder if his many glances our way meant anything. He sometimes rode beside me, speaking from time to time in friendly fashion and acting as if I truly was part of his family. I didn't know what to make of him but always answered politely. I tried not to look at him, but if I glanced up he was was always looking straight at me. It made me blush.

A day or two on, we began climbing into foothills, and I began to wonder why I must keep waiting to speak with Selim about his plans. His family was surely far enough away now; there was no danger of their learning something that might endanger them. One evening we stopped in a little village nestled in a high valley by a tumbling stream. I tried to approach him, but he was busy with his men and moved away just as I came up, almost as if he was avoiding me.

Finally I gave up in frustration and retired to the roof where Anna awaited me, most unhappy that I had left her alone for so long. She was wearing her amulet around her neck again and clutching it tight. I was feeling most unhappy, too, and answered her shortly before I lay down. And then I felt discomfited. There was no reason to take my feelings out on Anna. For a long time I stared up at the thickly starred sky. It seemed that the stars, so beautiful and mysterious, at one moment began crowding in upon me about to rain upon my head; and at another, they drew so far away that I lost all sense of up and down. Perhaps I would fall up, off the earth. They slowly swept overhead in a great arc, or was I asleep?

The next day we wound up a small mountain, red and rocky, stopping at a pass where snow hid in sunless crevices, the air was as sweet and crisp as a fresh apple, and the scent of lavender floated up from below. Before us lay barren foothills, a few little green valleys wedged between them. A glint of river wound around some distant bend. In the distance, massive mountains reared up, crowned with snow and sharply outlined against the lapis sky.

Kerim spoke from behind me. "Those are the Elburz Mountains before us, and those are the Alamut valleys below us. The river is called the Rudbar, and one of its tributaries leads back to our master's castle.

Another two days of easy travel and we will be there. The tallest mountain far to the northeast is Solomon's Seat. No, look over there, where its twin peaks resemble the arms of a throne."

I glanced back at him in surprise. "The King Solomon of my Holy Scriptures?"

"And ours. Legend says that when he was old and ugly, he married the Queen of Sheba, who was a lovely maiden, and magically transported her to that peak. She had to choose between freezing to death and entering his wedding tent." Kerim laughed softly, but I frowned and turned back to where Anna was standing.

After a brief rest, we plunged down a trail so dizzying that I had to keep my eyes shut part of the time and trust the man guiding my mule. At the bottom of the narrow ravine, we passed a little guard station by a swollen brown river where an armed guard solemnly greeted Selim. We crossed a rickety bridge that threatened to collapse under our weight—or so it seemed to me. A cliff rose on the other side like a prison wall, cutting off the sun, and a little track looped back and forth up to the top. I was glad my mount was so surefooted because the rock-strewn path seemed so narrow that I had to close my eyes or faint. The drop to the river below made my head spin the one time I opened them and looked down.

It was late afternoon when we reached the top where a meadow mantled with dazzling red and white poppies greeted us. More armed guards saluted Selim respectfully and led us to a small castle. While his men were unloading the mules, Anna and I wandered about. Finding a stairway up to the parapets, we went up to try to see where we were going. But the view before me was of mountains in all directions, marbled with snow and streaked purple and black in the setting sun. It was austere, remote, and utterly beautiful.

I retreated to the yard, feeling that I could not continue in darkest ignorance any longer. Finally, having summoned my courage and told Anna to wait for me, I dogged Selim while he worked. Finally he turned to me and said, "You wish to speak with me at last. I know it, and I have already set aside tonight for that very purpose since we arrive at my master's castle soon. I must beg your patience for a little longer until we are all settled here."

I had to accept his polite reassurances and withdraw to stand by Anna. There was nothing to do but watch the beasts be unloaded and fed and feel less important than they were. We submitted to God as the sun set, ate with the others, and were led to a small room where she and I were to sleep.

We were laying out our bedding when Selim joined us, followed by a manservant carrying a tray with a pitcher and cups. "I have brought you some mint tea," said my friend. And as he sat on the carpeted floor, "Please join me."

"Anna, do you wish to come and sit with us?" I asked.

"No, Mistress, I am so tired!" She knelt in brief prayer, crossed herself, rolled up in her quilts, and turned away from us.

Selim served the tea in solemn silence and with fewer flourishes than usual. At last, while I cradled my hands around the warm cup, he spoke in low tones, a hand over his heart.

"It must seem strange to you that I have said nothing about the future since returning from my travels. They took me longer than I expected, and I admit that I indulged my joy in being with my loved ones at the expense of your curiosity. For all of this I offer deepest regrets. As your host I must have seemed most ungracious."

I tried to disagree politely, but he held up his hands in a gesture that expressed regret, apology, and a refusal to be interrupted. "Please understand that my extreme caution came from a desire to protect my women. Now that we are safely away from Qazvin, I can unfold my plans to you." He paused to reflect.

"First, I want you to know that not even my own wife knows the secrets I now entrust to you, nor do any of the women under my care. Indeed, only my elder sons and a few loyal servants like Da'ud are part of my ... other life. I will tell you as much as I can because I hold you in such high esteem, Sofia. As you once said, you are an educated woman, an unusual woman. In some ways you are more like a man and most unlike my wife and girls. Although," he smiled, "it would seem that they are more capable than I once thought them. Effat has taught the younger girls to read." I smiled, but ironically. No matter how highly he thought of me, I could not share his small view of his loved ones.

"You once warned me that Batu Khan suspected I was a spy. I will confess that in part I am. But the question is, for whom? Not for the bloodsucking landowners who govern us for their Mongol masters. Nor for the scraps of Khwarizmian devils whose arrogant shah drew the Mongol storm down on us! He deserved his shameful death." I recalled that Argamon had once given me jewelry from Khwarizm, and Da'ud had mentioned that shah, but Selim was rushing on with his story and becoming ever more stirred as he spoke. "And the Seljuks who overran the Dar al-Islam," he made a spitting gesture, "our bitterest enemies—ignorant upstarts who claim to support true Islam! Someday the world will be purged of them and their false Khalifs and of the false teachings of all Sunni—and false Shi'a, too!" I had seen him so serious and so bitter only one other time, in the Mongol camps when I had chided him for cheating. And now this: such a long and alarming list of people to hate!

He took a deep breath. "No, my allegiance is to a higher sovereign, to Allah the Omnipotent and All-seeing. Sofia, life is more than appearances. Through the Prophet Muhammad, peace on his name, Omniscient Allah revealed that all streams of existence lead to the same great Ocean: surrender to Him and absorption into His True Being. He taught us how to surrender to God at every moment, so that every breath becomes an act of worship." That I somewhat understood because of that glimpse of wholeness I'd had in Batu Khan's camp. Could Selim have had some similar experience? But then he added, "And a chosen few of us are destined to cleanse the earth of evil and make manifest the full truth of Allah the Almighty. I am called to that sacred task, as are my sons; and Da'ud and his boys; and Habib who brought you into Iran; and many, many others. Every day our numbers grow, for many men will heed the call to martyr themselves as the end grows near. You see, these Mongol invasions are a clear sign that the final days of the last cycle are upon us.

"So yes, I am indeed a spy and much more, but for a nation that appears on no map, although we hold territory here and there in Iran and Syria. Ours is an empire of faith that stretches across Iran and Syria and beyond, even to Hungary in faraway Christendom. It is an empire of the spirit and truth and loyalty—true Islam, true submission. As a subject of that domain, I would do everything in my power to help usher in a new world dedicated to the glory of Allah, the All-Seeing!

"Sofia, I take you to the holiest man you will ever meet. He is our Imam, the direct descendant of the Prophet, blessings on his name. He is the Mahdi himself, the Rightly Guided One, who reveals Allah's truth to the faithful by his mere presence on earth. He is the Grand Master of our brotherhood, known to each other as the Nizari or the Faithful. We endure persecution and lies from Sunni and Shi'a heretics, but we cleave to the true line of Imams. Ours has always been the lineage of martyr-dom, so we bear our secret burden gladly.

"I have told you before why I want you to come to him. How fortu-nate you were to be so close to Batu Khan, to have witnessed for yourself how his generals work together, even to have written his orders to them, and been privy to his most intimate secrets. Not even his physician Ben Hasan, who is secretly one of us, can offer the wealth of knowledge you carry in your memory. My master will want to know everything about your life among the Mongols and about Batu Khan and his brothers and cousins in particular. He and his entire vermin breed must be wiped out in the great final struggle for justice. I know that my master will be most grateful to hear your story and that he will reward you handsomely."

All this talk of cleansing and martyrs and struggle! Selim was reveal-ing a side of himself that was neither expected nor welcome. I wanted the kindly humorous merchant back, the man who had bravely saved my life—purely out of friendship, I had thought ....

But he had also destroyed his beloved concubine. And now I had in effect married him!

And gentle Ben Hasan was "one of us." Who was this "us", for was the physician not a Jew?

Selim had fallen silent and was looking at me expectantly. But what could I say? Until Effat had told me Muhammad's life story, I had always thought he was some misguided mystic who had claimed to amend the Holy Word of Christ and set himself up in His place. I was still shocked that a Prophet would rob caravans and fight wars of conquest. And this Imam-Mahdi-holy man was his descendant? I sensed I was in grave danger, not just from deeds but from ideas.

"Selim," I finally answered, "As you know, I am Christian, and some of what you say is familiar. I too wish the Mongols to be gone from our homes forever, not from only Rus' or Persia but from all the places they plague, so I would help you on those grounds alone. But I know too little about Islam and nothing about this holy man and his empire of the spirit. I do not want to be a weapon in a struggle I know nothing about!"

He responded with frightening fervor. "Then I will tell you all you need to know!" He paused only a moment before plunging into a story that I was not prepared to hear.

"I will begin at the beginning, with the Prophet's death, peace on his memory. It was a terrible loss, and the Pure Faith nearly died with him. Many streams of Islam turned dry and empty, while his wisdom was sucked away like rain falling onto driest desert. In its place sprouted weeds of petty strife, grasping, injustice: everything he wanted us to abandon! The sweet fragrance of his teachings lingered in the air for a chosen few, but most men turned their backs on the brotherhood of Islam and marched straight into the wilderness of worldly ambition.

"Even his closest disciples, his Companions, lost sight of their true goal. Debate and struggle arose over who would represent him on earth as his Khalif, to lead Islam and be lord of the immense dominions the Prophet, peace on his name, had brought into the shelter of the True Faith.

"These men saw with the eyes of the blind. They turned their backs on their Prophet's own wishes, that his saintly nephew and son-in-law Ali be elected his Khalif! For the sake of harmony, Ali, peace upon him, would not press his claim. Instead, he shared the essence of the inner life—true submission, true peace—with his sons, Hasan and Hussein, blessings on them, and with his chosen disciples. He was finally elected Khalif, but only after three of our blessed Prophet's Companions were elected and had died. The last two were murdered, one by a fellow Muslim! But when Ali gained his rightful place, it seemed a sign that the True Faith had triumphed before selfishness and strife could destroy it from within.

"Alas, civil war broke out, led by one Mu'awiya, cousin to the last Khalif. Ali's army had almost crushed Mu'awiya's, but when this deviser of evil plots saw defeat before him, he cunningly had his troops tie pages of the Holy Quran to their spears so that Ali could no longer fight them. Instead, when Ali tried to make peace, one of his own men, a lunatic who put his judgment above his Khalif's, murdered him! Then Mu'awiya simply usurped the Khalifate. Thus, after only four reigns and within one lifetime, Islam had fallen so low."

I was feeling increasingly bewildered and upset. "Selim, you must forgive me, but I cannot take in so much at once. I had no idea you would try to tell me everything right now."

Selim looked a little wounded, but he nodded politely. "I will await your pleasure, then." He stood, bowed, and would have left.

I cried, "Please, I do want to hear more, perhaps tomorrow, but let me say this now. I have not traveled such a long way in order to forfeit my life or my freedom for another's cause. Promise me you will live up to our marriage agreement and take me away as soon as I have spoken with your master. And if you cannot do it yourself, you can send me west with one of your sons' caravans to a place where I can find my own way to Constantinople."

"Agreed, Sofia. More than what you offer I would never ask, even if I cling to hope that you will accept my invitation to truth. I imagined you joining us in our holy struggle for the One God's true justice … well, so you will in your own way."

We bade each other a good night, but I felt miserable. Everything Selim had told me had served only to confuse me. None of it helped me understand what was to come. Indeed, he had left me with more questions!

Just before dawn, a dark dream came to me. I was lying on a divan like the ones that ran along the walls of the women's room in Selim's andarun, but it was built onto a high cliff. It suddenly began tilting under me, rolling me off, and I was tumbling through darkness into an endless chasm. I awoke feeling as if I had fallen from a secure world of kindly women into an abyss of unknown dangers.

That morning we followed a path slippery with shale down into the first of the Alamut valleys and spent the rest of the day traveling beside the racing river, going up and down, over or around rocky hills where more forts were perched. Sometimes cliffs rose almost straight from the water, forcing us to edge along the riverbank; or we might have to cross a shaky bridge over a stream where it met the river. Now and then, a valley would open out before us into brilliant broad green, and there a village would stand, surrounded by bright orchards and gardens. But the further we went, the more those stark hills seemed to loom over us, trapping the heat, while they shifted in shape like djinn, turning from red to purple to blue as the sun grew lower.

Late in the day, we passed a village where the river broadened and ran more softly. The land seemed so peaceful and prosperous, with poplar and willow trees dotting the riverbanks, wheat and poppy fields beyond them, plum and cherry orchards outside the village walls, and a few meadows on the hills where shepherds tended small flocks of sheep. Lit by the lowering sun, everything glowed softly, although spurs of the Elburz Mountains thrust up around us like jagged bones tearing through the earth's skin.

We turned north along a narrow river valley enclosed by steep hills that led up to even steeper snowy mountain cliffs. It was almost dark when we arrived at a hamlet of flat-roofed houses clinging to a hillside. The headman came out to welcome us—he and the other villagers seemed to know everyone in our caravan but Anna and me—and we were introduced as "new converts to our cause." After dark, lying on the flat roof, I heard voices wafting from the headman's main room where all the village men had gathered. I fell asleep listening to scraps of long, fanciful stories and songs about local doings and wondering when Selim would finish his explanation to me. But I knew it was already too late.

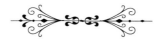

The next morning as the rising sun and the sound of prayer woke me, I got my first glimpse of our destination: an immense rock that bulged out before the craggy mountains like a massive wave frozen into stone. I thought I saw watchtowers and a wall that followed the rocky wave's uneven crest, though it seemed an impossible place for a castle. After breakfast we began to climb away from the river through a ravine whose towering rock walls nearly touched each other.

Once onto a more level area, Kerim, who had been walking near us, spoke as he drew abreast of me. "Look up there and you can see a little of the castle. It is called the Eagle's Nest. And the rock it is perched on is the Rock of Qasar Khan." As if summoned, an eagle appeared overhead, soaring and wheeling about the castle.

I shivered, though it was growing warm. "How will we get up there? Fly like eagles?"

He laughed. "No, this path twists up around the Rock and takes us in an arc to the north of the castle. It is wide enough for one horseman at a time but impossible for any army to reach—and more than one army has thrown itself against the Eagle's Nest and been shattered. We cross a natural bridge when we reach the top, and we are there. There are also secret entrances, but those I know of only from rumor."

Soon thereafter we reached the spot where the Rock adjoined a soaring mountain, and then our true ascent began. Armed men stood guard at a pair of forts, one above the other; but recognizing Selim, they let us by. Up and up and up we climbed. The trail seemed to have grown from the mountainside itself—surely no one could have tried to carve it from the stone and survived. And it seemed to me to be barely wide enough for walking even in single file! The air was so thin and sharp that I was soon out of breath. It even tasted rocky. I looked back only once at the ravine behind us and had to look away, the view was so dizzying. But above us, the cliff and surrounding mountain peaks loomed so rugged and steep that they too made me feel giddy.

At last we reached a metal-plated bridge of rock that connected the Rock to the mountainside, and before us stood the castle. With its massive walls and heavy round turrets, it too seemed to have been carved rather than built from the narrow slanting crown of the Rock. As I crossed the bridge, surrounded on all sides by peaks and sheer drops, I began to feel sick with dizziness. I closed my eyes. Happily, armed guards quickly admitted us through a narrow lead-covered gate guarded by watchtowers. I had seen aright from below; several more towers reared up along the castle's thick boundary walls.

Just inside was a fairly level courtyard, lined on all sides with small buildings built right into the walls. Its center held a small marketplace where a few men were displaying bright brass vessels, turquoise bowls, a saddle that seemed rather out of place, rolled-up carpets, and foodstuffs. One man poked among some onions while another haggled over a pot. Channels carried water downhill into the fort from what might be a deep cistern located to my right. Well-kept vegetable gardens were wedged between some of the buildings. Everything seemed clean, bright, and orderly compared with the ruination I had witnessed in my journey through Iran. A few men were purposefully crossing the square, and though one or two were armed, none looked ready to embark on any holy mission.

To my left a pair of buildings stood against the courtyard wall, one of which was a mosque. The larger building—clearly the citadel—lorded over the rest of the fortress. Selim led our group past them to an arched gate in the yard's wall, where steps led down to a second courtyard that doubled the size of the fortress. We stopped before the gate and I looked down. Along the wall nearest the cliff stood what must be a barracks; but there seemed to be no outer fortifications anywhere, just small houses divided by narrow alleys and tiny gardens. The little dwellings seemed to tumble down the rocky sides until they met—or became—the lowest castle wall. Down that far there were no alleys, and men were crossing rooftops and climbing ladders to get to and fro. All this I took in while waiting for Selim to finish giving instructions to Da'ud and his men. Only after they had departed down the steps did Selim lead his sons, Anna, and me toward the heart of the castle: the citadel. I was reminded suddenly of the time Argamon had delayed taking me to his father for the first time. Was Selim afraid, too? He seemed not to be; if anything, he seemed full of contained excitement.

We passed a few bearded men in gray or black kaftans talking with each other outside the beautifully tiled mosque, a clean scent drifting from its half-open doors. On another occasion I might have wanted to linger to admire the mosque's turquoise tiles, made more brilliant by the sun, but the citadel commanded my attention. Surrounded by high, thick walls that were pierced by a gateway with a pointed arch and guarded by a heavy door. Its impressiveness came not from any beauty but from its solidity. It looked as if it would never fall into enemy hands, even were the rest of Alamut somehow taken. Severe-looking armed guards stood at the entrance, but they let us in straightaway. We followed Selim across the small courtyard, where another guard opened a plain, heavy, iron-bound door for us. Selim beckoned us all to follow him and strode inside with rare eagerness.

Anna tugged at my sleeve and looked at me beseechingly. She still knew nothing, for I had not wanted to cause her any unease, but now I regretted my decision. Was I not treating her just as Selim treated his women? I leaned close and whispered, "Anna, we're summoned by a great man to help him rid the world of our Mongol enemies. I'm to tell him all I can about them, and then they'll send us on our way."

She clutched at my hand. "As long as I'm near you, I feel safe," she whispered back. I hoped her confidence was not misplaced, for instead of the keen interest I was trying to feel, dread was creeping into my bones. Thank God that in a day or so this final trial would be over and I would be on my way to Constantinople and a true home.

The day had grown increasingly warm, but once inside the stronghold, I began to shiver. Reminding myself that I was not being dragged before a one-eyed chieftain to be displayed as a war captive, I hurried behind the men up a flight of stairs, through another guarded door, and along a smooth-tiled corridor. We stopped before a simple arched door guarded on either side by yet more armed men. Selim spoke to a man in gray robes, who seemed to be a sort of major domo, and who said, "Yes, he expects you," before slipping through the door and closing it softly.

We waited.

My mouth dried up like a pond in drought, my hands felt sticky with cold sweat. Who was this mysterious holy man? And why was he making us wait for so long? Selim finally turned to me and whispered, "When we come before my master, you should remain silent at first and I will speak for you. Your time for speech will come very soon."

At last the door opened again, and the gray-robed man beckoned to Selim. We followed him into a modest but well-proportioned room that faintly reminded me of the audience hall in Papa's city palace in Kyiv, although instead of wood and marble, this room was of dressed stone; in place of well-swept marble floors, dazzling carpets lapped over one another like waves on the Caspian Sea; and instead of isinglass-paned windows, there were narrow slit-like openings that might serve as places from which to shoot arrows in battle. But there was also, as in Papa's hall, a dais with a low seat where a bearded man in a green dulband and black robes sat, looking just as stern as Papa had in the old days when he dispensed justice. Clusters of men stood silently along the sides of the room. And, just as in Kyiv, there was an air of serious purpose about this place.

The man in the chair was surrounded by other solemn, bearded men dressed in white or gray. I remember the beards clearly because there was only one fellow there without one, a sweet-faced youth of perhaps thirteen or fourteen who was seated on a stool before and below the holy man—for who else could he be?—looking utterly miserable.

I followed Selim and his sons in making deep obeisance at the door and walking the suddenly-endless distance of the room until we were right before the dais. But when Selim and his sons prostrated and kissed their master's feet before rising and looking down reverentially, as though praying to God, I decided not to follow their example. Anna reached for my hand. Hers was shaking. I heard mutters of disapproval from several men around the room. We stood in complete silence for a small eternity while Selim's master looked us over. I tried not to show my unease, though I also did not dare to look at him directly. Somehow he seemed not at all pleasant to me.

He finally spoke. "Welcome, my sons." Another long silence followed. I tried not to be afraid.

"Selim al-Din, is this the young woman you spoke of?"

"Yes, Lord."

"Why is she dressed in men's clothing? It is an abomination!"

I flinched, but Selim seemed unruffled. "My deepest regrets, Lord. She is dressed thus because it was the safest way to transport her here, and I brought her directly to you without stopping for her to change into women's attire. There are those who would sell their own mothers if the Mongols paid them enough, even among my own men, perhaps. And I know that Batu Khan, from whom I stole this woman, has sent out inquiries as far as Qazvin and as recently as last month." Stole? Well, in a sense Selim had. And if Batu had sought me as recently as last month, no wonder my protector had been so cautious!

"She must be very important to him, then," the Lord of Alamut was saying. He smiled without humor. "And now we have her. Very good!"

"There is more, Lord, if you consent for me to speak …." Selim waited to go on.

"Yes?"

"I could have dressed her in women's clothing before entering your holy presence, but I did not because she is almost like a man: intelligent, observant, with a deep love of learning. She will be of great value to our cause, I believe, and she will gladly tell you everything she knows about the inner circle of Mongol power. Furthermore, she can become another weapon in our war against the unbelievers who infest this sorry world."

I could hardly believe it! I had already told him I would be no one's weapon. Had I not been so daunted by all those harsh-looking men, I'd have cut in to correct Selim's false picture of me. But I held my tongue, and I will never know if I was right or wrong.

The holy man sat for some time as if in thought. He beckoned to one of the men standing behind him, and they spoke together in low tones. "I see some virtue in your answer. But beyond revealing what she knows, how else can she be of use to us?"

"In this way, lord: I have promised her that after she has opened her treasury of knowledge to you, I will take her to Constantinople, where her uncle lives. It might be useful for our cause if, at the same time, I were to travel there, too, to complete whatever mission might be useful on your behalf." Well, that would not concern me. I almost sighed with relief.

"Ye-ess," the Imam began, when his counselor bent and whispered something in his ear. "Yes, that is one possibility. There are others, too. I need time to consider them all. Now you may bring the woman forward to salute me."

I decided that if I were thought to be so like a man, then I had best act like one. I took a confident-seeming step forward and salaamed as Selim presented me to his master: Muhammad III Ala al-Din ibn Hasan III, Imam of the Nizari line of Islam, the Faithful, who are known less respectfully elsewhere as the Hashishiya, the rabble, as I was to discover much later. I sensed Ala al-Din's displeasure, but before he could reprove me I spoke, looking politely down at the floor, "I am not one of you, my Lord, but if I can give information that helps you in your quest to free Iran from the sharp claws of the Mongol tigers, then I do so gladly."

"You are a bold woman," he said. "And you speak our tongue. How did you learn?"

"I studied with Selim al-Din himself, and I stayed in Qazvin as his family's guest this winter. I read and write Farsi and Arabic, my Lord, as well as several other languages."

"Ah, so many talents. Selim sent me word that you were Batu Khan's concubine as well as his translator, but it seems there is more. Yes, I think he is right. You could indeed be a powerful weapon for justice. What do you think, my son?" He prodded the boy at his feet. The youth, I had noticed out of the corner of my eye, had been staring at me fixedly in violation of all the rules of propriety.

Recalled to himself, the boy straightened up and exclaimed, "I think that under that disguise stands a beautiful woman who would make a perfect jarya for a prince."

Selim stiffened at those words, but the Imam clapped the youth on the back and laughed. "A good thought indeed, little Rukn. I may make a man of you yet."

I had never heard of a jarya. Hopefully it was another word for translator.

The boy flushed deeply. There was something innocent, even pitiable about him. What I could not know was that he had just twisted my fate into a new direction.

Selim exclaimed, "My Lord, I gave my word of honor to this girl, even to marrying—"

"I gave you no leave to speak," Ala al-Din cut in. "Do you put your trifling word above the needs of our sacred mission?" I glanced up to see him glaring down at my friend. He seemed as severe as the holy men I had met in Rus': deep lines carved into his face, heavy brows, a beard streaked with white. He might be in his late forties or early fifties.

I glanced over at Selim, who looked frozen with fear. He fell to his knees and shakily said, "No, Master. Please forgive me."

The Imam sat stonily in silence for several heartbeats. "You overstep yourself in too many ways lately, Selim al-Din: too much luxury makes you soft. You even allow music among your women—and wine at weddings! Remember to whom you owe not merely allegiance but the light of life itself! You are to obey without doubt or question."

Selim hung his head, looking utterly crushed. I was frozen to the spot. This was not at all like my friend, and his master was clearly dangerous if he had spies in Selim's household! And though I could understand his condemnation of wine if Muhammad had forbidden it, what was wrong with music?

After an agonizing silence, the man finally spoke again. "I forgive you—this time. But this is my will: I will think on where to send you next, but meanwhile you and your sons must return to Qazvin on the morrow. This young woman will stay behind in your lodgings for now. I shall send for her later once I decide how best to make use of her talents."

"Yes, my Lord," said Selim. That seemed to be the end of the interview, for Selim prostrated before backing away. His face had stiffened into a mask. I too was almost stiff, with anger for Selim and fear for myself.

Anna and I followed Selim and his sons out, across the square; down through the lower castle courtyard; through a series of steps and alleys between houses until we were almost halfway down the rock; onto a narrow alley; and into his dwelling, a small compound that reminded me a little of Musa ad-Din's home in Derbent. We crowded into his biruni, but there was nothing to do but stand aside as he paced back and forth, fists clenched and brow furrowed. Only after prayers, with Anna and me pressed awkwardly against a wall, did he even invite us all to sit. Two servants brought in a midday meal, but I could scarcely eat, I was so worried. It was not until his sons begged to be excused that Selim even glanced at

Anna and me. I was bursting with questions by then, and I wanted no more replies that were more air than substance—yet still I hesitated to speak out of dread of what his answers would reveal.

Selim finally took a deep breath and said, "I am sorry, Sofia. What you witnessed was less about you than about my master purging me of sin. Please don't worry. He sees into all the hidden places of our souls, but to do so, he must cloak himself in human emotions. How else can he treat us in ways we can understand? And he is right to consider how best to use the gifts you bring us … but you are still under my protection. I would never abandon my duty."

"Selim, you are shedding no light on what just happened. You must stop treating me like a child—or a woman—and started trusting me to understand complex affairs. It is time for complete truth. Please: what just passed between you and your master, and why am I in need of protection, and from whom do I need to be protected?"

He sat in silent struggle with who knew what inner enemies, while I waited with less and less patience and Anna sat dumbly. "You are right. I will tell you as briefly as I can, but there is so much to say. Yet without it how can you understand me and the cause for which I live and breathe? Will you listen to the end this time?"

I nodded, unhappy at the thought of another long story. And I had a right to be: as he spoke, it felt as if the rock on which we were perched, already so alarmingly slanted, was slowly tilting beneath me until I was falling off into nothingness.

"You recall that the true Khalif Ali, peace on his name, was murdered and the evil Mu'awiya usurped the Khalifate? Until Ali's death, his followers across the Dar al-Islam, the true Muslims like us, the Shi'at Ali, had been struggling against the Sunni faction." I looked blank. "There are those are those who corrupt our religion for their own ends, starting with arrogant Arab nobility who saw newer converts to Holy Islam as upstarts and lesser men. They call themselves Sunni, but we call them traitors to the Prophet's great vision, blessings on his name!

"But back to what you need to know: seemingly, after that terrible murder, the Shi'a lost. Ali's first son Hasan became a holy recluse, only to be murdered by poison, while his second, Hussein, agreed not to claim the Khalifate until after Mu'awiya's death. Instead, when at last Hussein was on his way to claim his rights, Mu'awiya's wicked son sent troops against him and his followers. They slew Hussein and almost all his male relatives—even though Hussein was dressed in the clothing of his grandfather the Prophet, wearing the green turban of a descendant of the Prophet, and bearing the Holy Quran on his head! Even Sunnis still cry out against this terrible crime!

"Of the true lineage of the Prophet, only Hussein's infant son survived. Yet in him, we Shi'a found an answer to our thirsty cries in the wasteland of Sunni Islam, for Hussein had passed his deepest essence, the heart of holiness, to his son. He in turn, though raised in imprisonment, led the outer life of an upright Muslim, but his was also the perfect inner life. He passed his holy essence to his heir, and he to his, and so on. In each generation only one man is the Rightly Guided One for his time.

"But after six Imams came a great test of our faith: the future Imam Isma'il died before his father. By then the Shi'a brethren were torn apart by disputes, and his death caused another. Nonetheless, his legitimate line continued unbroken though his son.

"Meanwhile, corrupt Sunni Khalifs ruled most of the Dar al-Islam. Only once was there a true Khalifate: in Egypt, where a Rightly Guided One founded the Fatimid dynasty, named in honor of Ali's wife, Fatima. Through holy war and right argument, we reclaimed much of the Dar al-Islam. Alas, over the centuries false courtiers, minions of Satan, overcame the true Khalifs. But a hundred and fifty years ago, before that tragic fall was complete, Hasan-i-Sabbah came forth from Iran. He had trained in Egypt and been a da'i, a missionary, both in Syria and here. Then the last true Khalif died and his rightful heir Nizar was imprisoned and purportedly murdered by an evil vizier.

"At first Nizar's disciples despaired. But in truth he had escaped! Hasan-i-Sabbah revealed to his closest disciples that he himself was Proof that the true Imam had chosen the life of a Hidden One—as had other imams before him. Hasan-i-Sabbah rekindled hope in the hearts of all those of steadfast faith. Thenceforth he acted for the Hidden Imam Nizar. He had already seized Alamut castle for the Khalifate, but he prepared the way for Nizar's line, directed many Faithful to take other castles, and spread his true teaching. Thus was it passed on to future generations.

"And then some fifty years ago, it was revealed that the hidden Imam's grandson had actually been among us all along! Now his descendant guides both our inner and outer lives. One day we will overthrow all those who defile the Holy Prophet's teachings and dwell in worldly darkness. If the sacred line of Ali is to be saved, it will be by us!"

His voice grew strong again as he faced me, radiant. "Sofia, you are privileged to be in Alamut, the capital of our Nizari domain. Everywhere we Faithful go, we spread the truth. Where we can, we teach. That is my role; I too am a da'i. I find those with open ears and hearts and pour the holy wisdom of Allah into them. But if someone stands in our way, persecutes us, or tramples on the True Faith by his actions, others among our Faithful—our fida'i—martyr themselves to stop him. Soon the mouths of all defilers will be filled with dust, and mankind will arise as one to overthrow the old order and bring Heaven onto Earth!

"And very soon, at the end of time, we will enter Paradise, where Allah's perfection absorbs all being. Until then we follow the path of righteousness, not only the outer commands of the Prophet, peace on his name, but his inner teachings, and most especially the secret teachings of his true Khalif Ali, peace on his name, and of Imam Nizar's descendants: Allah's emissaries and God's light on earth. We know that the gates of Paradise will open to us because the true khalifs alone show us the truth hidden in every word of our Holy Quran—indeed, in every beat of our hearts, in every trembling leaf, in every drop of water! All, all is God's, and to live in His light is to live in Paradise now." He stopped for several heartbeats, his face alight with rapture, while I sat stunned and overwhelmed.

"You see, with the passing of centuries, many imposters have come forth calling themselves Shi'a and fooling the unwary until false imams stand in every marketplace proclaiming theirs as the only voice of authority. When a man's soul hangs in the balance, it is vital not to be deceived. Only one of faultless lineage is the true Imam, and you met him today, Muhammad Ala al-Din, who descends directly from Nizar. He is the Mahdi, the Rightly Guided One, who not only leads us but also shelters us from our own frailty. Mohammed Ala al-Din is the Imam of this, the last age."

Selim fell silent, and I prayed he was finished. But he spoke again, so softly that I could scarcely hear. "And, though I sometimes struggle to understand his will, I always find the wisdom in it when I search my heart deeply enough. Today he gave me new tools to search my soul, to root out the weeds of pride and indulgence that had sprouted there …."

"But what has all this to do with me?" I was shaking by then.

Selim's glow faded. "As yet, I do not know, Sofia. But I was wrong to use words like 'protect' when you are already protected by one who is the voice of Almighty Allah Himself. You are in no danger. The Imam's son, the boy at his feet, spoke rash words of youthful folly. I saw him staring at you—most unseemly!—but you have made a conquest, and he wanted you as his own jarya. It would be laughable were it not so sad. Rukn al-Din is still learning, too slowly and too painfully, that duty to God and our cause must come before his own desires. He must learn, for he is the next Imam. But his father would not use you thus, I am certain. He understood his son's intent and used it to teach him where his—"

"Selim, I do not even know what a jarya is!" I shouted at him.

"A slave concubine, Sofia. But you will never be one. First of all, you are my wife and under my protection."

"And what protection can you possibly give us when you are gone? Tomorrow Anna and I will be left among strangers who might decide to enslave us at their whim!"

"Allah has always protected you. Rely on Him, and your path will become clear."

I was ready to burst into further protest when Kerim came into the room and bowed to his father. "A message just arrived from the Imam, Father. He summons you now. Also, the messenger confirmed that Sofia is to live here with your servants. Umar has taken it upon himself to have Maryam brought from her house. He begs your forgiveness if he has done wrong. But she could be a companion to Sofia and Anna if you wish."

Selim's inner glow had faded. "Yes, he does well to think of her. Sofia, please accept my regrets, but I must answer this summons. Kerim, see to the women's comfort." He rose, bowed, and was gone.

I turned to Kerim to ask him what was happening, but he merely shrugged and rang a little bell that sat on one of the low tables in the room. "I can tell you nothing. I obey my father, and he obeys the Imam. But please, I heard the fear in your voice just now. You must set aside your worries. You are safe here, I assure you."

I bowed politely, trying not to panic. Anna had waited patiently ever since we had been to this Imam. Even with her poor understanding of Farsi, she knew that something was terribly wrong. Now she plucked at my sleeve. "What happened?"

I could not tell her that we were to be abandoned by the man I had trusted with our lives and our future, so I said, "We are to stay longer than

I thought. Don't worry; everything will work out soon."

A veiled maidservant appeared, and Kerim ordered her to show us to the andarun. We were at the threshold of a single small room when I stopped short. Another guard, a heavy door with an outside bolt, grillwork over the windows: no matter how lovely its carpets and elegant its appointments were, this room was meant to pen me in! Just inside the door, hovering in the fading light was a shapeless shape, perhaps this Maryam who was to be our companion, though why would we need one?

At that thought, a dam of rage and fear broke. I cried, "No! I will not be locked up in there!"

The poor maidservant was horrified. "But Master says—!"

"No doubt, but I will not be locked in that room! You had best take me back to Selim's biruni where I can await his return. After all, I am his wife!"

She stared at me without understanding but with a fear that made me see myself through her eyes: a fierce, half-mad man-woman who claimed to be married to her master. She turned to the guard for help, but I turned on him as well. "I am going back to the biruni, now! Do not try to stop me!"

The two of them froze, horror written on their faces. I took Anna's arm and marched back. Both maid and guard rushed after us, her begging us to return, him exclaiming angrily. Selim's room was softly lit and empty but for Kerim. Probably having heard me shout, he had arisen from some piled cushions, and was looking both alarmed and confused. A bowl of dark pills had spilled from his lap.

"What is it, Sofia? Are you ill?"

"No, but I am sick at heart, and angry, too. I refuse to be locked away in an andarun again. As the Imam's guest and Selim's wife, am I not already inviolable?"

For a moment Kerim seemed to lose all presence of mind, and I almost regretted my outburst. Finally, motioning to Anna and me to sit, he dropped down among his cushions. "Without Father here to decide what to do....

"Well, you are family now. You can await Father's return and join Umar and me for the evening meal. Would you care for some of my pills? Opium, very good for resting the mind."

"No, thank you," I said, and he scooped them up and set them aside.

But inwardly I was surprised, remembering Perijam and her little opium pills. Had she gotten them from her husband?

We sat and waited for Selim, drank mint tea, nibbled on dried fruit and nuts, and tried to make conversation. Kerim told me a little about his journeys to the west; I spoke about my hopes for finding my uncle and a new life. Nothing was said about the old woman in the andarun. Hopefully she had gone home! Servants brought lights, Umar came in and grunted unhappily on discovering us women, the muezzin called, they prayed, and we dined in near silence.

Selim finally returned. His dismay on finding Anna and me alone with his sons was clear, but when I explained, he actually smiled his familiar kindly way. "Well, well, Sofia, you may be right. I invite you to use the biruni at your pleasure. We have only this room and the two bedrooms, but you will not be locked into yours. Will that do?"

I nodded reluctantly; it was better than nothing.

"Also," he added, "the Mahdi and I spoke of you at length, and I can put all your other fears to rest. As I supposed, when I asked him outright if he had been disciplining his son with his words, he nodded. And I reminded him of your marriage to me and our agreement. He grants my request to take you on the rest of your journey home when the time is right. And be assured, you will never be anyone's jarya." Relief washed over me.

"However, you are being given a different sort of opportunity, one you will be glad of, I believe. The Imam will send for you soon, and he only asks that you fully answer his questions about the Mongol swine you served. In return he will allow you to study from the books in our library. You are even to attend classes. This will be a great honor, for men come from every corner of the Dar al-Islam to sit at the feet of the scholars and men of science who make their homes here.

"Alamut, as you will discover, is a haven of peace, untouched by the lawlessness and strife of what remains of Iran. Not all of the men who seek refuge here are Nizari—indeed, not all are even Muslim. But all enjoy our hospitality and find respite from their cares in this castle. You will find here, Sofia, a world of learning such as you never dreamed of, and you are to benefit from it all!" Trying to smile, I mouthed polite thanks, but I only wished to leave as soon as possible. I see now what a strange twist of fate it was: I was to fulfill my childish dream of becoming Sofia the Learned, but I could not properly value it then—and it certainly led me into trouble years later.

When we retired for the night, Selim himself led us to the andarun. There, sitting on a cushion in the dim light of a single brazier, was the shape: a sad-faced old woman, short, rather broad, slightly bent over as if carrying some great unseen burden. She awkwardly stood.

"Sofia, Maryam is Ben Hasan's mother. You recall the doctor I left with Batu Khan as a so-called slave? In reality, he is one of the Faithful. Maryam owes me a boon and offers to repay my kindness toward her son by helping you and Anna."

Maryam and I bowed warily to one another. "I trust yours was a safe journey here," she said. "Selim al-Din's son Umar has already spoken of you, and I look forward to getting to know you." Maryam's voice was as wispy as fog, but her sorrowful dark eyes were keenly observing me from under her straight brows.

I replied courteously, and then Anna and I were shown the pallets where we were to sleep alongside her and the serving woman. I listened for the drawing of a bolt, but it never came. Finally I fell into exhausted slumber.

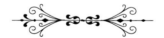

I awoke at dawn to the muezzin's call. The maidservant had risen to pray, but Maryam seemed deeply asleep. I hastily dressed and, after shaking Anna awake, hastened to the public room ahead of her. Selim and his sons were rising from prayers as I entered. Bundles were already stacked by the doorway.

After we had bowed and exchanged greetings, Selim said with what seemed to me to be false joviality, "Ah, Sofia, I was afraid I might have to leave before you awoke. I wrote you a letter, but this is better. I would have been sorry to miss saying farewell in person."

So Selim had meant to slip away. "I'd have been sorry, too, had you left in that way."

He must have caught the edge in my voice, for he spoke a little contritely, "I know you are shocked that I must leave you here, but I truly have no choice. You rest in the holiest of hands, for my master assures me you are under his special care. I will return as soon as I can, if Allah wills it, and when the time comes you may be sad to leave. You can become a fragrant rose in the garden of knowledge, Sofia. I pray that you avail yourself of it fully."

Again I suspected that Selim meant something particular by this, but I merely asked, more mildly than I felt, "When do you expect to return, then?"

He turned to his sons and waved to them to leave just as Da'ud came in to fetch the bundles. All three bowed toward us and were gone. "Now that my master knows about the rift between the great khans, he wants me to return to Sarai, which will take all summer. But when I return next fall, I can take you to Constantinople."

"But that will make it almost a year since I left Sarai! Please, if you cannot take us yourself after I speak with your master, then send one of your sons back for us in a week or two. Or let me leave with you now and I'll find my own way!"

Selim looked pained. "Sofia, we have no choice. Were I to take you from here now, I'd be branded a traitor, hunted down, and killed. At best you'd be brought back here, never to leave again. At worst you would be sold into slavery again or even killed as punishment. I have made sure that yours will be a safe and fruitful stay. The rest is up to you. And if the Imam sends for my sons to take you home, they will gladly obey, but it is up to him to decide that. I must bid you farewell now, and may Allah's blessings rain down on you."

He briefly pressed his hand to his heart, turned on his heel, and left. I rushed after him. "But I am being given no choice, and I want to leave now! Wait! How dare you walk away? I'm not some child to be set aside at your whim," I shouted—most childishly, I see now. Selim did not even turn his head. A manservant by the door made to shut it, but I tried to push past him.

Instead, a strange hand caught hard at my arm, and I turned, ready to strike the man who dared touch me. It was Maryam. "Let me go," I cried. "He is leaving without me!"

"I know, child. I know. Thus did he take my only son and leave me behind, too. Selim al-Din is a hard man. You could rail at him until you had no voice left, and he would be as deaf as stone. He did not even give me time this morning to write to my son!"

I stared at her and glimpsed Anna behind her, white with shock. I suddenly saw myself through their eyes: a silly girl trying to fight, weaponless, against the world of men.

"Come with me, come sit and break your fast, and weep if you need. But do not throw yourself against a mountain, for only you will break."

She spoke the truth. I looked around and saw the stony-faced guard glaring at my feet over his crossed arms. He was the man I had clashed with the night before; I was probably turning him into an enemy. Anna was standing in the same way, but she was shaking with fright, while Maryam stood like a small fortress. The sounds of departure faded. And, I realized, like Maryam I had been given no chance to write to my dear friend Dorje, the old monk who had saved my life and my heart and given me hope that I might escape the Mongols. Despair flooded over me, for what hope was there that I might ever leave this strange place? I did burst into tears.

Maryam gently led me back into the public room, speaking quietly to the maidservant. She placed me among the soft pillows and stroked my head while I sobbed over my betrayal, my helplessness, my sudden lack of future. It was a bitter hour, but I finally ran dry of tears and found mint tea at my elbow, delicacies kindly offered, and most of all the presence of two good women, one of whom wished only to befriend us both.

Of course I knew Maryam was a Jew, but that was hardly on my mind then. And even now, no matter what others say, I cherish my friendship with her as a fellow traveler in the sad dim places of the heart.

She was a healer like her son, a mistress of herbs and remedies. I tasted but a sip of tea and realized there was something more in it than sugar. I pushed it away but Maryam said in a kind voice, "It is just a little calming brew to help you regain a steady mind. You will need it. A summons just came for you."

"Who summons me? That so-called Mahdi?"

"Yes, he grants you an audience this very morning, and you must prepare yourself."

"He *grants* me an audience?" But an inner voice told me that if this was indeed an opportunity, I must not spoil it by betraying violent emotions. And I had certainly learned how to hide my feelings when I was Argamon's slave!

Anna had been hovering by me like a baby bird suddenly expected to nurse its mother. I tried to smile reassuringly and she timidly smiled back. Maryam led us to our room, where the maidservant had laid out a thick white cotton veil that would cover me from head to toe. After washing my face I picked it up, feeling even more freedom bleed away.

Having shown me how to wear the veil so that only my eyes showed, Maryam patted me on the shoulder and said, "Just keep your mind steady and remember all the courtesies you have learned from Selim. He is a master of those, at least! Your escort awaits you." I heard the bitterness in her voice. How had Selim betrayed her? He had said she owed him a boon. Why then did she seem not at all grateful? Well, the answer lay to hand, for she had said herself that he had taken her son from her.

Anna was following me to the heavy front door where the angry-faced guard stood. But he did open it for me. I was about to step out, Anna right behind me, when he thrust his arm before her. "She stays here. The summons is only for you and her," gesturing toward the maidservant who had appeared behind me, also heavily veiled.

I turned to my servant. In Hungarian, I said, "Listen, Anna, you must stay here. Remember how I kept you from Batu Khan's sight in order to protect you? It's the same here. You'll be with Maryam, who is our new friend—and not a Muslim—and she'll teach you about this place. I didn't mean to frighten you with my tears. I was just weary. Don't worry. I will return."

"Tell her it is much safer for her to stay here with me. No one should get any closer to the Grand Master than they have to, "Maryam advised. "Luckily, he never wants to see me! And tell her she can teach me some of her language so I can speak with her."

So Anna unwillingly stayed behind while I just as unwillingly followed the escort awaiting me in the courtyard. I doubt the maid was any happier than I was. I turned. "What is your name?"

"Shirin," she answered sullenly.

"Shirin, I regret frightening you last night. Can we have peace between us?" She looked at me with startled eyes, but thankfully she nodded yes.

This morning as we retraced our path to the upper castle, I felt as if the entire fortress had somehow shrunk and was scarcely larger than Papa's country palace with its outbuildings. Perhaps it was on account of my mood. The man led us into the citadel, but not to the same room. Instead of going upstairs, we passed straight along a corridor that led to another staircase, narrow and cut from the rock. It twisted around and down to a torch-lit corridor and an arched wooden door where another man was waiting. He knocked, and a voice told him to enter. Our first guard melted away, while the new man waved us in. Motioning to Shirin to sit on a carpet just inside the door, he led me across a chill room.

It was actually a deep cave, plastered and whitewashed, and bare except for a few carpets, some scrolls upon a low table, and a divan in one corner. The cave entrance had been enlarged and shaped into a rough pointed arch, and an outer lip had been made into a sitting area surrounded by a a low parapet of rock. Selim's Mahdi was standing by it looking directly down into the long valley below. Across from the cave lay raw-looking hills, still green at their bases but pale red at their bare summits. In the early morning light, they were sliced with blue shadows. Behind them reared the mountains, their snowy peaks blinding in the morning sun.

As I approached, Ala al-Din turned suddenly and, glancing toward me, sat down among some green silk cushions and colorful bolsters that lay heaped at his end of the carpet. A low table sat to one side with a single tea glass, half-empty, resting on it. The attendant bowed, as did I, and the Grand Master motioned to me to sit across from him. His servant poured him more tea and left. I was facing the man who was to save the world.

I sat with eyes lowered and tried to keep my heart from racing out of my chest while he studied me, silent as stone. We sat for so long that my attention finally wandered. Just then he spoke, and I almost jumped with surprise. "I see you can practice hejab properly—and that you can keep your tongue and eyes still. That is good. Selim al-Din sang your praises last night, but now I see some of your qualities for myself." I had no idea what he saw, but a polite bow seemed in order.

"So," he went on, "you are to pull back your chaador, for I want to see your face, to know whether or not you speak the truth. There can be no false modesty before me, who can look into your soul, and besides," he laughed in a most unsettling way," I have already seen you unveiled. Your beauty holds no power over me, so neither of us is in danger!" I did as he commanded. I had felt suffocated by the close-drawn fabric, anyway. I felt more than saw him nod approvingly. "So! You are from Rus' and were captured and enslaved by the Mongols. How did you come to the attention of Batu Khan?" Thus began his questioning.

By midday I felt like a rag used to scrub a floor. It had grown hot, and my body felt stifled in that chaador. And although my mouth grew dry as dust, no tea was offered me whenever the manservant came in to refill his master's glass.

At last the Grand Master said, "That is enough for today. You may veil yourself again." While I readjusted the chaador over my head, he added, "Whether you like being here or not, you are my guest—oh, yes, I know you are unhappy with my decision that you stay and your so-called husband leave. But if you continue to answer as honestly as you did today, you will be amply rewarded." I did not know it at the time, but that was high praise from the man.

He waved his hand in dismissal. I stood, stiff and weary, and looked out. Below in the far distance was the village where we had stayed: tiny houses, even tinier people and animals visible only as a trace of movement, and the distant river sparkling in the sunshine.

"They look like ants from here," he said as if reading my mind. "And without me they would live like ants. Instead, they live in spiritual safety, following Almighty Allah's commands as He intends."

I bowed and escaped his presence, wondering if those "ants" felt safe from him and hoping I could soon resume my journey.

How mistaken I was: for weeks, the Grand Master virtually attacked me with questions while I, wrapped in that chaador, nearly smothered in the ever hotter, drier weather. I spent almost every afternoon with him. Often Shirin and I were taken to the cave—his private retreat—and sometimes I was led to the audience hall before his advisors while she was left in the outer corridor. There I must repeat what I had said to him exactly as I had said it the first time if I did not want to be questioned yet more closely. I could never think of Ala al-Din as a rightly guided messiah, although he was almost as frightening to me as they say Christ will be on Judgment Day. With a nod of his head I'd have been dead on the spot. He knew I was afraid of him, and he found it amusing!

He was strangely changeable, too, at one moment cheered by my answers and at another plunged into a dark humor. His advisors seemed to dread his moods as much as I did. I thought the questions would never end. They were all about only one matter: what I had learned as the khan's interpreter or from writing out his orders. Clearly these men's sole aim was to find the weaknesses in the Mongol chain of command and to make the most of them. They wanted to know how the ordus were structured, both individually and as combined armies; who stood where in the hierarchy, from the great noyans down to the common soldiers; how the armies were assembled and deployed; how orders were passed along; how men were promoted; whether a non-Mongol could join the ranks without eyebrows being raised. They asked about battle tactics, about supply lines, about those close to Batu Khan.

They were, of course, fascinated—as well as pleased—by my description of the quarrel between Batu and his rival, Kuyuk Khan, but they also wanted to know about Batu's friendship with Mongke Khan and why Mongke would have returned to Karakorum.

They even wanted to know all about Mongol customs and courtly behavior. After the first round of questioning, I was made to repeat what I knew but in different ways. I was never asked to make sense of anything. That task belonged to the Imam's advisors, and they cut me short if I tried to explain more than what they wanted.

Often the Grand Master's son Rukn al-Din was there at his father's feet, and it seemed to me that he often stared at me. And because I had once been unveiled in front of these inquisitors, probably the only woman's face he had ever seen besides those of his mother and any sisters he might have, he seemed fascinated. He rarely dared to speak in the presence of his father and the stern, bearded advisors who surrounded him. I kept my eyes downcast at all times, but once the Grand Master ordered me to raise them and look him in the eye to see whether I was speaking the truth. As I raised my head my eyes also briefly met young Rukn al-Din's. We both blushed as red as beets and quickly looked away.

But it was one of the few times he dared challenge the Imam. "We cause our guest pain, Father. We insult her by making her meet a man's gaze directly, and before other men! I am certain she speaks truth, for her story stays the same no matter how you try to trick her into contradicting herself. Besides, other witnesses give us similar reports."

The Grand Master must have been startled to hear his son speak so boldly, but he did allow me to lower my eyes again. And I was grateful to the boy. Of them all, Rukn al-Din seemed to be the only one who thought of me as anything more than a living book of facts.

Though I was still upset with Selim, after the first few days of questioning I resigned myself to my captivity. Other than the tense hours with the Grand Master and his ministers, I actually had more freedom in Selim's tiny house than in Qazvin. And at least I was allowed to leave it every day. I would glance curiously through every alley and stare down at every roof that we passed, or at the bazaar and the mosque, which also contained a madrassa and the great library Selim had mentioned. And on the women's days, we all went to the public bathhouse: a small, steamy room set against the dividing wall between upper and lower courtyard where the women of Alamut stared at my red hair and whispered to each other secretively.

In the evenings with little to do, Anna and I became friends with Maryam and Shirin if not with the two menservants, who kept a cold distance from me after my first outbursts. Every day while I was gone, Maryam and Anna learned more of each other's speech, which meant that all three of us could soon talk together. Within days the woman was speaking simple Hungarian to Anna and coaxing her into learning more Farsi. I was glad but a little jealous that my friend would learn from her and not from me.

Indeed, Anna formed a far deeper friendship with Maryam than I did. She never realized that our new friend was a Jew. She only knew that Maryam was, like us, an unwilling guest of the Grand Master, and that Maryam liked Muslims, or at least Nizari Muslims, no better than she did. That was enough for her. And after they grew so close, why would I say anything that might divide them from each other?

One evening early on while we sat in the little garden, Maryam asked us how we had "fallen into the clutches of the Nizari." She shook her head at our stories. "Yes, just as it was with us," she sighed. "We too lost everything to the Mongols, everything but our lives, and I sometimes wonder whether we didn't lose them as well."

"What happened?" Anna asked.

"We fled when we heard that Mongol armies were almost upon us— that was about twenty years ago. We lived in Rayy then, southeast of here. Nothing remains of it now, I hear, but then it was a great trading center. My husband was a master potter, and he sold his workshop's wares not only in Iran but all the way into Syria. Such beauty of shape, color and decoration: turquoise or emerald or rich brown … all gone now.

"Because of his trade connections, we heard about the Mongols in time to flee. He even tried to warn everyone he knew, but people thought their soldiers could resist the invading armies or they felt they weren't well off enough to leave or that they would survive this army as they had others in the past. So we fled in haste to Qazvin with tears on our cheeks, taking what we could. Alas, when we arrived, the merchant we had hoped to stay with was already preparing to escape to some safe haven in the mountains. He offered to ask his guide if we could join them.

"That was how we met Selim al-Din. He was young then, but already wily. He agreed to take us, too, in exchange for much of our wealth. He first took us to another castle not too far from here, called Lambasar. When my husband died, Selim brought my son and me here and offered to support me while Benjamin studied medicine at the madrassa. He was a bright boy; he had learned much from me already. Many healing plants grow in the mountains, and he had often gone out and gathered them for me around Lambasar. Little did I realize that his doing so would bring him to the attention of these so-called Faithful!

"Now my husband has been dead for some twelve years, my son is lost to me these two years, and I am left alone at their mercy...." A rancorous, nervous look crept into Maryam's face, and she darted a glance at me as if to say, 'I could tell you much, much more.' Instead, she said, "That is enough for now," and firmly turned to other matters.

As spring softened into summer, Maryam undertook to educate Anna. I had always thought my servant simple, and she never did master difficult things. But really her mind was more like a flower that had always lived in drought and had grown stunted. Maryam watered and nourished it, and it throve and blossomed. Every day on my return, Anna would share what new thing she had learned. I recall one afternoon in particular.

"Look, Mistress! Letters! Maryam taught me how to make letters! See, this is Latin, here is Greek, and here are some in Farsi, and this is Hebrew, which was used to write down the first Holy Scriptures long, long ago. You see, each letter stands for a sound—these here all stand for 'a'—and when you put letters together, they make words. Then you put words together and you can write your thoughts down or even send them to someone!"

I hid my amusement. "Wonderful! Whose script will you learn to write first?"

Anna took a deep breath, her eyes alight. "All of them at once," she decided. And we laughed together. Maryam smiled, too, losing her care-worn look for a moment.

So when it was still light and Anna was learning letters with Maryam, and Shirin was preparing our meal at the outdoor stove, I had the luxury of time alone. I used it fully, to pray or practice peace, or write in my journal—indeed, I now regretted tearing up the second book that Batu Khan had gifted me, for I could see I had much I wanted to save in memory, more than two books could hold, not only what had been happening on my long journey to nowhere, but also my precious childhood memories, like the perfume of the meadows at haying time, Papa's beard tickling my cheek, our seasonal festivals with such laughter and feasting. Alas that so much was lost to fire.

I also recall that there was some great festival in late spring that I believe honored the prophet Abraham's willingness to sacrifice his son. But it also had something to do with the pilgrimage that every Muslim should take to Mecca; this much I gleaned from Shirin, who was far too busy cooking a kid slaughtered for the occasion to have time to answer more questions. We had little to do with it, other than my being let alone for a few days, but we were treated to some tasty dishes, and we heard sounds of celebration outside. Maryam mumbled something about Muslims trying to steal Jewish traditions and remake them for their own purposes. But then things went quiet again.

AUTUMN INTO WINTER
ANNO DOMINI 1243-1244

One morning I awoke to the muezzin's call and began to steel myself for another long day of questioning. Shirin got up looking somber, dressed herself in black, and did not put on her usual bracelets or earrings. And instead of her regular daily prayers, which I knew by then, she whispered new prayers and began wailing, "Oh Hussein, we were not there!" More cries came from outside.

Maryam, who slept in when she could, awoke. "Ah, Muharram; what a day for it to begin. Well, at least the Grand Master will leave you alone for a while."

"Why?"

"Muharram is a holy month, especially for these Shi'a. They mourn the death of their second Imam, Hussein, who was killed at a place called Karbala, along with his family."

"Oh, Hussein was the martyred son of Ali, I think."

"Yes. For the next two months, there will be what they call majlish in the mosque here—and everywhere else that the Shi'a aren't likely to get killed for practicing it."

The usually quiet Shirin spoke up. "These are especially holy days, Lady Sofia. An infidel should not be telling you about them."

Maryam shrugged. "You tell her, then, if she is even interested."

"Well, it is only partly as Maryam says. Muharram is the first month of the Islamic calendar. The Prophet, peace on his name, also decreed that we fast on certain days, but we true faithful also mourn the siege and murders at Karbala by performing Majlish at the mosque where our men act out Hussein's horrible murder while we lament for him. Many men even strike themselves for having let such an evil fate befall our Holy Imam."

Maryam could hold her tongue no longer. "Yes, with chains, or they walk over burning coals." She shook her head. "As if that does anything, since the man has been dead for centuries and we'd have been dead, too, if we had been there. And as if only Shi'a Muslims suffer or are martyred!"

Shirin turned red. "Beating themselves helps them relive Hussein's suffering! We need to let out our sorrow! Besides, it is not only about that. The men also give out water and the juice from fruits to us who watch, to remind us that Hussein's baby son and the rest of his family suffered tortures of thirst. We can only learn what someone else feels by feeling it ourselves."

Maryam retorted, "Then learn how it feels when an infidel steals your son from you!" She fled to the garden. I followed her to find her sunk onto the bench, sobbing quietly as if to echo the wails outside our gates. I touched her shoulder, but she turned away from me.

"I need to be alone, Sofia. My son was taken from me exactly two years ago today. What a bitter irony that this year Muharram begins on the same day."

So I left Maryam to her sorrows and went into the biruni where Shirin, still weeping, had already set out a breakfast. Anna was there, looking bleary. "Why is Shirin wailing like that? Where is Maryam? And what is going on outside?"

"This is a Muslim holy month—I gather that for the next few weeks, Shirin and the people in the castle will mourn for the martyr Hussein, just as Selim's family did. And Maryam is in the garden grieving over her son, who was taken from her on this day." Anna was heading for the garden, ignoring my cry of, "Wait, Maryam wants to be alone."

After a moment's hesitation, I went to the door to see her and Maryam clinging to each other, sobbing.

I turned at a noise behind me. Shirin and Selim's manservant Yusuf—the one I had offended—were there, dressed from head to toe in black. "I leave you food for the day," Shirin said. And they were gone. They did not return until that night. Only the guard at the gate remained, also clad in black. All day it felt as if some stealthy army of gloom had invaded the house and was attacking everyone's heart, including mine.

For several weeks, surrounded by the cries and wails of people passing our gates, I felt almost crushed by melancholy. It reminded me of so many sorrows that I was glad when it was over, even though it meant I must return to the Grand Master's inquisition.

More days of his relentless questioning followed. Autumn was approaching, and he and his advisers were still hammering at my memory. But early one morning, I arrived at Ala al-Din's cave expecting to have yet more nits of information picked from my memory and found him speaking to one of his advisors. I had noticed this one because his full beard was still mostly black, making him seem like a veritable youth among so many graybeards, though he wore the same stern, intent expression. I tried to fortify my mind for yet another round of questions.

To my surprise, the Grand Master was in an agreeable mood. He was saying, "You will ensure that she has every opportunity to learn." The man bowed, but there was a certain stiffness in his bearing.

The Imam turned to me and said, "You have done well, Sofia. This is Nasir al-Din al-Tusi, who is one of my most honored guests and a supporter of our mission." I bowed to Nasir al-Din and he nodded in return, but again I caught that undercurrent of some darker emotion in his manner.

"I now put you into his learned hands. Study hard and prove that Selim al-Din's faith in you is not misplaced. I am also allowing you to use books from my library, one of the greatest in the world. I hope you will see what a special opportunity I grant you, far more valuable than mere worldly riches."

I bowed again, although I felt a little insulted. Had I not already proven my abilities? The Master dismissed us both with a wave of his hand. I realize now that I never saw him again, though his commands set the course of my life.

I followed my new tutor out into the corridor where my guard waited. Nasir al-Din al-Tusi turned to stare angrily at the air beside my head. I kept my eyes modestly lowered, for I did not like it and only wished I could say so. But best not to speak unless spoken to—my inquisitors had taught me that. "Well, if I must," he finally muttered. "Follow me."

He marched off so swiftly that I had to trot to keep up with him, my guard close behind us. Along a dark corridor lit by oil lamps in sconces, down another long, rock-hewn, twisting flight of stairs, through an arched door, and we were suddenly in a hidden walled garden that backed onto the mountainside below the citadel. It was lovely. I could not have guessed that such a place existed in such a homely keep as Alamut.

Nasir al-Din turned to look back in my direction. He seemed surprised that I had kept pace with him without difficulty. "You even walk like a man," he said disapprovingly.

But he did slow down, which allowed me to look around. The yard was laid out with formal paths of crushed stone that wandered amidst beds overflowing with mountain blossoms or grass still as green as emerald. Four little streams, each lined with a different color of stone, ran through the garden. Nightingales in cages hanging among the trees sang out their delight, bright red and yellow butterflies floated by as if protected from the seasons, white-breasted blackbirds flitted in the trees, and I felt a sudden rush of well being.

Nasir al-Din seemed to feel it, too, for he stopped briefly to breathe in the garden's mingled scents. "This is as close to Paradise as mortals can come in this life, a pale glimpse of the glories that await the faithful after death. You are most fortunate, young woman, to pass through the Mahdi's private garden and to be allowed to study with me. If your understanding is as good as your ability to recount from memory, your mind will become a garden, not merely of knowledge, but of wisdom."

He marched through another door, out of the garden, and into another part of the citadel. I rushed to follow. After sweeping up more stairs and crossing an alley, we turned into a small, neat compound where two men stood guard—an honor guard, I found out later. From inside came boyish laughter that stopped as we entered the small biruni. On its carpeted floor sat five youths of varying ages, one of whom was Rukn al-Din. They rose to kiss Nasir al-Din's hand, casting curious glances past my shoulder or toward my feet. Rukn al-Din stumbled and blushed when he stood.

"We have a new student," Nasir al-Din announced. "Sit behind the boys, young woman." At his summons, a woman clad in black from head to toe entered the room and sat in a corner behind me with spindle and wool. She set to work while Nasir al-Din turned to his students. "Enough time is wasted already. Let us begin."

All morning we students sat and listened. Or I tried to. Nasir al-Din spoke of things I had never heard of before, and he made no effort to include me. At first I thought I had stumbled into a theology lesson, but I slowly realized that the subject matter was some kind of stargazing interwoven with references to the greatness of Allah. All the young men had dark boards and pieces of chalk, which they used to work the mathematical problems he set them. Each then read his answer aloud and told how he had solved his problem. Their answers mostly agreed, but if a youth failed, Nasir al-Din rapped him on the head with a rod. After some time, I grew so weary that I peeked around the room. On a nearby table sat scrolls, open books, and strangely shaped instruments and bottles. That was all. After awhile I began to doze off.

A sharp pain on my head startled me awake. Nasir al-Din towered over me, rod in hand, looking angry and self-satisfied. "Never fall asleep when I am teaching you! Attention is a gift from God and our thanks to Him!" He certainly taught me one thing in that moment. He was nothing like my gentle and much-missed tutor Alexander, who had instructed me not only with patience but with more thoroughness than I had wanted.

I sat with my head down, fighting back tears, for the rest of the lesson. Finally, my ordeal seemed over, for the youths rose, bowed and kissed their teacher's hand, and departed. I stood to leave too, though I was determined not to kiss this hateful man's hand!

"Sit down. I have agreed to tutor you, but until I have some feeling for what you already know, I cannot teach you anything."

I glared straight at him. "And until I am treated with respect, I refuse to learn anything from you, since so far you have shown me nothing but rudeness, contempt, and lack of hospitality!"

Nasir al-Din stared back at me in shocked silence for several heartbeats. "You are probably right. I forgot myself in my anger at being burdened with an infidel woman who thinks herself as good as a man. Well, since you walk and talk like a man, we will see if you think like one. But first, we shall have some refreshments."

Somehow, after the ritual of tea and slices of sweet melon, I felt better. At least Nasir al-Din was trying to act like a proper host instead of a tyrant. He even introduced me to his main wife, the woman spinning in the corner. She was polite to me but not friendly, either then or ever. But then, I was the infidel woman who wanted to learn like a man.

After tea Nasir al-Din began questioning me almost as closely as the

Imam had, but about my education. Where had I gotten it? What skills did I have in languages, mathematics, philosophy, history? At the end, he said, "It would seem that for an—" He stopped himself. "You are reasonably well-informed in certain ways. Your mastery of languages surpasses my own, for I speak only Farsi and Arabic. It surprises me, but Allah the All-Merciful grants us wonders every day. However, you know nothing of the scientific arts. No astronomy, no geometry or algebra; indeed, your command of mathematics is woeful." He stroked his beard. "Yes, I can see how you might excel at languages or history, for do not women spend every day chattering and gossiping? But the true test will be whether you can master difficult calculations and whether you can observe clearly … Yes, I can teach you much, or at least I can try."

I wanted to say something extremely quelling to this rude and arrogant man, but his mention of scientific and mathematical arts aroused my curiosity. I did wish to learn more about them, so I only answered, "For my part, I will try also. But I must say this: I was born a princess, and I never learned well under the rod. My childhood tutor, God rest his soul, never hit me. Instead, he poured his love of learning into me, and it never drained away, even after I lost him. For the sake of his memory, and to prove you wrong about 'infidel women,' I wish to study with you. But I will accept no more punishment, especially before your other students."

Nasir al-Din looked most displeased for a moment, but then he nodded curtly. "Agreed. But do not expect me to dim the light of my teachings for you. You must learn just like any man would, without any special help from me."

I laughed aloud. It had been a long time since anyone had offered me special help. I still so angry with Selim that I saw even his protection, his very hospitality, as a betrayal. "Agreed."

And thus ended my first lesson under the renowned Nasir al-Din al-Tusi, who, I discovered later, is famous all over the Muslim world—even more now, serving the Mongols, than he was then. After that, five mornings a week I went to his private classes for the sons of the Nizari elite, a special privilege for all of us since the future Mahdi was among them. Nasir al-Din also taught at the madrassa in the afternoons. In addition to the regular lessons, when I sat veiled and invisible behind the boys, he allotted some time afterwards to tutor me. To maintain seemliness, one of his wives—he had three—was always present in the room.

Each day was much the same. Nasir al-Din spoke, we students wrote, and when the muezzin called at noon, we ended with prayers. I soon became accustomed to his flowery language, full of the praises to Allah that are second nature to Muslims. He divided each session into lessons on what he called physics, on mathematics, and on astronomical arts. He made certain that we all knew how famous he was for his works on mathematics and astronomy! At first I was not able to follow much, as the boys were far ahead of me. I think in those early days, Nasir al-Din wanted to show me how inferior my education was, possibly hoping I would give up in despair, so he pushed his boys hard. If so, he was disappointed, for I paid close attention. And in our private lessons, I worked hard just to show him that he was wrong.

Though I disliked him, he was a good teacher. "We will start at the beginning," he told me at our first lesson. "All knowledge can be sorted and classified, thus making it easier to understand. The best tradition devised is that of Al-Farabi. Even the great Ibn Sina followed his method, and so shall we." I had never heard of either man before, but Ibn Sina— Avicenna, the great doctor and philosopher—has been renowned across Europe for almost a century. And they use Al-Farabi's system in Paris and perhaps elsewhere. What an irony: our Muslim "enemies" have given us so many gifts of learning.

Happily, Al-Farabi's system made perfect sense to me. It began with the arts of language, which I easily mastered and thoroughly enjoyed. We covered not only what everyone hates to learn, like grammar and syntax, but also poetry and elocution. There is so much wonderful poetry in Arabic. And Farsi, with its great epics and tender love ballads, even excels Arabic in my opinion. Then I learned about logic and proofs and learning to discern false arguments.

From there we proceeded to the mathematical arts. I had always thought that being able to add, subtract, multiply, and divide numbers was all there was to know. Now I learned algebra and geometry, which I mastered and, much later, taught to my daughter in turn. There are practical uses for these formulas, like building bridges and churches and palaces, but I just wanted to prove myself to my teacher.

There was even more, for he explained the relationship between numbers and music. I had never played any instrument, but now I learned about harmony and chords and other wonders whose perfect order offered proof of the perfection and order of Allah's creation, as my teacher never tired of telling me. Indeed, that was why a lesson always seemed as much instruction in religion as in a subject, for so it was. Nasir al-Din explained that the prophet Muhammad had enjoined his people to explore everything on earth and in the heavens, not in order to rule over them, but to witness God's greatness in all things.

My teacher was also happy to learn that I had studied the Quran a little. According to him, the Quran contains four levels of meaning in every verse: an outer meaning clear to anyone, an inner meaning that is implied, a secret meaning, and a cosmic meaning. And the whole world is like the Quran. Everything has a hidden meaning pointing to God, if only we are willing to solve the mystical riddle He sets before us. Of course, according to Nasir al-Din, only the Nizari know the key to the riddle. Yet despite his self-important claims, something wondrous, almost mystical, did happen to me. I remembered what a joy it is to learn new things. It was like plunging into a vast lake of delight.

Once I proved my understanding, Nasr al-Din allowed me to take home scrolls and bound books from Alamut's library. "Study these well, Sofia," he ordered me, "and you will glimpse worlds within worlds—if you are deserving of your name." Such words always felt like little pricks. Nasir al-Din often tried to find fault with me or to belittle my understanding. Well, in all fairness, he did that with all his students, but I took it as a personal attack. I was resolved to study all night every night, if necessary, in order to prove myself. Yet I know that despite his imperious manner, he meant well. It went hard with him to accord me respect in words, but letting me study books on my own spoke for itself.

In those first manuscripts, I learned the sacred meaning of numbers and chords that are hidden from common view, although I remember very little of all that now. I never found it that compelling. I do remember a sacred triangle made of ten points and a Greek theory about the music of the spheres, and there were complex systems of numerology connected with the ancient philosopher Pythagoras and with Jewish lore. It was all concerned with emanations from God and how spirit descends into matter. Contemplating such teachings was supposed to bring disciples back into harmony with Him.

Reading these treatises always made me feel as if I stood poised on the edge of some other, greater, more mysteriously perfect world. I felt light-headed and full of wonderment. But afterwards that sensation felt hollow, as if I had tricked myself into believing I had actually become wiser simply by thinking lofty thoughts. And I felt a little cheated, too, since I was still merely Sofia with all her little jealousies and grudges and ambitions!

From time to time, Maryam looked over my shoulder at some of the scrolls to see what I was studying. Once she snorted her contempt. "These Nizari borrow from the ancients, clothe old ideas in their language, and think they add something new by adding layers of secrets over it all! That text comes straight from the teachings of the Kabala, old as Egypt, which my husband and I once studied together. Through it I learned many healing arts, as did my son."

"Well, is there truth in it?" I asked, somewhat irritated by her airs. After all, Pythagoras the Greek had written much in that scroll, too.

"Of course. But truth can be twisted, so watch out for these Nizari philosophers. They are tricky and can lead you down a path to perdition if you aren't wary. That's what happened to my son. When Selim al-Din found out that Ben Hasan was studying the Kabala and practicing cures, he stole him away into their world. And what did all his knowledge get him? Slavery to a foreign master!" She strode out of the room, muttering, "I curse them all!" I suddenly remembered what Dorje had once said about not allowing my outlook to be poisoned by hatred.

And then I realized that by holding a grudge against Selim for bringing me to Alamut, I was poisoning my friendship with him. After all, he had helped me again and again: rescuing me in Batu Khan's ordu the day my guard and good friend Asetai was murdered, sending Da'ud and Nasr and Ali to guide me into Iran, hiding me among his beloved family, even clearing the way for me to study at Alamut.

Nasr al-Din also introduced me to astronomy and astrology. Astronomy is especially valued in Islam, as Muslims must know exactly when various holy days begin and end according to phases of the moon. Also, for knowing where Mecca is at all times, since they must face their holy city when praying. And with so many deserts in Muslim lands, people need to follow the stars, just as a sea captain does when he steers his ship out of sight of land.

I later found out that some branches of Islam condemn astrology, though Nasr al-Din and the Nizari did not. "Astrology guides a man's inner as well as outer life, for it shows how Allah's purpose is interwoven throughout all creation. It guides us to make wise and timely choices," he told me as we looked at a map of the stars. "If I know a person's date and place of birth, I can find out where the stars were placed in the firmament, and from that I can tell how they influence his life. Allah thus tells us of His plans and teaches us to follow them."

"Can you draw up a chart of the stars for my birthday?"

He smiled. "Yes. But then you must accept Allah's will, you know. Something you seem to have trouble with now and then."

"Well, maybe that will help me become more obedient," I answered.

He smiled again, more grimly, and agreed to do it.

Now, perhaps he had learned enough about my past to devise some clever explanations of how it fit into this chart. But when he gave it to me and explained it, he also knew things that I had never told him. At the end, he added, "I see four long journeys before you have passed your second decade, and many more journeys after that. Mars has oppressed your life, and Scorpio has brought you much pain mixed with fleeting pleasure. Other influences will lead to more loss. See how these planets all cluster in Aries? They are lined up like a knife stabbing a fire. You must remain strong in your faith, for only All-Merciful Allah will carry you through dark trials to a time of peace."

When he told me all this, it frightened me so much that I threw the chart away after I got back to Selim's house. Especially the part about a knife stabbing a fire—it reminded me of the Mongols' belief that it would bring ill luck. It was as if ill luck had been hovering over my life from the beginning. I never turned to astrology again!

Of all the subjects he taught us, my favorite was physics: learning about the beasts of the world and about plant life and medical lore, though they too are intertwined with astrology.

And there was al-kimiya, the study of how matter can be made to change form. During his lectures, our teacher would often show us what would happen if we mixed different substances and heated them over fire. Some melted, some grew hard or changed color or shape, some turned into steam. It was spellbinding. A person could spend the rest of his life studying al-kimiya alone and never reach the end, I think.

Possibly most important to our teacher, we studied different philosophies and religions, mostly so that Nasir al-Din could have his students prick holes in their logic—all but his own philosophy and, of course, the

Nizari doctrines. They were the standards against which all others were judged. Thus did I get a narrow glimpse into the hidden teachings of the Grand Master and the world of his Faithful. As far as I could tell, Maryam was right. They differed little from the teachings of Pythagoras and the Kabala. One thing that surprised me was their belief that souls are reborn again and again as they journey to perfection. At least I think that was what my teacher was saying.

Listening to Nasir al-Din's arguments, I also began to realize how many branches of Islam there are and that they vie with each other, claiming theirs as the only truth, just as we Christians do among ourselves. Especially, like Selim, Nasir al-Din seemed to hate the Sunni. But he also showered contempt on a group called Sufis and on fellow Shi'a and even other kinds of Isma'ilis, whose beliefs, as far as I could see, were no different from the Nizari, except that they followed a different Imam.

And just as everywhere else, there is much ill will between all these branches and spilling of blood from time to time. Nasir al-Din especially hated Manichaeism, of which I knew nothing. I found most of his logic tedious and tortuous. And there were secrets that not even these elite boys knew yet.

But one thing became clear. Since the Nizari, or perhaps all Isma'ilis, had come into being, there had been many upheavals in their history that their historians matched to various cycles or epochs, as they called them. During some cycles the Imam was "in concealment," or Hidden, like Nizar. It sounded as if each Imam, whether concealed or visible, added some new and subtle interpretation to the Nizari doctrines he inherited. And always, someone like Nasir al-Din came along later to reconcile the contradictions between one Nizari Imam's teachings and another's.

For instance, over a century ago the Nizari accepted their Imam's declaration that all Islamic law—what they call the Shari'a—was null and void because the Resurrection was here and now. But after that Imam died, they accepted his son's declaration that his father's commands were null and void and that Sunni law was to guide them! Nasir al-Din himself had written a learned paper that he read to us, which asserted that the Resurrection was only for the lifetime of that particular Mahdi, and that in other "epochs" the law was to be enforced due to outer circumstances that this same Mahdi had foreseen. And the correct understanding of this was the task of the Imam who followed him and whose wisdom guided his generation in turn. Always, our teacher told us, the task of each rightly guided one was to point the way to truth and to protect the faithful who relied on his wisdom.

I must admit that one whose faith was already established might be satisfied with such logic, but as an outsider I was not convinced. With no one to contradict him, what kept a Mahdi from following his own whims? Allah? After all, Chinggis Khan's Tengri had supposedly commanded him to conquer the world, and the result was mayhem! Could that be true vision or was it merely ambition cloaked in faith?

But the boys enjoyed it all. I would listen to their lively debates and wonder why they got so emotional about their points of view and felt so determined to best the others. For me it was interesting to discover yet again how many different ways people can see the same world. Clearly every person on earth carries around a personal way of looking at things, and the great miracle is that we ever understand each other at all! Perhaps, I theorized, through God every heart in this world is linked to every other heart, and opinions and theories only get in the way of our finding and feeling that link. But I never shared that thought with anyone else, for how could I prove it?

Over time I felt I came to know each boy, though I cannot remember all of their names now. They must have ranged in age from perhaps eleven to fifteen. There was one, bigger and slower than the others, who looked over the shoulders of his neighbors to get his answers. Another was the wit of the group. He was forever offending Nasir al-Din and enduring pinches on the ear and tongue lashings for his too-ready tongue—not to mention the rod! The others I remember for their liveliness, which was only contained by Nasir al-Din's freely given raps on their heads. When studies were over and the ritual of bowing and kissing his hands completed, they were scarcely out the door before they were racing each other down the narrow alleyway. How I envied them!

But the boy I remember best is Rukn al-Din. As the future Mahdi, he was treated with respect, but none made him their friend. He seemed slightly weary, as if the burden of his future already weighed upon him. He seemed not to know what to do after lessons were over—he clearly hated having to be accompanied by the two honor guards who stood outside during every lesson. He often lingered afterwards, finding excuses to converse with Nasir al-Din. I felt sorry for him.

After my lessons I would return to ever-shorter afternoons and eve-nings with my friends. Anna could read now. Maryam and she were like mother and child. In the afternoons, all of us seated on bench or carpet and a plate of sweet Persian melon slices by our sides, they murmured together while I wrote in my journal. Alas, that became slow work. I had too many painful memories. Sometimes, weary with work and study, I might watch shadows chase the sun's rays up its walls until all sunlight was gone or simply delight in the clear mountain air, until it grew too cold to be outside for long.

But always I was drawn back to the texts that Nasir Al-Din had let me take back to Selim's home. Though I might lack outer freedom, I still was free to roam among ideas.

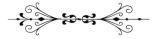

Frost blighted the last roses, the air turned as sharp as broken glass, and we had to light a fire in the biruni's little round hearth. If I went onto the roof, I could look down and see autumn tinting the valleys below in reds and golds and greens. My sixteenth birthday and Saint's Day must have come and gone, though the Muslim calendar could not tell me when.

One day in early winter, having braved a bitter wind and snowfall, I arrived at lessons to find Nasir al-Din and his students ranged around the table reserved for books and scientific instruments. They were poring over a pile of scrolls and books that had just arrived. Some documents were rolled and sealed in long leather cases, some were bound into pages, and one book even had a lock on it. A Nizari merchant had brought them back from eastern Iran, where so much had been destroyed that to save anything written was regarded as meritorious. Our teacher announced that he would sort through them to determine which were worthy of en-tering the Alamut library. Of course I could not join the boys, though I'd have loved to see more. I had glimpsed Uigur script on one scroll.

After the group lessons were over and the boys were gone, both Nasir al-Din and his wife left the room briefly. I got up to look for that Uigur manuscript when suddenly, as if he had been waiting for this moment, Rukn al-Din reappeared at the door and strode toward the table where the manuscripts lay. I stepped back and modestly turned away from him. Behind me I heard the rustle of papers and then felt more than saw him flee the room. I returned to the table intending to look for my document again. Rukn al-Din had disturbed the pile of manuscripts, and one now stood foremost among them. As I picked it up, a folded piece of paper fell onto the table. How I knew it was for me I cannot say, but after finding my Uigur text, I tucked the bit of paper into it. Just then Nasir al-Din returned to the room, and I almost jumped in surprise. And my chaador fell back.

It was a doubly awkward moment, for I had been at something secretive and now I had violated womanly decorum. Yet if that paper was a note from Rukn al-Din, I felt I had to remove it or compromise both him and myself. I had to hastily cover my face again as Nasir al-Din averted his eyes, but I saw a gleam in them that I had seen before in other men. I was suddenly most happy to have his wife there. To cover our mutual confusion, I lifted the manuscript in which the piece of paper lay and asked, "May I take this one to translate, master? It is written in Uigur, a language I know."

He curtly agreed.

My private lessons took forever that day, and the way home seemed longer and more twisting than usual. As soon as I was alone, I opened Rukn al-Din's paper. It was indeed meant for me, though it did not name me, so at first I thought he had a scrap of sense! I supposed he had imagined that if I did not pick it up, it would just mingle with the other manuscripts and not be connected to either of us. It was a love poem in quatrain form, so flowery and overblown that I almost laughed.

But I grew serious when I read his postscript. "I love you. My heart aches for another glimpse of your face. Your emerald eyes sparkle with the promise of Paradise, your copper hair is more precious than gold." Now, that would have compromised me. I regretted having even exchanged even one accidental glance with him. There would only be trouble if he revealed any more of his feelings for me. I must ignore him from then on, not to mention behave with complete circumspection in the presence of all men!

The next day when lessons were over, Rukn al-Din did not leave with the other boys. Instead, he ambled over to the pile of manuscripts still sprawled upon the table, looking as if he had won some secret prize. Nasir al-Din summoned me to the table as well.

"I must finish sorting through these books, Sofia. Many of them are in scripts I do not understand, and you may help. We will suspend your private lessons for today. Rukn al-Din also offers to help me—indeed, it was his suggestion that I might use you in this way."

So my young admirer had found a way to be near me no matter what I did! And my teacher was completely unaware of the way he was being used. I confess that in that moment it seemed more a jest than a risk, I so resented Nasir al-Din's high-handed ways. And today Rukn al-Din did not seem to be any threat. I was also grateful. Now I would be allowed to pore over that enticing display at leisure. Out of the corner of my eye, I could see the poor boy blushing as though he had swallowed fire, as in one sense he had.

"We will divide them according to language and then determine what each says," Nasir al-Din was saying, oblivious to these undercurrents. "The ones that none of us can understand will have to be burned unless I can find someone to translate them for me and prove them useful. The Grand Master wants no books in his library that might offend the eyes of a True Believer." How I hated that thought, even before I knew what the books contained.

We set to work at once, silently sorting everything by language. Of course most of them were written in Persian or Arabic script, but I found several written in Uigur, some written in Turkish, and even a few in Greek and Latin. It was hard not to stop and read them on the spot. And knowing they would otherwise meet their fate in the fire, I also set aside a few written in unfamiliar languages. I recognized Hebrew lettering from Anna's lessons, but in some scrolls there were letters I had never seen before. Sometimes the characters ran from top to bottom like the Uigur script, but each character was made of different strokes crossing over each other, while in a few papers I found a beautiful script that was all curves and dots, connected by lines along the top of each word.

But then I realized that in order to save them, I would have to invent what they said. Reluctantly I put all but the Hebrew manuscripts into the rejected pile. Then I came upon one that was written in columns, each devoted to a different form of writing, including Latin and Greek. They seemed to be greetings and so forth, things a merchant would need to know, and words were paired together: Latin beside Hebrew, Farsi, and the one with curves and a connecting line. If they all said the same thing, or expressed how they sounded, I might even teach myself languages I did not know!

I spoke eagerly, holding up my pile of Latin and Greek scrolls. "Master, these I can translate myself. Perhaps I could take the ones written in Hebrew home, and the Jewess Maryam could translate them for you. And this manuscript seems to contain side-by-side translations of the same words. If I can puzzle out those unfamiliar to me, I may be able to translate other works in those languages."

Nasir al-Din's face lit up. "Yes, take them and work on them at home."

I was thrilled, not only to save more books from the fire but to have such an interesting puzzle set before me. That afternoon back in Selim's garden, I entirely forgot poor Rukn al-Din, I was so happy sorting through books and scrolls. Some really were not worth saving: lists of goods to be transported by some merchant, or letters or official documents written years earlier. Their authors were probably all long dead. Others would bear more study.

The following day, I was so eager to return to the delights of my new treasury that I could scarcely pay attention during the group lessons. How I wished Nasir al-Din would let me go early for once. However, after all the boys but one had left, he spoke my name sharply. He had seemed more annoyed than usual during our lessons, and I feared he would take me to task for something I had left undone.

Instead, he said testily, "It seems that you are to become a teacher yourself, Sofia. The Grand Master orders that his son," and he gestured toward Rukn al-Din, who had wandered to the manuscript table and was innocently looking at a scroll, "receive lessons from you. Our young master here was evidently so impressed yesterday by your command of languages that he wants you to teach some of them to him. He claims that he will find use for them when he succeeds his father as Mahdi. You are to teach him here, under my protective eye." He snorted. "The Imam's ways are unfathomable. But understand this: I will allow nothing to happen to

Rukn al-Din! I know a woman's wiles are vast and deep."

Blood rushed into my head, dividing me between anger and guilt, for while I had done nothing to encourage the boy, I had not exposed *his* wiles, either. Besides, I had seen how Nasir al-Din himself had looked at me, and I had not exercised any wiles then, either. Anger won out.

"What makes you think I practice wiles? And what makes either of you think I would agree to be anyone's tutor? I find the very idea insulting!" And I turned away, ready to sweep out of the room in haughty fashion.

"How dare you! You have no choice, and your ingratitude to the Imam and to me is monstrous! The Grand Master is much mistaken in you— you are a mere, infidel, woman!"

I turned back, enraged in turn. "That may be, but I have my pride and my virtue, something neither of you can understand, who regard women as nothing more than—than—wombs waiting to be filled! And you, sir, think far too well of yourself." With that parting insult, mild enough, I reached the door and would have left.

"No, wait, come back, I beg you," called Rukn al-Din, who had stood stiff with shock during these outbursts. I did stop, since the poor boy could hardly be blamed for his master's insults or my outrage.

"I am sorry, it is not your fault," we said together, each looking at the other's feet.

"Please stay," the boy added. "I must understand my enemies' speech so I can parley with their envoys directly. Think on it before you turn away. You know so many languages: Mongol, Turkish, Greek, Latin. It is my solemn duty to protect my people from possible threats, and you who lost your own home to invaders must surely understand."

Nasir al-Din still stood with his hands on his hips, his face marred by with anger, and I almost turned away again despite Rukn al-Din's touching plea. Had I left, my life would have turned out very differently. Instead, I paused and thought. How it would please my arrogant teacher to see me walk away—less trouble for him and everyone's poor opinion of me as an infidel, a woman, and a student would be carved into stone. But even more, how could I turn away from someone who needed my help?

I addressed the air beside the future Mahdi. "Rukn al-Din, I will agree to tutor you, but you must promise never to take my courtesy for womanly lures. Indeed, I am married! If needed, you must think of me as a man and not as a woman. On those terms alone will I teach you. But while your virtue is safe from my so-called wiles, mine must also be safeguarded."

"Yes, I promise."

"Well, well, I am sure we both regret any hasty words we have spoken." Nasir al-Din smiled, much to my surprise. "After all, if the Mahdi approves this arrangement, who am I to argue?"

I was still tempted to argue, but there seemed little point, so I simply agreed to do as I was asked.

From then on, my afternoons were no longer my own. After my lessons, Nasir al-Din left for the madrassa while one of his wives chaperoned Rukn al-Din and me. My pupil was not only an eager learner but was also a model of courtesy, which eased my concerns about his letting slip something about his passion for me. We began with Mongol speech, and toward the end of the summer I introduced a Kipchak dialect. But truly, Rukn al-Din was more interested in hearing stories about life among the Mongols. He seemed to thrill to the idea of a nomadic life, and who could blame him, who had never seen anything beyond Alamut castle?

Meanwhile, at what I now regarded as home, I was happily ending the day by examining my Uigur texts. They were fascinating. Several were Christian scriptures, possibly Nestorian, and a few were Buddhist. One told the life story of the Buddha, and to my surprise, it was our old tale of Barlaam and Joasaph! Nor did they borrow it from us Rus'. This Buddha lived about five hundred years before Christ. I imagined that story slowly making its way across so many countries, passing through different languages and religions before settling in Rus', and it made me feel a deep bond with my fellow men.

I also found several scrolls about Manichaeism. I did not think much of it, or about it. It offered salvation to its faithful through spiritual truth, a familiar creed. But its founder, who called himself Mani, claimed that life is nothing but pain and evil, that our pure souls are entrapped in matter, and that Satan and God are equally powerful and in an eternal struggle for them. There was much more, but I finally set it aside in impatience, wondering why, if life was so evil, all Manicheans did not just starve themselves to death and reenter God's light without more ado!

I do not suppose my thinking was any clearer than this Mani's, but I kept feeling how ungrateful he and his disciples were for this world's most basic gifts of life and love and understanding, not to mention its manifold offerings of sky and earth and wind and sun. Indeed, how could he or his disciples even know what good is, or find their so-called salvation without life here and now? No, God's word in Genesis still rang true. This world is good and so are our lives, which also partake of God's goodness. Later I learned that much of what Mani taught is what the Cathari heretics believe. What an irony. I rejected their beliefs long before I stood accused.

A foggy, snowy winter dragged on forever with nothing but lessons, translating, and weekly baths to mark its passing. As the days slowly grew longer again, I began to wonder when Selim would come for me. No matter how fascinating my lessons were, they could not make me forget my only goal, to find a true home with my uncle in Constantinople.

SPRING, ANNO DOMINI 1244
TO SPRING, ANNO DOMINI 1245

Ramadan came a little earlier than the previous year, to my surprise. Remembering Selim's family celebrations and how much we had shared then, such deep loneliness welled up that I thought I might drown in it. But shortly after Now Ruz, and to my great joy Selim and his sons returned without warning. I was at lessons at the time, and when I got back, the biruni was in chaos. We women had made it ours. Scrolls and manuscripts were piled here and there, writing utensils set out on a low table and pillows piled for our ease. The servants were hastily rearranging everything, and Anna and Maryam had vanished.

"Well, Sofia," Selim said after we had exchanged greetings, "I see you have availed yourself of the opportunity to learn after all."

I had to smile. "Yes, despite my ill humor when you deser—left us, I have appreciated my lessons with Nasir al-Din. For those, I thank you heartily. And I am sorry I did not know you were coming, or I'd have cleared away all these manuscripts."

"Think nothing of either, and let us dwell no more on what is past. Will you join my sons and me for the evening meal? And Anna, too, if she wishes. She has retreated to the andarun rather than be left alone with us men. A natural modesty that one can only admire."

I overlooked the little sting of judgment that seemed to lie under

Selim's words and sent word to Anna. However, she claimed she preferred Maryam's company.

"She has been studying, too, with Maryam," I said, "and they are now close friends. She can even read to us in Farsi and a little in Hebrew, a language still unfamiliar to me." Selim smiled strangely and raised his eyebrows, which drove me to add, "Maryam is also translating some scrolls written in Hebrew to assist Nasir al-Din."

Selim merely turned the talk elsewhere. "Having already been admitted to the holy presence of the Mahdi, I must pass on his words. He told me you were most helpful to him, Sofia. He praises you twice over, for I also hear you are teaching various languages to our future Imam."

His sons arrived, Umar as cool and Kerim as brotherly as ever, and our conversation was cut short. After they had prayed, we ate together. During the meal I asked a few polite questions about their journey, but Umar stayed stonily silent and Kerim seemed loath to say much, either, although he glanced at me several times and smiled. At least he regarded me as family, even if his brother did not.

It was Selim who talked. "I am again a grandfather, and Kerim is a proud father. Perijam was delivered of a fine son, whom we have named Sayeed. She sends you her love. The rest of the family is thriving, too. Banu is now with child, and we expect it to be born before next Now Ruz." She must be fourteen by now, and pregnant. I offered a silent prayer for the health of both mother and baby before returning to other questions, especially about his journey back to Sarai. Selim spoke little about his travels, though he said that he had seen Qacha and Dorje. I was thrilled.

"How is Dorje?"

"He is well," he assured me, "and though you do not ask, so are Qacha and Argamon. I was able to tell Dorje that you arrived here safely. He sends his blessings and says that Batu is still furious with you. He wondered why you'd been so unwise as to insult the khan, but then he added that your letter, whose contents gossip had relayed to his ears, may have had an effect on the man. At least Batu is now called the Sain Khan for the wisdom and justice of his rule. 'The Good Khan'—it makes me laugh! Dorje tells me that Argamon's first wife joined him from Karakorum, he has taken a second wife, and he may well be a father again by now."

I do not know why, but I felt faintly jealous. Pushing those feelings aside, I asked, "And what is happening in the larger world? Have they elected a new Khakan?"

"No, nothing but rumors as solid as mist. I only know that Batu Khan still makes no move toward Karakorum. But Kuyuk will be elected, anyway. That is one of the reasons you were so helpful. This growing split between the cousins has already spurred the Mahdi to make plans that, I hope, will not include me. I always feel defiled among the Mongols."

After the meal, while Umar and Kerim were outside seeing to the animals, I raised my most important question. "Selim, once you are rested, will we be leaving?"

"So you feel no desire to stay here and complete your studies," he said. "I confess to being a little disappointed. I had hoped … Well, I suppose it was not to be."

"No, Selim, it was not. I beg you to take me away before another winter sets in. I thank you from my heart for arranging for me to learn from Nasir al-Din, but my deepest wish is to find my uncle. For all I know, he is dead, but still I must try. Please, you know how it feels to lose family and friends. Take me home."

Selim was clearly moved, but he only said, "I can promise no clear date, Sofia. This is a decision only my master can make. But I promise to ask him on your behalf." And with that I had to be content. I was rising to bid him goodnight when he touched my sleeve.

"Sofia, tomorrow I seek another audience with the Mahdi, and I will ask permission for you to leave with me. I will speak plainly to him of my obligation to you."

"Thank you, Selim," I smiled, hope rising in my breast. "Until tomorrow, then."

As I knelt for prayers, though, an image came unbidden to my mind: English John, long dead, and his toast to no tomorrows. A chill swept over me, but I tried to banish it by praying fervently for everyone I knew, including myself.

For the next few days, both Selim and I waited to hear when his master would grant him an audience. Meanwhile my life continued in the usual way. I was proud of my good work, my intact honor, and my dignity. Nasir al-Din even deigned to praise one of my translations. More and more of the scrolls that I had taken back to Selim's were opening their secrets to me. Especially exciting were those that allowed me to piece together the meanings of one language through another.

And I had found wonderful collections of poems and ancient tales written in Uigur, although when I showed them to my teacher, he laughed. "Those are the old songs and legends of Persia herself! Some of our literature dates back thousands of years, almost to the Creation. Ours is such an ancient civilization, and everyone who comes in contact with it is perfumed by its greatness. Indeed, those in the past who forced Iran under their yoke were always yoked in turn by our culture, even the Arabs who brought us the teachings of the Prophet, peace on his name." How his prideful words reminded me of my much-missed friend Q'ing-ling and her praise of her Chin homeland!

So since Nasir al-Din did not want them, he allowed me to keep the manuscripts and I formed my own little library. Though most of it was also lost to fire or blood.

Alas, Selim was made to wait almost two months to see his Mahdi. He took it even harder than I did. He left early every day, and I would return from lessons to hear that he was still waiting outside his Imam's door. So I in turn waited for him in the courtyard and when it grew dark, the biruni, joining his sons at supper time. Our speech was often strained, as Umar was so cold and Kerim, as if to make up for his brother, almost too friendly. And when Selim arrived, the news was always the same. No audience. After dinner I would retire, discouraged, to the andarun.

More and more often, waking at night, I could smell a faint pungent odor. "Opium dissolved into a tea," Maryam told me one morning when I commented on it. "A good medicine when used in moderation. When we first knew him, Selim used to drink or chew it sometimes when he was ill, but these days he takes far too much of it, far too often, and now Kerim turns to it. Taking it too often is dangerous! It slowly entraps a man's mind and makes him into a dumb animal. Umar is the only sensible one."

I tried to turn a deaf ear to her judgments, but she was right. Selim was becoming ever more withdrawn and unhappy, and he was turning to opium daily.

Finally Selim was admitted to the Imam's presence. I knew nothing about it, as I was at lessons. But as soon as I got back home, I smelled the opium tea and my heart sank. He never drank it so early in the day. I found him in the main room by himself, not only with his cup but also chewing a little dark pill from a pile in a bowl on a low table beside him. He seemed to have drifted into a waking sleep and was scarcely able to rouse himself from his torpor, but when he saw me, he did sit up and greet me, but with a frown.

He forgot his usual polite greetings. "Oh, Sofia, it is you. Alas, I bear ill tidings. I saw the Grand Master today. He refuses to let you go."

"Why?"

"Oh, many, many good reasons," Selim answered, waving his hand vaguely.

"Please, do give them to me!"

Selim shook his head as if to clear it. Using his fingers, he counted off reasons. "First … he sends me south. Next … west is too dangerous. More and more Mongol ordus moving into Azerbaijan … already destroyed western cities … slaughtered everyone…." He seemed about to fall asleep, but he took a deep breath and added, "and third … they now move into Syria … so the main route west is cut off. Troops and scouts everywhere … you might be caught and brought back to …." I was able to finish that sentence for myself, although he was not, as he seemed to be drifting back into his dream world.

"Selim, those are your reasons, not the Grand Master's. If I am willing to brave those dangers, then why should he care? I gave him what he wanted. I am of no more use to him. And if you worry about the Mongols punishing you or your sons, then send me with Da'ud and his boys!"

Selim sat up straight and regained his clarity for a moment. "Sofia, you are twice mistaken. I do not fear for myself. And you are still useful to Nasir al-Din."

"What? How dare he! Why did you not take my part?"

Selim frowned. "He is a great scholar, Sofia. You should feel honored."

"Well, I do not! And I will tell him so, too."

Selim looked alarmed. "But there is more. Rukn al-Din wishes to learn more from you. He says he honors you above all other women, Faithful and infidel alike."

Selim fell back onto his cushions as if he had used up his entire mind, and I fled to my room. When supper was served, I did not respond to the summons.

The next day when I arose, late on purpose, Selim and his sons had quietly departed. He had at least left me a letter, but it only said something like, "The Imam has chosen to discipline this wayward disciple's heart by sending him straightaway to southern parts. Because of the season, I will probably have to spend the winter there, gathering information and new disciples. But when I return, I swear on my life that I will find a way to fulfill my promise, Sofia. I am a man of honor, and it pains me deeply to leave you in this way. I am your slave." And so forth.

I refused to attend lessons that day. When the guard came for me, I claimed to be ill. Instead, while Anna and Maryam worked together, I spent hours brooding and listing all the ways in which I had been ill used, ending with this latest abandonment. It was like a seal of doom. Anna and I must remain virtual prisoners in Alamut at least through the winter. Ironically, she was happy with her new friend, who had as good as adopted her as a daughter.

When I finally told Anna and Maryam about what Selim's hasty departure meant, Maryam frowned and patted my arm. "I feared it might come to this. This so-called Mahdi is like a dog with a bone; once he has you between his teeth, he never lets go. And Selim al-Din has the spine of a worm when he's around the man."

Tears started to my eyes. "I only wanted to go home. Anna, I'm so sorry."

"But I'm happy here, Mistress. I can wait. Or if we never leave, that won't be so bad, will it? Life is good here, and I—we—have Maryam … and each other." At that I ran into the andarun to weep until I was empty of tears.

I resumed lessons with Nasir al-Din the next day. There was nothing to be gained by hiding in Selim's house, nor even by showing my bitterness to my teacher or my young admirer. Even if they could understand, their needs came before a woman's.

Summer came and went, marked by little but warm weather; the autumn passed as slowly as the leaves drifting from the poplars dotting the valley below us; the weather grew bitter and the days short, and the snows began. I felt like a rock stuck in a streambed, looking up at sun and storm passing overhead, feeling my life flow away like water. I bowed to Rukn al-Din's eager study with no joy, I no longer cared when a new bundle of texts arrived. Even Nasir al-Din remarked on my lassitude. The winter passed like a dark dream.

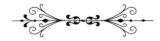

Ramadan came again, even earlier than the last year, and put an end to lessons for a month. Shirin left us a cold repast each morning before she and Yusuf disappeared to the mosque for the day. Maryam and I played backgammon with Anna or chess with each other, so at least I could put to rest my fear of being shut out from their friendship. And between my Hebrew lessons and my attempts to unlock the secrets of more manuscripts, I kept busy. I had set aside my journal. With so little to write, I would not reach its end anytime soon.

Now Ruz passed with much noise and celebration outside our garden walls, but we took no part in it. I returned to Nasir al-Din for lessons, and more days passed like water dripping slowly on stone.

Then one night a true dream came to me in the darkest hours when I lay between waking and sleeping. I was at the gates of the castle just before sunrise, and the sky was glowing red-gold. The gates slowly opened, and I saw the Alamut valley below, all hidden in darkness. A caravan began wending its way past me and onto a much wider bridge than the real, waking life bridge, and suddenly I was in its midst, dressed as a man, with Rukn al-Din walking beside me. He was pressing my hand and assuring me that he had arranged everything with his father; I was free to go. I sat up, wide awake. Rukn al-Din no longer seemed in love with me, but if he still was, surely I could persuade him to arrange for my release! The only question was how I might even ask for his help.

Ironically, it was so easy to ask that I felt foolish for not thinking of it sooner. The very next day during his lessons, I simply said, "Translate this from Mongol speech into Kipchak Turkish," as I wrote on the chalkboard, 'Read it silently. Answer in writing.' I paused, at a loss. 'Do you still care for me?' I handed the board to him, my hands atremble.

Rukn al-Din read and reread it. Finally he took up his chalk and wrote, "I love and adore you!"

I wrote, "Then why do you imprison me here? All I want is to find my family."

He looked stricken, then hastily wrote, slipping into familiar address, 'I wanted only to be near you. You are my dream of love.'

'But your dream has become my nightmare,' I wrote. 'I am alone and friendless here. I beg you to help me leave with Selim al-Din so I can find my home again.'

Rukn al-Din hesitated before writing, 'I am your friend. I promise, but I must persuade not only my father but also Master Nasir al-Din.'

'I have faith in you.'

He blushed and smiled, and we continued our lessons in a more ordinary vein.

Now all my hopes grew from the slender stem of that promise.

In fact, after that nothing changed. I studied hard, taught Rukn al-Din, translated texts for Nasir al-Din, and collected a few manuscripts of my own. Nasir al-Din did give me several fascinating histories of Iran to read, and I was soon awash in lengthy, extravagant tales of ancient emperors, mighty shahs, and even petty local chieftains. Such a litany of wars; such a procession of kings, proud heroes, and tragic martyrs, not only Iranian but Syrian and Egyptian and even Greek and Roman. Persian history did seem to reach back to the beginning of time. Among those stories, though, I remember only one tale with perfect clarity, for it spoke not of great wars and mighty deeds but of a shah and his jarya. I took a personal interest in that!

According to this history, a powerful king had a huge haram with many concubines. One jarya in particular pleased him beyond measure when he first brought her into his bed. But she pleased him too much. He was so consumed by lust for her that he decided not to summon her again. But he could not resist, and she gave him another night of sublime pleasure. He sent her away again, but again his lust for her was too great. The shah became possessed by such passion for his lovely, biddable jarya that he lost interest in governing his kingdom. Finally he decided that his obligation to his kingdom was being compromised. So he had her beheaded!

To say that I was aghast scarcely expresses my outrage, defenselessness, panic. His jarya had only served her master as he wished, but instead of affection or gratitude, he felt only lust. And because she was merely property, rather than send her far away where he would never see her again, he killed her! Although this story was a famous illustration of duty before pleasure, I have no doubt that this supposedly great man grew old and died possessed by the memory of his jarya, for why should her death kill his lust? And I was equally dependent on the pleasure—and whims—of men who saw me only for what I could do for them.

My old nightmares returned: the rape, the murders of those I had loved, the utter helplessness of captivity. I suddenly recalled Argamon telling me he would have killed me had he believed Qabul and I were lovers. At the time, too much else was going on and I had forgotten it quickly. Were his threats not the same? He had later claimed he loved me, but love would not have stayed his hand.

At the end of summer, I began studying Hebrew to fill the time. So while the days grew short and cold, I learned to read the Torah, which is also called the Books of Moses. Maryam taught me always to begin by reciting a special blessing.

I learned to my surprise that we Christians know the Torah as the oldest of our Holy Scriptures, so some of it was familiar. But there were also chapters that we Rus' knew nothing about. It made me wonder what other Scriptures I might never have seen.

Maryam also brought me her other holy writings, which she called the Tanakh. It includes laws and customs known as Halakha or path of walking, and the Talmud, which means learning drawn from the Torah, plus the oldest oral traditions, which are now preserved in writing. That was the most sense I could make of it, anyway, for there were so many categories of study that I got lost.

What seems to be most important in all these writings is for Jews never to forget all their rituals and laws and what they mean. These books have guided them everywhere since they lost their kingdom to the Romans and were turned into wanderers without a home. I could certainly sympathize with that!

So though some customs and practices were as strange to me as were Mongol or even Muslim ways, I could still respect the Torah and the laws that bind the Jewish heart to God—almsgiving, honoring one's parents and guests, being kind, visiting the sick, honoring the dead, praying, being peacemakers. I felt devotion rise from every page. There was so much to study that it took months of reading, a little at a time, with my scant knowledge of Hebrew. I never finished it all.

Still, as I learned more and more about Islam and Judaism, I found so much that they both shared with my Christian faith. I had never realized how much of Christianity arose from Judaism. Other than forms of worship, our deep difference lay in their not believing Jesus was the Messiah and Son of God. That was difference enough, but all three religions teach love and justice and goodness. Thinking on the Grand Master or on how bitter Maryam was, I wondered why we could not simply follow those guidelines and not meddle with how others worship or what they believe, since not one of us truly thinks like anyone else even when we do share the same religion. I finally decided not to dwell on such questions, as they only added to my bleak mood.

I still could take pleasure in learning, and all autumn and winter I fell further in love with Iranian letters, especially with the poems. There were delicate love songs, usually quatrains or ghazals, and animal fables, and great epics filled with long ago shahs, warriors, and lovers—my favorite was still the Shanameh. All delighted me and allowed me to endure my lonely hours. I still recall word-for-word some lines that conclude the most famous of the tales of the Simurgh. I fear my translation will sound clumsy compared with the elegance of Farsi, which delights as much in sound as in imagery:

> *Seeker, Journey, and Road*
> *Were but my self drawn toward My Self, and the*
> *Arriving but my Self returning Home ...*

And here is the final image:

> *Return, you lost fragments, to your Center and Be*
> *The Infinite Mirror where you saw Me:*
> *You rays that strayed so far into Darkness*
> *Now your Sun draws you back to rest.*

SUMMER
ANNO DOMINI 1245

With spring the garden had begun to bloom again, and hope had again tried to bloom inside me, but it was blighted. Several times over the winter, I had risked using the same ruse to ask Rukn al-Din if he had spoken to his father yet, but he had always written the same answer: 'no.'

Once he had added, "I await the right opening in Father's mood when his heart favors me. Alas, that happens rarely."

In all that time, my only contact with the world had been through Rukn al-Din, for Nasir al-Din did not think it worth his time to tell me any news. But my pupil sometimes passed on what he had overheard in his father's council room. For instance, a message had once come from another mountain stronghold called Mazandaran to warn the Grand Master that more Mongol troops were moving west. I almost wished then that I truly did live in haram, knowing nothing of the dark clouds growing on the horizon, for if the Mongol storm blew Iran into oblivion, I might be forced to stay in Alamut until I died. I was a fully grown woman now, sixteen or perhaps even seventeen by my count, but my life already seemed over.

But one early summer's day after Nasir al-Din had dismissed the other students and I had sat down across from Rukn al-Din, he cried, "I bring you good news, Sofia! I was with my father when he received word that

Selim al-Din has returned to Qazvin from the south. He will be here soon!" I wanted to ask more, but our teacher frowned and interrupted.

"You are here to study, Master Rukn, not to gossip like an old woman."

Our teacher could not burst the bubble of joy that rose up from my heart. I went home full of plans for what I would take with me or leave behind as gifts to Maryam, which books to pack, and so forth. The day after that, not only Rukn al-Din but all the other boys seemed to simmer with excitement, and Nasir al-Din struck out with his rod again and again to no avail.

After the others had raced off, Rukn al-Din waited until our teacher had left the room and said hastily, "I have more news for you, Sofia. Father has sent some of his men on a holy mission against Qazvin. We are all wishing we could go to defend Islam! A man lives there—Farhad ibn Ali—he and others guided my father in his youth but were turned out of Alamut for abusing their power. They have been slandering Father ever since, especially that Farhad. He's been a thorn in the side of the Nizari for years. But out of respect for a great Sufi Sheikh who lives in the same quarter of Qazvin and who has always tempered Farhad's actions, Father has left him and the other Qazvini traitors alone until now."

Before he could continue, I interrupted. "But I thought you despised Sufis."

"Most of them we do. They see no further than personal union with Allah; they have no sense of mission! But Sheikh Jamaluddin Gili was secretly one of us. Alas, he died recently, and Selim al-Din sent word that Farhad ibn Ali has been recognized as a Sunni mullah. Unless we meet Farhad's demands for many gold dinars, he threatens to expose all our Faithful in Qazvin! We must stop this apostate's mouth before he does any damage.

"Besides, some of our supplies grow thin and our people grow hungry."

"Well, he sounds like a nasty sort of person, but what do thin supplies have to do with him? And what does any of it have to do with me, anyway?"

Rukn al-Din looked at me pityingly. "We will strike a blow against the unbeliever while reaping rewards that Allah the All-Just sees fit to grant us! As to what it has to do with you, my father has ordered Selim al-Din to delay coming here for a few weeks."

"Why? And beyond that, why not just purchase supplies from the Qazvinis?"

The boy laughed bitterly. "You speak of our enemies," he said. "They would sell us nothing, or poison what they sold!

"As for Selim al-Din, he must spy on them for us."

Nasir al-Din returned, and we had to begin our lessons. It was not until later that I had time to think about Rukn al-Dins' news. I tried to assure myself that I must only wait a little while longer, but the thought of the Nizari raiding their own countrymen made me uneasy.

More than a week passed after Rukn al-Din had told me about the intended raid on Qazvin. One day he and the other boys arrived for lessons, all of them in a frenetic mood that lasted for the entire class. After Nasir al-Din dismissed them early, having given up on his rod, Rukn al-Din turned to me and burst out, "Father's raid on the unbelievers was a great success, Sofia! I only wish I had been there. His men swept down on the apostate's settlement on the city's edge, crying glory to Allah and smiting every man they met, and they cut that false imam Farhad down where he cowered in his mosque. They arrived home this morning, their mounts loaded with bags of grain, and they captured many sheep and brought them safely across the mountains—a dangerous journey with snow still lingering in the higher passes! They even brought back a few infidel women as slaves. Praise be to Allah, who grants us such bounty!"

"What?" I cried. "Is this how you Faithful advance your cause? By killing in your holy places? By stealing women and sheep? How does it differ from banditry?"

Rukn al-Din turned red as beets and snapped, "You forget yourself, Sofia. You cannot talk that way to me! Those infidels are spiritually nonexistent!"

Spiritually nonexistent? Fiery words sprang to my mind, but I quenched them. If he could think of and use fellow Muslims in such a way, then what was I? Another jarya to discard, even murder, if I pleased him too much or too little? I took a deep breath and sat unmoving until I could speak with some calm. "Perhaps, then, we should turn to your lessons."

We spoke no more about the raid, but at the end of our session, as Rukn al-Din rose to leave, he said, "I wish for no quarrel with you, but sometimes I forget who you are. I can hardly expect an infidel woman to understand our difficult and dangerous spiritual mission. Just understand this: there is nothing that is not spiritual to him with eyes to see it. Until he conquered Mecca, the Prophet Muhammad made holy war on its caravans and Allah rewarded him with many riches! This is holy war, too!" And with that he left, trying to look as dignified as a fourteen-year-old boy secretly in love with an "infidel woman" could!

Murder and banditry were spiritual? It made me sick. But I still might need the boy's help. Once I had thought myself above women's wiles, but now I saw I might need them!

At any rate, Rukn al-Din recovered from his pique within a few days, and when Anna happily pointed out that Selim's servants were serving us handsome portions of mutton again, I found my scruples hard to maintain. At least Selim would be back soon, and I could leave.

Another mournful Muharram passed. I clearly remember only one thing. A swallow flew into the biruni one morning. It flitted about in panic until Shirin shooed it out the door, exclaiming, "We rarely see swallows here. Poor thing, it must have lost its way flying south."

"Swallows flying into a room are bad luck," Anna half-whispered to me.

I knew this omen, too, but I tried to shake off my forebodings. "Well, we're not in Hungary or Rus', so it surely doesn't mean the same thing here." We both smiled in relief.

A few days later I returned home one afternoon after lessons. The stony-faced guard opened the gate, but this time he seemed grimmer than ever. Bundles stood in the courtyard and the door was open. My heart flew ahead of me in delight. I hurried into the house to greet Selim, but only Kerim was in the biruni. To my great surprise, he was helping Perijam to sit; she looked as pregnant as when I had left her! A little boy slept in her arms—that must be Sayeed. Anna and Maryam were nowhere to be seen.

"Perijam! Kerim!" I rushed to embrace my friend and admire her son. Only then did I see that her face was streaked with tears and that Kerim looked wild-eyed and pale.

"What happened? Perijam, what could bring you out of haram? You are carrying another child!" Selim's servant Yusuf entered with food and drink.

"Terrible tidings, Sofia," Kerim began without a word of greeting, his voice cracking with emotion. "Here, Perijam. You must eat something for the baby's sake. No, what am I thinking? Yusuf, call Shirin to take my wife and boy to the andarun and see to their needs."

Racking sobs seized my friend and woke her little son. He began to cry too. She awkwardly stood and drifted out of the room behind Shirin.

"Sofia, sit down." All welcomes forgotten, I did as he said.

He rubbed his face and then burst out, "Father is dead, Mother is dead, Umar and Effat and little Ali are dead, Akbar is dead; and Aftab and Sarah and the maidservants are taken away—I can only guess to be sold as slaves. Our home is ransacked and ruined, all Father's menservants are killed."

"No!" I cried in disbelief. "How? When? Dear God, why?"

Kerim groaned. "Father and Umar and I were home awaiting a summons from the Imam when Perijam's family sent word that she must hasten to her father's house. He had fallen from his roof and was dying. A good man though a Sunni, loved and respected by everyone. She was his favorite daughter—the youngest. I took her straight to him. We stayed more than a week, and she was there when Allah took his soul—

"Then a neighbor arrived bearing evil tidings—a raid across town—a mosque attacked—vicious killings, pillaging, women kidnapped—the bandits fled into the mountains. Outside neighbors began calling to each other in outrage—not bandits, they cry, but the Hashishiya—what the Qazvini infidels call us Nizari! Rioting spread in the streets—men and boys dragged from their homes, tortured and slaughtered on the merest suspicion—their wives and daughters, maidservants raped and killed—or seized and sent to the slave market.

"Father had sent a warning to the Imam about a foul traitor—he knew the Qazvini Nizari were in danger. Grief, horror clawed at me—what if someone had betrayed Father?

"I knew I should go straight to him, yet I could not leave my mother-in-law alone—she had no sons. She clung to me for help, so I stayed on to arrange for her husband's funeral—"

Kerim buried his head in his hands. "I sent word to Father, begging him to flee to Alamut with his household. We would follow when we could. He always knew he was at risk, he had always meant to move us here. But always there was another secret mission and another delay....

"We waited out the riots with Perijam's mother. They spread like Greek fire throughout the city—the rioters even turned against each other!

Finally I could wait no longer. I returned home alone to gather a few things for Perijam, to see whether Father had taken everyone away, for I'd received no word."

Kerim sat staring dully before continuing in a strangled voice. "Our gates were smashed in, our guards' rotting bodies lay inside. Father's house was partly burned, his garden hacked to ruin. I found his remains there, and Umar's—hewn into pieces, floating in his pond, bloated and— I went through every building. Everything not stolen had been burned. In the andarun I found four charred bodies, two large and two small. Only by bits of their garments could I tell that one was—Mother—and—"

He could not finish. A wail tore from my throat. My friends, those lovely women; Selim, my protector. The little boys—the girls! We sobbed and wailed together.

At one point Maryam appeared with two cups. "Here is some lemon balm tea to soothe your raw heart. Kerim, your wife told us what happened. I gave her something that will allow her to sleep; she is worn out with grief and travel. You must rest, too. You are now head of the family, and you will need your wits about you."

He nodded and drank her remedy gratefully, as did I.

I finally left. Anna awaited me in the andarun, her face pale with shock. Even though she had been so unhappy in Qazvin, she felt the cruelty of these murders. "No one deserves to die like that," she said, bursting into tears. "Just like my family!"

That woke little Sayeed, who began to cry, but Maryam picked him up and calmed him with soft words and gentle touch. "Anna, dear one, now is not the time to relive your own grief. Come help me with the little boy. Bring him some water, please." Anna wiped her tears and dutifully obeyed.

That night while the dark hours slowly passed, misery flooded my heart: not just horror at such murders and grief at losing my friends, but anger at Selim for lingering among enemies and rage at this Imam, whose retribution mingled with greed had cost so many others' lives! Again and again terrible imaginings arose: Layla and Effat and the little boys, Aftab and Sarah. Would word ever even reach Banu? And I had lost my way home, too, though I put that thought aside. Nearby, Perijam tossed restlessly, often crying out in her sleep. Little Sayeed slept soundly beside Maryam.

The muezzin's call still hovered in the air when I finally arose and went to the biruni, intending to send a letter to Nasir al-Din and Rukn al-Din excusing myself from all lessons for the foreseeable future. Kerim was rising from his prayer rug, candles were burning, and writing materials were laid out. It looked as if he had been writing even before dawn.

"I never in my life had more difficulty writing a letter. A son must always obey his father, but now that Father is gone, I confess that I never felt the same devotion to …," and he gestured with his head toward the Imam's citadel, "that he and my brother felt. His Imam was forever turning him inside out—Father was always struggling to find some secret meaning behind his commands—even to breaking his promise to you. I witnessed how much pain and shame it caused him. Now I must guard my own feelings while seeking the Imam's aid. I fled here only because I could think of nowhere else to turn, yet I am terrified of compromising Perijam's family. The Imam must help me after all this!"

"Perhaps I can assist." I sat down beside him, and together we composed something simple to the Grand Master, to which task I brought all my abilities as an interpreter.

"Thank you, Sofia. Your help moves me deeply."

"This is a terrible time for you and Perijam. I must do everything I can."

I turned to my own letter to my teacher and student, better prepared with my mind cleared somewhat. I think my heartfelt words must have touched them both.

For the next few days, we women tended to Perijam and little Sayeed. As well as her adopted family, she had in effect lost both her parents, for Kerim had told her she could never return to Qazvin. Sayeed, less than two years old but aware that something was wrong, fretted constantly. Only Maryam seemed able to comfort him when his mother lost herself in grief.

Meanwhile Kerim was often in audiences with the Grand Master. After the first one, he arrived home distraught to find me removing scrolls and so forth from the biruni. He sat down and poured out his feelings to me. I was aware only of his need to grieve.

"A stone would have more feeling! The Imam told me Father was a great martyr for 'our' cause, that he and my murdered family now rest in Paradise. Perhaps it is so, I pray it is so, but I cannot find a way out of the desert of my own bitterness. My beloved mother, Effat, the little boys:

they knew nothing of our secret lives. Why were they sacrificed? I keep reliving their last moments and praying that Allah has wiped away their fear and pain—He has done nothing for mine! I—I am angry with my own God!" He burst into tears and impatiently brushed them away.

"And I am left alive. Was I a coward for not returning home at once? Is this Allah's punishment? How am I to go on?" There was much more; he was chained to an endlessly turning wheel of pain. I listened, nodding now and then, for I had felt just the same both at the Dnieper and after the fall of Kyiv. I offered a few words of consolation, but no more. I am sure of it.

Finally Kerim ran dry of words. He sat slumped with one hand over his eyes. I stood to leave, but he spoke again. "I can tell no one else of all this. Perijam has borne too much loss. Thank you, Sofia." He reached up his free hand in what I thought was gratitude.

I touched it, meaning only sympathy, but he suddenly clasped mine tight in his. I felt its heat flow into my palm. He looked up into my eyes and started to draw me down into an embrace, or so it seemed to me. I wrenched my hand from his and fled.

Back in the andarun, I busied myself with organizing my papers, all the while trying to regain a steady mind. I could not know whether I was right about Kerim, and there was no safe way to find out. I decided that unless I was surrounded by others, I must stay in the andarun whenever he was at home. That night he kept his wife with him. Somehow, his doing so added to my suspicions.

Soon thereafter the odor of opium tea came floating from the biruni. When Shirin returned from serving, Maryam asked, "Did you brew opium tea for Kerim?"

Shirin shrugged. "Yes. And he asked for pills, too."

"That fool! I hope he's not giving it to his wife. It would be an ill deed!"

"What can I do? I am but a serving woman!"

"It's not your fault, Shirin. It is just that I know what can hap—well, never mind."

When Perijam returned the next morning, her eyes were red, her lids drooping, her movements listless. Maryam cried, "I know what opium can do to a person, Perijam. My husband took it in his last illness. It is good medicine in small amounts, but if you take it often, you will keep wanting more and more of it while it does less and less to help you. Your baby may even be born craving it. I have seen lives ruined by it!"

Perijam burst into tears. "But it gave me release and let me enjoy my Kerim's embrace. We both needed it! And it was the first night I rested in peace since—that day!"

Maryam relented and patted the girl's arm, and the moment passed, at least for them.

But not for me. My fate lay in the hands of a man who gave opium to his pregnant wife! And I knew what Maryam did not: that Perijam had been using it when she was carrying Sayeed. How could I flee now when I could trust neither Kerim nor the Imam? I put no faith in Nasir al-Din and Rukn al-Din. What could an opinionated scholar or a brash youth do?

Perijam began spending every night with her husband. We could smell the opium.

At least at supper, Kerim shared his conversations with the Mahdi. After repeated visits, he had begun the painful task of claiming his heritage. I remember one conversation in particular. "The Grand Master is not entirely made of stone: he grants me substantial monies and goods to establish my own trade connections. He wants me to take up Father's role—whatever that means—but I tell him I am not ready yet. Well, in truth, I will never serve him! At first he was very angry, but now he relents and offers only generosity to us until we can depart for Tabriz to start anew."

Perijam exclaimed, "How brave you are to stand up to this Grand Master!"

I said nothing. If Selim was right, Kerim might have signed his death warrant by not submitting to the Imam straightaway. On the other hand, since no retribution had fallen on Kerim so far, perhaps the Grand Master was patiently waiting for him to make up his mind. He would then want to test his disciple, I suspected, which might mean other kinds of trouble. Or else Selim had lied to himself all those years and nothing would come of Kerim's hesitations. Only one thing was clear. If he was my only hope of escaping Alamut, the sooner we left, the better!

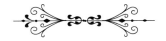

ays passed, and Kerim's plans grew no clearer. Once I asked him at supper about what would become of Anna and me. He started and said, "I am so sorry, Sofia. I have been thinking only of myself and my family these last few days, but you are Father's widow. He was to help you find your way home, and I must do the same. I will ask the Imam."

But his face grew long when he saw me the next night. "Oh dear, I forgot. I'll ask him the next time I have an audience with him. That will only be in a day or so."

So I waited an endless week, each night smelling the opium. Even when the Grand Master summoned him again, Kerim's mind seemed so clouded now that he might forget to ask.

Finally I decided not to depend on him any more. The only other men I knew were Nasir al-Din and Rukn al-Din. Although I felt little hope, there was no one else to turn to.

At the next meal I said, "I must resume my studies with Nasir al-Din and begin teaching your future Mahdi again. I must let them know I will return tomorrow."

After the meal Kerim sent Yusuf off with my letter.

A guard arrived for me the next day. When I entered the classroom, my teacher waved me to the back of the room. He kept repeating parts of earlier lessons I had missed, so I could follow him almost as easily as if I had not lost over two weeks of study.

After the group lessons were over, he spoke directly to me. "You stay behind, Sofia. And you, too, Master Rukn al-Din. You can resume your lessons."

The other boys left, casting a few curious glances back at us.

Nasir al-Din let out a great sigh and held his hand over his heart. "Sofia, I speak for Rukn al-Din as well when I ask you to accept our sympathy for the terrible murders of Selim al-Din and his family. And please offer it to his son, who, I understand, was the sole and miraculous survivor of that heinous slaughter." Rukn al-Din nodded, his eyes bright with unshed tears.

My teacher continued. "We are so sad for you and your people and yet so glad that you have returned—I have wanted to send for you."

"I thank you both." Silence fell. I did not know how to begin my request.

Nasir al-Din spoke first. "Alas, when I first wanted to send for you, it was to encourage you to continue your studies, but now … I must tell you, you must find a way to leave Alamut as soon as you can. In honor of your hard work, Master Rukn al-Din and I will both try to help you." The youth nodded agreement.

"He approached me a few days ago with news that affects you and your hosts directly, and he also told me about your wish to go home. Sofia, I delighted so much in drawing on the jewel casket of your mind to enrich my studies that I never realized that I was keeping you here against your will."

Rukn al-Din added, "I too am to blame for your overlong stay. I will do all I can to help you find your way home, since all travel may soon grow more difficult—I cannot say more right now—but you must not wait for Kerim ibn Selim, whose future is … hidden."

This was such unlooked-for kindness in both of them that tears started to my eyes. "Again, I thank you from my heart." When I could regain control of my voice, I added, "I place my fate in your hands."

"I will seek a way for you to leave," said Nasir al-Din. "Be ready to go at any time. Meanwhile come to lessons and stay behind as usual, when we can speak together freely."

I nodded, feeling both humbled and grateful for such unlooked-for kindness. But on my way home, questions crowded my mind. What was this secret knowledge that prompted them to suddenly urge me to flee? Had Rukn al-Din overheard his father express displeasure with Kerim? Was the man toying with Kerim while plotting harm against him? It would be simple to imprison or even murder him if he thought him disloyal to their cause, and Perijam and her son might be disposed of just as easily—indeed, all of us. Or perhaps the Grand Master was playing some more hidden game, to use Rukn al-Din's words, perhaps waiting until Kerim had left before he had him killed. Batu Khan had played a similar trick on his Hungarian prisoners; it seemed entirely possible.

Maybe I should not wait for Nasir al-Din to find me a caravan, or maybe I should warn Kerim. Caught up in worry, I returned to his house to find all the women clustered in the little courtyard. Perijam especially seemed both excited and panicked. She jumped up to take my hands and spilled out a disjointed tale as she led me to sit with them.

"I wanted all of you to hear this together, Sofia, to help me make sense of it. Kerim was just here. I've never seen him in such a state! He says revenge is at hand, that the infidel Qazvini who murdered our 'Faithful' must die. His Imam has called for jihad, and many of his closest followers, his Fida'i, have come forward to martyr themselves. Then Kerim left to join the chosen martyrs. I know so little about all this, but I think there is to be some kind of public killing, and I fear more people will lose their lives, including my husband!"

I stood in shocked silence, but Maryam said, "Listen, I know more about this than any of you do. You are right. Whatever mullahs or imams led the butchery in Qazvin will find a knife stuck in their hearts very soon. They had best avoid open places, for these so-called Faithful always kill in public expecting to be cut down themselves. They call their murders justice and their deaths martyrdom. The fools expect to enter Paradise on the spot!"

Feeling as if walls were slowly closing in on me from all directions, I cried, "That means more slaughter on both sides. Perijam, you must get Kerim away from here as soon as possible. Whatever you do, do not return to Qazvin! Get him to take you to Tabriz or somewhere far from here. And I beg you to ask him to take Anna and me with you."

She nodded slowly. Soon thereafter, Kerim returned home, wild with excitement. "Perijam, Sofia, at last I have taken a stand! I will personally avenge my family! Soon I join my brethren in holy martyrdom! Allah wills everything, and I put my trust in Him alone."

Maryam and Anna left for the andarun, but I stayed with Perijam, listening to Kerim. Perijam soon got caught up in his martial spirit; clearly I could not count on her.

Finally when I could take no more, I spoke. "Kerim, you know how I grieve for you both. I loved your family, and I understand your desire for revenge. I once felt the same toward the Mongols who killed everyone I loved. But to martyr yourself also sacrifices your wife, your son, your unborn child, and even Anna and me, none of whom are the Grand Master's disciples. You have obligations to the living as well as to the dead. When he married me, your father vowed on his life to take me to Constantinople, and you inherit his vow."

"But how else can I prove my bravery, my very honor? Sofia, this world will pass, and only those who—" But I caught a hint of doubt in Kerim's voice and cut in quickly.

"You can prove yourself by taking your loved ones and those you are honor-bound to protect away from this place! Let the Imam's true followers be the ones to martyr themselves, while you begin a new life and raise fine sons. You feel no loyalty to him and what he stands for! Once you are no longer under the Grand Master's sway, you will see differently. Do you really want to leave your sons fatherless, dependent entirely on him and his whims?"

Kerim flushed and looked at the floor for so long that I was afraid he was angry. Finally, he looked straight at me. "I hadn't thought about that. Perijam has neither family nor friends in this castle. My sons brought up by the very people whose heresies caused my mother to die so horribly.... What you say makes sense, Sofia, but it is too late. I cannot go back on my word. Were I to break it, the Imam would have me killed, anyway."

Sick at heart, I left Kerim and Perijam for the andarun, where I poured out all my fears to Maryam and Anna. Anna only said, "Well, they'll still take care of us, won't they? I like it here. Maybe we can go live with Maryam once Kerim leaves."

But Maryam frowned and said, "No, my home is a hovel compared to this. There is no room for two more people. Let me think a moment." I waited, but without much hope.

"So Kerim feels no real devotion to the Grand Master," she slowly said. "It sounds as if his guilty heart is telling him to martyr himself just to prove that he's not a coward. But Sofia, you must keep arguing to him that defying the Grand Master and escaping for the sake of his wife and child is just as brave as martyring himself, that he can simply feign commitment to this mission. You can do it. I have seen how he looks at you."

I frowned. "You think I can use ...?" She nodded. "I must think about it." To use his lust for me violated my sense of honor. No, I decided, my best hope lay elsewhere.

The next morning I sat impatiently through lessons, and for once Nasir al-Din would have had every right to strike me. But afterwards, alone with him and Rukn al-Din, I spilled out my story.

"Yes, this was part of what I meant yesterday," said my teacher. "And now Kerim ibn-Selim offers to martyr himself, too. Very bad. You cannot count on him at all."

"But how else are all of us to leave? And even if only Anna and I went with another caravan, how can we travel alone through Iran to—I know not where! Besides, Perijam is my friend. I couldn't leave her alone."

Rukn al-Din spoke. "Well, even though our cause is just, I say it is dishonorable for Kerim not to fulfill his father's vow to you. In a way you are his widowed mother! You must make him see, and soon; men already leave for Qazvin on this mission. I would take you away myself if I could. But I do have some wealth of my own, which will help pay for your journey home. And you must tell Kerim that the future Mahdi blesses your journey and commands him to fulfill his father's pledge. Even if he does martyr himself, you women can go without him—there are trustworthy men for hire in Qazvin that I can send word to. I also can get something from my father that might be of use. It's a metal token called a paize that is supposed to give you safe conduct through Mongol-held lands, or so I am told."

A paize from Rukn al-Din—almost like my dream!

"I too can help with monies, and I can give you some scientific manuscripts of great value to sell," added Nasir al-Din. "Many a wealthy man would want them for his library."

"Thank you, thank you both. I will do as you say."

I returned home feeling more hope than I had in two years. That night after supper, the other women retired to the andarun, but I braved being alone with Kerim. He had lost his earlier eagerness and was in a pensive mood.

"Kerim, may I speak with you as one who is almost your mother?"

He looked a little alarmed. "Yes, and I wish to speak with you, too. I have been thinking about what you said yesterday. Now I feel torn between protecting my family and dying bravely. You say Father swore on his life to help you?"

"Yes. It was in our marriage agreement. Would you like to see it? Or his last letter to me? I saved them, clung to them as my thin thread of hope."

"No, I believe you. He was a man of honor; he never willingly went against his word, and only the Imam could make him violate it...." He glanced at me sideways as if to read my face, then hastily looked away. "I have been thinking that I would be wrong not to fulfill his promise to you. But I gave given my word to the Imam, and now I see no way to go back on it."

"Well, his son Rukn al-Din told me to say he commands you to honor your father's vow, and he must be obeyed, too. But I have an idea. Nizari often disguise themselves, yes? Your father hid his purpose behind his merchant life, which allowed him to travel freely."

Kerim's face lifted hopefully. "Yes, go on."

"You can approach the Imam and tell him you wish to serve him, not only as a martyr but first as a spy." His face fell again. "You must, Kerim, or he will think you a traitor. Offer to go back to Qazvin and reestablish your father's secret connections under cover of his former trade. Part of your disguise will be settling your family there, which gives you a reason to take us all with you. You will say you can use Selim's spies to follow the movements of those the Fida'i wish to strike down, to tell them when and where it is best to strike. Add that when the Grand Master orders it, you will join them in martyrdom."

"Well … he may agree to that. But I no longer want to kill—or die—for him."

"You will never need to. You will not actually return to Qazvin. You will pass it by and go on to Tabriz, which is far to the west, yes? There you can find refuge among your remaining family, even perhaps send for Perijam's mother. And from there you can either send me or take me to the borders of Christian-held lands. We will all be able to start a new life."

Kerim was nodding vigorously by the time I had finished speaking. "A workable plan, Sofia. I will try to speak with him tomorrow."

I stayed home the next day, waiting for Kerim. When he returned late in the afternoon, I was alone in the little garden. Perijam had lain down for a nap with Sayeed, and Maryam and Anna were studying together in the biruni. He sat down by me and, after the usual polite preambles, he said, "I waited forever to speak with the Mahdi, but I did as you said when he admitted me to his presence. He saw the merit of my plan and offers to give me men and camels to add to my disguise. I gratefully refused; I said my own servants would gladly martyr themselves with me. Was that not clever of me, Sofia?"

I nodded just as I had seen Perijam do. "Yes. And it is also brave of you to rescue us all from a man who freely sacrifices others while he hides in a dark cave of safety."

But Kerim's face did not brighten as I had hoped it would. "Yes, but when I asked about you, he was not willing to let you go at first. Finally he agreed, but only when his advisor Nasir al-Din persuaded him. But I had to lie a little to them both. I told them that that I had married you and taken over my father's responsibility for you, that I had taken a solemn vow before almighty Allah to take you west straightaway. "

"What?" I was startled into staring straight at him.

"Well, we can have a contract just like the one you had with Father. And it would only be for a short time…." He must have seen the fire in my eyes because he added, "Well, at least think about it. It would deliver you safely from the Imam."

It was the only argument that could make me even consider the idea! Kerim was changeable, dependent on opium, and he lusted after me. Was he expecting more than he was saying? And Perijam was reeling from grief. Had he thought about her feelings? My heart said agreeing was dangerous, but what other choice did I have?

Finally I spoke. "I have your solemn assurance that this would not be a real marriage like yours to Perijam—you know what I mean—but like the one I had with your father. It would only be to get me away from here safely, and it would last only until you took me as close as possible to my home."

"Yes, yes, of course" he spoke, looking away from me and blushing. But then he turned back to me, slipping into less formal speech as though we had already married. "You'll be much safer this way, believe me. But we must do it right away, or the Imam will find out and be angry. We'll need to leave within a day or two. And I must write the contract now and we must sign and date it for yesterday, and I must show it to a mullah tonight because the Imam demands to see it right away. Without it, he'll know I lied to him and he'll kill me and maybe you and the others."

"Well, that does leave me with no choice."

"Let us waste no time," Kerim urged. He led me back into the house, where Maryam and Anna hastily left for the andarun, and eagerly took over their writing materials. I felt as if I had been thrown off a cliff. I could only trust the fact that so far I had been guided onward at the right time, and surely the right time for leaving Alamut was now!

So once again I helped Kerim write something. At least I was able to ensure that he put what I wanted into the contract: a clear promise to deliver me onto a safe route to Constantinople. This time I demanded a time limit of two-months. We both signed the paper, and he rose.

"Now we are married. I will take this straight to the mullah and then to the Imam. We must leave soon. Tell the women to begin packing now."

We parted, he in high spirits, I with mixed emotions. Again I was married—but while Kerim was handsome and kind enough, just as I had always dreamed, he was also distraught, torn in his loyalties, and not of my faith. Well, at least he would not claim conjugal rights, which should make it a little easier to tell the other women about it. I still dreaded Perijam's response, but I had no time to plan what to say. As soon as Kerim had left, my women friends appeared at the biruni door almost as if summoned. I told them what had just happened and why.

"Sofia, you didn't!" cried Maryam, while Perijam just stared at me in surprise.

"But it is not a real marriage, just a way to escape from the Imam. Kerim loves only you, Perijam," I said, turning pleading eyes to her.

"No, no, I was just surprised, that's all. When I think on it, I could not wish for a better sister to share him with. I only wish you were married to him for life, for then you and I would never be separated again!" And she rose to embrace me.

"And what about me?" cried Anna.

"Anna, you don't have to marry anyone this time."

She burst into tears. "But why do we have to leave? I was happier here than I've ever been in my life!" She looked beseechingly at Maryam, who was gazing back at her with sad eyes. They clearly hated to part with each other.

"Anna, you could stay with Maryam. You are under no obligation to go with me."

"So I must be parted from one of you!"

"Or Maryam could come, too." I looked hopefully over at the older woman.

Maryam sighed, blinking back tears. "No, that would part me from my son forever. As long as I have even a slender hope of hearing from him or at least about him, I am bound to this place. Anna, while I will miss you terribly, I could never part you from Sofia."

Perijam burst into weeping, too. "Why are you all so unhappy? You haven't just lost your family and seen your dear friend suddenly become your husband's new wife!"

I burst into tears, too. I did not want to be married to Kerim.

We might have continued our fits for the entire afternoon had Shirin not come in and handed me a message from Nasir al-Din. I read it aloud.

'Sofia, please forgive my brevity. Regarding your marriage to Kerim ibn-Selim, I did the best I could for you, seeing that the Imam was in another dark mood and might well have refused to release you. He is certain that everyone plots against him, and he believes the worst of Kerim, who changes his mind at every turn.

'After Kerim left, the Mahdi insisted that he sees through his ruse. He is certain that Kerim is bent on betraying our cause. It matters not if this is true or false. I fear you are all in danger. I have persuaded the Mahdi to allow you all to leave, but instead of sending Kerim to spy for him, the Grand Master will order him straight on a death mission. His spies will kill Kerim if he fails to obey. Beware!'

At the end I looked around at my friends, wishing I could think, plan, decide something. "This only confirms my worst fears without offering a new way to elude the Imam!" Perijam and Anna burst into louder sobs.

But Maryam, in her most practical voice, said, "Well, Kerim must still seem to obey the Grand Master's commands. You must begin packing at once." We all were about to follow her back to the andarun when she suddenly stopped, put her hands to her cheeks, and turned to Anna. "My dear, this means that a choice has been made for me. I cannot stay here. I know too much. If the Grand Master suspects Kerim of treachery, he might question me after you leave and have it all out of me sooner or later and one way or another—he has a hold on me that he'd not hesitate to use. Then he'd send his men to slaughter all of you!"

Driven by the whip of fear, we all fell to, and soon the andarun and biruni were littered with bundles. Thus when he returned late in the day, Kerim found everyone almost ready to leave. He looked as troubled as we felt. "The Imam admitted me right away, but he says I am not to spy for him in Qazvin but to find a certain apostate mullah, Dadbeh al-Qazvini and to kill him in public at the first possible opportunity. I know that other Fida'i will be watching. I am a dead man now."

Kerim looked ready to weep, but Maryam cut him short. "Yes, Sofia's friends already warned us. You must feign obedience to the Grand Master's commands, Kerim, or none of us will escape. Sofia, tomorrow you must go to Nasir al-Din's class and afterwards ask Rukn al-Din to meddle with his father's plan somehow. There are malcontents here in the castle whose loyalties are already fastened on the son, unknown to the father—this I overheard from your servant Yusuf, Kerim. Perhaps Rukn al-Din knows men loyal to him who could come forward to follow and guard us while the Grand Master thinks they spy for him."

A faint hope, but one I seized eagerly. That night after the other women went to bed, I stayed up writing some pieces to give as farewell gifts to my teacher and my student. What sleep I got was broken by dreams of pursuit by killers with daggers.

The next morning I went for my final lesson. It seemed an eternity before the other boys departed. Finally I could speak freely with my new protectors! I began with, "I threw myself on your mercy." And I repeated everything that I knew.

"Yes, I think I can 'meddle' with Father's plans," Rukn al-Din said thoughtfully. "I know a few men who might willingly serve me, but as Father also has his own spies who pose as traitors, I must tread carefully. I did take the paize, though. I wish I had brought it with me!"

"Well, it is too late now," I said, feeling a little disappointed. "We leave early tomorrow. This is our final farewell."

I suddenly felt awash in sadness over our parting. Nasir al-Din stemmed its flow, however, saying in his no-nonsense voice, "Well, here is money and here are my gifts for you: a history of the world, a few of my famous treatises on science and philosophy, and a pair of maps in honor of your travels. And a fine little astrolabe, which you may sell when you reach another civilized area. You were an excellent student, Sofia, and I am forced to admit that even an infidel woman has merits I never dreamed of!"

Of course, as he was my teacher and not family, I had to pretend to reject his gifts at first, but after several polite refusals and insistences, I accepted them. "I thank you, Master al-Din. I have little to offer to you other than gratitude and these manuscripts that I translated for you from the Greek. I hope they prove of use."

And we went through the ritual again. Finally, Nasir al-Din replied, "Thank you, Sofia. I am certain they will be useful." He quickly unrolled them and glanced over their contents. "Already they perfume my library with the sweet scent of knowledge."

"And Rukn al-Din, I also brought you a gift. I wrote down all the laws and customs of the Mongols that I could recall. If you have future dealings with them, this might help you. As well, since I know you love poetry," at this he blushed, "I wrote down a few verses from one of their epic poems for you to translate. I hope they please you."

A third round of polite refusals followed, but at last he said, "These do please me, more than I can say." With tears in his eyes and hand over his heart, he added, "I wish I could summon to my lips the poetry in my heart. But now I must take my leave and see what I can do for you. I may try to send word later today, and the paize, too."

"And I must go, as well."

We all bowed to each other in farewell, calling down the blessings of the God we shared and wishing each other a green future. With a heart filled with hope and foreboding intermixed, I returned to Kerim's home. He had been summoned for a final audience with the Mahdi, so we women finished packing a last few things while the guard at the gate brought a pair of mules into the little courtyard and Yusuf, Shirin, and Kerim's other menservants loaded them. All but Yusuf and Shirin set out at once, planning to meet us at the village in the neighboring valley the next day. We women were all abed before Kerim returned late that night.

The sound of the door closing woke me, but worry kept me awake after that. How trustworthy was he, really? What if something happened to him before I reached Christian lands? I quietly crawled to my bundles and found my sewing kit and the cloak from my Papa. I set to, painstakingly ripping out one seam and then another, until I had found some rubies, a few pearls, a diamond, and an emerald. I was tempted to rip out all the seams, but this must do for now. I found a length of fabric from my kit, used it to wrap the jewels around my waist, and repacked everything. Then I lay back down and fell into uneasy sleep.

SUMMER'S END
ANNO DOMINI 1245

We arose well before dawn. Kerim was in the courtyard looking haggard, but he was already at his prayers along with his men. We all joined him, each praying in our own way. I supplicated our shared God for a safe journey and complete escape for us all from the Grand Master and all his designs. The sun had just touched the highest mountain peaks when we stole out of the gate and up the street toward the castle entrance. Despite the wealth of learning I had received, I felt only relief at escaping that prison of a castle. Maryam was the only one with tears in her eyes.

I overheard her behind me whispering to Anna, "Now I'll have no way to get word of Ben Hasan … but I cannot betray you all … Well, it is time for me to admit that my son is lost to me forever, whether I stay or go. At least you have a chance for a new life."

Anna made no reply, but I imagined her slipping her hand into Maryam's.

We were almost at the large gates when who should appear by my side but Rukn al-Din—truly as in my dream! Hand over heart, he greeted me, adding in a low voice, "I have done everything I could for you, and now you are in Allah's merciful hands. No time to argue; take this." He thrust a small package into my hands. "When you travel through Mongol-held territory, it may ease your passage. Keep it secret from Kerim ibn-Se-lim—he is not trustworthy—and use it only if you must. Had I been less honorable, I would have taken you from him and married you myself! I will never forget you, and I pray that Allah's blessings rain down on you wherever you go."

"Rukn al-Din, you are a true friend. I will never forget you, either. Farewell and God bless you." At that moment Kerim looked back and Rukn slipped into an alley.

I thought the youth had turned back, but as we reached the gates I heard his voice calling softly from behind us, "Farewell...."

I looked back just after crossing the bridge and saw him standing alone near the stone-faced guards at the gate, still watching me as the sun flamed over the mountain tops.

When we met the rest of Kerim's men in the village down below, sure-footed mules awaited us. All day we hurried through the Alamut valleys, Anna and me suffering in the heat under our veils, Sayeed excitable, Perijam weeping off and on, and Maryam simply looking miserable. We passed by the high fortress late in the afternoon and somehow got over the mountain pass just after sunset. When we reached a village, exhausted beyond belief, it was a miracle that they let us in, as the sky was dense with golden stars. After settling at the headman's house, we went straight to sleep.

The next day Kerim hurried us until long after dark when we stopped in another little village. But early the next morning, to the surprise of all us women, he led our little caravan straight to the northern outskirts of Qazvin itself, where he put us into a women's room in a small caravansary! He was turning to leave when I cried, "But Kerim, why are we here and where are you going?"

"Last night the Mahdi ordered me to come straight here and martyr myself. I must seem to obey him at least, for other eyes are upon me, per-haps even among my own servants. So I decided to ask after this Dadbeh al-Qazvini as a feint. And I want to find out about Aftab and Sarah and to send a message to Banu and to my mother-in-law. You would like that, Perijam, would you not?" Kerim smiled at her.

"Oh, yes, yes! Maybe you can find your sisters and free them. And my mother—do you think I could see her to say goodbye? It would mean so much to me."

"We'll see. I think a visit with her would be good after all your travails," he answered tenderly. "Such rapid travel cannot have done our unborn child any good."

I wasn't sure that Kerim was following the right course, but my opinion, had I even formed one, had not been sought. Now that he had made up his mind, my new protector—I could not really think of him as a husband—seemed to want no more advice from me. Indeed, he had scarcely seemed to notice any of us on our journey from Alamut. So I held my tongue.

After noon prayers and a meal, we women decided that in Kerim's absence we would like to bathe, so we arranged through Yusuf to have a few of Kerim's men take us to a local bath house. There we enjoyed a good soak and scrub. Surrounded by strangers who took merely friendly interest in us, I could only contrast this place with Alamut, where the bath house had seemed so full of whispers. But on our way back to the caravansary, a shiver went down my spine; unseen eyes seemed everywhere. I looked around, but there was no way to tell if someone was following us.

Kerim was there waiting. "Good news! I learned where Dadbeh al-Qazvini is. He knows what fate awaits him and surrounds himself with guards, which was perfect for me! I could only send him a message begging humbly to meet him tomorrow at his mosque to plan my wedding, a good ruse, if I say so myself—not that I will be there. I don't trust him not to have his guards waiting to seize me, and I even lied about where I live!

"And Perijam, I went to your mother's house and spoke with her. She wept with delight to see me, and she had a wonderful surprise for me. After we left Qazvin, she had sent a manservant to the slave market to see if he could find my little sisters, and thanks to Allah the All-Merciful, they were both there! He bought them and brought them back to her. She has adopted them. They are still in shock, but safe and well-loved. And of course she begged me to let you and little Sayeed go there and stay the night. I have agreed, but we must leave right away, as the day draws to a close."

Perijam smiled fully for the first time since our reunion and was soon gone with Kerim, surrounded by guards and carrying greetings and small gifts for the girls from me.

"Well, it seems we have the evening to ourselves. Shall we play a game of backgammon, two against one?" I spoke lightly, but in fact I was feeling most uneasy about being in Qazvin. Anna eagerly pulled out the game board and opened it, ready to play.

Kerim returned with surprising swiftness. We found out when Yusuf knocked on our door and called out that his master wished to see me. I left Maryam and Anna to finish the game, wondering what he could want. Maryam sent me a sharp glance as I shut the door.

I followed Yusuf to a front room that smelled of incense, where he left me alone with Kerim. "Come in, Sofia, and lock the door." I was surprised and not too happy, but I did as I was bid.

"Come sit with me. I bought you some wine, and if you want it, here is a glass of opium tea."

Refusing the tea, I sat down on a cushion beside him and gratefully accepted a cup of sweet, mild Persian wine. Kerim seemed oddly elated, staring at me with too-bright eyes that made me wonder if he had already drunk some tea himself.

After an uncomfortable silence I finally said, "It was kind of you to take Perijam to see her mother and your sisters. It must have been both painful and happy for them all, knowing they may never see each other again after tomorrow."

"Well, that leads to what I wanted to tell you, Sofia." Kerim paused, looking at the carpet. "I was right. I am being followed, but it is by my father's men. Da'ud and his boys are guarding our backs. I saw them today when I went to the apostate's house.

"But that surely means enemies are watching me, too. We must leave well before dawn. I have arranged for us all to join a merchant caravan … but I am leaving Perijam and Sayeed behind with her mother where she'll be safe and happy. Her family never knew about our other life, and no suspicion rests on them. And Perijam must think of our unborn child. I will send for her and the rest of the family as soon as I reach Tabriz and find a new home for us."

I was taken aback, but I supposed he made sense. "It is good to know that you have guardians; not good that you need them. Does Perijam know that she'll stay behind?"

"Oh, yes," he said, still looking down. "She accepted my judgment without question, and she'll be glad of the time to rest. All this travel was hard on her. She is accustomed to waiting for me."

"I wish I had known; I'd have bidden farewell to her properly."

"Well, this way is better. It would have drawn unwanted attention to us had I led away a weeping woman while others stayed weeping behind. And she did weep, but only a little, and less over staying in Qazvin than over what she knew would come next. I spared her much with my plan, for I feared she might be jealous once I claimed my marital rights."

He raised his eyes to mine, smiled, and pulled off my veil before I had time to react.

I shrank back in shock. "Kerim, you agreed that this was not a real marriage. And if you mean what I think by marital rights, you promised me you'd not claim them! Since signing that contract, this is the first time you've ever hinted that you thought you had any!"

Looking confused, he countered, "Well, I could hardly ask anything of you before now. But this is what marriage is about. And I didn't promise not to claim my rights, I only agreed that it would not be like the love that Perijam and I share. Why did you think I put you under my protection, indeed why I even had the idea of marrying you? Surely you knew. I thought you were just speaking with delicacy because you care for Perijam."

"No! I told you it must be like Selim and me."

"Don't be foolish, Sofia. He'd have done the same in due course, as soon as Mother came to accept it. Besides, you cannot deny your sidelong glances at me, full of meaning—I've seen them again and again since we first met! Now, no more teasing."

And he was suddenly upon me, covering my face with kisses and tangling my hair in his hands. His mouth found my neck and then tried to move to my breasts. Torn between fear and rage, I began kicking and shouting. He pulled away from me in alarm.

"Don't you like making love? I want to please you. After all, you were once a concubine—"

I stood up, shaking. "Selim should never have told you that. And you tricked me into this so-called marriage. We made a pact, but you never really felt bound by Selim's promise to me, did you?"

Kerim looked up at me and smiled slyly. "Well, if you had been less desirable…."

I rushed to the door, groping for the latch. "You make me feel like a whore! I would never buy my freedom with my honor!"

Kerim looked shocked. He stood and came toward me. With a voice of reasonability he said, "Sofia, I am sorry. I never meant to make you feel that way. Please, try to understand. Father's death left you alone, and I will honor my vow to fulfill his promise. On the other hand, you must honor your vows, too."

I ignored him and with shaking hands tried to unbolt the door, but Kerim put his hand over mine. "Why, you're trembling! Please, come back and sit with me. I promise you a gentler courtship than I gave you just now. Perijam accounts me a good lover ... and you and I could learn much from each other. How often I have longed to explore every part of your body, to learn secrets of lovemaking from you that I could only guess, and to give manly passion to you in return. You are everything a man could desire."

Knowing he could force himself on me if he wished, I stopped struggling with the latch and slowly looked up. He was smiling in the way I had mistaken for brotherliness. Why had I allowed my desire for family to lead me so far astray? Had I forgotten how to read people?

Swallowing my fear, I took a deep breath before answering. "Well, you did give me quite a shock. I too am an honorable person, but I truly did not understand about this marriage. I do now, and I honor my debts. But tonight is a bad night, for my moon cycle will begin at any time. I would wait until I am clean."

Kerim's face fell a little, but he tried to admit defeat graciously. "You will let me know when you're ready, then?"

"Oh, yes, I will let you know when I'm ready. May I go now?"

He nodded, picked up my fallen cap and veil for me, and once I was properly veiled again, unlocked the door himself. Yusuf almost jumped back when it swung open. I fled down the corridor without him. Back with the other women, I locked our door and went straight to bed, where I lay awake most of the night trying to devise a plan to escape Kerim's demand for his "marital rights." I had escaped one trap only to fall into another! I had lied about my moon cycle, which was never regular, but that lie wouldn't protect me for long.

How unpredictable men were! I knew that both Nasir al-Din and Rukn al-Din had desired me, but only once had either of them overstepped the bounds of propriety. Had it been lack of opportunity or a sense of honor that held them back? And had Kerim been right about his father intending to bed me someday? There was no knowing, and I could only vow never to look any man in the eye again!

We left Qazvin the next morning. I never saw Perijam or Banu or Aftab or Sarah again, and I can only hope for their happiness. It is a dim hope.

On our way to the new caravansary, I told the others that Perijam was staying behind for now, and Maryam declared, "Kerim shows good sense for once. This is the best course for the poor child. She'll be happier with her mother and likelier to bring a healthy baby into this world!"

"Well, there is more to it than that." And I told them about the night before.

Shirin shrugged and turned away as if to say I should have expected nothing else, but Maryam spoke sharply, "I knew he had some reason besides your well-being when he suggested that marriage. We must simply surround you at all times. At least you have a week's respite, and after that we'll seek another excuse for you to avoid him."

Kerim had found a large caravan that was making for Tabriz and had arranged for each of us women to ride in a howdah, which in this case was an arched, cloth-curtained wooden box just large enough for one person, each balanced opposite its twin on either side of a camel, and each box shaded by a parasol. He made a special point of helping me into mine, showing such concern that it softened my heart somewhat. But so much for a howdah being better than riding on a camel! It was as close and hot as if I'd been rolled in a carpet and as jarring as if I'd been slung over a beast of burden. Although I did pull my chaador from my head, I could not see out except through a crack in the curtain. It seemed that summer had come. The wildflowers I remembered from two years earlier had withered away, and the hills were brown and desolate.

That day while we rode, I had ample time to think. Ironically, I missed the exchange of passion so much that had Kerim been subtler and gentler the night before, I might have been tempted. But fear of another rape had killed any desire I might feel for him now.

We encamped at sunset in a green valley with a little stream running through it, and for the first time in two years I slept in the wild. We women were not allowed out of our tents, but after living so long in seclusion I felt ill at ease being outside at all. The ground seemed harder than I remembered, too. I longed for a soft pallet like the ones from the andarun. When we finally reached a largish town with a caravansary on its northern edge, I was most grateful, despite worrying that Kerim might renew his demand that I fulfill our agreement.

While we were settling into a private room for women, he knocked on our door and entered. I stiffened, fearing that this time he had come to collect me in person, but instead he told us, "In case someone is still following us, we part company with this caravan. I will find another at the caravansary on the other side of town. I will see about it tomorrow morning." With that, he bowed out, leaving each of us enclosed in our own thoughts.

It seemed as if dogs howled all that night, disturbing our sleep, and Anna especially seemed uneasy. After silent morning devotions—three traditions in one room—we ate a meal handed in to us by Yusuf, finished packing, and awaited word from Kerim. Our inn had held only our caravan, and I could hear the men departing, leaving a loud silence behind. Maryam and Anna murmured together, Shirin sat gloomily on her bundle, and I sat and thought.

The morning passed slowly. Maryam and Anna played backgammon and then worked on lessons; Shirin only moved when she heard the call to prayer. At first I entertained myself by imagining what Constantinople might be like, and then when time began to drag, did the practice of peace. It helped somewhat, but it also sharpened my sense of something being amiss. Finally I began pacing back and forth.

At some point, perhaps mid-morning, I had heard sounds of men below in the courtyard, but now empty silence reigned. No one else seemed to notice. I had no idea what happened in a caravansary in the daytime, and though I knew the noises and ensuing quiet might be completely ordinary, my thoughts began to race. What if Kerim thought he was still being followed by his enemies … and had taken all his men … and left us here? After all, if all he wanted was to flee for his own safety, he might abandon us women as unnecessary burdens. Or had he been found and murdered by some Nizari spy? Were Da'ud and the boys still following us? Could they truly offer any protection to him? I had to fight back my rising unease.

Finally after waiting for what seemed like hours, I unlocked the door and looked outside. The courtyard was silent, and Yusuf was no longer standing guard in front of our door. I saw only a sweeper whose back was to me.

I turned to the other women. "There's no one out there besides a man sweeping the courtyard. All of Kerim's men seem to be gone, and so is Yusuf."

Shirin jumped up in alarm. "But Yusuf would never leave without me; I'm his wife!" She rushed to the door and began to wail.

Why I had never realized this before is beyond me. "But where is he, then?"

I turned to Maryam, who would surely know what to do. "Well," she said after long thought, "I suppose I could go out into the streets and find the other caravansary and ask about him. I doubt anyone would pay attention to an old woman."

Anna cried, "Oh, Maryam, don't leave us! We're lost without you! I know something bad has happened—those dogs howling all night—I knew someone in the house would die!" And she threw her arms around her friend and burst into tears.

My hair stood on end. It was all I could do to think straight. But I had to. While we had all come to depend heavily on Maryam's wisdom, and she might even be right about being invisible, something in me cried a warning.

"No, Maryam. You cannot go. What if something terrible has happened to Kerim? Perhaps his men seek him now out of concern. Worse, what if some of them betrayed him and have lured away the rest and cut them down? If anyone you know from Alamut sees you, you'll be in danger, and the rest of us will be at their mercy!" Shirin burst into tears, and Anna clutched at Maryam even harder.

Maryam frowned, absently stroking Anna's dark hair. "You may be right. Well then, I suppose we must trust in God and wait."

"No, if Yusuf is gone, something is wrong. I must go. I still have my men's clothing in one of my bundles. I've passed for a boy before, and I can do it again."

No one liked this plan any better than Maryam's, but I ignored their protestations, found my clothing, changed, tucked my hair as thoroughly under my cap as I could before wrapping the modest dulband, and patted my jewels tied around my waist. I might need to bribe someone. "I am leaving. Bar the door behind me." I tried to feel brave.

I slowly opened the door and looked around. Suddenly all pretense of bravery deserted me, and I stood rooted to the spot for a small eternity. But the sweeper had gone and the courtyard was empty, so I took a deep breath, stealthily crept down the stairs, slid to the wall, and peered out the entrance. A few men sat in the shade of the caravansary wall, looking on while one halfheartedly hawked his wares to indifferent passersby. With a timidity that was not feigned, I approached and, eyes downcast for fear they would see my green eyes, asked where I might find the main marketplace—that seemed innocent. One of them looked me over kindly and said, "Who are you, and where is your master, my lovely boy? Will he be angry with you for straying out?"

Thinking that he might be familiar with the men who worked here, I thought quickly and answered, "My master was traveling with a caravan that left several days ago. He fell ill, and now he is worse. He sends me to the bazaar to seek a physician, or at least medicine for him." I think my worry gave an illusion of sincerity, for the man looked around at the others, one of whom gave a small shrug. "Well, let me draw you a map in the dirt."

Having memorized his directions, I raced off in search of a nonexistent healer. It suddenly struck me as odd that lies always sprang so easily to mind when I needed them, yet I thought myself so honest. But this time I was glad! Once out of sight of the caravansary, I slowed my pace, keeping to the walls as much as I could. Men passed by bent on their own errands, but none gave me a second glance. Alas, the alleys closed around me and the walls towered above me, both heavy with threat. I felt as if the slightest slip could mean my death. At one point I grew so afraid that I had to stop and lean against a wall.

It came to me that living in seclusion had somehow shrunk me, making the world seem large and hostile and me utterly small, foolish, and alone. Finally I reminded myself that I had once led Anna across a wasteland with much less of a map. Forcing myself on, I prayed someone in the marketplace could tell me where the other caravansary was.

It was not a large town, and I found the bazaar easily enough, small and facing a square bordered on the opposite side by a lovely little mosque. I knew that bazaars were crowded, but there seemed to be a surprising number of men gathered in the square. They were all pushing and shouting to each other in a waterfall of words. I could make out, "Allah is great… Curse the foul infidel … Justice is swift in the hands of the righteous."

To one side of the market stood a cluster of camels, bawling and peering over men's heads. Perhaps a camel had gotten loose and strayed into the crowd and angered these men. And some poor soul was probably taking the brunt of their anger—unless someone had discovered Kerim was Nizari. Though it seemed unlikely, I shuddered.

To reach the bazaar, I would have to push through the crush of men, and I was not eager to do that. Nor did I dare ask anyone for news—there was an edge to their voices that chilled me. But the crowd seemed to be breaking up now. Men were leaving, some racing out of the square, call-ing to each other that they would meet at such and such a place. Slowly I began to work my way around the edge of the milling mass. I had almost reached the stalls when a heavy hand fell on my shoulder. I almost started out of my skin!

"What have we here?" a familiar voice rumbled. I turned and looked up, and there was Da'ud smiling grimly! "I was looking for you, my son. Come away! You are supposed to be helping your brother." He gripped my arm hard and fairly dragged me away. I looked back just as another group of men turned to leave. Now I could see what everyone had been gaping at and shouting about. On the ground before the mosque lay a head, severed from its bloody body, its eyes glazed, its face waxy. It was my young guide Nasr's, his death grimace a mockery of his usual friendly grin. Over him stood Ali, his face crumpled into sorrow as he gaped at his friend's remains.

I sagged and might have fainted had Da'ud not kept a firm grip on me. "Come away, I say! I'll not have you wasting your day gaping at executions."

He kept talking as he pulled me through the crowd, speaking as though Nasr was some stranger! A newcomer stopped him to ask what all the excitement was about.

"A beheading," answered Da'ud. "Swift justice for murderers is best justice in these unholy times! I was at the southern caravansary early this morning when it happened, and I saw it all. The fellow came right up to a merchant haggling with a caravan leader. Crying 'Allah is great,' he stabbed him dead in full daylight!

"The merchant's servants fled like cowards, but several brave men seized the murderer and dragged him to the mullah here in the mosque. Strangest of all, the fellow proudly confessed, claimed to be a Fida'i—an accursed Hashishim—and demanded to be put to death for the glory of Allah! Well, his wish was granted. Right here in the middle of the square, they—," he finished the sentence by chopping his hand at the back of his neck. "Well deserved, I say."

My gorge rose.

"Your son looks ill. You should take him home." The other man made way for us. I looked back to see him trying to press forward to see for himself.

Da'ud dragged me away from the crowd, chiding me as if I was a naughty but beloved son. Finally, when we had turned a corner and then another, he pulled me into a quiet alley and wiped his sweat-beaded forehead.

"Merciful Allah protects you at every turn. Praise and thanks to Him who led me to you before you came to harm. Why were you here and not at your caravansary? Are your servant and the Jewess still there? I sent some local Fida'i to guard the three of you."

I slid down against the alley wall and put my head between my knees, trying to breathe deeply. "How can you even ask such questions when Nasr lies dead? How could anyone think that sweet boy was a murderer? And how could you talk about him like that?"

"He was no murderer—he was an agent for justice, albeit an overeager one! We were to dispatch the man quietly in private, not in public as if he was someone important. But once the deed was done, I had to send Ali after Nasr to make sure he died quickly. He would have killed his friend himself rather than let him be tortured by infidels." Da'ud sighed. "At least Nasr now sits at Allah's right hand, and justice is done. Kerim was a foul traitor who defiled the honor of his father and of his Imam!"

I looked up in shock. "Nasr killed Kerim? The Imam sent you and Nasr and Ali after him? We all thought you were protecting us!"

Shouting still came from the square, and a cluster of men armed with long knives ran by crying, "Allah is great! Death to all infidels!"

Da'ud looked around cautiously and crouched down beside me. "Keep your voice down, or we might be taken by our enemies! All the town's gangs are gathering, and it grows more unsafe the longer we linger here. Listen to me. Kerim ibn-Selim was a foul traitor. Not even his father fully trusted him. In Qazvin he may even have sent the rioters after his own family."

I was doubly shocked. "No! He was wild with grief over losing his family."

Da'ud snorted. "No doubt he acted his part well. But how was it that he escaped?"

I wiped away angry tears that insisted on flowing. "Kerim's father-in-law had died suddenly, so he was at his mother-in-law's when the riots began, riots that your Imam caused with his absurd raid! He sent a warning to his father, but then he stayed to help his mother-in-law and to—for that matter, how did you escape?"

Da'ud looked taken aback, but only for a moment. "I was away with the boys on a mission for Master Selim. When we came back, signs of rioting lay everywhere, and tales of slaughter were still on everyone's lips. We found our master's home looted and burned, his body torn and rotting—Umar's, too. We looked everywhere but found no trace of Kerim.

"We of course sent word to the Imam. Kerim had been to Alamut and gone again. We heard back. The Mahdi wanted us to follow him. He was certain he would abandon his mission. We witnessed him flee from his duty to kill Dadbeh of—"

Another group of armed men raced by, talking excitedly, but one man noticed us and stared back in curiosity. "Come with me to a safer place." Da'ud stood, pulled me up with him, and began to walk back along the alley toward the street.

I tried to twist out of his grip. "No! You have murdered my only protector here! You go your way and I will go mine. I will find some way to get home by myself."

"You do not understand. I am here to help you. My master entrusted me with your safety, even beyond his own death. It is a matter of honor. Nasr died partly to protect you!"

"Let me go or I will scream and reveal that I am a woman!"

Da'ud dropped my arm and cursed. "For what? To die here for nothing?" We stood glaring at each other. "This is what comes of a woman trying to act like a man," he finally snarled.

"And this is what came of your blind obedience to an idea!" I shot back. "Kerim also vowed to protect me, and Nasr sacrificed his life to kill him! And it was all based on lies! Kerim meant to return to Qazvin; he left his wife and sisters there. And now you expect me to trust you?" I knew I was not telling the exact truth, but I was wild with anger and panic and revulsion.

Da'ud looked like he might burst asunder with rage, and he even turned on his heel and strode a few steps before stopping. The shouts were getting louder and coming our way. I was already looking around, trying to orient myself, for he had not only taken me far from the streets I had followed, but emotion was clouding my mind. He slowly turned back.

"Listen, before we ever met, back when I was sent to await you at the Caspian, my master made me vow before Allah to protect you with my own life. And I will! If you wish no direct help from me, so be it, but I will follow you until I know you are safe."

I burst into sobs, oblivious to the passersby gaping at me. I had no idea what to do.

"Come, come, that is enough weeping. Let me take you back to the caravansary," Da'ud finally said, returning to my side. And he added in a whisper, "Please, in the name of Allah's mercy, let me get you out of this town. We are surrounded by enemies."

I saw no help for it. There was no escaping him anyway. Da'ud had been an unfailing protector before, and had he meant me harm, he'd have done it by now. And, I now recalled, Selim had included him in our marriage contract as my guardian.

So I nodded and he led me back to the caravansary, him marching ahead, me trying to stanch my tears, as the noise behind us grew. A few men and boys ran past us, shouting. Some brandished sticks or carried stones, others carried those long knives. Happily, Da'ud soon turned off the thoroughfare and away from the noise.

"I think they go against a Shi'a neighborhood. Soon the entire town will be rioting. I must find Ali before we leave."

"I saw him back there," I said. "He was weeping over his friend's body."

Da'ud shook his head. "That is bad news. Very bad news."

It took a surprisingly short time to get to the caravansary. The men who had given me directions all jumped up when they saw us. So they were Da'ud's men sent to guard us! Despite my misery, I almost had to laugh at the surprise written on their faces.

"We must leave now," Da'ud said to the men. "Violence gathers. There will be many martyrs today, but we cannot allow our guests to be among them."

He turned to me. "Go and tell the women we leave right away. If they have not packed, they must leave their belongings behind."

The urgency in his voice drove me up the stairs. I pounded on the door, calling, "Maryam, Anna, Shirin, it's me. Let me in! We must flee!"

Maryam flung the door open. "Thank God! We thought you lost!" Anna sat on a bundle behind her, her eyes red from weeping. Shirin and her belongings were gone.

"Where is Shirin?" I closed the door. "We must leave right away. Riots are starting, and Da'ud is here to guide us out of the city."

Anna whimpered, "What if you hadn't come back?"

"Well, I'm here now. What happened?"

Maryam was already picking up bundles and handing them to Anna. "Come, dear, dry your eyes. We must make haste." She pushed my women's clothing at me. "Here, Sofia, you cannot stay in those clothes. You're violating every law of decency, and it's too dangerous.

"As to Shirin, Yusuf came back shortly after you went to the market, and she left with him. He told us what happened to Kerim—do you know?" I nodded, tearing off my men's clothing, throwing on women's, and donning hejab once again while I listened.

"When the other men came back here to gather their things and flee for their lives, they told him about the murder. At first he stayed behind to guard us, but doubts were tearing up his heart, as he put it. He finally decided he must go find out about Kerim for himself. He got as far as the main square and turned back. He and Shirin took the one camel Kerim's men had left him. He offered to take us with him, but how could we go without you?"

I had finished dressing. "I'm surprised Da'ud's guards let him and Shirin go—maybe they thought they worked for the caravansary. Anyway, we must leave at once. I'll tell you what happened to me after we're on our way."

Da'ud was waiting at the foot of the stairs. Behind him five or six men held the reins of several horses. "I must leave without Ali," he said grimly. "He never could hide his feelings, and showing any sorrow over his friend's death would betray him. I bribed the landlord and his servant to forget they ever saw us, but if the rioting spreads I doubt their tongues will stay still for long. Here are your horses. Let me take your bundles; praise Allah you brought so little."

"What are you doing here? Why didn't you protect Kerim?" asked Maryam. She had stopped on the stairs and was staring at him angrily.

"I am here to deliver Sofia and her servant Anna to safety! And you can count yourself lucky to join them," he growled. But then he added, "Come, Maryam, let me help you mount your horse."

Although she first flushed with anger and then protested that she was too old to ride such a lively animal, Maryam grudgingly accepted his help. Within moments we were all galloping away, out of the town and onto a road that led, not northwest toward Tabriz, but southwest into the unknown.

We rode for the rest of the day, avoiding all settlements and stopping only to rest our horses. I glanced back often to see if anyone was following us, but the road behind stayed empty. At first we were too bent on escape to speak, which gave me plenty of time to think, but I could not get past my confusion. Such senseless deaths! And I was torn between fear of being caught and relief that anyone was helping me. It felt as if every journey I had made since leaving home had been some form of flight. I could no longer imagine one that did not feel like a plunge into new dangers.

At one point Maryam rode up to my side and said, "Sofia, we must talk. What happened when you went into the town, what is he doing here," pointing at Da'ud, "why is he guiding us, and why didn't he prevent Kerim's murder?"

"I still cannot grasp what happened back there. Da'ud was never trying to protect Kerim. The Grand Master ordered him and two youths who were once Selim's servants to pursue and kill him. I can only be grateful that they didn't kill all Kerim's servitors, too, though for all I know, Da'ud may go back and try at some point!"

Maryam's eyes widened and she gasped, "The filthy murderers!"

"I feel sick at heart. For all his faults, Kerim didn't deserve to die, especially at the hands of men who should have been loyal to him. And I feel just as sick about his murderer, a boy I knew, who was merry and kind: Nasr. Did you know him and Ali?"

"Yes, slightly. Selim al-Din's converts."

"They and Da'ud helped me escape the Mongols and guided me to Selim's home in Qazvin. Selim appointed Da'ud as my guardian, and he vowed to guide me to safety. Maryam, I had no choice about him. He already knew where we were and had left guards at the caravansary. He swears by his God and in honor of Selim's memory that he will take me—us—at least part of the way to Constantinople. And he did save us. Riots were starting, I think because of Nasr and Ali. Had anyone connected us with them or Kerim, we'd have been killed, too. Even if he helped murder Kerim, I think we should count ourselves lucky that Da'ud is so loyal to Selim's memory."

Maryam did not look convinced. "Well, we'll see. I just pray we don't end up being sold in a slave market. That Da'ud is the snake who led my son and me from Lambasar castle to Alamut."

"Please don't frighten me any more than I already am," I pleaded.

She sighed. "I'm sorry. It has just been a terrible day. I have lost all sense of myself. I feel like I shriveled up living in that accursed castle until I'm afraid of everything."

"Me, too."

She leaned over and squeezed my hand. "Well, I suppose we must trust in God. He has led us this far, and we are unharmed."

We spoke little for the rest of that day. Anna, beside herself with terror, insisted on riding between Maryam and me. It had been so long since I had ridden that I spent most of the time managing my horse over rough ground.

That night we encamped in an empty valley near a stream. Da'ud put guards and a screen around our tent and campfire like the one that had surrounded us at Now Ruz, but it only made me feel isolated and more afraid. I heard him berating his men and them defending themselves over letting Yusuf and Shirin go—and not stopping me.

After supper he entered our little enclosure. Sitting down beside me where I was tending our little fire, he spoke, looking into its flames the entire time. "I will take you at least as far as al-Mawsil, where I can find merchants whose caravans travel to Frankish-held lands. If all goes well, I can leave you in good hands. Otherwise I must take you on to Halab, where you can find Christian merchants to take you to the coast. From there you can take a ship to Constantinople. But Mongol troops are everywhere now. And I must go back and find out what happened to Ali. He is my nephew, and my sister will never forgive me if I do not let her know what happened."

We sat in silence for some time, each with our own thoughts. Finally I thought to ask, "Da'ud, how did Kerim die?"

"Allah foresaw and planned all. We were staying with a fellow Fida'i near the other caravansary. The two boys and I were in a tea house across from it this morning when Nasr saw Kerim. Without a word he jumped up and rushed out to martyrdom. It happened so quickly, and then… shouts, men crowding and pushing, Kerim's people fleeing in terror, Nasr arrested and bound and dragged away …." He stopped for so long that I glanced up at him. He was staring into nowhere. Unshed tears sparkled in his eyes, tinted red by the fire.

After a painful silence, he continued, "I sent Ali after Nasr and told him I would follow as soon as I had made sure of your safety. I went to my host, and he sent his men to protect you three. Then I went to fetch Ali at the town square. At first I could not get anywhere near there because of the crowds. Then I found you."

How strange the man was: so loyal to his own family yet willing to betray his master's son on the word of that unpredictable Imam.

He was standing up. "I leave you to sleep." I glimpsed his frown in the firelight before he bowed and strode off into the dark.

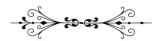

Because Da'ud followed an indirect route and avoided settlements, several days passed before I got any sense of where we were going. At first we rode north and stayed in a concealed valley overnight, but then we turned west, climbing into rocky hills that overlooked a little village and changing direction to avoid a shepherd with his flock. But in general, we continued to head, not north, but slightly southwest through desert country toward new mountain ranges. I decided they must be the Zagros Mountains. My geography lessons with Nasir al-Din were proving useful, since Da'ud rarely spoke to us and told us even less.

The travel was hard on Maryam. "My poor bones," she would moan every night. A few times, her groans woke me. But only Anna could comfort her, brewing willow bark teas or asking if Da'ud's men could collect dried grasses to make Maryam's bed softer.

I passed these requests on to Da'ud, since Anna would not speak to any of the men directly anymore than they would look at us directly. But that was as much as I could do. Maryam seemed angry with the world, and I took her misery to heart. I felt like begging everyone's forgiveness for wanting to flee Alamut instead of taking our chances with the Grand Master, since Rukn al-Din and Nasir al-Din would surely have protected us. It was too late now.

Finally Da'ud relented. "I doubt anyone following us will pick up our trail now. We will rejoin the main road tomorrow, and then we can rest at a caravansary."

We women were glad for that. Camping was no longer delightful. It was cold at night, and rocky, and so very exposed, and I yearned for four solid walls around me. But as it happened, we did not have to wait another night to find at least the walls. Late that afternoon we discovered a desolate settlement where only a handful of families lived. The walls surrounding the village were rubble, and most of the buildings were deserted.

Both men and women fled inside their houses when they saw us coming, except for one man who leapt onto the only donkey in the village, kicked it into a trot, and disappeared among the hills. But by calling out friendly words and assurances of our peaceful intentions, Da'ud convinced the men to come out and deal with us. An argument followed over allowing us to stay, until Da'ud finally exclaimed, "What happened to Islamic hospitality?"

The headman answered, "The Mongols, that is what!"

It took some more talk before Da'ud could convince them, but finally they decided to let us stay at the far edge of the village in an empty hovel for the night, and with that, everyone seemed to feel more at ease. A pair of old women even came to the door of their house and motioned to Maryam and Anna and me to come inside and rest out of the sun.

Their home was as bare and poor as the one Anna and I had sheltered in on the Caspian, but it was such a relief to put off our chaadors and sit still for awhile, even on threadbare rugs on a dirt floor. One by one the few other women in the village joined us, mostly to gape. One of our hostesses disappeared outside to her stove and returned with a kettle. She dipped out small servings of hot water into cracked cups and handed them to us. The water looked a little muddy, but we all sat around the empty hearth sipping it and smiling at each other. Everyone—all nine of them—seemed worn out and sad faced, but glad for an excuse to stop work for the day. A toothless old woman sitting next to me boldly reached out and fingered the edge of my silk gown. "Pretty, pretty," she mumbled.

I suddenly wanted to do something kind. Stripping my fine sash from my waist, I handed it to her. The other women looked so surprised that I wondered if they too would expect a gift. Or would they try to rob us all? I thought quickly. "For the wise eldest woman, such a gift is fitting, yes?" They all nodded and almost sighed together. It seemed I had said the right thing. So we whiled the afternoon away, and I even joined in their prayer session. Maryam and Anna did not, but I just said, "People of the Book," which seemed to satisfy everyone.

That evening while the men sat together around a small campfire in the courtyard and talked, we stayed on with the women. We had shared our food and been treated to some tough flat bread, and now they seemed to be truly warming to us. By asking a few friendly questions Maryam and I finally got them to talk about their lives a little: this woman had just lost her sixth baby and was too old to try again, that one had lost her husband to disease. But none of that explained why the village was so ruined or why there were no young people at all.

I finally asked outright, and the answer made me both afraid and sick at heart. A troop of Mongols had been there within the year, possibly only scouts, although it was hard to tell as the numbers grew in the telling and no one seemed to know how to count. 'As many as the stars in the sky' was what the women all agreed upon.

The two worn women who were hosting us told most of the story. "They killed anyone who tried to resist, and they stole all our young people. When they left, one said, 'Get to the nearest city if you can, or else stay here to rot.' The only one who even spoke in our tongue."

Her older sister—or another wife?—added, "That was not all. They found every qarez, our water tunnels from the tops of the mountains, and they destroyed every well and even the entrances to the tunnels! Now no water runs down to us, much less to the plains! It happened so fast. In a few days, they wrecked the work of a thousand years! Almost all the villages along our qarez are empty now, but we stay. We scratch out a living on poor soil with the little grain we have left and too little water. But how will we live without water?" Everyone shook their heads.

The first woman spoke again. "We get some from the cistern, but summer is almost over and no rain in sight. It is almost gone. And the Mongols cut down our fruit trees and took the wood away, so no more plums or apricots. By Allah's kindness we have a few sheep and goats hidden in the hills, or we would starve."

An older woman suddenly moaned and began rocking back and forth, and soon all the others had joined her in supplications to Allah for mercy. One woman spoke up angrily. "But Almighty Allah does see, and He judges. Someday, they will have to answer before Him, and I will speak out against every one of those flint-faced monsters!"

They all nodded agreement, adding other insults and imagining what tortures they would use if they got their hands on them. "And watch out," one of them added, turning to me. "My husband's brother saw Mongol scouts out in the hills again a few days ago." I shivered and had to keep from crossing myself.

Soon after, I stood up. "I share your grief and anger. But it is time to sleep now. We thank you for your hospitality and I pray for a greener future for you all."

The three of us women walked in gloomy silence back to our ruined building. Only Anna had been spared this litany of horrors, but she felt our mood. As soon as we were inside, a pair of Da'ud's men stationed themselves nearby. I lay down on my bedding and looked up through the beams of the ceiling. Part of the mud roof had already collapsed with no one to repair it. Stars sparkled in the night air, serenely distant.

Maryam whispered, "My heart breaks to see such misery."

"Not as bad as what happened to my village," Anna said. "They are alive at least. I wish we hadn't stopped here. It just makes me afraid and angry."

"Yes, I feel all those things, too," said Maryam. "Yet those Mongols couldn't destroy their good hearts. They treated us with such hospitality, and Sofia, you made everyone's lives glow with your gift."

But my mind was on Mongols. If they were everywhere, how could we avoid them? I got up and searched through my parcel of belongings until I found the paize Rukn al-Din had given me, along with some gold coins my young friend had added as his parting gift. And I pulled out the white cotton chaador I had worn when facing the Grand Master.

"I will wear this tomorrow. Indeed, we should all hide our faces from now on. Maryam, have you another cotton chaador you could offer Anna?"

"Indeed. It is well thought, Sofia." She rummaged through her bag of belongings and found one for her friend. Anna took it, looking rather sad.

"Must I not wear my pretty one anymore?"

"Well, why not wear it under this one? You can be pretty in secret," I suggested.

Anna smiled happily, and I lay down feeling a little safer, though I still patted my little store of jewels from Papa's coat, hidden around my waist and now supplemented by the coins.

"We should try to sleep now. I'm certain the men here told Da'ud the same things the women told us. He'll want to leave early tomorrow."

They had indeed warned him. Waking us well before dawn, he ordered us to pack and leave straightaway. He was in such a hurry that I could not get him to speak with me, so I just followed him out and quickly handed him the paize.

He raised his eyebrows in surprise. "How did you get this?"

"From Rukn al-Din, your future Mahdi," I answered curtly before turning away.

"Allah is endlessly merciful," I heard him exclaim behind me.

After prayers and hasty goodbyes, we hurried in single file south along a goat track that the village headman had pointed out. It took us over a hill, through a little valley, and then up another, higher hill out of sight of the village. We were about to crest its rise when Da'ud's forward man exclaimed in alarm and pointed ahead. At least a dozen Mongol horsemen were rapidly approaching. I looked behind us and saw more soldiers cutting us off from behind. We had ridden right into a trap.

"That man who fled yesterday had something to do with this," Maryam muttered.

"Or a Mongol scout saw us—or someone sneaked away from the village and betrayed us last night," Anna cried.

"Let us push our imaginings aside, try to keep calm, and cleave to faith. Whatever comes next is out of our hands, anyway," I cautioned.

Da'ud motioned to us to stop and rode forward, paize in hand. It was a round silver one, with a griffin embossed on its face, which meant that we were important. In my heart, I thanked Rukn al-Din and our Savior that I had given it to Da'ud.

To my surprise, he spoke a respectful greeting in Mongol speech.

The captain of the scouts looked at him suspiciously and said, "Where did you get such an important paize?"

"Sir, I only know greetings."

If Da'ud had thought this would save him from questioning, he was wrong. One of the soldiers, a Persian by the looks of him, rode to the captain's side.

"Speak Farsi, then!" Da'ud managed not to flinch too openly. Several of his men stirred and exchanged frowns; clearly they thought the translator was a traitor.

But Da'ud managed to speak in a calm voice, "It belonged to my master, a wealthy merchant, and I was given it in order to take his widow west to al-Mawsil."

"And why do you travel on this hidden path and stay in half-empty peasant villages? Why not follow the main road?" The fellow seemed to be enjoying himself.

"That is where we were headed, but we stopped last night at a village to rest. We rode many weary days, trying to avoid enemies who would take our lives and enslave the women."

"And who are those enemies?" The translator looked disbelieving.

"It is an old, old conflict, both tribal and religious, which has just broken out afresh east of here. Revenge killings on both sides, and then riots across the entire town. My master was murdered on his way to the mosque, may Allah have mercy on him. Now his widow," Da'ud gestured back, not at me but at Anna, "fears for her life and that of her unborn son. In al-Mawsil, she has relatives to care for her and her women."

Anna recoiled when Da'ud looked back toward her, and her chaador slipped, revealing her silk veil. Her look of terror was enough convince anyone, although Da'ud's interweaving of truth and lies seemed a mighty gamble to me. The Mongols' man translated to the captain, who scratched his scarred chin and looked hard at each member of our group before speaking.

The translator in turn told us exactly what his superior had said. "It was not right of you to use such an important paize for such a small mission, but we honor it nonetheless. We will escort you to the main road. Perhaps you can share useful information with us on the way."

"We are most grateful, sir, and I help you gladly. My master had good relations with Baiju Khan. He would be distressed to hear of his death."

The mention of Baiju Khan seemed another gamble, for who knew what politics prevailed among the Mongols in this part of Iran? Were these troops loyal to this Baiju?

The Persian soldier translated again, and our luck held. Baiju's name seemed to open a door for us. The Mongol captain nodded and spoke in low tones. The translator bowed before turning to Da'ud. "You can stay with us tonight. We will guide you further along your journey now that we know of your master's loyalty. What was his name so that I can send the news on to Baiju Khan?"

Da'ud promptly gave a name I had never heard of, and I could only pray he had not invented someone, that he truly knew of some man who had recently died. A lie might be our undoing, given the swiftness of the Mongol arrow messenger system.

At least for now, we were relatively safe. The Mongol captain signaled to his men, who fell into line before and behind us, and without casting a single glance our way, he led us on. I sighed deeply. Not only had no one mentioned a runaway slave woman, now I had both a convincing disguise and yet another unsuspecting Mongol protector! Thank God Anna's veil had slipped. I even felt almost grateful to Chinggis Khan and his universal laws. For once, they were working in our favor.

That night we women stayed in a black felt Mongol tent, reminding me of a past I had hoped to leave far behind. At least we were hidden away from the soldiers' eyes, as the captain had granted Da'ud's request that we women keep to haram. I tasted airag for the first time in years. Da'ud had been forced to accept it or risk offending his hosts, and they even insisted we women accept some, too, along with several strips of dried horsemeat. We sat in that dark tent and worked our jaws just as sore as my fellow captives and I had once had to do—how many years ago? Was it five years since Argamon had captured me? Or six? I could not remember exactly. Time had lost all meaning for me … just as it had for my friend Q'ingling. Thinking of her and Dorje and my other friends brought on such a wave of sadness that tears came to my eyes. I could hear Farsi mingled with Mongol speech, but the men spoke too softly to know what lies or truths Da'ud might be telling them. Finally I went to bed and tried to sleep.

The next day a few of the Mongol captain's men guided us over more hills to a wider track that led to the main caravan route. Reaching the main road, they saluted us and turned away. It was so lacking in drama that only fright kept me from laughing aloud.

After they were out of sight, Da'ud dropped back to speak with me. In a rare burst of talkativeness, he said, "That man who fled the village accused us of banditry! He hoped to curry favor with the Mongols and protect his village. My little trick at Derbent has been used against me." He laughed bitterly. "Had you not possessed that paize, we men would be dead now and you women would be enslaved. Allah is wise beyond human reckoning. He foresees all." And he spurred his horse forward.

We rode all that day in silence. My mind kept returning to the sash I had given the old woman. How strange that we had been betrayed by her fellow villager when we had come in friendship. With so little trust and so many chances for things to go awry, how did anything ever go right? And yet here we were, safe. How harsh, tricky, and yet miraculous life seemed.

The rest of our journey over the Zagros felt almost ordinary. We found a caravan to travel with, so the Fida'i who had accompanied us from Qazvin left us. Da'ud, brief as always, said only that merchants had traveled this road as long as Persia had existed.

As we reached higher altitudes, we passed under the shadows of steep, snow-clad peaks, the narrow trails clinging to their sides and often bordering sheer, dizzying gorges that plunged down to boiling cataracts or noisy rivers. Occasionally, riding through some desolate hidden valley, we passed what looked like small hills of dirty snow—or perhaps they were salt. Other valleys, watered by nameless rivers, were green and hospitable; we might pass a small mud-brick village surrounded by fruit trees, small fields of grain, and vegetable gardens where men and sometimes women worked, their lives untouched by wars or invasions, at least as yet.

Nights we often spent at a well-kept caravansary in a small town, or we might be offered hospitality at the headman's home in a tiny village, for our route was not only well-worn but, even with Mongols about, well-traveled. It seemed that they were leaving the trade routes alone, at least.

We had already passed a few caravans coming the other way when we stopped for the night in a hill town that Da'ud called Hamadan, a sadly destroyed city of ruins, both old and new.

"Much of it is rubble now," he told me as we rode toward the caravansary, "but it is the oldest city in Iran, one of the oldest in the world. The Mongols razed it when they first invaded, although all around here are rock carvings and ancient monuments from our great past that they did not bother to destroy. That was some twenty years ago—I told you about Subodai and his fellow khans passing through here and into the north. When they beheaded my father."

"Yes. I knew about them before you told me. They tortured and killed my grandfather, too, after defeating our Rus' armies at River Kalka," I said. He raised his eyebrows in surprise. I supposed he had never before thought further than the damage to Iran.

Hamadan's caravansary was new and relatively busy. Da'ud found another caravan that was going in our direction and immediately arranged for our party to join theirs in the morning. He even found howdahs for us women to ride in again. I think only Maryam was glad not to have to ride a horse anymore, but I was bitterly disappointed. I had accustomed myself to being outdoors again. And I wanted to see where we were going, if for no other reason than to see danger coming.

A few days' journey took us over yet more mountains. How I hated being stuck inside that little box! Anna and I were slung like baggage on either side of one camel, while Maryam was put by herself opposite a load of merchandise. If we had wanted to, Anna and I could have called out to each other from time to time, but we had nothing to say. Whenever we stopped she went straight to her friend.

I soon lost the vigor to feel left out, for it was on my account that they were forced to make this journey. I sometimes felt overwhelmed by regret. Not only could we have stayed in Alamut and been safe, but also Maryam could have awaited news about her son. What would each of us even do once we reached Constantinople, for that was my goal, not theirs? I scarcely knew what my desire for home and family meant anymore. All I knew was that I must make all this dislocation up to them when we reached my Uncle Vasily's protection.

Thoughts of Kerim and Nasr, and of Ali, who was surely dead, haunted me. All seemed doomed by fate, by their convictions, and by the world they lived in—as trapped as any woman in a howdah. I wondered about the Shi'a who had been attacked in Qazvin and in the town where Kerim was murdered—I had never even learned its name—slaughtered because they followed the lineage of Ali.

Shi'a of other lines of imams must hate the Nizari, too, if they were persecuted for Nizari crimes. And they would probably take revenge against

Sunni and Nizari alike whenever they got a chance. And then the Sunni or Nizari would get their revenge in turn, and on and on until no one could even remember who was right or wrong or even how things had gotten so terrible!

It struck me: if each man believes that his religion, his way, is the only truth, then he will feel free to destroy his enemies forever. But will the total destruction of everyone who believes differently prove that he is right or merely that he has become a monster? It was a dismal line of thinking, but it returned again and again while we bumped up and down mountain trails.

One morning at dawn, I heard snarls above us, as if some great cat might be stalking us. It took all my willpower to keep my imagination from running wild. Anna heard it, too, and ran to Maryam. The Jewess comforted Anna like a child, telling her, "Yes, that was a lion's roar, but lions sleep all day and only come out at night. And they are afraid of fire, so we were perfectly safe all night." I did not believe her.

One late afternoon we stopped, and Da'ud actually let us out of the howdahs. A lone chunk of mountain towered over us, as if it had broken off the main range standing at some distance and gone its own way. Lovely springs bubbled out of its side and ran down to a pool by the road at the base of a fairly steep cliff. The caravan handlers had stopped to water the camels. Other men and even a veiled woman or two stood nearby staring up.

Da'ud pointed up. "We are at the Rock of Behistun, sacred since time began."

My eyes grew round at that. I had read about the Rock in one of Nasir al-Din's histories, written by a Greek named Diodorus. Alexander the Great himself had stopped here over a thousand years ago.

"See high up there, where the afternoon sun hits? Those pictures and words were carved into the rock by an ancient Persian emperor. It looks very small from down here, but it is huge. We believe it celebrates his victories over his enemies, but no one can read the writing anymore."

Trying to keep my chaador in order, I had a hard time seeing much beyond a rock face and a few seemingly small carven shapes of men, strangely stiff as if frozen in the stone.

While Da'ud was talking, several men and boys had come into sight on an outcrop high above. They shouted greetings down to us all, and soon they were down among us, sweaty with the effort of climbing, grinning with delight, and full of stories about the magnificent carvings.

"The Prophet himself, peace be on him, would have marveled at such a sight!"

Another added, "When you climb up there, you find a flat place where there must have been a temple overlooking the western plain. And above it are wondrous carvings of slaves being led to a king. One is being trampled underfoot. And look, you can see it from here: the ancient Persian symbol for Ahura Mazda, the Lord of Wisdom, crowns the king!"

A third said, "How anyone ever got up there to carve that wall is a great mystery, for no man can reach it by climbing."

Those strange, ancient carvings were only part of the mystery. Partway up the cliff was an area that had been graven to look like a flat, closed doorway with a pointed arch. It had writing on it, too. And here and there lay huge boulders on which were engraved likenesses of ancient gods or conquerors, and a boulder-statue reclined with a cup in his hand—who knows who he was, for his history is forgotten, wiped from memory by the steady scrape of time.

Someday I too would be gone, with no one to remember me or anything I had done. I climbed back into my howdah.

We stopped the night in the nearby village of Behistun, which had been there since the very first caravans had ever passed this way, and which seemingly had never changed. Its water came from a stream that ran down from one of the springs above, the sweetest I had ever tasted. I would have liked to stay for a few days to rest, but Da'ud was relentless and we moved on early the next morning.

Our path dropped down onto featureless plains occasionally broken by rough hills. Looking through a crack in the curtain, I could make out mountains in the distance, flat against the sky and as indifferent as eternity. I had never been so hot. And though Da'ud had filled water skins for us in Behistun, even those sweet waters tasted bad after the sun heated them up. And there was nothing to do but sit and be jostled about until we stopped for prayers or a meal, or an afternoon rest under makeshift shelters when it grew too hot to travel.

We stopped at a fortified town that lay at the base of more mountains. I saw little of it, we women being taken straight to its caravansary and confined to the women's quarters. By then none of us was fit company for the others. Anna complained of motion sickness and Maryam of sore bones, so we spoke little and just lay down after supper and tried to sleep. Even in my dreams, I seemed to be rocking to and fro in a howdah.

And then it was back to that dreadful desert, seemingly devoid of life except for what were called oases, where everything sprang into greenness and people grew scanty crops, small spots of life in a red-brown wilderness. Over the next few days, we stayed at one town after another, but I learned few of their names and remember fewer; Kurind was one, Altun Kupri another. Sometimes we crossed softly murmuring rivers, either by fording them or on bridge. I knew which when I heard splashing or the camels' hooves treading over wood or stone. I could only guess from the way the sun moved over the sky that we were moving more or less north and west. After awhile, I could scarcely remember why I was making this journey—fleeing the Nizari? Seeking my uncle? Madness?

One night I dreamt that the howdah was a coffin and I was being buried alive in it. I could hear people wailing outside: Dorje and Argamon and the other women of his household, my old friends and fellow slaves. Most chilling, my lost family and murdered companions from Kyiv, from the ordus, and even from Iran, were among the mourners. I kept pounding on the door of the howdah and screaming that I was alive, but no one heard me. I was lowered into the earth and dirt was shoveled onto my coffin. It grew dark and silent, and I could no longer breathe. With a great gasp of fear, I sat up to find myself in a small room at the back of the caravansary, Anna and Maryam stirring sleepily nearby. I could not go back to sleep, so I prayed and then tried to practice peace.

The journey lasted for what seemed like months. One day we passed ruins of castles and of a great city. It stood baking in the afternoon sun, another relic of the ancient past. Not long after that, we reached the walls of al-Mawsil—or Mosul as the Franks call it—by way of a stone bridge over a river. The sun blazed straight into my howdah. Thankfully, once we were inside the city and following its twisting alleyways, the blank-faced buildings cut off much of the sun's heat. When I was let out, my clothes were stuck to me with sweat.

We stayed in a large caravansary that night, with a high arched roof and a good upstairs room for us women, which we shared with a few others. Da'ud even arranged for us all to go, heavily guarded, to a public bathhouse nearby. It was one of those rare occasions when I felt we were also people to him, not just burdens he must deliver before he could turn back to discover Ali's fate.

In the bath, which refreshed us all, I found out from listening to the flow of talk around me that the ruins we had passed were of an ancient city called Nineveh, that the river we had crossed was called the Tigris, that al-Mawsil was almost as old as time, and that we were no longer in Iran but in a land called Assyria—or was it Syria? The terrain and buildings I had glimpsed had all seemed the same to me, though the al-Mawsili women I overheard were speaking Arabic with a few unfamiliar words mixed in here and there. I never knew when or where we had left Iran behind.

The other thing I learned was that al-Mawsil had recently fallen into Mongol hands, though it had surrendered peacefully and was more or less governed by its own emir. Indeed, there seemed to be a certain ill will directed toward this emir, whose willingness to send his soldiers into Mongol wars had spared the city but not its men. And in general there seemed to be much battling back and forth for power in this part of the world, not only with the Mongols but between neighboring cities. I only prayed that we escape it all as soon as possible. It seemed that everywhere we went, danger from my enemies lay in wait, and sure enough, we passed Mongol soldiers on our way back from the baths.

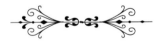

Although we lingered for several days in al-Mawsil to rest, we women mostly stayed inside the caravansary, sweating in the heat and doing little beyond drinking fruit juice and sleeping. Finally Da'ud found us a caravan that was traveling west to Halab, which the Franks call Aleppo, and put us in the hands of a fellow Nizari, a merchant named Thābit ibn-Ahmad who had contact with Christian merchants there.

Much to our delight, Da'ud and his men took us to stay in the man's house, where his wives and daughters hosted us in the andarun for a few days. Like the homes in Derbent or Qazvin, it sat inside a guarded compound with a pleasant courtyard garden. A pool adorned its center, flowers bloomed in pots, and a pomegranate tree cast welcome shade. Our hostess offered us kind and fulsome hospitality. She welcomed us to sit in the courtyard whenever her husband was absent; and like Mother Layla, she straightaway began plying us with delicious foods like flat bread with spicy ground chickpeas, which she called hummus, or a cracked wheat dish mixed with minced lamb and spices that she called kibbeh.

We took to sitting in their garden every morning, delighted to be free from howdahs, camels, and even dour Da'ud for a few days. Sometimes Fatima joined us, along with two young daughters whose liveliness reminded me painfully of Aftab and Sarah.

We had been there perhaps three days and were all sitting in the garden. I was talking with my hostess, learning a few new words of her speech while Maryam gave lessons to Anna when the Jewess stopped and exclaimed, "I just remembered! My husband had relatives in al-Mawsil."

Later that evening after supper, we were back in the haram, as Fatima called it, trying to keep cool, when Maryam spoke again, pensively. "After we first fled to Qazvin and found it wasn't safe, we almost came here. How different our lives would have been had we done so instead of joining Selim al-Din's caravan! Hah, now that I'm here, I wonder if I could contact them."

She turned to me. "Sofia, you speak Arabic better than I do. Would you ask our hostess if she knows whether your husband has ever heard of Salman bin Abram? He's a merchant here in the city. If he still lives, that is."

When I relayed her request, Fatima answered, "I think my husband has spoken of him. Jewish, yes? If she wishes, I could ask him to send a messenger tonight."

Maryam paled when she heard Fatima's answer. "God is wise and provident indeed."

What Maryam did not see in her eagerness to meet her husband's relative was Anna's face. I doubt it had ever crossed her mind that Anna did not know she was Jewish. The girl reddened, and tears sprang to her eyes. She turned away and avoided both Maryam and me for the rest of the day.

Meanwhile our kind hostess sent word to her husband, who did know the man. Thābit ibn-Ahmad arranged all, and Maryam wrote him a letter that very night.

When bedtime came, Anna lay down on her mattress, her arms wrapped around her and facing away from Maryam, clearly deep in misery. I almost felt sorry for her, but after all she and Maryam had shared, how could she hold Maryam's religion against her? Maryam was too happy to notice, either then or the next morning when she received a reply.

"How kind. Salman bin Abram sends condolences, though my husband has been dead these many years. He says it would be very difficult for him to meet me here, but that he will see us off when we leave al-Mawsil. And he offers to send letters of introduction to his friends in Halab! If we stay there for awhile, I could meet them. It's been so many years since I saw any fellow Jews, and he says that there are many who would welcome me there!"

I glanced over at Anna. Her lower lip was trembling. She feigned a headache for the rest of the day, and when poor Maryam tried to nurse her, she refused her friend's ministrations and insisted she only needed to sleep. The next two days grew increasingly awkward, with Anna trying every trick she knew to avoid Maryam. Only the woman's eagerness to meet this Salman bin Abram kept her from falling into a black mood herself, for she was clearly bewildered and then wounded by Anna's sudden coldness.

At last we were able to leave. After bidding farewell to Fatima, offering her little gifts that I had brought from Iran, and receiving several generous gifts in return, we set off on foot, much to my surprise and delight. I was able to peer around at winding streets, faceless walls, open squares, and various passersby, almost all of them men. The few women I saw were like us, heavily veiled and almost always escorted by servants or guards. All of them hurried by, eyes to the ground. Other than the sound of other languages in addition to Farsi, a few differences in attire—loose-fitting striped or embroidered cotton robes, for instance—and unusual cooking smells, there was surprisingly little to tell me I was in Syria. Walls are walls, streets are streets, and I felt I could have been in Qazvin or a dozen other cities I had passed.

Interestingly, on our way to the area where the caravan waited, Thābit ibn-Ahmad and Da'ud spoke freely together before their men. It became clear that there are many Nizari in that part of the world who quietly maintain their allegiance to the Grand Master and who have their own mutual protection societies—which were what Da'ud had called gangs when they were Sunni.

Maryam's cousin-in-law Salman bin Abram was waiting to meet her, and they had a brief, tearful visit together amidst the bustle of men loading the last bundles onto camels. Rather than meet him as Maryam clearly wished her to do, Anna climbed straight into her howdah, a nasty box with a roof and curtained windows, but I exchanged polite greetings with him before stepping aside to allow him and Maryam time alone. I could not bear to enter my own howdah yet, wanting to enjoy the small freedom of being outside as long as I could.

As promised, Salman bin Abram gave Maryam a packet of letters for his brethren in Halab as well as a few small gifts. And just before I entered my little howdah prison, I bade farewell to Da'ud and thanked him as best I could, given my mixed feelings about him. I also gave him a ruby and all the pearls I had taken from my Papa's coat, which was the first time I had revealed I had anything of my own. He was both surprised and grateful.

"Half are for you, or perhaps for your sister who may be bereaved. The others are for Kerim's widow, Perijam, and his orphaned sisters, who most certainly are bereaved." I was unable to keep sharpness from my voice.

He smiled grimly, looking past my shoulder. "Yes, I will do that. It is only right." He offered the salaam and disappeared into the thronged streets with his men without another word. I never saw him again. And I never found out what happened to Ali or to Perijam and her family.

Thus began the next stage of my seemingly endless journey to Constantinople, which was much the same as the trip from Hamadan to al-Mawsil. All through it, Anna seemed subdued, though she said nothing to Maryam or me. Whenever we stopped, Maryam would ask her why she was so quiet and she would claim she still did not feel well. That sounded reasonable, as we were traveling in such hot weather. But their mutual misery made me gloomy, too.

I could see little, but I guessed from the way the sun rose and set that we were heading west. It was so hot that we could only travel early and late in the day; it must be August by now. Even putting my chaador off inside the howdah gave me no relief, especially since there was then the problem of where to put it. I finally just folded it up and sat on it. Sometimes I peeked through the crack between curtain and window frame, where I glimpsed a softer landscape, often with men and women working in small fields and orchards, but it was nothing like the green world of my childhood. I suddenly missed my home, my dear Rus', where it was plenty hot in the summer but with moistness in the air, not like this oven. Yet in the heat, nothing mattered for long. The remorseless sun bleached away even the horror of Kerim's and Nasr's senseless deaths.

It was really only a week later that we reached the city of Halab, The White. It is encircled by hills, surrounded by rich fields and abundant orchards, and adorned with cypress trees. As we dropped down into the valley, I grasped at little views of it. It was a striking city surrounded by massive gates, with a great flat-topped hill in its midst. Atop the hill stood a great, once-unassailable citadel, but that is gone now. The Mongols took and destroyed it some months back. I can only imagine the ruination that followed—and I still recoil at the fact that Frankish Christians allied with them and joined in the slaughter!

But when I was there, Halab was still whole and proud. Disappointingly, though, her walls were not white but the same ochre I had seen so much of already. I was not to learn how it got its name until I had been there for some days. Maryam told me the story one evening.

"It seems that in ancient times after the city had been laid waste by a war, the Patriarch Abraham stopped in its ruins leading a single white cow. Islam regards him as the first Muslim, if you can believe it. It's one thing to share the same roots, another to claim he was not a Jew! Anyway, he prayed before milking her, and she gave so much milk that it saved the starving survivors and allowed them to rebuild their city. In honor of this bounteous miracle, they named it Halab." Whether this story is true, I cannot say. I only know that from the way she told the story, Maryam thought Muslims were either stupid or arrogant. Even if I still feared the Grand Master and mistrusted the Nizari, neither view felt quite fair to me after the kindness so many Muslims had shown me. People only believe what they have been taught, I think, and many Christians I know have some strange ideas about Jews, Anna among them.

While in Halab, we were hosted by a friend and trading partner of Thābit ibn-Ahmad. His magnificent home was hidden behind thick walls. This man was truly wealthy, with his luxurious mansion and many servitors. He had four wives, who were all courteous but incurious about us, and several concubines who were more interested in bathing and dressing and gossiping than in dust-laden strangers. One woman was fair-haired and gray-eyed; another had skin almost as black as her eyes and tightly braided hair. After a few days, I learned that the fair concubine was Christian and that yet another was Jewish. You could get lost in his many rooms, which I sometimes tried to do in order to escape Anna or Maryam. It was heartbreaking to witness the two of them in the same room.

One night soon after we arrived, I took Anna aside and tried to speak with her about her change of feelings. She answered slowly. "I suppose I knew in my heart that Maryam was Jewish, but I told myself she couldn't be, since she never acted like a Jew. She prayed differently from me, but so do you. But she had no horns on her head and she never ate Christian babies or … did the other terrible things my parents told me Jews do. I told myself that since she hates the enemies of Christ like I do, she must be Christian. And she was so kind to me, so loving. I felt I had a mother again, and that made it even worse when I saw the truth.

"Now Maryam looks at me with her sad eyes, and I know I'm hurting her. And I am still grateful to her, but I feel so torn, too. I was taught to hate Jews for murdering Christ! How can I forget what her people did to Him? For that matter, how can you?"

That stopped me short. The only two Jews I had met were kind and gentle people. Maryam had not killed Christ, nor had she ever uttered a word against Christianity. But Anna was like most Christians I knew. I saw no way to argue with her.

Finally I said, "I don't know how to help you. I can only repeat what my father told me: judge a person by what he does, not by how he worships. He said that in his travels he had met good and bad people of every faith. I let God take care of deeper judgments."

Anna shrugged. "I suppose you're right." But she was unable to do more than be polite to Maryam. That lovely trust was gone. As for Maryam, the old set of her shoulders came back and wrinkles of sadness ate ever deeper into her face. Although she never turned to me for consolation—I suppose she thought I was too young—I did my best to be kind to her. The only thing that comforted her was sending Salman bin Abram's letter of introduction to his people.

One afternoon a message came for her. Soon after reading it, she sat down beside me and announced, "You know that I sent word to our Jewish brethren, and now they have replied. It makes it much easier for me to do what I had already been considering. I will stay on in Halab, among my own kind. Anna no longer needs me, and if she can turn on me so easily,

I know I will face worse in Christian lands. If I go on with you, I will find nothing but hatred and oppression, far worse than in Iran. In Rayy we Jews were often treated badly, much worse even than when I lived in Lambasar or Alamut. But I hear that you Christians are even crueler to us—not you, Sofia, of course—but you're unlike most Christians. The stories about our people in Europe that reach our ears: riots, rapes, murders, synagogues and homes burned! My brethren warn me that even in Halab, men spit on our people in the street, pull the rabbis' beards, threaten the women, and worse. They were very frank about life here when they wrote to me, so I know what to expect."

"Maryam, I'm so sorry. I wish I knew how to help heal the breach between you and Anna."

She shook her head sadly. "There is nothing you can do. I spoke with her about it last night when you were out of the room. She can no more help herself than a cat can help fearing a dog, even if the dog is friendly. It breaks my heart, but I always knew that sooner or later we would have to part. And the Jews of Halab welcome me with open hearts and arms. I am invited to share a roof and bread with another widow in the community. I can be with my own people here, worship freely, and try to begin life anew. And who knows? I may even be able to get word of my son from time to time. There are so many Nizari living here that I can send a letter, and it may get to him in a few months. Once I cross into Christian territory, that hope will most likely be lost."

Tears filled my eyes. "I understand, but how I will miss you! You've been so kind to us both, Maryam, and I owe you such a debt of gratitude."

"Yes, I'm fond of you, too, Sofia. You've shown me that not all Gentiles are vicious!"

I was shocked, but when I looked through her eyes I could not deny what I saw.

So when the day came to leave, Maryam was not with us. Someone had come for her from her community two days earlier. She and I had parted with sad affection and the exchange of little gifts. I also gave her the emerald and the gold coins I had taken from Papa's coat, to help her begin again. That brought tears to her eyes. Even Anna came up and embraced her just before she left. I was glad for that moment, though I was soon made sorry that I had never found a time to remove the rest of Papa's jewels from my cloak.

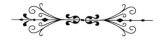

Our next stop was to be Antioch. Because we were under Thābit ibn-Ahmad's special care, he placed us far forward in his caravan just behind a corpulent, wealthy, and very outspoken man. I heard him throughout the day, calling for dates or for water or for some item he must have that very moment. The first night we spent in a caravansary, and I was glad of the respite from him.

But the next day, he fell ill. I could hear his groans, as well as complaints from my camel handler to his companions. "He ate too much halvah and now he insists that we stop until he feels better. What if he takes all day? We could roast alive out here."

I could hear Thābit ibn-Ahmad arguing with him, and we wasted much time before the man came to his senses and we moved on. It was a miserable day, since we were passing through desert with no settlements nearby.

We stopped at small oasis midday. Thābit ibn-Ahmad came by to see after our needs, as we had to stay in our howdahs. "We should have been further along by now, but Allah wills it," he sighed before ordering everyone back into line.

An eternity later, after we all had endured the heat of hell, he began calling out orders to set up camp. He came by again. "The sun is setting; we must make the best of it."

Anna and I were more or less herded into a tent together with two other women, where we spent a difficult night trying not to hear the wails of some large cat in the distance. Anna even begged me to hold her hand for a while when she could not sleep.

We broke camp right after dawn prayers, as the heat was building up fast. I was already in my howdah when I overheard my camel's handler speaking with one of his fellows. It seemed that before we reached the safety of a Muslim village, we would be forced to pass near a Christian castle and might have to pay baksheesh to "the accursed Franks" who lived there, but that it was the lesser of two evils.

After listening to the two of them cursing all evildoers for awhile,

I pieced together that our path led through a mosaic of lands held by Christian or Muslim, and that uninterrupted travel was never assured. I thought that they meant the Franks might take too much baksheesh, perhaps at worst harass us; and although I had no reason to trust Franks, their nearness seemed like good news to me. We would reach Antioch shortly, and I would find a ship bound for Constantinople!

Then I heard Thābit ibn-Ahmad's voice and step; he was moving down the line of camels, urging everyone to hurry up, that his scout had heard rumors that "the accursed polytheists" were nearby. "We must make for the safety of the village before nightfall." It was the way he said safety that made me question the nature of the threat—too much baksheesh did not seem enough reason for him to sound so uneasy. For the first time since leaving Halab, danger crossed my mind. And in looking back, I do not know why I had never been afraid of bandits, since we may well have been in danger all along. Perhaps the heat had stolen my mind.

By midmorning I could barely breathe inside my howdah. It was so hot that sitting on my chaador felt like sitting on a hot, wet rag. Thābit ibn-Ahmad was again calling to his men to hasten and to the guards to keep their eyes sharp. I peeked through the curtain and glimpsed steep, rock-strewn slopes rising on either side of us.

We had gone no more than a hundred paces further when a storm of hisses filled the air, then screams of fear or pain, shouts from above coming nearer, and the beat of hooves thundering down upon us. Our camel handler shouted in alarm, and Anna called out to me, "Mistress, what is—," when he grunted softly and our camel began to dance sideways with great hoarse bellows, a sound I hope never to hear again. When I tried to see past the curtain, the man lay bleeding on the ground, his hands plucking uselessly at an arrow in his chest. I knew the worst was upon us.

I panicked in that coffin of a litter. I must get out, run, hide! I had just gotten the howdah door unfastened when the camel screamed one last time, staggered, and slowly toppled over toward my side. I jumped free, rolling onto the stony ground as my howdah burst into splinters under the beast. Its harness snapped like cracking whips, and Anna's howdah slid to the ground to stand upright between the camel's flailing legs. Anna was screaming—little short bursts of pure fear. I tried to catch my breath, all around me a frenzy of rearing horses, bellowing camels, shouts, screams, swords thrusting, spears stabbing, arrows whistling, men wrestling, grappling, strangling, slashing, dying.

My chaador had fallen on me and clung to my legs like a shroud, but I shoved it away. Blood was pumping from a spear through the camel's throat, and its legs were still thrashing. I had to climb onto the dying beast to drag Anna out and over it. Slipping and tumbling over its quivering flanks, she lost her chaador, too. The camel's blankets and harness suddenly tangled around our feet like shackles, I slipped and fell, and Anna slid onto me, screaming, knocking the wind from my chest.

And then a shadow passed over us and she was lifted clean off me, like a mouse snatched up by a bird of prey. I sat up gasping to see a man in a dulband thrusting her onto her back with one hand and loosing his payjamas with another. I leapt up and threw my arms around him from behind, but he just shook me off and finished with his payjamas.

I screamed NO! He was leaning over her and ripping at her garments, he was pulling out a wicked curved knife. Thinking he meant to cut her clothing from her, I was already searching the ground for something to hit him with—there was my fallen camel driver's knife! Then I saw the flash of the blade arcing down toward Anna's throat. My hands seized the knife and of their own drove it hard into his back, bright blood spreading where I had stabbed him. He arched backwards and fell onto me. The haft of the knife punched me in the belly, something struck me in the head, and a fierce blackness overtook me.

How long I lay there, I do not know. When I came awake, at first I had no idea where I was or what had happened. My head was pounding, and I had to wipe crusted blood off my eyelids before they would open. All around me was empty silence but for a strange humming sound: flies. Something weighed on me like a great slab of meat: a corpse. When I struggled up, flies seemed everywhere. I nearly fainted again, but that image of Anna and the knife brought on a rush of panic. I began frantically pushing and struggling, head and belly shrieking with pain, until I had worked free, all the time crying her name.

Finally I staggered up and looked around, my head spinning so fast that I could scarcely stay upright, my eyes covered with a veil of red mist. The man I had stabbed lay at my feet. More corpses lay strewn about, hacked and bloodied, fallen over each other, some of whom I had known by sight—including the rich man. Flies and greedy carrion birds were picking at them. Here and there dead men and camels lay befouled in their own blood and offal, bundles and packs lay ravished and emptied of their contents. I fell on all fours and vomited.

Where was Anna? I tried to find my bearings. There was our camel, here at my feet the man who had attacked her. But the bodies of two strangers lay where she should be. No, there was a corner of her gown underneath. I pushed and strained until one and then another corpse rolled over, the screaming pain in my head and body almost blinding me, my heart squeezing ever tighter, trying to release her, hoping against hope that that fiend had not killed her, yet expecting to find her lifeless, too. And there she was, eyes closed, her throat streaked with caked blood.

Groaning in agony, with my little remaining strength I shoved the last corpse's leg off my friend and gathered her into my arms, brushing away flies from her face while tears streamed down mine. "Anna, Anna," was all I could say. She still was warm, still had color. Was that a trick of the hot day? I scarcely dared touch her throat, it was so like my old dreams of the dead. It took all my willpower to put one finger on it, but what I found made me even shakier—with hope. The man had not had time to slit her throat, and her wound was only skin deep. I stroked her cheek and felt a slight mist of sweat. She was alive! In a panic of joy, I embraced her and felt faint breath stroke my cheek in turn. But when I tried to smooth out her bunched up skirt, I saw that her ankle was bent at an unnatural angle.

Only then did I feel the sun beating down on us like a fiery hammer, crushing my skull through my hair. Water. She would need water. I looked up and met the eye of a buzzard that had stealthily edged up within a few feet of us and was standing with head cocked. It seemed to be reckoning how long we would survive in this wasteland.

"Shoo! Get out!" I cried. It just stared. I gently let Anna back down on the ground, stood up and flapped my arms, which made me feel sick and even dizzier. The bird hopped back a few steps and started picking at the eye of a corpse, then stopped and looked back at me as if to say, 'You are next. I can wait.'

Swaying with pain, I searched the ground until I found a piece of bloody cloth large enough to spread over Anna, hoping to hide her from both bird and sun. After covering her with the cleanest end, I looked around. No one else was alive. Where could I find water? Our camel lay with the broken shaft of the spear still sticking from it neck, its legs stiffening on either side of Anna's howdah like a bony fence. Her litter might still hold her water skin. I stumbled over bodies and crawled between the beast's legs; there lay the skin on the floor, an offering of life in the midst of all that death.

After staggering back to Anna and forcing a few drops of water between her lips, I took a swallow, too. Above, the sun was reaching her zenith. Never before had she seemed so cruel, so unrelenting. I looked at the water bag. Almost full, but not enough for two people for more than a day. I must build us a shelter, find more water, then … what?

Wait to be saved or to be enslaved by strangers, or to die.

I moved without hope. It was a wretched business to seek food and water among so many dead, not only because of their terrible empty lifelessness but because I hurt so much and felt so sickened by the sights and smells of death that it was all I could do to force myself on. Almost everything had been carried away, but here and there the bandits had overlooked things in their haste to kill and be gone. Near the head of the ragged remains of the caravan, I found Thābit ibn-Ahmad, sprawled face down, birds pecking at his legs and cheeks. I shooed them away and covered him up as best I could, realizing with dim horror that his wife would never know what had happened to him.

But I took his water skin out of panic that Anna might die of thirst while I was gone. There were other skins of water here and there, too, a few scraps of food, some lengths of cloth. I gathered them all onto a carpet that was too soiled even for bandits. It took all my strength to drag everything back to her side. At least the buzzard was gone.

"Anna, here I am." I kneeled and removed the cloth, but though she was alive and her eyes were open, she was staring into space and seemed not to see me at all. I gathered her back into my arms. "Here, I've brought you food and water. We'll build a shelter and wait until we're rescued. Someone will surely come for us."

"Mama?" she asked, finally turning her eyes to mine. "I thought I was in Hell. It is so bright and hot, and I hurt so. I'm so afraid. Hold me tighter."

"No, Anna, it's me, Sofia. I'll take care of you. I won't leave you."

She did not seem to understand, but she at least accepted water from me, almost choking as it spilled into her mouth. "I knew you'd take care of me. I always trusted you," she smiled. "Thank you, Maryam. I'm sorry...."

There was no point in trying to get Anna to understand. I must build a shelter quickly, or we would be cooked in this terrible heat. The howdah might make a good frame, and though the camel stank horribly, its flanks and legs could serve as crossbars. I had to shove the frame around little by little until its door faced inward toward the camel's belly. Anna's ankle dangled uselessly, and I half dragged, half carried her past the beast's fore-legs and into her howdah. I also slowly towed my laden carpet as near to it as I could get, though so many bodies blocked the way. After spreading out the bloody rug and awkwardly carrying everything into the narrow space between the litter and the camel's belly, I draped several lengths of cloth from the howdah to the beast's body and over its upper fore-leg. Flies attacked relentlessly, and several buzzards flapped over to watch before deciding that the dead were more interesting than the living.

As hellish as all this may seem, part of me felt like laughing at the absurdity of our troubles. Why set up house amidst a hostile desert in a foreign land with little or no hope of living past the next day? But I could not give up. I even found another carpet, too shabby to steal, and spread it on the first, to cover the blood and soften the feel of rocky ground. Anna was slumped inside the howdah, unable to move.

"Anna, it's too hot in there. Come rest in my arms." She almost fell onto me, she was so lost to her surroundings, but she smiled as I fed her dates and sips of water. My head and belly hurt so much that I could eat nothing and drink little, but I bathed both our faces often. There seemed no point in hoarding the water. Finally she fell asleep, cradled like an infant in my embrace, while I hunched over her and brushed flies from her face.

At first that task absorbed me completely, but as the day wore on, I could not escape my terrifying lack of future. Although we were surely not far from a settlement, I could neither leave Anna to go for help nor take her with me with her ankle broken. But if no one knew we were there and came for us, we would either die of thirst or heat, starve to death, or be attacked by wild animals and torn apart. Uncaring death awaited us both, no matter how I tried to find a way to cheat it. I had eluded it again and again, had felt guided past so many threats. But always, beneath my faith, had lain a deep and subtle arrogance: I was special, I was chosen. As the afternoon stretched longer and longer, surrounded by that field of death, I had to face the truth that I was in no way special. My life was smaller than a mote of dust on the mirror of the universe and as fleeting as a wave in the middle of the sea. It was a crushing understanding, and it pressed in on me from all sides. Our time had come, and every choice I had ever made, every event in my life, had led me to this empty day. There was no escaping it, and no prayer would make it less painful.

How long was I sunk in misery and pain? I will never know. Yet as I sat, emptied, despair slowly dissolved into surrender. Stillness flowed over me like the delicate river mists I remembered from childhood. It rose past the ruined caravan, across the silent desert, over the hills and distant mountains, and outward into the sky itself, softening my every sensation. Perhaps it was only acceptance or even brain fever, but it filled and lifted my mind and heart, carrying me beyond little Sofia into a peace as sweet and strong as that day back in Batu Khan's camp. Pain and weariness fell away, and I drifted into sleep.

It seemed that I floated up into the air and hovered over our ruined caravan. Anna was floating nearby, looking down at our makeshift shelter, and I looked, too. It was as if I could see through it to our sleeping bodies. A great ochre-colored cat was prowling among the ruined caravan, sniffing here and there. How small it all seemed from here, how unimportant.

I turned to Anna and said, "We have a choice now. We can leave this world and enter the realm of death with no hope of entering Heaven, or we can go back to the world with all its troubles. What do you wish?"

And Anna answered, "You choose. I only want to stay by your side." But even as she was speaking, she was drifting farther and farther from me.

I called out, "Then we must go back now or we'll be parted." She nodded, but continued to grow smaller and smaller, while I turned and saw the sky above me, black beyond all nights and full of blinding suns. Its vastness terrified me and I fell down, down, down into this world and a dark, dreamless sleep.

AUTUMN INTO WINTER
ANNO DOMINI 1245

When I opened my eyes, I was immersed in an ocean of love so profound that I could not tell whether it was coming to me or from me. I was lying on something soft, perhaps a cloud. An angel stood guard nearby, outlined in gold. The mist cleared from my eyes a little, and I made out the familiar curve of cheek, the curl of beard, and the way his hair fell.

"Papa?"

My heart soared with joy. I had died and this was Heaven after all, though the sun was setting, my head was pounding, and my belly hurt, which seemed strange if I were dead.

The angel turned and became a tall man wearing a dark cloak. He bent down to me and his cloak parted to reveal a plain split tunic with a white cross sewn over the breast. Underneath it was chain mail armor. It took me several heartbeats to realize that he was not Papa but a stranger with sun-streaked brown hair and gray eyes. Only the curve of his cheek was Papa's.

That all-embracing love faded. I was alive, Papa was still dead, and that was why I hurt so. Then I truly saw: a goodly-looking man with kindness written on his face. That was like my Papa, at least. And there were other men moving around nearby, some with white square crosses marked on their dark cloaks. My guardian spoke to me in simple Arabic. "Can you sit a small way up? I can give you water mixed with wine."

I nodded, and he helped me sit up enough to drink. My belly felt clubbed, and the back of my head began to pound. When I tried to touch it, I realized it was wrapped in a bandage. It felt moist, perhaps from blood. There were other men moving throughout the camp, setting the dead in order, dragging lifeless animals away, picking up stray objects, and burning what was ruined. I had taken a few sips from his water skin when I remembered my dream.

"Anna! Where is she? Does she still live?" I tried to sit up, but he stopped me.

"Your friend? The black-haired girl? By your side there. She is very ill. Her ankle broke, and she needs a surgeon. Do you follow my words?"

"Yes." I turned and saw Anna lying on a sheepskin. Her face looked like a pale dead flower. She was asleep, but her breath came in shallow gasps. "Oh my poor little Anna," I said in Hungarian, pressing my hand against her hot forehead. And then I remembered my Latin. Turning to him, I asked, "You are Christian? Frankish?"

Surprise crossed his face. He nodded. "You speak Latin, then?"

"Some, and Greek if you know it."

"Only greetings. I speak Langue d'Oc … French … Latin … fair Arabic."

Returning to Arabic, I asked, "Why are you here in this wasteland?"

He smiled grimly, looking around at the havoc. "Today it seems that way, but in truth you are but a few miles from a castle and safety." He nodded his head toward the other men. "We were out hunting for a lion's den. We try to discourage their taste for sheep—and sometimes for their shepherds. We saw horsemen leading burdened camels too fast for such a hot day. When they saw us, they turned and fled. We knew who they were: Bedouin bandits, a plague to everyone in these parts. We gave chase and caught the slow ones unwilling to drop their booty. One of them led us here in trade for his life. The others…." He shrugged.

"We found you and the other girl. You made a strange shelter," he nodded toward our howdah—the camel and my makeshift tent were already gone, "but it saved your lives. It kept the buzzards and the sun off you. And deceived a lioness whose den lies near here. She must have been wakened by the noise of battle. Her prints led right past your camel."

I shuddered. "I dreamt that Anna and I had ...."

"Did you find the lion?"

"One of them." He paused. "May I ask your name?"

"Sofia Volodymyrovna, once of Kyiv in Rus'," I said, feeling a rush of sadness.

"And I," he said gravely, "am Sir Joscelin of Braissac, once of Occitaine. The castle—or rather convent—where we take you belongs to the Order of Saint John. The Hospitallers." Seeing that neither name meant anything to me, he added, "They are a monastic order of knights. They, at least those who remain, guard pilgrims journeying to Holy Jerusalem and provide for the sick and the needy and the orphaned. They also fight. Their castles host pilgrims and the sick; our infirmary may offer hope for your friend. We will take you both there now that you are awake. She ... we wanted to wait for you ... She will suffer from the ride. She was awake for awhile, but lost in fear. She kept calling out in a strange tongue."

I stroked Anna's hair. "Hungarian. She is from Hungary. Will she recover?" I glanced up and away—it had never been safe to look a man in the eye—and his face was grave.

"Only God can tell. Meanwhile, you must rest until it is time to move you. He must have watched over you, though. You are the only survivors."

I shuddered, and bile rose in my throat. "My God, I killed a man! He was about to slit Anna's throat, and then—take—her body!"

He looked shocked. "She is lucky to have such a friend!"

But I sank back onto the sheepskin and felt tears trickle into my hair. I had killed—for Anna, yes, but I had murdered someone without even a thought. I'd had no choice. And I would do it again if I had to, but it made me feel sick! I wiped my eyes and hair and realized I had no veil. "My chaador—or at least a veil—most unseemly—"

He had risen and now towered over me. "You are not well, your thoughts wander. But I will see if I can find something for you—oh, I must tell you this. Your friend—Anna?—her possessions were still in her howdah; they lie next to her now. We found nothing of yours, though; the other howdah was splintered into kindling under your camel. We burned it along with everything that was too covered in blood to save. We only stay now to bury the dead."

I nodded and, suddenly too weary to think any further, was asleep. I did not wake until I was lifted onto a litter. I heard Anna cry out and turned my head to see her eyes open, but she was staring up at the sky as if through a dark door into Hell.

"Anna, I am here. Take heart." She looked over, but she seemed not to know me.

"Mama, don't leave me!"

I touched her hand, but the men carrying our litters separated into single file, and we were pulled apart for a few moments. "I'm right here, Anna," I called into the gloom.

Someone had brought up a wagon, and we were placed in it side-by-side. The sky had suddenly grown dark but for the stars, and the only helpful light came from torches.

My servant was still staring into space, her eyes glittering in the torchlight. "Anna, we're safe, someone found us. We go to a castle to be healed. It is a miracle."

"Oh, Mama, how I hurt. Make it stop, I beg you!"

"Here is my hand. Hold onto it. I won't leave you."

On the way to the castle, Anna cried out every time the wagon rocked and jolted her. I tried to soothe her, but she did not know me. When we hit an especially rocky part of the road, she screamed and fainted—or so I thought. Soon thereafter I saw lights ahead. I must have drifted to sleep, too, because I awoke as I was lifted and set onto a cot in a dim, cool room with stone walls. I heard other voices nearby, moaning or weeping. Crying out for Anna, I tried to start up again, but gentle hands forced me back down. I opened my eyes to see a square-jawed, tonsured old monk covering me with a thin blanket. The guardian knight was there, too.

The knight said, "Your Anna is right beside you, though we may have to move her soon. Her ankle snapped in two, and the bone has broken through the skin. It needs setting quickly."

"Thank you, thank you," I murmured.

"Here, drink this," said the monk. I took a few sips—wine infused with something herbal tasting—and fell into uneasy slumber. At one point in the night I half woke, thinking I heard screaming, but all around me was darkness and silence. I fell back asleep and remembered no more until sunlight streaming through a window woke me.

My whole body ached, especially my head and belly. Above me was a stone ceiling of curved ribs that flared from thick pillars and met halfway between each in graceful arcs. The mist over my eyes had cleared. I carefully turned my head and saw a few more cots, all of them empty but for two occupied by an old woman and a little girl who were asleep.

"Anna!" In my panic, I half sat up and was sorry for trying.

The square-jawed monk from the night before rushed to my side. "Ah, you wake—good!" He spoke in simple Latin. "Do not sit up. You have good fortune to be alive. A spear butt perhaps nearly cracked your skull, and you are bruised all over." I must have looked shocked, because he added, "Oh, take no alarm. I am dead to fleshly desires. I had to dress your wounds. I am Brother Dominic. I work here in the women's infirmary."

"Where is Anna? The girl who was with me last night?"

"The hakim—lucky for her he is both physician and surgeon—has set her ankle; he says she may walk with a limp when she heals, but she will live...." Yet the monk looked as sorrowful as if she had died.

"Are you hiding something?"

"As you are unwell, I dislike giving you sorry news, but ... Last night, she seemed merely ill: called out over and over for her mother, for someone named Maryam, and for you, Sofia Volodymyrovna." My guardian must have told him my name.... "We almost came for you to be with her in the surgery room while the hakim worked, but she fainted from the pain when he began setting the bones, so you were not needed. And knowing you are hurt, too, we felt it best not to wake you. He decided to leave her where she lay, to let her rest, too. That may have been in error. This morning when she woke, it was as if she did not know we were there. At least we got her to eat and drink a little, like a babe in arms."

"I must go to her!" I tried to sit up, but pain overcame me.

"No, you must rest. They will bring her back here soon. Meanwhile, I will put a fresh poultice on your head and bring you some breakfast."

I tried to endure Brother Dominic's well-meant ministrations with patience, but by the time Anna was carried back to her cot, I was ready to defy my pain and go look for her.

Her eyes were open, her ankle was bound to a neat splint and covered with a clean dressing, and she seemed to feel no pain, but when I spoke her name, she did not answer.

"Please," I asked the monks who had brought her in, "would you push her cot close to mine so I can watch over her?"

They kindly obliged, although when I reached for her hand lying limp at her side, one of them said, "She will not know you."

"Why, has a broken ankle blinded her?"

"No, but demons have stolen her mind from her. She neither hears nor sees."

Tears started to my eyes, and I forced myself to lean over my young companion. "Anna, it is I, Sofia. I won't leave you. But please, don't leave me here alone, either!"

She gave no sign, just stared blankly at the ceiling, while I lay wondering whether it had been a miracle that we were found, whether we had been saved after all.

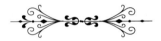

Anna was in that strange stupor for two weeks. My health took a long time to return, too. I was so weary and my head hurt so much that Brother Dominic insisted I drink several doses of his herbal wine daily. I slept much of the time, sometimes wakened by bells sounding the hours of prayer, but when I drifted back to sleep, nightmares haunted me. Several times they relived the attack, but at the point where I plunged the knife into Anna's assailant, I felt its blade pierce my own back. I would startle awake, shivering and yet covered in sweat. And if I turned to Anna, sometimes her eyes would be open, yet if I called her name she never answered. Then I would reach out and take her resistless hand in the empty night.

But one morning Brother Dominic announced that I must go outside. "You are turning into a ghost haunting your Anna's bedside. Besides, Old Agathe claims she cannot do her work with you in her way." Old Agathe, a scrawny hen of a woman, swept the room now and then and called it clean.

Letting me lean on him, the monk slowly guided me through a cool arched passageway to the infirmary's little garden, where I could sit on a stool protected by the shade and watch the few other patients wander or hobble past the trim beds of healing herbs and fragrant flowers. For the next week or so, I spent every morning there, breathing the clean, dry air until the sun's heat and dazzling brightness drove me back inside.

Nor could bright sun chase away the dark thoughts that dimmed each day: the brevity of life and certainty of death, my shocking ability to kill without thinking, Anna's alarming ailment, my empty future. And I thought of the knight, Sir Joscelin of Braissac, whom I had briefly mistaken for Papa. There was little hope that our paths would cross again, for Brother Dominic had explained what a knight was. He would have other duties besides waiting on a pair of stray survivors.

Happily, I was wrong. It was morning, Anna was asleep, and I was sitting in the shady part of the garden with the old woman, called Blanche, and her little granddaughter, whose name I forget. Sir Joscelin came out into the sunshine, no longer clad in armor but in flowing robes that reminded me of paintings of ancient saints. A solemn-faced, dark-bearded Muslim by his side alarmed all but one of my fellow patients, an old knight, into leaving. Old Blanche urged me to come away with her, but I held my ground.

Sir Joscelin had not seen me yet, and again I was struck by how at one angle he looked just like my Papa and at another so unlike him. Something about the way he held himself, too, made my heart turn back to a younger, more innocent time when love between man and woman had seemed possible. Seeing me he approached, limping slightly, and greeted me gravely. Faced with two men in their prime who were not monastic, I suddenly realized that my face was exposed; I felt naked. Thanks to Blanche I at least had a proper veil, which I drew before my face.

"I would like you to meet Adar al-Mas'ūdī, a hakim who sometimes visits here to exchange methods of healing with the brothers in this castle—although they learn more from him than he does from them! He is well-versed in cures for the body, but he also seeks remedies for wounded spirits. That night after the bandit attack, we sent for him to set your Anna's ankle, and he came today to find out how she does. Now he hears that she is still gripped by this strange torpor. If you are willing, he asks to speak with you about her."

With my eyes downcast, I thanked Adar al-Mas'ūdī courteously in Arabic. All I could see of him were his flowing blue robes. They were similar in cut to Sir Joscelin's, though they were of silk instead of wool and would be lined with cotton, and the weave was finer, the dyes softer and more even. I almost laughed at myself, noting things as though I might be a merchant instead of a lost woman.

After a few more polite exchanges, he asked, "Was this young woman ever badly hurt in some way before the bandit attack? Some injury to her spirit, perhaps?"

I had to decide how much or little to say to this stranger. "Yes, about two years ago, evil men—Mongols—murdered her family in front of her. And she was both victim of and witness to other unspeakable acts." I glanced up, fearing even that little of her story might have been too much. Given how shocked Adar al-Mas'ūdī and Sir Joscelin looked, I was glad I had not told them everything. "She never recovered from those first terrible events, and since then she has suffered more shocks ….

"Do you think that is why she is …?"

The hakim stroked his beard. "It seems likely. Sometimes when people cannot bear any more blows from life, they become like empty shells, in some cases forever."

I blanched. "Will she never get better?"

"It is hard to say. She might. I would like to visit her daily if I may be permitted, with you present, of course, and I come to ask your permission."

"Yes, of course you may. She is my servant, although in some ways she is more like my daughter. But who knows what anyone is now? I seem to have lost everything in that raid, and she has lost her mind."

"May I offer my sympathy for your travails?" After a suitable pause, he added, "If we may go to her now?"

I nodded and stood up so suddenly that I nearly fainted. I had to sit down again.

"Oh, of course you are still ill, too. Brother Dominic is in the infirmary. If he is enough warranty for your servant's honor, you need not go with me."

Too dizzy to move, I accepted Adar al-Mas'ūdī's kind offer and watched the two men reenter the infirmary before sitting down and folding my hands in prayer for my poor Anna. The old knight who had also braved the infidel presence, and whom I knew slightly as Sir Foucald, came over to me. "You pray for the girl with the broken mind? We all know about her. I will pray with you."

And he did until, to my surprise, Sir Joscelin came back. Foucald melted, or rather hobbled, away. I was so wary of speaking with a vigorous, fine-looking man that I blushed, or perhaps even then it was more.

There was a subtle heat about him—I could not have said then whether it was of his heart or his loins. He took Foucald's place, saying, "I hope you will forgive my intruding on you, but I thought to speak with you about the raid. We did recover some goods from the caravan, and when you said you lost everything I wondered if any of it might belong to you. There were things like carpets and swords, but also some books and manuscripts and some other things seized from the Bedouins we caught. When you are better, I could escort you to the storeroom where it all rests for now."

Hope lifted my heart and I eagerly raised my eyes to his. "Did you by any chance find a worn deerskin cloak—it would look foreign to your eyes. It was given to me by my father, and it was all I had to remember him by. And chests and bags were packed on our camel. In one were a pearl and ruby collar, a gold neck ring and some other jewelry, and some gold coins."

He shook his head. "No, your cloak was probably burned, and we found no collar or jewelry." My hope sank again. "The papers and books had been rifled through and strewn about, but we collected what was not too bloodied."

I shuddered. "They may be mine. I had an astrolabe, too, and some maps. If I could find a wealthy scholar—oh my, how my mind leaps to silly conclusions."

He smiled for the first time. "And what would those conclusions be?"

Blushing, I said, "Some things were to sell, perhaps in a port city like Seleucia Pieria—I saw it on one of my maps—where ships go to Constantinople, which is where my uncle lives. But now I have no way to leave here, nowhere to go, and no one to whom I could sell my goods—if what you found are even mine. I had my own little book collection that I valued, too. Two of them I had been using to write about my journeys." I sighed. "I have no hope for the valuables, but my cloak and books meant much to me." That cloak was not only a reminder of Papa's love: for so long now, it had offered me hope for a new start. And now, when I could have truly used the gems hidden in it, it was gone.

"Well then, we must find out soon. If your papers are complete enough, I think you could find a buyer for them, but your finery is surely lost to the handful of bandits who outraced us."

"I—I think I could manage going now, if you are free."

He shook his head. "Perhaps I should have waited to speak to you. You must not try walking so far until you feel better. But I can help you back into the infirmary to be with your servant."

I blushed and then with a shock remembered how much Anna hated Muslims! "Oh dear, I really should have forced myself into going with the surgeon. What if she wakens? She—she was raised to think of anyone not Christian as a mortal enemy. She never relented, even though we lived some two years as … guests … of Muslims."

He raised his eyebrows. "You seem to have an unusual past."

"Yes, I suppose I do." I must be more careful of my speech. How would these monk knights view my life? If I were stranded here, the less anyone knew of it, the better.

"Perhaps one of the brothers can lead me to this storeroom later."

He looked a little disappointed, or was that simply what I wanted to see? Already I felt a new, interesting tug of the heart. Certainly I liked Sir Joscelin's answer!

"It is no trouble to me. I have little to occupy myself with at present, and the brothers are often very busy. I will come back another time and take you. Soon."

"Thank you, thank you so much. I am indebted to you twice over!"

Leaning on his arm, I walked along the dark corridor toward the infirmary. Adar al-Mas'ūdī suddenly appeared, so I withdrew my hand to hide my face. I felt even more exposed before this Muslim hakim than I did before the Christian knight.

"I must make my farewells for today," he said. "She may recover. At least when she saw my 'imamah," and he touched his dulband, "she flinched and cried out with terror, which means that she begins to recognize some things. I worried that she thought I was the man who tried to violate her, so I retreated in haste. It means that there will be little I can do for her directly." He shook his head. "But, as the saying goes, 'For every malady Allah has appointed a fitting remedy,' so perhaps this shock was just what she needed. You, lady, may be able to help her if you go to her now. She may recognize you and feel less troubled."

"Yes, of course." I turned to Sir Joscelin. "Thank you for your kind offer. And thank you, Adar al-Mas'ūdī. You both give me new hope. I thought my Anna was lost along with everything else."

They each bowed gravely.

"Let me see you safely to your room before we part," said Sir Joscelin.

When I gratefully took his arm again, Adar al-Mas'ūdī looked shocked. He quickly bade us farewell, turned and strode off.

I looked after him thoughtfully. "Who told him about Anna?"

"He knew something was wrong when he set your servant girl's ankle; and when he came to see how she was doing, I told him everything. I did not want to intrude on you, but I have been asking Brother Dominic about you both. I wanted to help."

I stuttered surprised thanks. He smiled rather sadly. "I have younger sisters."

He left me at the infirmary door. My heart was trying to soar out of my breast, but whether from hope or fear, whether for Anna or myself, I could not say.

Brother Dominic had moved her cot to face the morning sun, and she was sitting up looking utterly desolate. But to my delight, she knew me.

"Mistress, you're here!"

"Indeed I am." We embraced, tears spilling down our cheeks.

Finally we pulled away. "That terrible man came at me again—I remembered the raid—and I was in this strange room and he was holding my ankle and his face was—I screamed and he went away but I thought you were dead—I remember a dream where you and I were together and we nearly died—and, oh, I'm so happy to see you!"

"Anna, that was not the bandit who attacked you; he is the surgeon who set your broken ankle—he was looking at it to make sure it's healing properly. We both owe him a great debt. He saved your ankle and your memory and perhaps your life!"

"But he wore a dulband the same color! I was certain … And he is a Muslim!"

"My dear, you cannot go on thinking someone is your enemy just because he doesn't share your faith. This kind man's name is Adar al-Mas'ūdī, and he wishes to help you. If you'll let him, he'll visit you again to see how your ankle heals. You knew no one, not even me, for many days, and it was all we could do to get you to eat."

"Really? I remember the attack now, and a little bit about you sitting with me in the desert. And then I woke up here."

"Anna, this man might be able to heal you. Will you allow that?"

Anna shook her head doubtfully. "I don't know … perhaps. But please don't leave me again. I'm nothing without you."

"I'm going nowhere. You can rely on me."

I let it go at that. Anna was trembling like a cornered rabbit. I worried that she might retreat back into her terrible torpor if I pressed her beyond her limits. And it was too true: I was going nowhere indeed.

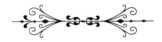

I tended Anna daily. Brother Dominic showed me how to make a poultice of wine and honey to keep the torn skin from rotting; as well, it seemed natural to help him in the infirmary whenever I felt able. He was a kindly old man, perhaps fifty years old, with white tonsured hair, a square chin, and bushy eyebrows. He had joined the Hospitallers out of devotion to Christ the healer, not to fight but to help pilgrims on their way to the Holy City. His family was dead, and this was now his home. If no other duties claimed him—he went to weekly meetings to deal with convent business—he went to every hour of prayer. He put me in mind of my friend Dorje.

Besides Old Agathe the house-keep, the only other women there were Blanche and her little granddaughter. Their family had been traveling to Jerusalem on pilgrimage when illness carried away her husband and daughter. Her son-in-law was recovering in the men's ward. I helped bathe and feed the child, who could not have been more than two years old and did not understand that her mother was not coming back. Whenever she cried for her, it reminded me so much of losing my own mother that tears would spring to my eyes. I knew that that would not help her, and then more tears would come: of frustration. There was so much suffering in the world and so little I could do about it!

Five days after Anna came back to me, the diminished family of three left, praising God on the one hand and lamenting their losses on the other. Blanche gave me a parting gift, too, of a garment her daughter had never worn—her other things had been burned in case they carried the illness. And she left one of her worn gowns for Anna, too, so we both had more than one garment again and could put off our bloodstained clothes. I was sorry to see Blanche and the little girl go. They had given my life a sense of purpose and helped fend off the panic and despair that continually hovered around my heart.

I know that five days had passed because I was counting them. Sir Joscelin had not returned, and I wondered if he had forgotten his promise or simply had more important things to do.

Anna was slowly reclaiming her wits, although she often fell into moods of terrible sadness beyond tears. I could do nothing about them, since I felt just the same, but they made me wearier than ever, and sometimes it took all my will to be patient with her. At least with the aid of some crutches—Brother Dominic's gift—she could join me in the garden in the cool of the morning. Adar al-Mas'ūdī had not returned, either, perhaps not wanting to frighten her again.

And then one morning when I was picking herbs for Brother Dominic in the garden while Anna sat nearby, Sir Joscelin reappeared, this time alone. Once again I was taken unawares and thought I was looking at Papa. But then I saw the larger frame, the slight limp, the gray-green eyes with their keen gaze. I know it was keen because it fell on me and, like a spark from flint, set my cheeks aflame. I quickly lowered *my* gaze.

He strode up to me and bowed. After a few courteous exchanges and my making him and Anna known to one other, he said, "My lady, I am sorry not to have returned sooner. I was kept away by those self-same bandits who attacked your caravan. We were searching for them and found them just in time to stop another attack. Their leader was slain, and the rest of them fled into the desert. Then I helped escort the caravan to Antioch. I returned last night."

He paused and added hesitantly, almost shyly, "If you desire, I could escort you to the store room now."

Desire? Sir Joscelin's speech was entirely friendly and correct, but I trusted no man after Kerim—or did I mistrust myself? I bowed my head, and an awkward silence followed.

"Only if you wish," he finally said.

"Oh, yes. Please. I think I am well enough." I stood up carefully, avoiding the hand he offered me. Was it shyness or fear of a comely man?

"Anna, Sir Joscelin is taking me to look at the spoils he and his men recovered from the bandits; perhaps some of my things were saved. Will you come with us?"

She shuddered when I said 'bandits'. "Are there stairs?"

I translated her question, and he nodded solemnly. "It would be hard for her."

I sighed. I could not leave Anna, nor was I ready to be alone with a stranger, even a kind one. "I fear it must wait until she can join us."

"Well, then, I must come every few days and see how she does. And then I can report to Adar al-Mas'ūdī, since he is interested in her condition."

After the knight departed, Anna said, "Why did he leave without taking you?"

"For your sake, he says he'll wait on the storeroom until you're well enough to come, too. And I don't know who he is, only that he fights bandits and escorts caravans."

Anna sat silent for several moments. Finally, she spoke in a quavering voice, "Mistress, I want no reminders of that day. I don't want to come with you, even after I'm well. Next time the knight comes, I must stay behind. I know you want to find your things."

"Are you certain? I can wait. It would be more seemly if you came with us, too."

"No, someone else must go with you, and I must learn to trust being alone more.

"I … I've been thinking a lot lately about all the bad things that happened to me. There was always one good thing: you. You always took care of me. Not only the other day, but when we were escaping and when I was ill, and even in Selim's family. You could have turned your back on me, but you never did." Tears welled up in her eyes. "And I did turn my back on someone, so I know how much it means that you never did."

I took her hands in mine. "You can write to her, you know. And in a sense, you saved her life. Maryam would be dead right now if she had been in that caravan."

Anna wiped her tears. "Perhaps. Anyway, you must go look for your things. And that knight—I don't think he'll do you any harm, especially here in a monastery."

I had to laugh. I suddenly felt happy that I could go with "that knight" alone.

So when he did return in a few days, just as he had promised, I was ready to leave her alone in the garden where we had been sitting with old

Sir Foucald. After suitable greetings and talk about small things like how the heat was abating now that autumn was here, I stood, defying the dizziness that would still strike. "I won't be long, Anna."

We had almost left the garden when she cried out, "Mistress, please don't go. I—I'm not brave enough yet." And I had to turn back.

I was afraid Sir Joscelin would be angry, but he simply said, "Another time, then." And with a polite bow he was gone. I stifled a sigh.

Anna looked at me closely. "You like this knight, I think."

"Yes, he helped save our lives. He's valiant and kind."

She shrugged and might have said more, but grandfatherly Sir Foucald demanded that I tell him why I hadn't left with Sir Joscelin. I had learned that the old man was a monk-knight who had taken vows many years earlier and now lived here on a small pension. From him I had also learned a little about these Hospitallers and their mission, and how they and it were slowly losing ground. This castle, called Sa'amar, was one of their last northern outposts. Mostly they lived farther south and spent as much time fighting battles as healing or shielding or sheltering pilgrims, which had been their original aim.

But Sir Foucald still wanted to shield someone: Anna. He was even learning Hungarian from her. After I explained why I hadn't left, he nodded and turned back to her. He always made her smile with his quaint mimes when the right words did not come, and today while they chattered on, I was able to sit quietly with my new, interesting feelings.

But as the heat climbed and Anna and I made ready to leave the garden, he spoke to me. "I am glad that Sir Joscelin watches over you. He is a good man, and brave. He was nearly killed in battle last year, and he lost his younger brother there."

"Oh my!"

"It was at the great Battle of La Forbie, as they now call it: October 17, 1244, a date that will call up dark memories for as long as history lasts. First we lost Jerusalem to barbarian tribes called Kwarizmians, thanks to the perfidy of the Egyptian Sultan, who broke his treaty with us and sent them to do his dirt for him. They killed everyone and razed the Holy City! And then when we tried to recover the city, we lost that dreadful battle. For two days we fought the Egyptian host and their mercenary Kwarizmians, but our Heavenly Father decided to punish our sins. Over five thousand brave souls died, including most of the Hospitallers, the

Teutonic Knights, and the Templars—oh, they are other military orders. Most of our Muslim allies were killed, too, though others fled: cowardly Turcopoles and Syrians and Bedouins with no honor." He shook his head. "The flower of Christian chivalry, cut to pieces for relying on barbarians.

"I was not there, of course—too old to fight but no home to return to, which is why I live here—but those of the defeated and wounded who were not made prisoner slowly found their way north. Some went on to Antioch to return home, but others with nowhere else to go were simply looking for shelter. Sir Joscelin was among them. His squire Hugh had tied his litter to the back of his one remaining horse and led it here, where Sir Joscelin's brother had taken Holy Orders with us Hospitallers. Joscelin was wounded in many places. It was a miracle that he lived—not that he thinks so. He blames himself for his brother's death, as though that had not always been in God's hands.

"At any rate, he was fortunate that that Saracen hakim is such a good man and was willing to treat his wounds. Do I surprise you by saying that an infidel can be a good man? Well, there is nothing like old age and loss to cool your head. Some of our Muslim neighbors are our allies, and they have proven to be worthy friends."

"And now that Sir Joscelin is recovered, why does he stay on?"

"I have no idea—could be he has no home."

"What are you saying?" Anna asked, so I repeated Sir Foucald's tale to her.

"Well then, he is a good man, yes?" I nodded, suddenly wearied by my own feelings of age and loss as time swept me on and away from my goals. Good god, how I had lost track of time. If it was now 1245 and late autumn, then I must be eighteen years old!

More days passed. When not with Anna or resting from my almost endless headache, I helped Brother Dominic in the herb room next to the women's infirmary, hanging herbs to dry or crushing various substances to use for liniments and so forth. It kept me out of Agathe's way, too, not that she cleaned the rooms well enough to matter if anyone was there. But she was so relentlessly unpleasant that both Anna and I wanted to get away from her. Whenever I was able, I day-dreamt that my knight might visit soon.

When he did arrive one morning, carrying an ornate box, Anna and I were sitting outside with Sir Foucald. She was telling him how much her ankle still hurt, and he was making much kinder replies than I had been able to muster for some time.

After courtly greetings, my knight said, "I brought a chess set. Do you know the game?"

"Oh, yes, how lovely," I cried.

"So you already play it. I have time today … and sometimes many days in a row … when I can play it with you … if you wish."

"I do wish. I enjoy chess very much."

"Good, since my friend Adar al-Mas'ūdī is not always free to play it with me."

"He is your friend, then?"

The knight paused. "Yes, as much as Muslim and Christian can be friends in this place of deceptive courtesies. If war broke out again…." He shrugged. "I sometimes visit the castle where he lives. It lies not far from here." He pointed in the general direction of some hills on the other side of the valley.

"If you would like, we can move over to the other bench and play there."

So, while Anna and Sir Foucald sat together and his jests made her forget to complain, my knight and I played a game of chess, although I found it hard to think clearly and he defeated me soundly! At the end he said, "If you wish it, I can come tomorrow." I nodded, unable to look at him but equally unable to hide my smile. I felt more than saw him smile in return.

"I thought you might enjoy a little amusement during Anna's long days of recovery, for long they may be. I spoke about you both with Adar al-Mas'ūdī, and he commends your devotion. He says she needs someone to trust—he has seen love work miracles in the past."

And he bade my goodbye, leaving me pondering his words.

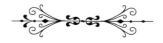

ir Joscelin visited several times over the next few days, always raising the question of the storeroom, but Anna clearly did not want to be left behind. Though I was learning more about him—that he had an older brother and three younger sisters, for instance—it was hard to be patient. The days were getting shorter, I was penniless and dependent on charity, and I wanted to learn whether I had anything left to call my own. A slow panic was worming its way into my chest: I might be just as trapped in castle Sa'amar as I had been at Alamut.

It was Sir Foucald who freed me to visit the storeroom at last. He spoke with me one cool day after Sir Joscelin had left. "I have learned enough Hungarian to understand Anna a little better. Ah, how she reminds me of my own daughter, dead from plague these many years." He sat in silence for several heartbeats, his watery eyes looking into a distant past.

"Well, that is not what I meant to tell you. I see how your mind falls into heaviness when Sir Joscelin leaves, and Anna told me why. I think I can persuade her that she will be safe with me while you go see if any of your goods were spared. What do you think?"

Suddenly, my eyes felt watery, too. "You are so kind. Yes, please."

And when Sir Joscelin next arrived and heard my good news, he said, "Well, I hope our chess games will not come to an end." He smiled, and I thought I glimpsed special warmth in his eyes.

"Oh. Oh, no, of course not." I felt my cheeks grow hot.

So at last Sir Joscelin escorted me toward the corridor into the castle. This time when we reached it and I looked back, ready to be disappointed, Anna and her elderly knight happily waved me on. So I followed my own knight down the corridor past the infirmary and out into a little courtyard. Sir Foucald had not spoken falsely when he called castle Sa'amar a small outpost; it was not only small but thinly manned. Only two sentries patrolled the battlements, far fewer than in Alamut, which was much less exposed to attack. We wound our way up a short flight of stairs and through another, larger castle yard with a double door in one wall that must lead to the world outside.

We passed only a few people: menials, knight-monks, ordinary monks, and one or two soberly dressed women who might have been servants or even nuns. A pair of young men was practicing with wooden swords in one corner of the yard. Like all the monks, they wore dark gray, and their tunics were marked with square white split-ended crosses. Instead of helmets, tight-fitting white caps, stained by sweat, were strapped under their chins. We passed a few other monk knights, but I only knew their occupation by the chain mail under their gowns, the bulge of a sword on one side, and the occasional helmet or shield borne by a squire.

I looked at Sir Joscelin's attire to see if he too was a Hospitaller, but though his cloak bore a small white cross, it was unlike theirs. And his neatly trimmed beard set him apart, too; these Hospitallers were clean shaven. So perhaps he was not a monk—at least I hoped not.

Leaving the courtyard and passing down another stairway and along a dark hallway, he stopped before a door and took out a large key. "I drove the steward wild borrowing this every time I came to visit you," he smiled as he opened the door. "Now I can justify myself to him!"

"Oh dear, I am sorry for causing so much trouble."

"No trouble at all. In fact—"

But he stopped speaking and simply waved me into the dark, chill room. Casks of wine and jars of oil were set in neat rows, while mysterious shapes hung from the ceiling, almost touching closed chests or bulging sacks. At the far end, the remains of the caravan's goods lay on the floor in a sad heap, like the corpses of their former owners.

"Please," he said, waving me forward, "if you can use anything here, you should take it. The rest will be sent to Alexandretta soon, to be sold for the benefit of the Order." While he lit a small torch and put it into a wall sconce for me, I fell to my knees and silently sorted through the mess. Much of it—clothing or torn packs—was marred by dried blood; if this was what had been deemed worthy of saving, how utterly spoiled everything else must have been! I did find one of my maps and a few scrolls and books, including, to my great happiness, my first journal! Alas, the second one was not there, so both of Batu Khan's gift books were now gone from my life. And the astrolabe was there, but who would want it in a monastery? Perhaps I could give it to the hakim in thanks for his saving Anna's life.

But, though I searched through every pathetic remnant of other peoples' lives, Papa's cloak was missing, probably burned or stolen. My last embers of hope died.

Tears filled my eyes, and I had to sit for several heartbeats before I could bring myself to speak. "These things are mine, although most are of little use now. A few books and a map. I want nothing that belonged to others.

The Order should have them."

Sir Joscelin said nothing, but when I stood up, still shaky, I felt the kindness in his hands as he helped me steady myself. I blushed and drew back, clutching my journal.

"Nonetheless, I will have my squire bring your books and scrolls to you rather than you carrying them. It is too early to despair. I know that learned men might be glad to buy them from you—yes, even damaged by a little blood. Learning is valued by some."

I heard an edge to his voice, but he said no more.

We were silent on the way back, but when we reached the infirmary, he said, "I will look into selling your books and map. Adar al-Mas'ūdī may know someone."

"Thank you. Also, if you would do me another kindness: I wish to offer him this astrolabe. I have no other gift of thanks. Would you give it to him when you next meet?"

"Gladly. Until then, when I hope to bring you heartening news." He smiled, silently guided me back to the women's infirmary, bowed, and left.

I found Anna inside, sitting on her cot looking through the things that had been saved for her from her litter and that had sat, bound together in a bundle by one of our rescuers, untouched all this time. She was holding a small lidded box that Mother Layla had given her as a parting gift.

"Did you find anything?" she asked eagerly.

"Only a few of the books from Nasr al-Din; and my first journal was there but not the one Batu Khan gave me. Ironic, is it not, that I tore up one of his books to set our ger on fire, and now the other was probably also lost to fire. At least Sir Joscelin may be able to sell the remaining books for a little money …." With a sigh I sat down on my cot.

"And your jewelry?" I shook my head. "Your father's cloak: was it there?"

I looked at her in surprise. "How did you know it mattered to me?"

"Well, you've carried the dirty old thing everywhere with you yet you never wore it. And you often said it was all you had left to remember him by … and it held secrets that would have helped you now."

"How did you know that?"

"The last night in Alamut, I woke up and saw you ripping out one of its seams. And then later you had jewels to give away. I could guess where they came from."

Had Anna always been so sharp-eyed? "You're right. I counted on my Papa's cloak to bring me safely to Constantinople, and now I feel so bereft. I miss it more than the jewelry Argamon gave me or even my Mama's collar. It would have taken me—us—home to Constantinople."

She sighed and closed the box. "I am sorry ...."

"Mistress, would you help me write a letter to Maryam? Perhaps your knight could find a way to send it."

I nodded, glad for a task to fend off more despair.

Sir Joscelin came again the very next day, his cheery-faced squire behind him. The young man was carrying my papers, which seemed on the verge of spilling from his hands and flying in all directions.

"You look desolated. Perhaps my good news will lift your spirits."

"Yes, I am a little sad. But you say you have good news?"

"Well, as it happens, Adar al-Mas'ūdī himself is interested in your map and your manuscripts, if there are not too many missing pages. He may want to purchase them all, anyway, as his love of learning is so strong. A most unusual man—a man of great heart. Oh, and he sends many thanks for the astrolabe.

"I will not stay today. You will want to sort through your papers now."

I almost told him that sorting could wait if he would keep me company, but the words came up against a barrier of fear. So I said nothing beyond a few words of thanks, and after a few awkward moments he left me with the remains of my library.

Over the next few days, I spent my free time wishing Sir Joscelin would visit again and trying to put the papers back in order and sorting through the books. Some were worth saving, but much was spoiled: pages torn or too bloody to be readable.

While he was gone, I also had time to think. My feelings frightened me. Too often men had mistaken mere friendliness for lust, and now I had no idea how to behave toward a man who did attract me.

Finally, late one afternoon Sir Joscelin returned. "Have you had time to sort through everything? I missed our chess games; you make it so easy to win."

I blushed and laughed. "I missed them, too, and once I fully recover my wits, it will not be so easy for you anymore. But I finished sorting my papers and even found one complete manuscript. And if I can find paper or parchment, I can copy stained pages that are readable, which will complete another book. If you wish, you can take the complete one to ... the hakim." I had almost said "your friend."

He took the manuscript and then stood looking a little foolish, as if he did not know what to do next. So I invited him to stay for a chess game, and he gladly accepted. Thus I was able to spend a happy hour stealing glances at him while he pondered his next move on the board. If only I knew how to ponder moves. With no skill in the game of love, I was afraid of a misstep that might checkmate me. I did not think he was aware of my secret gaze, and shortly after the game was over—he won again—he departed, saying nothing about returning.

Another few days passed. I tried not to think of Sir Joscelin, the longing was so intense. Then one morning, I had just finished changing the wrappings on Anna's ankle when he appeared at the door of the infirmary. She saw him first and said, "There's your guardian."

I turned and caught a most unguarded look on his face. He looked more like a boy in that moment than a battle-hardened warrior. "Mistress, you should go to him," Anna whispered in a voice loud enough, I was sure, for him to hear. Luckily, he did not speak Hungarian.

Cheeks aflame, I did go to him. After a few courteous exchanges, Sir Joscelin handed me a pouch, saying, "Adar al-Mas'ūdī wishes to buy your manuscript, for which he sends this."

Thanking him gravely, I opened it and five gold coins, none alike, spilled into my hand. "Oh," I gasped, "this is far too generous!"

I tried to hand them back, but he held up his hands in refusal. "He tells me that considering how far it traveled, and with such travail on your part, and that it was written by a very famous scientist, he thinks the price exceedingly fair."

I was startled into looking up at him. "He knows of Nasr al-Din al-Tusi?"

"Yes, of course, but I am surprised that you do." His question hung in the air.

"I...."

Anna called from her cot, "Mistress, what are those for?"

"For one of my manuscripts."

"Are you not taking them? Why?"

"It's too much, Anna."

"Well, if he doesn't think so, why should you?"

I laughed. "It's the hakim's money, not his."

She looked surprised. "Well then, why not take it? Let this hakim help us out even more. Once I get better, we can use it to go to your big city and be free from all these bandits and infidels. At least we're in a Christian world again."

I frowned. "Adar al-Mas'ūdī saved your life, Anna. You could show some gratitude."

I turned back to Sir Joscelin. "My servant wants me to keep the coins. She seems to be gaining a little spirit now that she is in Christian lands again."

"They are not Christian," he said grimly. "It would be a grave error to think so. We had a mission at the beginning, I suppose, but the men who seized these lands and turned them into counties and principalities for themselves never truly possessed them, no matter how they tried to delude themselves—many still do! People have fought over this desolate desert since the Creation, and now we Franks add to its misery."

"You feel strongly about this," I said.

"And I know whereof I speak! I have read all the histories and listened to the arguments. Our forebears rushed to war understanding nothing but how to strike random blows, and not all of them for God! Too many thought they would find fabulous riches here, and that drew them into cruel excess. Now we have lost Jerusalem, and the rest will fall soon unless a new expedition to reclaim the Holy City changes everything."

"So you are not one of them, then?"

"Oh, I have fought battles, if unwillingly, but I came to this convent as a final penance for my sins, and I stay for the same reason. I doubt I will ever return home. But at least I will die with a clean heart, having done everything that God and my conscience have asked of me."

Anna, now struggling up with her crutches, cried, "Why is he angry at you?"

"Not at me; he just spoke about the folly of the Christian efforts here. He says these aren't Christian lands. And you must lie back down, Anna."

"Well, we're in a Christian castle at least. And when my ankle heals, we can go to your uncle, who does live in a Christian land, and we'll both be happy! I do wish it would stop hurting so. You should go outside with him and I will rest."

I conveyed her orders to my knight, who shook off his grim mood and led me to the garden. We began a game of chess, but he seemed distracted, as was I. Never leave here? Would he perhaps leave for my sake? If so, how was I to rework my past to make it acceptable to a man I scarcely knew but wanted to know in every possible way?

WINTER INTO SPRING
ANNO DOMINI 1245-1246

The next few weeks seemed to stand stand still. Only the cooler weather and an occasional thunderstorm gave any sign that time was in actuality rushing on toward Advent and Christmas. Though I did not feel right about praying in a Catholic church, I helped Brother Dominic tie dried herbs into bunches to decorate the chapel. He had offered to take me there to pray, but I always claimed that Anna needed me. Once I did follow him part of the way, but alas, the monk crossed paths with the Master of the convent, a battle-scarred, gray-haired warrior-monk, and they stopped to talk. The Master spoke as though I was not even there until he glanced over and frowned at me. His harsh demeanor frightened me into retreating to the safety of the infirmary. Still, I did feel the need to pray, and sometimes my knight came upon me there, sitting in prayer or trying to practice peace.

Sir Joscelin was often away leading pilgrims to Antioch, but he unfailingly looked in on Anna and me on his return, her health being his excuse. Happily, he usually stayed play chess with me. One day when Anna was sitting with Sir Foucald and I had already lost our game, Sir Joscelin asked if I would like to visit the chapel to pray. "I noticed that you only pray here and never attend Mass—because of Anna?"

I nodded. "And because I am unsure of my welcome. I am a stranger and a woman. But I would like to go."

We made our way to the chapel in silence. Following him, I had time to admire his broad back and how the gold streaks in his hair looked like waving stripes of sun. His limp seemed almost gone, too. I wondered what his legs were like, and from there my mind leapt to an image: mine entwined around his. A hidden coal of lust, which had been smoldering deep in me all along, burst into flame and almost consumed me. I might find myself alone with my knight in the chapel; he might turn, sweep me into a deep embrace, kiss me here and here and here, and take me! I had to stop and shake my head to banish my unholy thoughts. How ashamed they made me feel! I must seek out a time to go to confession ... if I would even be allowed.

The chapel was empty and a little dusty, though the bunches of sweet holiday herbs smelled wonderful. Its quiet, its bright stained glass windows, and its crude but lovingly decorated surfaces should have been a balm to my spirit. Saints were painted on the walls, which curved up into the vaulted ceiling, and a wine-colored velvet cloth and golden candlesticks adorned the altar. But I was still burning with both lust and shame.

And when I bowed to the shrine and crossed myself after finishing my prayer for forgiveness, Sir Joscelin looked taken aback. "You are Greek Orthodox, then?"

"No, Rus'."

Before he was able to hide it, I saw discomfort on his face. "I did not realize."

"Thank you for bringing me. I will come here often now that I know the way. And I would like to attend Mass here if I am allowed. And confession."

"I will ask." The way he spoke: did he hold my religion against me? My lust sparked out, leaving me only with shame.

After Sir Joscelin had led me back to the infirmary and departed, still courteous but distant, I sat down and sighed. My life had shrunk into such a tiny space. Once I had thought that having escaped the Mongols, I would see it blossom with possibility. So much for that! I was shriveling from my constant need to guard against a slip of the tongue—or the body—that would betray me. Now I had probably snuffed any hope of friendship, much less courtship, with Sir Joscelin. And simply by crossing myself differently from a Catholic!

Even though he returned the next day with the news that I was permitted to attend Mass and even the hours of prayer if I stayed in the back of the chapel, I felt like a trespasser the first time I went there and had to choose how to cross myself. And not only the Mass but all the psalms and so forth for the hours of prayer were different from what I remembered. Not that I had paid close attention when I was a child. It was like having to learn religion all over again. And I missed confession, though I was afraid to expose my sins to the dour old priest who presided over the Mass. I did celebrate the Christmas Masses, standing at the back as ordered; and despite the odd looks I received from some, probably for crossing myself in the old way, I even felt comforted by these ways of worship that seemed odd to me.

At least my knight did not stop visiting, so either he truly loved chess or he was using it as an excuse to be with me despite our differing faiths. Neither of us spoke much while we played. I was so afraid of saying something that might compromise me that it was like walking on that rocky bridge into Alamut: a slip and I might fall!

How I wanted to belong somewhere, how helpless I felt: dependent on strangers, waiting endlessly for Anna to heal, betrayed by my own body. I knew so little about this new world or my hosts beyond small hints I had snatched from their speech. They didn't even celebrate the new year after Christmas!

Anna, on the other hand, seemed more and more transformed by her near-death. Although she often complained about her ankle, she had also become more reflective about her life. For instance, her letter to Maryam had been filled with loving apology. I had asked Sir Joscelin to find a way to send it. I think he was surprised, and not especially pleased to see her writing to a Jew, but he said nothing. I believe he used Adar al-Mas'ūdī as a go-between, and after that, Anna even admitted that the hakim must be a good man. I wished he would return and treat her again. She was taking forever to heal.

Several high born women arrived, heading home to a city called Pisa, which seemed to be a world unto itself, in a faraway land called Italia. They minced about and put on airs and were more demanding than sick people! So Brother Dominic gave Anna's care entirely over to me and virtually hid from them in the chapel. Her ankle seemed to be getting worse, but I kept doing what I had been shown to do.

Thank God, Sir Joscelin finally took the women off to Antioch. I was changing Anna's dressings when Brother Dominic returned, rubbing his hands and smiling with relief. He leaned over to examine her ankle and sniffed at it as he usually did.

"Good God, what is this? It smells like rotten meat. And look here, a red streak up the leg under her skin." He gently squeezed the wound, which was bright red, and a thick yellow liquid oozed out. Anna winced and tried to pull away. "Pus is a bad sign."

"Oh no, I knew something was wrong, but I know so little about healing!"

"No, it is my fault for running away from prideful women. The question is what to do now. My remedies are too weak for such an infection. I will have to call Adar al-Mas'ūdī. Will your servant let him see her?"

I quickly explained everything to Anna, who still had only the slightest understanding of Latin. She was almost rigid with fear by the time I had finished.

"Will I lose my leg? Just let me die; I know it will kill me anyway," she wailed.

"Don't be silly. But you need help now! We must call for the hakim."

She began to cry. "I'm so afraid!"

"Don't be like this!" But her only response was to sob even louder. I sat there feeling more and more helpless and angry. "Well, then, I am deciding for you. We're calling him in, and if you're afraid, just cover your face while he examines you!"

Brother Dominic wasted no time sending a message to Adar al-Mas'ūdī's castle. By the afternoon, the hakim was at Anna's bedside. She did indeed cover her face, although after he had finished examining her ankle and had moved away with Brother Dominic to discuss her condition, she peeked out and called to me.

"What are they saying? Will they cut off my leg? Don't let them do it—I lost a brother that way—he broke his leg falling off a woodpile and when it didn't heal they cut it off. He was eaten up by pain and fever and then he died screaming!"

"There's been no talk of cutting off anything. You must calm yourself."

Adar al-Mas'ūdī returned to my side, and with eyes averted, said, "Give her this to drink," and he handed me a cup. "It is a cordial of pomegranate juice mixed with a few healing herbs that I brought to help reduce her fever and regain her strength."

Anna had to sit up to drink the juice, and her covers fell away.

"Paugh! Too bitter," she exclaimed after a sip. The hakim, caught by surprise, I think, looked at her briefly. But then his eyes softened at the sight of Anna's pale, frightened features before he hastily looked away again, his face bright red.

"I need to find a stronger remedy for her ankle than what you use," he said to no one in particular, his attention seemingly on finding and removing some bandages from a pack he had brought with him. "One problem is that you should have been cleaning the wound with hot water and soap every day. I truly will never understand why Christians think dirt is holy!"

Brother Dominic looked offended, but I could see the infirmary through Muslim eyes: the rat droppings, the dust that constantly sifted in from the desert, the patched and seldom-washed blankets. More than Old Agathe could or would ever master.

"From now on I will wash Anna religiously. I only want her to get better!" How I wished I had known that bathing a wound would help it heal. I had been missing baths, but I had never known that cleanliness was more than a luxury.

"I will return tomorrow morning with a special unguent I will prepare tonight. But let the wound breathe in the air for a while, and then use these clean bandages to wrap it after you have washed it." Having offered courteous regrets for his outburst to Brother Dominic, he left.

He returned much earlier in the day than I had expected, examined my friend's ankle, spread his special ointment on her wound, and departed after telling Brother Dominic how to care for her.

As he left, Anna seized my arm. "Please, Mistress, would you thank him for me?"

I did. He blushed and smiled slightly. "I only do my duty to Allah's fellow creatures. Here," he handed me a flask, "Make sure she drinks some of this thrice daily. I sweetened it this time. I will return soon, but I must take a short journey before then."

A few days later, Sir Joscelin arrived, his chess set under his arm and in a jolly mood. "Greetings, my ladies! I just returned from escorting those noblewomen to Antioch. What a pestilence is pride—no wonder it is a deadly sin!" But when he saw our long faces and heard about Anna's infected wound, to my disappointment he stayed only long enough to speak a few words of comfort to us both.

Despite my best efforts—and Brother Dominic's—Anna's ankle grew worse over the next few days. She had been restless and querulous for some time, but now I realized that her behavior was not due to selfishness but to a rising fever. I tried to be more patient, but it was all I could do to get her to lie down. She wanted to be up and wandering around on her crutches, and the monk finally had to hide them from her. At least he allowed Sir Foucald to visit from time to time.

As well, he made me stop tending her and take a walk out in the garden whenever the old knight came to visit. "You need to get better yourself, or you will do no one any good."

When Adar al-Mas'ūdī returned from his journey and saw how poorly Anna was doing, he began coming every day to see to her. That should have made me happy, since Sir Joscelin always led him in. The knight would ask after our patient and then invite me to amble along the garden paths with him, but I could not enjoy his company.

I was pushing myself too hard. Finally, after staying up well into the night bathing Anna's forehead and failing to think of anything encouraging to say, I was so tired and angry, and my head was aching so, that I could scarcely stand when the sun woke me the next morning. Brother Dominic banished me back to my own cot for some much-needed sleep.

So I slept and dreamt of urgent voices calling. I opened my eyes, but no one was there. Where was Anna? The voices were growing louder, more alarmed. Panic gripped me and I leapt up to seek Anna, but every step was an agonizing push against an invisible barrier. The voices seemed to echo from a stone staircase that appeared in front of me, but as I strained up the spiraling stairs, they kept going up and up and up. I would never reach the top. I was panting with dizziness and exhaustion, and then I heard Anna scream.

I sat straight up in bed, shaking with fear and half-trapped in the dream. Anna truly was screaming—and struggling with Brother Dominic and another monk, who were trying to lift her onto a litter. Adar al-Mas'ūdī was hovering near them, almost wringing his hands.

"Don't touch me, you villains! Don't cut my leg! Don't cut my leg off!"

"No," I cried, staggering from my cot, "stop!" Brother Dominic and his assistant released Anna, who fell sobbing back onto her cot. She pulled her blankets over her head, painfully recalling to me the shrouded outline of my mother's corpse.

"What happened?"

"We were only trying to help," said Brother Dominic, his face as flushed as if it had been slapped. "I thought she trusted me, but her fear is so great—" He shrugged helplessly.

Adar al-Mas'ūdī cried, "When I arrived and saw how much worse she is, I knew I must act quickly to save her foot and perhaps her entire leg. I wanted to take her to a clean place where it will be safe to drain the pus and cauterize the wound. I know it will hurt her terribly, so I offered her an infusion of cannabis and opium for the pain! Brother Dominic was trying to explain, but she seemed to think we wanted to poison her and cut her leg off!

"Brother Dominic tried to waken you then, but he could not. We were all getting desperate, so we decided to let you sleep and carry her into the surgery. But the moment the monks tried to lift her, she began screaming. We were too hasty, but all of us were so worried. I must do this soon. Otherwise I will have to remove her foot, and that is dangerous! Please, try to make her understand. All this flailing about surely makes her worse."

The other monk, middle-aged, stooped, and also red-faced, added, "I have other patients. Send for me in the men's ward if you need me." He left, shaking his head.

"See if you can argue some sense into her," Brother Dominic begged me.

I nodded and hurried to Anna's side, the surgeon right behind me, but fear made my steps feel as slow and hard to take as in my nightmare. At least she had quieted down, and when I spoke to her she pulled her blanket off her face. Her eyes were bright with tears, her lips swollen from crying. She looked so forlorn and yet, oddly, so beautiful, with her hair tousled around her face like a dark halo. I rapidly explained all to her, ending with, "They were not trying to harm you. The hakim and the monks thought only of your well-being."

"But burning me isn't any better," she cried.

"Anna, if you don't let them try, you will either lose your foot or die or both!"

Anna sulked for far too long before saying, "I want you to go with me."

"Of course I will, but you must first take his pain-killing syrup. I promise it will only help you. If Maryam were here, she would say the same—yes, despite her warnings about opium. You are only taking it this one time, not every day." Anna looked unbelieving, but she nodded and took the cup from Adar al-Mas'ūdī's hands.

"We must wait until she grows drowsy, and then we can move her."

Anna was finishing the cup—sweetened, to her happy surprise—when Sir Joscelin appeared at the door. "How can I help?" He strode in, looking most worried.

"You can help Brother Dominic move her once she is ready." The hakim retreated to the door, and both waited outside. I wished I could join them, just to be near my knight, but Anna needed me.

At last the medicine took effect and Anna drifted into sleep, clinging to my hands. Sir Joscelin and Brother Dominic were able to carry her to the surgery, which stood between the men's and women's infirmaries. They laid her on a table that Adar al-Mas'ūdī had hastily covered with a clean cloth. A brazier stood by it, coals alight and an ugly flat iron tool heating in their midst. Though Anna was asleep, I held her hand while the surgeon examined the infected skin. She cried out once in her sleep, which drew his eyes to her face. He looked away, blushing.

"Now, my friend," he said to Sir Joscelin, "once I begin, you must hold her shoulders down so that her mistress can soothe her in case she wakes. And then Brother Dominic can hold her legs while I apply the hot iron. But first I must drain the wound."

Alas, as soon as Adar al-Mas'ūdī pierced Anna's flesh with his knife and I saw the blood and pus spurt out, the world went gray. I heard a faint moan before a roaring sound filled my ears. When my sight cleared, Sir Joscelin's arms were around me and Adar al-Mas'ūdī was saying, "You must take the lady away. Brother Dominic, please call the other monk to assist me."

"No, I must stay with her," I protested feebly, but Sir Joscelin firmly led me away like a child, his arm around my waist.

As we left, the hakim called, "Be of good comfort, Lady. You can pray for little Anna. I am certain that Allah the All Merciful will hear your prayers."

"I will stay with you," Sir Joscelin said as he pulled my thin blanket over me. Without thought, I reached for his hand and kissed it.

"Thank you," I whispered. We began to pray.

I must have fallen asleep, though, because it was dark and torches were burning when I opened my eyes. Sir Joscelin was helping Brother Dominic lay Anna back on her cot, while the hakim hovered anxiously behind them. Her ankle was splinted and bandaged neatly, and she seemed to be sleeping peacefully.

When he saw that I was awake, Adar al-Mas'ūdī knelt near my cot, although his gaze was still upon Anna's ankle. "I would like to make a request, lady," he said in a low voice. "I know it is unusual, but in order for me to watch over Anna properly, I must beg your permission to take her back to my home where my mother and sister and I can care for her. There is no Islamic hospital near here, or I would suggest taking her there where it is clean and many kind hands would be at hand to help her heal."

He must have sensed my unhappiness, because he added, "Please understand. She will be more likely to heal fully this way. You have done your best, but you are not trained to recognize signs of progress or decline. My mother and sister and I know what to look for. I know how much you love her, and I wish to help her recover, both in body and in spirit.

"If you want, my friend here," he nodded toward Sir Joscelin, "can bring you to the castle often to visit her. Indeed, you might wish to stay with us, too, if you grant my petition."

"But why would you take so much trouble over a strange infidel girl?"

He blushed. "I suppose you could say that her plight interests me. Not many people recover their wits so readily … and besides, I hate to see an innocent girl suffering so … and my mother is Christian, so I can scarcely disapprove of infidels."

What could I say to that? Dismaying his request might be, but Adar al-Mas'ūdī was right. I knew so little about how to care for Anna, and I did love her; and if I wanted her to get well, she would be better off with him than with me. Indeed since his mother was Christian, Anna would not be alone with people she feared and hated. I sighed, certain that she would not like it.

"If you think it best. When do you want to move her?"

"Tomorrow morning right after prayers, I will come with a proper litter and several men to help carry her smoothly."

Sir Joscelin spoke up. "My squire and I will gladly escort you, Sofia Volodymyrovna."

When Anna awoke late that evening, bedeviled by pain, I purposely waited until her medicines had gotten her drowsy before explaining to her what I had done.

She scarcely resisted. "He is saving my leg, isn't he?" She paused, looking somewhat shamefaced, and then burst out, "Mistress, I had the strangest dream today. You were carrying me across a nasty stinking marshland. I was so afraid that I screamed, and you nearly sank trying to save me. And then I awoke, and there you were, right next to me. I see it now: I have been so ungrateful to you … and to everyone. I must be braver and stop troubling you so much."

Now I felt ashamed. I took her hand. "You're never trouble to me, Anna," I lied.

She smiled wanly. "But you will visit me often, won't you?"

"Of course. If you want me to, I will stay there with you."

She smiled dreamily. "Oh, no need, you must stay here near your knight. Though you should visit me often, and he can bring you. Would you not like that? And perhaps Sir Foucald can visit me, too, sometimes."

Suspecting that she would be in haram again, I doubted that Sir Foucald could visit, but I was too happy that she was being agreeable to spoil her hopes.

The next day dawned clear and bright, with a nip in the air. Adar al-Mas'ūdī appeared in the infirmary early, Sir Joscelin and his squire with him. The hakim first gave Anna a medicinal drink, "To ease any pain to while she travels, and sweetened with honey just as she likes."

She obediently drank the syrup. Brother Dominic and several fellow monks carried her outside on her cot and placed her into the surgeon's curtained litter while I trotted along beside her, holding her hand. The bright sunlight in the yard almost blinded me, and I had to stop for a moment and pull my veil further over my head to shade my eyes. I was dimly aware of people stopping to stare at us. Foucald appeared with a pitiful handful of greens, one wilting flower half-buried in them, and offered them to Anna. He looked so forlorn. And then the litter carriers were walking out of the gates with her. No one had even spoken to me. I stood stupidly, holding her belongings in a bundle and wondering what I would do without her.

Sir Joscelin broke into my daze, saying, "Here are our horses. You can give Anna's things to my squire Hugh. Let me help you mount."

"Why are you so kind to me?" I asked as he almost lifted me onto a little roan mare.

He smiled. "You make it easy, my lady. You are a lovely blossom in this harsh desert world."

He had never spoken to me so boldly before, and I surely turned redder than a beet. Hopefully my veil hid it. Not knowing how to answer, I simply bowed my head as he led me out the gate.

Outside the castle walls, we followed Adar al-Mas'ūdī down the rocky path. He rode right beside Anna's litter among a little caravan of guards. The way he leaned toward it, as though he would see right through its hangings if he could, suddenly opened a curtain into my understanding. I found myself smiling a little. If an apt moment arose, I would ask Sir Joscelin if he had noticed the same thing.

My horse stumbled slightly on the rocky path, startling me into my surroundings.

Suddenly the immense vista of road, fields, desert land, pale hills grayed by distance, and vivid sky rushed forward as though attacking me. They did nearly fell me with fear—outside again, with no protective walls around me, no true veil between me and the world, and so dwarfed by its hugeness and daunted by its fickleness that I was unsure whether I was in a body or was simply a mote of awareness floating in empty space.

I tried to reason with myself. This was mere silly panic. Where was the Sofia who had bravely fled the Mongols, who had put her trust in a God beyond thought? Was I not still alive? Had I not been saved from the wilderness? I must not give in to such childish fears! Nonetheless, I so wanted to flee back inside Sa'amar castle's protection that I turned in my saddle and stared back at it longingly. I had never seen it from the outside. How small it was, almost like an outcrop of its stony hill. Its crenellations framed by that brilliant canopy of sky, a tower at each corner, some arrow slits, and a thick double door that was already being closed behind us were all that spoke of human design. And where were my little garden and infirmary? Perhaps downhill at the back? Certainly out of reach.

I turned and forced myself to look forward again. The pathway twisted down past rocky outcrops and clumps of gray grasses, while below us lay a wide valley, surprisingly fertile where it was irrigated, and patch-worked with fields either lying fallow or dotted with laborers busy with their harvesting—or was it planting? I knew nothing of the seasons in this strange world. A bend in the path brought groves of palm trees into view, and orchards heavy with orange fruit, and two villages, one near the base of the castle's hill and another among the farther fields. Beyond them the empty valley stretched to distant hills. I had once thought that the world was always alive and speaking to me. Now, either it had closed its lips or I had become deaf. Or perhaps it was telling me how utterly displaced I was.

I looked over at Sir Joscelin, who seemed as calm and confident as I was anxious and timid. I could trust him. Nothing would happen to me with him and the surgeon and all these men guarding us! And I should be enjoying his company; it was rare to be alone with him. I stole a glance at him. Something about his face still reminded me of my Papa, and he was kind and upright like Papa, too. Certainly it was a miracle to have met such a man.

At that moment he turned toward me. We both started to speak and stumbled on our words. Sir Joscelin smiled and said, "Please, you must speak first."

No man had ever asked me to do that. "Is that the custom of your country?"

"Why, yes, I suppose it is. It is part of every knight's training to defer to a lady. One of our great French queens taught us that—that and how to love a lady from afar."

Did he mean me? My heart raced and stood still at the same time.

"Now I have forgotten what I meant to say. Perhaps you should speak."

"Oh, I just wanted to point out where we are going while we are still high enough to see clearly. There," he pointed, "lies Adar al-Mas'ūdī's castle on a ridge at the far end of the valley. It is less than an hour away even at our pace. Can you make it out? See, just above that village."

Fighting giddiness, I stared out across the valley. It was a clear, crisp day, and I thought I saw something at the foot of the distant hills, a patch of mixed browns and greens, yet everything seemed to be covered in a haze—then I remembered that the same thing had happened to my sight on leaving haram in Qazvin.

"I see little, I fear. My eyes seem to have grown weaker since coming to this convent. That happened to me before, almost as if we lose our gift of seeing very far if we do not use it."

He gave me an odd look. "An interesting observation. And would that have been when you were a guest of a Muslim family—in Iran, I think you said?"

"Oh! Yes, that was when…." What could I tell him? Now I felt unsafe inside and out, bereft of any words that could hide my past. An awkward silence followed.

"You need say no more, you know. I did not mean to pry a story out of you."

I took a deep breath. "It is just that my memories are so full of pain and loss. I—I was twice widowed in the space of a year. And most of the people in the family that took me in are dead now, killed in a riot. It is too terrible a story to tell…." I know this was not all the truth, but it was not entirely a lie, either. And though we all disguise our words and even our hearts from time to time to avoid taking hurt, I did not feel good about it.

"… And then there were the Mongols. Do you know about them?"

"Oh, yes, I remember. They hurt your servant badly. I take it you saved her from them."

I nodded. That at least was true.

"They recently forced Rum to submit: a great Turkish state in eastern Armenia and an enemy to us, but who knows which way they will turn next?"

"They are a terrible people," I blurted out, surprised at the heat of my feelings.

He looked surprised. "The Mongols? As far as I can tell, they are just one more brutal army destroying an already ravaged land even further."

"You speak like no warrior I ever knew."

He laughed. "I suppose not, but I never took pleasure in killing, even when I had to do it. Had things gone differently…." Awkward silence filled the space between us.

I finally said, "You need not tell me anything more, either." None of this was going as I had hoped—no light talk, followed by a little laughter. Instead, I felt lost.

"Strangely, I feel drawn to telling you so much. It is just that my tongue cannot find the words, and there is loss and sorrow in my story, too…."

His words lightened my heart a little, but they also reminded me that Sir Joscelin had recently lost his brother. Summoning what little courage I had, I said, "If I may, I do wish to say one thing to you. Sir Foucald told me that you lost your younger brother not long ago and that you blame yourself. I too have felt such a burden—even with Anna—and I honor your grief."

Sir Joscelin said nothing for several heartbeats, and I feared I had overstepped myself. Suddenly, he made an odd noise in his throat that startled me into looking at him. He was staring straight ahead; tears were sparkling on his lashes. I hastily averted my eyes, unnerved by the memory of Papa's freely shed tears when we had bidden each other that final goodbye.

After another long silence, he cleared his throat. "Sofia Volodymyrovna." I turned. He seemed to have made up his mind about something.

"I think we know each other well enough by now that I trust our friendship. If you wish, I will tell you a little about how my brother and I came here and how I lost him."

"Yes. Please. I have wanted to ask, but somehow the right words never came to me." But inwardly my heart sank. What did he meant by "friend" when I already knew I wanted so much more?

He smiled sadly. "I have the same problem with certain people...."

Did he mean me? Did he want to say what I wanted most to hear? My heart bobbed up and down on a little sea of hope and apprehension.

"I ... the short of it is this: my brother and I served a high-born noble here in the Holy Land and Robert was killed in battle while I, who had vowed to protect him, was merely wounded. And I cannot forgive myself. So now you know."

I already knew most of this. I said, "And what would be the long of it?"

Sir Joscelin laughed ruefully. "Are you certain you want to hear?"

"Yes."

"Well then, Robert and I were born in the land of Occitaine. We did not grow up there, though, but in Francia in the north, where we trained to become knights."

"Occitaine? Francia? I know neither of these places."

He was silent for so long that I glanced up at him. His face had hardened into rocklike crags and seams. "I see I will need to tell you more of my story than I intended."

"Please. We have time."

"Well then, I will start with my land of birth. In Occitaine we say 'occ' for yes instead of 'oui' as the Normans do, so our land is also called the Langue d'Oc, which means the speech of yes, most apt. In the words of our troubadours—oh, you won't know that word. They are travelling musicians who sing about love and life, and they once abounded there. Not anymore. Anyway, as one of their songs say, Occitaine is an Eden of fair meadows, silver rivers, and bold mountains; every crop grows as if God's hand lies upon it, and the wines are as sweet on the lips as a maiden's kiss."

He paused again, and added, as if to himself, "And though I will never see it again, it will always be my true home." He shook his head as if to clear it and spoke more boldly.

"Where a land is blessed with so much beauty and wealth, strife often follows over who will possess it. So I suppose you could say it is the most blessed and accursed place on earth; great and petty men alike have fought over it for centuries.

"And when heresy arises there, what a perfect excuse for invasion! When I was a small boy, we were invaded by one king of Francia after another—the Pays de Francia itself is but a few estates surrounding the city of Paris, but its king is feudal lord of great dukedoms and baronies farther afield. And these kings have always laid claim to much, much more, including Occitaine. In my eyes that, not heresy, was their real reason for unleashing their Norman lords on us. A plague of greedy nobles fell on my homeland with their equally greedy armies and stony-hearted Papal prelates behind them. They killed … burned … brought ruination everywhere! And then they wrested whatever they desired from us, including many loyal Catholic cities, castles, counties and more.

"The worst were the de Montforts, Simon and Amaury, father and son, who hounded almost every noble in Occitaine out of life and fortune. And always in the name of the Pope. Ha! Their Viking blood betrays the truth: they were simply plunderers garbed in false piety!" I flushed, for Viking blood flows in my veins. "Towns burned, castles stormed, good Catholic citizens slaughtered along with the handful of heretics in their midst. Old and young alike were burned at the stake—or slaughtered when a city was taken. No one had seen anything like this kind of warfare before. It was vicious and totally without scruple! A couple of decades ago, in Bezier, they killed every single person, including innocents who took refuge in the cathedral: the elderly, women, children, babes in arms. They even slew the dogs and cats! All in the name of Christ our Savior!"

I shuddered. Just like the Mongols in Rus'! These Normans must be just as savage!

"My father was a wealthy baron. He knew there were heretics among his peasants. They called themselves the Cathari, 'the pure'. Their holy man, whom they called a Perfect, was a man from the village who had gone to Lombardy to learn to become a Goodman, as he called himself. He worked in the fields with the villagers and was a tailor, too, a useful man who had dedicated himself to his faith. They had argued religion and even agreed on some things. The man had led a pure life and seemed harmless enough.

"But he was almost our downfall. When he was arrested and convicted, Father was much aggrieved. Being the civil authority, he was expected to burn the man at the stake, and so he had to order his men to do the deed. Father refused to be present, though. From then on he tried his best to protect the heretics among his people, since they were hard-working and honest and provided us with a good living. But he failed, and then came more arrests, convictions, and again he was expected to burn his own people, my people, too. Men, women, children I thought of as my.... And Father first protested and then resisted this time, to no avail and to his own travail."

I stared over at him, my own fears forgotten. He seemed lost in dark memories.

Suddenly Sir Joscelin said, "The burned homes, then the stench of scorching human flesh and the screams of my playmates floating up to the castle from the village—they haunt me even now!"

I shuddered. My own memory of passing by Kyiv still haunted me, but another rushed out at me now. I had once witnessed an accidental death by burning. The hut of one of our smerdi had caught fire and the family had fled, but the father, whose fault the fire was, had run out with his hair and clothes on fire. His death screams had been so terrible, so terrifying, that I had actually forced myself to forget it until Sir Joscelin's story brought it back. Even the smell of the poor man's scorched flesh came back to me.

"You know, too? You can never forget, but there were those who came to watch and laugh and jeer! It still disgusts me that some people are entertained by others' suffering." He fell silent for several heartbeats.

"For awhile my father was excommunicated—banned from the comfort of religion in that terrible time. He was publicly scourged before the

Church would accept him back, and he had to offer me to the local monastery as proof that he had repented.

"Luckily for Father and the lands he held, Simon de Montfort was killed in battle soon thereafter, and our southern armies soon chased Lord Amaury back to Paris, where he had the gall to offer his so-called holdings to the Frankish crown! Then a new king came to the throne.

"Father saw his chance and hastened north to offer homage to this new king, and he was there just in time for the hasty coronation in the cathedral at Reims—the year of Our Lord 1226—with my brothers Anchetil and Robert and me by his side. He took me back from the monastery in hopes that the new king or one of his nobles might take us younger brothers into service as squires, even though we would both be starting late. I was pleased. I had taken Christ's message to heart in the convent, but while I had easily mastered my letters, I was restless for action. I wanted to protect the helpless and poor of this world just like Father, and I wanted to be knighted as soon as possible! But Robert—how I wish he had been sent into the convent instead of me! He would have been happy there.

"Well, things rarely happen as we imagine they will, yes?" I nodded. "To my surprise, this new king of Francia, Louis the Ninth, was only twelve, a year older than me and three years older than Robert. The King, or perhaps his mother the Regent, agreed to my father's petition, but in return we had to become his personal vassals."

"I do not know that word."

"Oh. My father became the king's dependent in exchange for royal protection. But it meant that our family lands, ours for generations, could be taken from us at the king's whim! This was something new to the Occitaine, a kind of government unfamiliar to us and in conflict with our independent ways. I suppose it held Normans in check once and it certainly gives the king more power over us, but—

"Well, you are not interested in my musings. As for Robert and me, by ill luck we ended up in thrall to Lord Amaury de Montfort—this is a long story. Are you certain you want to hear it?"

"Yes, I do."

"Well, our father and eldest brother left for home, and Robert and I began training as pages." Sir Joscelin laughed. "I was almost too old, so I became a butt of the other boys' mockery. That is when I started brawling. I still bear a few scars." Grinning, he pointed to a white seam along his chin.

"And what is a page?"

"It is the first stage of training for knighthood—learning how to serve one's master, courtly manners, the basics of fighting, to read and write a little, although I was ahead of the other boys there at least—alas, that proved a curse, too. They thought me too bookish at first, another cause for quarrel. Our new master had many pages and squires, some of them tough bullies. Oh, a squire is the next step to becoming a knight; he serves his master at table and so forth, and he follows him into battle where he also sees to his horses and armor and belongings.

"At any rate, when we were not traveling in Lord Amaury's retinue, we lived in Paris. Robert and I learned more about serving at table and polishing plates and doing errands for arrogant men, not to mention caring for armor and horses and cleaning out stalls, than I had thought possible. I also mastered how to fight and ambush other squires, and sometimes hide from them!

"Robert was wretched right from the start. I should have found a way to convince Father to send for him straightaway. It was not only the boys who made our lives hellish. As soon as Lord Amaury learned we were from Cathari country, he hated us. But Father would not bend when I wrote him about it. He wrote back that we both needed to be tougher. So I spent the rest of my youth trying to shield Robert from Lord Amaury's random blows and petty taunts—almost as bad as the treatment we got from our fellow squires.

"Because our master was so close to the royal circle, we often traveled in the king's retinue over the next few years—there were so many uprisings, so many enemies—hence the hasty coronation—and King Louis and his mother the Regent put them all down!

"Then one day when I was thirteen—I remember it was shortly after a huge brawl, me defending Robert—Lord Amaury called us all together and announced that henceforth the king's own men would be in charge of our training. The squires from several great houses were to spend the summer receiving serious instruction in serving and fighting. 'I expect you to return to me acting like true squires instead of like dogs battling over a bone,' he said. He almost kept Robert and me back to abase us. Instead, praise God, at the last moment he relented and sent us, too.

"To my amazement King Louis and I met on the training ground when the master trainer chose me as the royal training partner. The king and I were well-matched in size and strength, and perhaps in our serious temperament. I was called upon regularly after that.

"We quickly became friends—that is, he spoke and I listened in complete awe. I sent word of our friendship to my family, who welcomed it as a miracle. No longer would we be tarred by suspicion, for the new king was already known for his piety."

He paused. "But for me, it was less of a blessing."

"Why was that?"

"Well, though I enjoyed mastering the arts of war and riding and hunting with him, King Louis could trust very few people beyond his stern mother and his equally stern priest. So he shared his secret thoughts and fears with me—and there were plenty to share! There was so much opposition to him and to his mother, Queen Blanche, who was hated for being a woman, and beautiful, and cold, though that did not keep people from spreading all sorts of lascivious slanders about her relations with her priest. I learned too much too soon about the dark side of life at court: the ambitions, the endless lies, the false smiles. Men even tried to bribe me to get at King Louis!

"He was no fool, and he faced those two-faced hypocrites bravely in public. But in private he was riven by fear of sin. His mother said it was better to die than to commit a mortal sin, but she never saw into the heart of a spirited boy—she even forced him to give up falconry as too worldly—

"Well, I have wandered from my story.

"I think my friendship with the king was a boon to Lord Amaury, too—at least King Louis and his mother showered honors on him—yet it seemed to me that he held my friendship with the king against me. I suppose it stayed his hand from truly hurting either Robert or me, but instead he indulged in petty cruelties."

"Why did you not tell the king?"

"Oh, they were things every boy refuses to bend to. Besides, I could never confide such small hurts to King Louis when he was dealing with much bigger concerns! And at least we were receiving excellent training, even if Lord Amaury laid a heavy hand over it whenever we returned to his service—well, in fairness, he was tough with all the boys. But Robert suffered more than I did. A few times, he begged Lord Amaury to allow him to join the priesthood, but our master refused. He taunted him, called him a coward. I suppose that is why my brother grew up with only two passions: to defend the weak and helpless and to serve Christ."

"You could not both leave and find another master? Is that not done?"

He shook his head. "Besides, Lord Amaury was too powerful. His enmity would have followed us everywhere, perhaps even to the king's council chamber. As long as I was in King Louis' confidence, our family was safe; but I feared that if I were to leave Lord Amaury's service, I would lose King Louis' favor and that my master might speak against me and my family. Ah, who knows? Perhaps I should have defied him and my father and sent Robert home...."

We rode for some time in silence. Suddenly Sir Joscelin spoke. "By 1229 I was almost grown. That year, with royal blessings, the Pope sent new inquisitors into Occitaine to root out the last weeds of heresy—rebellion was and probably still is rife—and Queen Blanche sent in the French armies again. Word of attacks, torture, and burnings soon trickled north. My king did protect my family and our people, but what did that matter in the face of the evils that befell my countrymen? Every time I heard of another village burned, of people cooked alive at the stake merely on suspicion, it made my stomach turn. And the soldiers and inquisitors are still at it, forcing confessions from anyone they choose to suspect, for I have seen torture extract lies from the hardiest man! It is no way to get at the truth, not to mention that people who know they will soon die anyway will accuse their enemies as a way to get revenge."

I nodded, remembering all the people Qacha had had tortured after Lady Q'ing-ling's death. More people had died from false accusations by their enemies than had ever been part of Lady Har Nuteng's plot against her rival.

"The holy war against Occitaine, as the Franks call it, was only part of a great movement to cleanse the earth of those who opposed Mother Church. We squires learned we were to follow Lord Amaury on a holy war to the Holy Land with one of the foremost French lords, Count Thibaut of Champagne. Lord Thibaut was to do penance for rebelling against his king and defying the Pope and, I think, for being in love with Queen Blanche and causing all manner of evil gossip about her. He is a bon vivant and a great troubadour, but too many of his songs were dedicated to her.

"Anyway, this war was meant to make the most of recent gains by the Holy Roman Emperor Frederick, who had made a long truce with the Saracens."

Vassals, barons, emperors, names—I was awash in foreign ideas and politics that meant nothing to me. I sternly forbade my mind to wander. At last the man I liked above all others was telling me his story. Later on I could learn what it all meant.

"For seven long years the great lords made their preparations while we lesser men waited. Lord Amaury was made Constable of Francia, second-in-command to King Louis himself. All the while, my heart yearned for Occitaine. My parents grew old, my father died, and my elder brother Anchetil succeeded him. But I saw my home only twice in all that time. I reached full manhood, yet Lord Amaury refused to knight us—me in particular."

"But you are a knight now," I said.

"Yes, I am now. I will pass over my master's reasons for refusing to knight me. But I have spoken far longer than I meant to. And about dark things. We left the mountain without once enjoying the view."

"I do not mind," I said. Between the view and his dark story, I preferred the latter!

"Nonetheless, I will try to finish my story quickly. We finally left. Sir Thibaut celebrated by burning almost two hundred heretics at the stake in his county—he who was once a friend to Occitaine—and then he led his troops to the ships, all singing one of his new, rousing war ballads. He had once preferred singing and eating and lovemaking to jousting, and as for his going to war: it turned my stomach—his hypocrisy, the waste of it all when we arrived, the…."

He fell silent again, while bitterness seemed to flow from him like a fresh wound. "I bade my friend and king goodbye, probably forever. I still carry the ring he gave me."

From under his robe, Sir Joscelin pulled out a gold chain, a heavy ring strung on it. He drew the chain over his head and handed it to me. I examined it: a band of what I later learned to call fleurs-de-lis, a large ruby enthroned in their midst.

"It is beautiful." I handed it back, and he reverently returned it to its hiding place.

"What with bad weather, rough seas, dishonest merchants, and money-squeezing ships' captains, we did not arrive in the Levant until the fall of 1239, at a city far south of here called Ascalon. It lies at the edge of the Gaza desert, not far from Jerusalem.

"But some of the nobles in our army were more interested in easy gains than in rescuing the Holy City. The trade route to Damascus lay nearby, and after several quarrels over what was to be done next, one party of knights grew restless and attacked and pillaged a merchant caravan. Their success spurred Lord Amaury and his companions to do the same. I was among the squires—the eldest by then—who followed him on that mission of greed. I thanked God that Robert was ill. It was to be my first true battle, 'my first blooding,' as Lord Amaury put it to me while I helped him don his armor. 'Not like those puppy fights you got into all the time. If you survive this, perhaps I'll even knight you and your baby of a brother,' he said, and he laughed in my face.

"But instead of finding a merchant caravan, we rode straight into a trap. Crossbowmen lay in wait among the sand dunes, and we were easy targets! The slaughter was beyond belief. Some of the great lords fell, but Lord Amaury was among those captured, as was I, his only surviving squire. Surprisingly, the Saracens did not harm us beyond blows and taunts. They wanted ransom, so before carrying my overlord away to Cairo, they allowed him to send me back to Ascalon to raise it, an irony as I would have gladly let him rot in Muslim chains.

"Lord Thibaut was not interested in rescuing him. When I finally gained an audience with him, he called Lord Amaury a foolhardy bastard who deserved his lot. I think there had never been friendship between them. Lord Thibaut left soon after, having lost one battle and signed one frail truce and done little else—he did not even wait to confirm the truce. Most of Lord Amaury's remaining knights and household went with him—their obligations were fulfilled and they wanted to get home to their crops and their wives.

"But I had to stay behind in Ascalon to await the ransom money that must come from Francia. Robert insisted on staying with me. We knew that even though Lord Amaury was a great noble, it might take months, even years for the monies to arrive. I had given up all hope of receiving a knighthood by then and wanted nothing more than to go home to Occitaine. Sir Thibaut's indifference had sent me pounding on moneylenders' doors, from Templars to Jews, but to no avail, so I would just have to wait. We had been in the Holy Land for almost a year by then….” Sir Joscelin fell silent again.

A soft breeze brushed against my skin. We were deep into the valley and had left the village far behind, but the overarching sky still seemed appallingly vast. I could not bear to look up at it. Only the mild warmth of the sun seemed friendly.

“Even before Lord Thibaut was gone, Robert would sometimes disappear and wander about on his own. One night about a week after everyone had left, he returned late to our inn, his face bright with holy joy. He had met a group of Hospitallers traveling north, and on hearing his story they had invited him to their convent to be knighted there and joined into God’s service. He was a grown man, anxious to begin his true life. The rule of the Hospitallers offered him everything he wanted. We had some money of our own—our eldest brother Anchetil had seen to that—so I helped equip Robert with horse and armor and a Turcoman squire, and I bade him goodbye. I thought never to see him again, truth be told. It was a black time.

“But things suddenly seemed to fall back into place. Only two weeks after Lord Thibaut left, another war party arrived, led by Prince Richard of Cornwall, brother of the English king and brother-in-law to Emperor Frederick. This truly noble English prince, who could have been our enemy, ransomed all the men captured in that useless battle.

“Imprisonment had destroyed Lord Amaury’s health, and I greeted a much humbler man. He knighted me when he learned how loyally I had served him and even gave me my own horses and hired young Hugh there as my squire—an English boy come with Sir Richard who had lost his master to fever and had no way home. And he released me from his service. He wanted only to return home, for he knew he would soon leave this life.”

I had never paid much attention to Hugh, but his story struck me as painful. I glanced back at him, wondering how he had felt, alone in strange country. He was such a serious-faced youth, his blonde mane falling around his head like a hairy bowl, his eyes such a pale blue. When he saw me looking at him, bowed, blushed, and lowered his gaze as shyly as a maiden would.

“Alas, Lord Amaury was outraged when he then learned that Robert had left without permission. Though there was little heat left in the man, he threatened to ruin our family if my brother did not return to his service. So when Sir Richard sailed away, having extended Sir Thibaut's truce, I was left behind, having promised to search for Robert and bring him back with me. But, though I did search for Robert, I had no intention of returning him or myself to that man. The pall of death already hung over him, and indeed Lord Amaury died on his journey home. As to Robert, it took a month but I found him here, already a consecrated monk-knight. He was so happy. Of course he had never been in a real battle. All he knew about fighting was a few bruises, a bloody nose, a broken arm. He had never seen arrows through a man's neck, guts spilled—what is it?" I was swaying on my horse, and he caught my arm to steady me. "You look pale."

I shook my head to clear it of terrible memories: arrows in necks, raids, brutalities—and my dead tutor, his guts cut out for nothing. "I would rather not hear the particulars."

"I forget myself. I am sorry. I should stop."

"No, I want to hear more."

Sir Joscelin looked at me closely for a moment before glancing ahead. "Lady, I would gladly tell you, but it seems I have used up our time. We are almost there."

I looked up and saw the fields, the orchards, the little village ahead of us, all so like those below the convent. A soft line of dust was marking the path down the hill from Adar al-Mas'ūdī's castle; reaching the valley road, the dust turned into a troop of armed horsemen.

"We should join Adar al-Mas'ūdī or we might be mistaken for enemies." Sir Joscelin spoke lightly, but nonetheless we spurred our horses forward. We had lagged far behind.

The troop passed by us before we could join the surgeon. It was a hunting party from the looks of their clothing, led by a richly dressed man who saluted Adar al-Mas'ūdī ironically as he passed by him. On seeing us, he nodded coldly to Sir Joscelin and glanced at me in surprise. I hastily pulled my veil over my face, and he looked away. Clearly this man knew both the surgeon and my knight, so why speak of enemies?

"That was Adar al-Mas'ūdī's elder half-brother, their father's favorite and heir to all the lands hereabouts: Mustafa ibn Husain al Mas'ūdī. He is not happy with his younger brother's lack of fighting spirit, not to mention his healing profession—he seems to regard it as below the family's dignity. There is little love lost between them. And it helps nothing that

Adar befriends infidels."

"Oh dear! I should have been riding by Anna all this time. She must be terrified!"

Sir Joscelin laughed. "I doubt that. Have you not noticed how the two of them feel about each other? Look at how tenderly he speaks to her through the curtain."

"Well, I had begun to see that he cares for her, but Anna hates Muslims."

"Well, perhaps I speak out of turn."

At that point, we reached the rest of our party, and I rode forward to speak with Anna. She seemed contented, even a little drowsy, when I parted the curtain and peeked in. "The hakim is being very kind to me," she smiled. "He has thought of everything. Look, he even brought me a little box of dates and a peeled orange. Would you like a slice?"

"No, thanks. I must drop behind again. We near the hill where his castle stands."

She smiled dreamily. "I'll see you soon, then."

So unless that pain-killing syrup was responsible, Sir Joscelin might be right.

We wound up the hill, me with my eyes firmly on the pathway. I only looked up as we neared the castle's gates. A fortress, larger and far better maintained than the Hospitallers', loomed on a ledge above us. Guards were clustered together on the battlements looking down at us in curiosity. One saw me and pointed, and suddenly a dozen eyes turned my way. I looked down again and drew my veil even closer over my face.

In the castle yard, crowded with servants, horses, giant jars, bundles and mysterious shapes, we dismounted. Sir Joscelin said, "I must stay here. You go with Anna."

I hurried after Adar al-Mas'ūdī, as a well-dressed man—a servant?— led Sir Joscelin and young Hugh through a corridor leading from the busy courtyard, Hugh looking as uneasy as I felt. We hastened past guards, along a hallway, and through an inner gate into a private yard a little like Selim al-Din's andarun garden in Iran, although flowers bloomed in pots instead of in the ground. A pomegranate tree offered shade next to a round pool, birds sang, benches were placed invitingly. Clearly this was part of the women's quarters.

No one was there at first, but as soon as Adar al-Mas'ūdī's men had set

Anna's litter down and left, the court filled with women fluttering about like butterflies, pulling back the litter's drapes, exclaiming about Anna's ankle, and to my surprise, over her beauty. Actually, there were only three women, one of whom the physician sent for refreshments.

He presented me to his mother, who invited me to sit by her and to call her by her Christian name, Adalia; and his sister, whose name was Jena. They could scarcely take their eyes off Anna, though, who blushed prettily as Jena arranged pillows under her head and offered her sweets and drinks from the tray that the maid set on a low wooden table. Of course they offered me refreshments as well, but Anna was clearly their honored guest.

Once they had settled her comfortably, though, Adalia turned to me and after a few pleasantries said, "We are so glad that my son persuaded you to bring dear little Anna here. We know how hard you worked to save her, and we are so grateful for all you did. You can rest assured that we will nurse her back to full health. And you can visit whenever you like. Just send a messenger. And of course you must stay overnight whenever you wish."

I murmured polite thanks, but my mind was in turmoil. How had they come to think of Anna as dear? What had Adar al-Mas'ūdī told them? They seemed almost possessive. Had I made a terrible mistake bringing her here? Would she be free to leave? I must make sure.

"And when she returns to me, we will both be grateful for your tender hospitality."

They smiled sweetly, but they scarcely seemed to hear me. And when Anna asked if she might sleep now, Adar al-Mas'ūdī almost leapt from his seat when I translated for her, looking at me expectantly.

So after again offering to stay and again being refused—"You must keep company with your knight"—I bade Anna goodbye. The hakim led me out and back to the main courtyard, me feeling as neatly severed from her as if he had performed surgery on me.

Sir Joscelin and his squire came out of the same door, Hugh wiping crumbs from his face. But I did not want to go. I turned toward the hakim. "I thank you and your family for every care you take of my dear little Anna. I will try to come often to see her, and I look forward to her full companionship again one day."

Neither of us could look directly at the other, but his body stiffened slightly. "Please, rest assured that she is in the safest of hands," he politely replied. We both bowed and he disappeared into the passageway that led back to the haram.

The journey back to the convent was made mostly in silence. I no longer felt the same keen interest in hearing about Sir Joscelin's brother Robert, and he made no effort to finish his story. Perhaps he understood how I felt. After parting with Anna, it was as if the sun had withdrawn all her warmth and the entire world been so stripped of meaning that only a vast emptiness remained. I had not expected to miss her so fiercely and so soon. In truth I had been secretly looking forward to resting and letting my aching head recover a little more. Now I could not imagine what I would do with so much time on my hands.

I almost absently thanked Sir Joscelin when we arrived back at the convent. Once we had parted and I had my chance to lie quietly, I could not. Instead, I busied myself, shaking and folding Anna's blankets and wondering about finding a way to wash everything before scrawny Old Agathe returned—it would fill the empty time. I kept thinking of that beautiful courtyard and those kindly women, scarcely real people to me, who seemed so ready to devote themselves to Anna and who had so much to offer. No matter what happened after this, she could never again be my little Anna.

Lost in this painful reverie, I was about to shake the dust out of her final blanket when a little packet tumbled onto the floor: a note to me, written on a scrap of bloodied paper from one of my ruined manuscripts. It was folded around several gems.

"These are for you, Mistress," her note read. "From Batu Khan's ger. Do you remember? You tried to set the ger on fire and you threw gems away. You said take what I wanted, so I picked these up. I tied them in a sash around my waist and hid them well if we stopped for baths or such. When Selim's wife gave me that box, I kept them there. I am sorry I said nothing when you were sad about your father's cloak. I was afraid of losing everything, and then other things happened. You keep them. If I die, please remember me. Your loyal servant, Anna."

I burst into sobs and threw myself on my cot, where I finally fell deep into weary, heartbroken sleep. The next morning, the noise of new pilgrims arriving wakened me. Brother Dominic bustled in with a pot of broth and some wine from the kitchen and bade me eat, but I was not hungry. Sir Joscelin would soon be gone again.

SPRING INTO WINTER
ANNO DOMINI 1246-1247

The pilgrims only stayed overnight, and without my knight I had no way to visit Anna until he returned. The convent celebrated the new year right after the equinox in March, on what Brother Dominic called the Feast of the Annunciation. A special Mass and feast marked it, but I felt little beyond loneliness. I tried to conquer it by helping Brother Dominic. One day he made a suggestion that at first I greeted with dismay.

We had finished copying out receipts for medicines and were storing the fresh copies in a casket when the monk said, "Once we finish grinding a few of these herbs for the infirmaries, there will be little else for you to help me with. If riding out to that Muslim castle gave you a taste for getting outside, I could send you on an errand to the village below us. Mostly peasant settlers live there, but also a few people who used to work for us—servants who grew too old and the like—and I have been meaning to send them some liniments and medicines for some time. Sir Foucald could go with you."

A dizzying journey down the hill with no reward at the end held little appeal, but I could think of no reason to refuse. "Yes, I could do that."

"Then I will arrange it for you."

The next day Sir Foucald came for me and announced how delighted he was to join my little mission, and we set off. Because it was such a short distance and because I thought it might help me feel less afraid of being outside the castle walls, I had decided to walk, but he rode a little donkey so that his leg would not pain him. He had to wedge himself between some panniers filled with Brother Dominic's Easter gifts, but he seemed not to mind. "I am so happy to leave the convent. It is too lonely since little Anna left, and now I can see how old Herbert does—he once served a companion of mine. I used to visit, but after my leg got so bad, I stopped going. I just needed a fair lady to inspire me again." I smiled without real pleasure.

"Look down there at the village. Here live the Christians. And see beyond it? That other village is where the Muslims live. They work their own fields and olive groves and pay us taxes. Before we took Sa'amar, this village was theirs, but we let them stay and build a new one over there. And they kept much of their land, too. Not everyone has been as generous as we Hospitallers are. At first our good Christian knights and princes often took everything, killed many of the peasants or drove them away, and then brought in Frankish settlers. Of course they ended up need-ing help from the natives, anyway, so we Hospitallers knew better." Sir Foucald rattled on, turning from this subject to that, while I pondered the nature of generosity.

Once we arrived, he led me down narrow dirt lanes from one tiny dwelling to another. Soon it seemed as if everyone in the village was fol-lowing us: first the skinny barking dogs, then half-clothed children, then their harried mothers who chased after them and then joined the parade to find out what was going on. Old men looked up from their doorway stools to watch us pass. The houses, so tidy-looking from above with their tiled roofs and whitewashed walls, were often in sad disrepair. Each time I went inside one of those hovels, I was struck anew by how poorly these people lived: a straw mat on the floor, a pot, a dish and cup, and little else.

I met a faded widow who had followed her husband to the convent to serve him when he decided to join the Hospitallers, had borne a daughter by him before he took his vows, lost him not only to the Order but to ill-ness, and who now had nowhere else to go. Her tiny home was scrubbed and neat, and she claimed to make enough money sewing robes for the knights that she needed no charity, just a little friendship. But the next place we visited was home to a grimy man with one leg. He lived alone in filth. Beyond the stench of so much that was unwashed, his house smelt of some pungent herb that he evidently smoked. At least I saw a dark brown chunk of something lying next to a pipe, where the smell was strongest. The man's name was Jean. Poor fellow, he was so glad to talk with me or anyone else who would listen that I soon learned his life story: his knight had been killed in battle and he was completely alone.

When I asked him why he had hired no one to help him, he seemed surprised. Having been a servant all his life, he had never thought to ask one of the village women to keep house for him. He was so grateful for the liniment I found among the baskets that I thought he might weep. And there were too many others like him.

I did go back to the widow to ask if she would clean for one-legged Jean and offered to pay her myself. She agreed to send her daughter, a shy, squint-eyed lass named Mary, but that was the only joy of the day.

We returned to the castle, Sir Foucald happily chattering on about how glad he was to have gone. "I saw Herbert while you were arranging things for old Jean. That was most kind of you. He has fallen into bad ways, smokes hashish like any Syrian peasant. It's the rabble's drug. But he is a good man, anyway. You should be proud of yourself."

But I was not. I felt helpless in the face of such deep poverty. I knew I would have to return, to do what little I could.

On Easter Sunday I went to the sunrise mass, standing as usual in the back of the room while monks, knights, squires, artisans, and menials crowded in front of me. There were only a few women, most of them in some way attached to the Hospitallers as laypersons. I felt a certain pride, however, as the room was again fragrant with the sage and rosemary that I had helped place about the altar and tie around the room. The priest spoke at length about their holy meanings, but I scarcely listened. I was praying to my patroness the Holy Virgin for Sir Joscelin to return soon. While it no longer mattered that this sacred ceremony bore so little re-semblance to my childhood memories of the same holiday in Kyiv—the sonorous chants and songs, the holy processions around Saint Sofia—on this day I felt so alone.

But nothing is more certain than change, and its seeds are planted in ways we can never foresee. Brother Dominic brought me two packets. One was a note from Anna, saying that she was recovering and happy and that she missed me; the other was a letter from Maryam. When I asked him who had brought the latter, he shrugged and gestured with his head toward Adar al-Mas'ūdī's castle.

The letter from Maryam spoke of her gladness to hear from us, her horror at what had befallen us, and her regret that there was no way she could help directly. "My new life is not rich in material ways," she also wrote, "though spiritually I am reborn. I have many new friends here, some with trade connections even as far as Constantinople. If ever you need my help in that way, please let me know. I will do my utmost for you both. And I was able to write to my son, as there are Nizari here who will send letters for a price. I hope for a reply in the months to come." I could almost see the tears in her eyes, the bitterness she still felt toward the Nizari.

Another week passed while I rested, helped Brother Dominic, and tried not to miss Anna and my knight too much. When Sir Joscelin finally returned, a strange veil of reserve had fallen between us. But he did offer to take me to see Anna the next day, and I accepted.

Once again in that vast, indifferent world, even escorted by the man I wanted to love, speech abandoned me: Anna's gift meant I was wealthy again and that we would be leaving once we were both well. A deep chill settled into my heart.

Happily, Sir Joscelin finally broke the thickening silence. "I am sorry you had to wait so long before you could visit your servant again. I had hoped that Adar al-Mas'ūdī might send for you. Perhaps he has been busy with other things."

"Yes, it has been lonely without her ... and without you—I mean your friendship—to take my mind from her. However, I did receive a letter from our old companion, Maryam the Jewess."

"You and Anna seem to have led most unusual lives."

"Yes, I suppose so." A long silence followed.

Finally, I burst out with a question that surprised me. "Sir Joscelin, do you think Adar al-Mas'ūdī means to keep Anna forever?"

He laughed softly and gazed out toward the surgeon's castle. "Well, if I may speak boldly, that depends on you and Anna. You must see now how love-struck he is. If he can persuade his father to accept it, he might well make you an offer for her."

"Do you mean he wants to buy her for a concubine?" I shuddered.

Sir Joscelin darted a sharp glance at me. "I do not know, but would that be a bad fate for a servant girl?" When I gave no answer, he added, "I did not mean he would offer to buy her. I do not even know what he intends. But living under his protection would certainly be a pleasant life for her: he is both wealthy and kind. And I gather that as Christians, his mother and sister would befriend her. On the other hand, perhaps he does want to marry her."

"Well, that is the only way I would consent to part with her!"

"You seem to value her honor."

"Well, what is any woman when she is stripped of it?" How sorry I was that I had brought up such a painful subject.

"What indeed?" There was a hint of sorrow in his voice, but he said no more.

A long silence followed, each of us locked in our own thoughts.

"Sir Joscelin, I am sorry. I have told you so little about myself, yet you have befriended me beyond what I deserve. I—it was hard to explain. Not so long ago, I thought I could remake my shattered life, and instead it shattered further. Anna and my friend Maryam—yes, I do call her friend—were part of the new life I was trying to build. I wanted to help them find a new life, too, and Maryam has, at least. Now it seems from what you say that Anna has a chance to do the same. I would not stand in her way if she decided that being with Adar al-Mas'ūdī was what she wanted. But it leaves me feeling more desolate than ever."

"I understand. Letting go was never easy for me, either. But perhaps it is best to scout out the terrain before making a false move, with him or anywhere."

The rest of the trip was made in unhappy silence.

But when we reached the hakim's castle and were about to part in the courtyard, Sir Joscelin said, "I look forward to hearing how your scouting mission goes." And he smiled.

Anna seemed radiant, and she was now able to walk on crutches again, human ones: Adalia and Jena. They hovered over her like bees at a flower; they drank her in like nectar! How had this affection been born so quickly? But instead of sitting in the garden, they led me into a beautiful white-washed room lined on floor and wall with shimmering carpets. Many braziers stood about ready to warm it, and refreshments already sat on a table. We all sat together smiling politely, sipping tea, and eating sweets until Anna spoke to her hostesses in a language I did not know. Her human crutches smiled covertly to each other and nodded to me before withdrawing.

"They teach me their speech, Sofia: Syriac! And look: they gave me such lovely clothing." Anna patted her rose-colored veil. "I am so glad to see you and that Maryam sent you a letter, too! I asked Adar to send it on to you rather than wait for you to come here. I have one, too, of course, and I will read it to you later."

So it was Adar and Sofia now—and when had she become so talkative?

"But first I want to know about you, Mistress, and how it goes in castle Sa'amar."

"The same—sleeping, helping Brother Dominic, praying in the chapel. Sir Foucald sends greetings to you." I took a deep breath. "I know you want no thanks, but the packet of jewels you left for me ... it means much to me. I will give one of them to the Hospitallers to repay their hospitality when we leave." We both laughed at my feeble play on words. "And what about you and your life among Muslims?"

"Oh, Mistress, even though I miss you so, I do love it here. Adar is so kind—he looks in on me every day and says I must call him by his first name, so I do. And his mother and sister take care of me, too, like I'm part of their family ... and his sister is Christian, too, not just Mother Adalia! I even met his father, though I had to veil myself and sit behind the other women. He seems a gallant man—I don't suppose you ever imagined me saying something good about infidels, but there it is. I seem as changeable as a bird dancing in the sky these days. In fact I sat out here under the stars with them last night and I saw a falling star and made a wish on it, so it must come true." She looked at me slyly. "Do you know what I wished?"

"No, but I hope you wished for a speedy recovery."

"Oh, that's already happening. No, I made a double wish, for you and for me, that we would each find happiness with the right man—

"What is it? Did I say something wrong? Are you angry with me, Mistress? Oh, please don't be." Anna looked ready to weep.

"No, Anna, don't be silly. It's just that I didn't see what was happening between you and the hakim—it all happened so suddenly—you scarcely ever saw each other, and you always hated Muslims so much that—and now you're so happy, and I miss you terribly."

Tears started from my eyes, and Anna burst into tears, too. So we held hands and wept for awhile. And then, to Anna's surprise, I had to laugh. What were we doing, falling into weeping fits? We might be in Muslim territory and in haram again, but in truth our lives had changed so vastly that it was like being reborn.

Finally, I wiped my eyes and said, "So do you like him? Perhaps love him?"

She nodded shyly. "He's so kind to me. And I think he likes me, too— no, I know it. He's so unlike that brute Argamon, so gentle and so caring. He was married before, but his wife died … and his little son Nasif likes me. Jena says they all hope I never leave them. But when I try to think about staying here, my mind gets cloudy. I don't know what to do. And Adar says nothing to me, so perhaps Jena is just being polite."

"I don't think so, Anna. Sir Joscelin says the hakim is in love with you. And he … he thinks you might be happy here." I fought back more tears. "I care so much for you, Anna … I would never stand in your way."

She blushed. "Oh, I forgot to show you Maryam's letter!"

But I suddenly felt the passage of time and stood up. "Well, perhaps next time; my escorts must be getting impatient. I'll return as soon as possible, and meanwhile you can think on what you want to do. Pretend I'm your mother and I am helping you plan your happy future. Yes?"

"Thank you…. And don't forget the second half of my wish." She smiled happily.

I suddenly felt better. And there were Sir Joscelin and the others, waiting for me with smiles on their faces. If Anna could find happiness in such an unlikely place, then the world was full of possibilities.

"You look happier, my lady," my knight commented as we left.

"Well, I suppose I am." We rode the rest of the way home speaking only of light things, despite a slight reserve in his manner.

A month drifted by. Anna not merely improved; she blossomed. I saw her weekly, thanks to Sir Joscelin, although he offered no more gallantries. Nor did Anna say anything about Adar al-Mas'ūdī's intentions, though every time she called him by his first name, my heart tightened into a little fist.

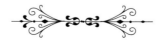

𝕹ot a week later, those seeds of change began to sprout. Sir Joscelin was away again, and I was in the garden helping Brother Dominic plant new herbs. No one else was about. I looked up, and there was Adar al-Mas'ūdī standing at the door of the garden looking frightened.

I rose slowly and faced him, knowing what was coming. After the usual greetings, the hakim handed me a letter from Anna. "Before you read it," he said, "will you walk around the garden with me? I would speak with you about something."

We slowly paced together to the far corner of the little courtyard, uttering polite nothings, where he stopped and turned toward me. Words spilled from his mouth so quickly that I think they surprised him. "Lady Sofia, I cannot contain myself any longer. I am deeply in love with Anna. I live to see her happy. It is my greatest wish that she stay on in my home as my wife. My father gives his permission, since he too fell in love with a Christian—and the Prophet himself, blessings upon him, married one. Father always respected my mother's religion, as I will Anna's. I will always treat her tenderly. She will be wealthy, too. And I will gladly write out a contract for your approval that safeguards her future. Please grant my deepest-held wish. And hers, too, I believe."

I had almost hoped he would try to buy Anna so I could refuse him. I must have paled, for he added, "I know this must come as a shock to you, but I hope not as a surprise. Anna says you once spoke together about it. Please sit down on this bench. You need not answer right away. Perhaps you should read her letter now."

I did, while he paced nearby, but I learned nothing new. She was in love with him, she loved his mother and sister as her own, she felt treasured, she felt safe. She had not told me sooner for fear I might think her ungrateful.

I looked up at Adar al-Mas'ūdī, fighting back tears. "She was always free to decide for herself. She served me long and well."

He smiled. "She thinks differently. As do I. I wish to give you the bride price for her." From the folds of his robes he brought out a small, ornate casket, opening the lid as he handed it to me. It was filled with gleaming gold coins.

"I cannot take this. Truly, she does not belong to me."

I tried to hand the casket back to him, but he refused to take it. "You will offend us both if you refuse it. She wants to thank you; if you wish, see it as a gift from her."

I had to wait several heartbeats before I could control my voice. "What can I do, then, but wish you both the greatest happiness?"

He smiled as though his face might split in half with joy. "We will be most honored if you stand in for her mother at the wedding. Indeed, I doubt Anna would consent to marry me if you were not there. Now with your blessings assured, we can seek an auspicious day for it."

Adar al-Mas'ūdī soon departed, floating on bliss more than walking on earth. Of course I was glad for Anna. She would be happy with her new family, and unless the Mongols came this way, she would be prosperous and safe. But I missed her, and now that I had enough wealth to journey in style to Constantinople, after their wedding I must leave Sir Joscelin behind without even knowing if he felt for me as I did for him.

My knight returned a few days later with an offer to take me to Anna. I gratefully accepted, but it was all I could do to keep from bursting out not only with the news but with all the contents of my sorry heart. Instead, I lost my tongue again. And a sharp glance from Old Agathe, who looked up from her scrubbing as I left, made me feel even warier.

As we rode down from the castle, I tried to turn my gloomy thoughts toward my companion. But soon I would again have to leave people I loved and be alone. How could I bear it? What choice did I have?

"You seem so sad today, Sofia Volodymyrovna. Is all well with you?"

I tried to smile. "Adar al-Mas'ūdī has asked my permission to marry Anna. And she wishes to marry him. So … I gave my consent, and … and now I will lose her."

"I see … and after the wedding you will go to Constantinople?"

"Yes, it will not be long before you'll be escorting me to Antioch."

I had tried to speak lightly, but the words caught in my throat and almost ended in a sob. I looked away, but there was nothing to see but ploughed fields and desolate hills. Silence stretched between us like a cord drawn tighter and tighter.

We parted in the castle courtyard. With Anna and her new family, I hid my feelings fairly well, since they did most of the talking. But it was hard to listen, since the only topic was the wedding. A date had been set, although they were using the Islamic calendar, so I did not understand exactly when. "Oh, a few months hence, once I am fully healed and the omens are right," Anna finally explained in a somewhat superior tone that caught me off guard.

After taking refreshments with them, I found an excuse to depart. Anna saw me to the garden gate. "See how well I'm walking now? Adar has worked wonders on me, yes?"

"Oh, yes indeed. You're a different person entirely," I said. I think some of my feelings must have leaked into my voice; Anna looked surprised. But before she could make more of it, I embraced her and whispered, "I wish you every happiness in your marriage, Anna." And I fled back into the outer courtyard, where Sir Joscelin and Hugh were just taking their horses from one of Adar al-Mas'ūdī's grooms.

On the ride back, Sir Joscelin asked, "Has a wedding date been set?"

"Yes. A few months from now. And then I have no reason to stay on...."

"You could—" But he cut off his words.

"What could I do?" I finally asked.

"It is nothing," he said. "We should go back."

We spent the rest of the journey back, each with our own thoughts. Sir Joscelin helped me dismount and led me inside the passage to the women's infirmary before he and Hugh led the horses away. After he left, I waited, wishing Sir Joscelin would return and tell me what he felt, but he did not. Finally I gave up and went inside.

Sleep eluded me that night. I twisted about in my narrow cot, getting tangled in the bedclothes and finding lumps of blanket under my back that refused to straighten out. It was as willful and tangled as my thoughts. Why had I hoped that my knight—who clearly was not mine at all—might now reveal that he felt a special liking for me, perhaps even love? One word from him and I'd have given up my dream of finding my uncle and stayed there forever. And then I had to remind myself that he had offered me nothing beyond a few gallant remarks, hardly enough to tell what he really felt. So many foolish dreams I had cherished, each to fail me in turn—like when I once dreamed of escaping the Mongols to single-handedly warn Kyiv. And was Constantinople just another figment of my desires? Perhaps I must learn not to dream.

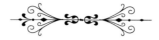

He stopped coming to see me. Days passed. I knew there had been no recent pilgrims, so he was not gone to Antioch. When I timidly asked Brother Dominic—we were standing at his worktable making some medicament—he shrugged and said, "I hear Sir Joscelin joined the hunt for another lion that is attacking flocks in the hills. A shepherd was badly mauled. He returns soon, no doubt, and knowing him, with a lion pelt over his saddle. He fought one before and killed it single-handed."

My heart leapt into my mouth, but I said nothing.

The next Sunday, with Mass over and the crowd flowing outside, I was passing along the courtyard to the women's infirmary when four knights rode in leading an extra horse. After dismounting, they gently released a makeshift litter dragging behind it.

Brother Dominic understood sooner than I did, and he rushed to the still form lying on the yard and fell to his knees beside it. "Does he live?"

One ruddy-faced man nodded. "Barely. His arm and shoulder—he lost much blood, though we managed to stanch the bleeding. The lion leapt on his horse from behind and attacked him. He needs the hakim."

"Who will go to the Muslim castle for him?" One knight remounted and rode off.

I was standing at the edge of the courtyard lost in the press of men and women gathered silently around this small tragedy. Pitiable man, whoever he was! I could see little, but it seemed best to stay well away since I was so faint-hearted around blood. Then I heard the word "lion".

I scanned the solemn knights, and Sir Joscelin was not among them. Now they were gently lifting the litter and carrying it away, beyond my sight. No, I could glimpse him now: it was he! His head lolled, his face was gray. Then he was lost from view.

I covered my face in horror. What if he should die? He might not be mine, but I could not bear to lose him!

The taut silence shattered into babble and chatter, although people seemed more excited over the great lion skin that had been borne off than in the fate of the knight. But it was all I could do to contain my raging, terrified heart. Finally the crowd thinned until the courtyard was empty but for me. I waited, shivering, by the castle gate for an eternity. Finally I saw Adar al-Mas'ūdī come galloping along the road at what seemed an ant's pace, the Hospitaller emissary by his side and a pair of servants behind them; now his horse was laboring up the hill, now bounding into the courtyard, lather coating its neck.

He dismounted almost before his mount had clattered to a stop in the yard. His imamah was rimmed with sweat, and his face was inscribed with anxious lines. "It is Sir Joscelin?"

"Yes. Oh, dear God, please save him!"

"If All Merciful Allah wills it." He tossed his horse's reins to the other knight and raced off with his servants into the passage leading to the men's infirmary.

I followed, desperate to see anything, but Adar al-Mas'ūdī had already vanished into the surgery by the time I got there, and the door was firmly shut. Faint sounds; a monk opened the door briefly and I stood back against the wall to let him pass. He returned shortly with a bowl of steaming water and shut the door again, not even glancing my way. After that, silence.

There was nothing to do but pray. It was hard even to make my legs move, but I forced myself to return to the chapel, where in despair I flung myself down at the back and began praying to the crucifix hanging behind the altar. As an Orthodox Christian, I used to be horrified by the gory Crucifixions that the Catholics worshiped, but that day I felt crucified myself. There were not even words for the frenzy in my heart, and after a few rote prayers to Christ, to Holy Mother Mary, and to Almighty God Himself, I fell still and sat in a huddle of misery.

The bell for None prayers rang, and the chapel filled, mostly with monk knights. I was still there when they left. None—Brother Dominic had once told me this was the very hour when Adam and Eve were driven from the Garden and when Christ died. I felt driven out and dead, too.

Only when the sun had set and dark seeped into the room, candles lit and people assembled for Vespers did I return to myself with a start. It was as if I had left my body and retreated into an empty trance. I leapt up, my head swimming, and ran through the thickening dusk back to the door of the surgery, feeling as if the very air was pushing against me.

The door was open now, but no one was there and the room was unlit. Somehow it seemed so small. Two people I loved had lain on that rough table. Even in the dark, I felt its scars from saw and knife, blood soaked into its core. The room's crude stone walls seemed to lean toward it as if drinking in all the suffering they had witnessed.

Steeling myself for the worst, I slowly approached the entry to the men's infirmary and peered through the door. It was like the women's but larger, with several round pillars holding up a high vaulted ceiling. There were many more beds, too, and the space, lit by flickering wall torches, seemed airier than the women's. Alas, with so many men moving around, I could see little beyond wavering lights and shadowy figures and a few cots where old men lay. Finally a middle-aged monk carrying a tray with a cup and bottle passed near enough for me to call to him softly. He was the same man who had tried to help carry Anna to the surgery all those weeks ago. He stopped short and looked at me in surprise.

"Please, Sir Joscelin. Is he—is he alive?" The words caught in my throat and I had to swallow a sob. "I have been in the chapel praying for him, but I—I needed to know."

The man's face softened. "He lives. God showed him mercy today. That hakim saved his life. I think he was seeking you after the surgery, and so was Sir Foucald. Look for Brother Dominic. He was helping, but he probably returned to his duties; he can tell you more." And the monk walked on.

I hurried back to the women's infirmary, and there was Brother Dominic at the door, deep in conversation with the surgeon, their faces weirdly lit by the hallway torch. "Sofia! We were looking for you. Adar al-Mas'ūdī has good tidings."

"Yes, I went to the men's ward to seek news. I never imagined anyone bringing word to me." I burst into tears.

"There, there, no need to weep now that the worst is over," the monk began, but Adar al-Mas'ūdī understood.

"Her tears are from gladness, I think. And Lady Sofia, you were much mistaken, for I knew to bring you word."

Brother Dominic nodded. "You may have matters to discuss that are no concern of mine. And I would go to Compline."

"She is safe with me; she is like my sister," Adar al-Mas'ūdī gravely replied. Brother Dominic bowed and disappeared into the shadows.

"Lady, will you sit? Here, wipe your eyes. I will light another taper. Sir Joscelin has deep reserves of strength; certainly Almighty Allah has denied his prayer for a valiant death." Even in the half-light, the surgeon must have seen my surprise. "Yes, he went after that lion hoping to leave his earthly travails behind. He sent me a message of farewell, and in it was one for you, too, once he was dead." As he spoke, Adar al-Mas'ūdī was pulling a bulky, folded piece of parchment from a wallet concealed in his belt and handing it to me.

I looked down at the parcel, completely confused. "He sent you a message to give to me? Why? Why did he not come to me to say goodbye? Why would he want to die?"

"As to that, I cannot say. You foreigners are a mystery to me. Read his letter and let his words speak for him. When he recovers, he may not be happy with me, but he came close enough to death that you deserve to read it. And now I must be on my way. My men must be hungry, I have missed my own times of worship, and my family awaits my return."

"Thank you, thank you for everything. You are such a good man."

After he had left I opened the letter, and out slid the ring that King Louis had given Sir Joscelin, still on its chain. I just caught it as it fell toward the floor. My heart beating wildly, I pulled the two tapers close together and in the flickering light tried to read, but the writing was too small. So I blew out the candles and lay down on my cot to await the dawn.

I tossed all night long, a seemingly endless night, and when the bell rang for Matins I got up and went outside to the garden where the rising sun would give more light. The letter said:

To Lady Sofia Volodymyrovna.

May 15, Anno Domini 1246

My lady,

   Your receipt of this letter and ring means that I am dead and can finally reveal my heart to you. But first I must confess my deep sin, which nearly cost me not only knighthood but the favor of my king. I beg you to forgive me both for my crime and my silence to you.

In my youth lust ruled me. A lowly servant girl or lady of the court would catch my eye and I would pursue her with a single aim. I justify nothing in saying that I was not alone in this. King Louis may be saintly, but most of us squires were not. There was a lady-in-waiting to Queen Blanche, Yolande, no more temperate than I was. I was fifteen, she was thirteen. We were discovered and she was sent home in disgrace by the virtuous Queen. Worse, the great lord who was affianced to her withdrew his offer.

I went to my king to beg for mercy for us both, but King Louis was so aggrieved that for days he refused to see me. When at last I was allowed into his presence, I fell at his feet and begged his forgiveness, but he said only Mother Church could remit a mortal sin. Yet so good was his heart, he added that once the Church had forgiven me, he would do the same. And he gave me a collection of writings, some by his great-grandmother, Queen Eleanor of Aquitaine.

To my surprise they were not about purging my sins. They explained what true courtship is and how to love a lady from afar with no hope of ever winning her. I confessed to my chaplain, accepted his penances, wore a hair shirt, told my paternoster beads countless times, went on pilgrimage, climbed endless church stairs on my knees. And read and reread those pages of courtly wisdom.

Six months later I was recalled to the royal court to learn that Yolande was big with child and that her father had come to Queen Blanche demanding redress. Of course a wedding was hastily arranged. We lived in Lord Amaury's castle, the butts of sordid jest, especially from him, who thought my only sin was getting caught. Robert alone stood by me.

Yolande hated me by then and never accepted my attempts to make up for the damage I had done to her. She spent day and night in prayer. Sometimes she fainted from fasting. Our son was born early and dead, and she died of childbed fever. I as good as killed them both. The rest of my life has been a penance for those two deaths.

I came to the Holy Land to die. Instead, Robert died in my arms, an arrow in his side, happy, and with a prayer for me on his lips, while battle raged around us. How often I have wished that arrow had found a truer mark. Afterward, I lingered on here at the Hospitaller convent like some ghost that cannot rest, having found a new penance. I went on missions of danger, seeking release into death.

And then like some radiant angel, you appeared. I loved you from the moment I carried you out of that mad makeshift tent. Now my penance was to be by your side as often as I could, but never to betray my heart to you. I regret even the few gallantries I could not hold back, for they fell from tainted lips. And when you go to your uncle, I will be fully punished, for I will have no reason to live. I leave my king's ring with you. Perhaps you can show it to him someday. It is only a dream, I know, but in it you would tell him that I not only conquered my lust but was able to give my heart to an angel—you—without ever violating your chastity. Then, perhaps, he could fully forgive me.

Sweet Sofia Volodymyrovna, now I can tell you. I love you without measure. I wish I had been a worthier man who could marry you and protect you as my friend Adar al-Mas'ūdī loves and protects his Anna.

Adieu.

Sir Joscelin of Braissac.

I had never felt such a chaos of emotions: shock, sorrow, heart melted and frozen and broken. What was I to make of this story? Sir Joscelin had done his best to make amends to this Yolande. Yet years later, he was still burdened with such shame. I felt as forlorn as if he had died. And what to do now? If he did recover, what should I say? I was no radiant angel. I could offer understanding, even forgiveness to him, but would he be able to forgive himself? And what would he think of my past if his own haunted him so?

I was lost in thought when Brother Dominic found me. "Lady Sofia, you must come inside. You are shivering."

"Am I? I had not noticed."

"Sir Joscelin awoke just now and asked for you. I know it is not proper, but it may be a dying man's wish…."

My hair stood on end. I leapt up. "Please, take me to him!"

"I did not mean to say that he is dying, only that sometimes when it seems that a man is recovering, suddenly he gives up his ghost. Here, come this way, not to the men's infirmary. We have put him in the cell where he lives. Young Hugh watches over him."

Brother Dominic led me through the main courtyard, down a dark stairway, and along a short hall. "This is where our honored guests have always stayed, and though he denies it, Sir Joscelin has always been an honored guest indeed. He has done so much for our little convent. If he dies, he will be much missed."

I supposed the monk had seen so much death or was so confident of reaching Heaven that dying did not frighten him as it did me, or perhaps it was because he was speaking of the man I loved, but I sagged against the passage wall, almost too faint to move.

Yet when Brother Dominic opened the door to the little cell, Sir Joscelin was sitting up against some pillows, bare to the waist but for a swathe of bandages covering his left side. Morning light from a high narrow window lit his face, making it glow. Hugh, who looked as if he had not slept for days, was spooning broth into his mouth and spilling a good deal of it on his master's beard and chest. The monk bowed to me and departed.

I had been so certain I would find my knight dying that I did not know whether to burst into laughter or tears, so I did both.

"Well, Lady, that is quite a greeting," he said with a faint smile. Then I saw that he was pale and weary and in pain.

"I thought to find you dying, sir knight, and confessing to the priest."

Sir Joscelin tried to shrug and winced instead. "And I had thought to be completely dead already, but instead I am doomed to live yet again. The lion took as much leather in her mouth and claws as she did my flesh. I fell and hit my head on a stone, and everyone gave me up for lost when I was only stunned. They killed the beast and brought me back here straightaway. Now I only need to heal. Nonetheless, it will be some time before we can resume our chess games." He stopped talking, and I saw that despite his brave front, his strength was ebbing.

"And did you summon me to tell me that?"

"No, something else." Sir Joscelin brushed Hugh's hand aside. "Enough, boy. Go tend to my mare. I don't know if the lion wounded her, too."

Hugh bowed and made for the door, the bowl of broth still in his hand. "Leave the bowl, my good fellow. I may want more." Flushing, the youth did as he was told.

"I think I have never heard Hugh say more than two words," I said to cover my sudden shyness at being left alone with this half-naked man.

"He is a good boy. I will knight him in a year, if we both live so long."

"Please, lie back down and rest. You should have waited to summon me. I can live without chess, but not without—"

I had moved close to Sir Joscelin's side, but now I turned away, not wanting him to see how I felt. "I should go. I will come back when you are more rested." But he reached out with his good arm and took my wrist in his hand.

"No, not yet. I … I wanted to tell you something. I wrote you a letter before I went out lion hunting. You will not see it, since I gave it to Adar al-Mas'ūdī and he was only to give it to you once I had died. So now … I will tell you myself what was in it." My whole body turned as hot as if I had been plunged into boiling water. "You blush. Have I said something wrong?" I shook my head, not knowing what to say.

"He … he gave you the letter?" I nodded.

"Oh, dear God. I am ruined. Why did I not die?" he moaned, closing his eyes.

"Because God wanted you to live." I turned to face him. "Because I can forgive you. I am no radiant angel, Sir Joscelin, just a woman whose heart has been deeply bruised, but who has never given up hope for love. A woman might dream her whole life of receiving such a letter as yours. I can only count myself doubly lucky: to have received it and to be able to respond." I knelt beside the bed, my hand somehow now in his. "I love you entirely, too. I do not want you to die. Please, please live, for my sake."

My knight stroked my face. "Yes, for you I will." He pulled me into the curve of his arm, moving slowly so as not to hurt his shoulder. Our eyes met, then our lips. A gentle kiss, full of warmth and promise. My veil fell back onto my shoulders, and I pulled back at last, sighing.

"You must rest. And I will come every day to watch over you and feed you broth without spilling it. I think I have it in my hair now! And when you are able, I will play chess with you as long and often as you wish."

"In truth, I only enjoy the game when I play it with you," he smiled, sinking back onto his bed, already half-asleep.

I touched his face lightly, found a rag and gently cleaned him, pulled his blankets over him, and stood by his side while he drifted off to sleep. When Hugh returned, we spoke briefly and warmly. The boy loved his master, and I think he was glad to confirm that I did, too.

I spent the rest of the day in happy dreams. When my knight recovered, we would marry and live nearby. I would send word to my uncle, and we might visit him someday; my ambition to find him was finally at rest. All good things would come in the right time.

By sunset I was fast asleep. And at dawn I awoke happy to the summons of the chapel bell and looked out the window at a soft sunrise that seemed to bathe the world in love. My heart cried out at such beauty. I hastily dressed and sought out Brother Dominic, who had already risen from his cot outside the infirmary and was preparing to go to Matins. So I followed him.

As we made our way to the chapel, I asked what was uppermost in my mind. "Would I be allowed to nurse Sir Joscelin back to health? It would … give me something to do with Anna gone." I had not finished the sentence as I had begun it: it would give me the greatest joy to nurse my beloved back to health!

Brother Dominic gave me a keen glance. "Well, I will ask. Certainly you may visit him with a monk or young Hugh present, but this is a monastic house."

I was shocked. Did he doubt my chastity? Or could he read my thoughts?

"Well, well, I meant no offense. But we all know how you feel about each other."

Now I was truly shocked! "Everyone but us, it would seem. I only just learned that Sir Joscelin … feels … as I do." I was overcome with shyness, speaking thus to a monk.

"Hmm. Well, now is the time to set worldly love aside and remember the only lasting love, that of our Savior." And he led me into Matins.

Afterward, I waited impatiently in the infirmary while the monk went to the abbot with my request. When he returned, he looked grim.

"He denies permission?"

"No, you may go with his blessing. It's just that … Sir Joscelin may be dying after all; the chaplain gives him the Viaticum as we speak. Go to him. Do you know the way?"

But I was already out the door, racing to my beloved. That was, of all the journeys I had taken, perhaps the longest. Every step I took seemed rooted in earth, every stone in the courtyard seemed ready to make me stumble, every knight or squire or servant seemed to block my way. And when I finally arrived, Hugh was standing outside the door, tears streaming down his face.

"Thank God you are here. He may die any time now. No, you cannot go inside just yet. The priest is in there giving him the … the …," and he burst into sobs.

Just then the elderly chaplain, whom I had just seen celebrating the dawn of a new day, opened the door. He looked scandalized at seeing me, but then he shrugged and muttered, "I have done what I can." He moved off down the corridor, clutching the bundle that must have contained his holy oil and wafers, shaking his head, and murmuring to himself. He threw one last sharp glance at me before I entered the small cell.

At least Sir Joscelin was awake, though he looked as if he was rapidly sinking into death's arms. He could not raise his head. His eyes found mine; they looked dulled; life seemed to be ebbing from them. His hands lay crossed on his breast. Even his skin looked gray. I'd have thrown myself on him were it not for young Hugh. Instead, I kneeled at the side of his cot and entwined my fingers in his.

"Please, I cried, "please do not die. I need you to live, to thrive, to be filled with my love." And, though the words never left my lips, my heart cried its need for him to live and love me in return.

Sir Joscelin smiled faintly. "That is in the hands of God," he whispered.

"Then let us pray together for His mercy on us both."

And I bowed my head over our hands and prayed. At first my prayer went out to all the images of God and our Savior and our holy saints that I had revered as a child. They had offered me such solace then. But today they seemed flat and empty, devoid of life. No answer came to me, only the sound of Hugh sobbing. Where had my faith gone? I tried to dive deeper into my soul, to seek that vast and deep God beyond thought that I had once felt in my heart and all around me. Why could I not feel it today when I most needed it? Too many terrible things seemed to have entrapped me, and now only fear and desperation were left. Still, I must try; my entire being cried out for a miracle. If only I could pour my spirit into my beloved, give him my own health, heal him with love.

I must have knelt there for a long time, lost to misery, unable to form anything like a true prayer, when I felt Sir Joscelin's fingers loosen. I looked up, certain that had died, and saw that he was only sleeping. There seemed to be more color in his face, and a look of peace lay on it. I looked around. Behind me, Hugh was kneeling in prayer.

He jumped up, a look of awe on his face when I smiled at him. "He lives? It is a miracle. Our prayers are answered!"

I felt like a vessel emptied to its dregs. I stood unsteadily and slowly released my hands from Sir Joscelin's. He shifted slightly but did not wake.

"Thank God." For several heartbeats Hugh and I stood staring into one another's eyes. His were red from weeping, but his face glowed with youthful earnestness.

"You are a saint."

I shook my head. "I am no saint."

The chapel bell began tolling. How long had I been there?

"Lady, you look pale. It is Terce now and you have been on your knees forever. You should go, or there will be talk. I will look after my master. Praise and thank God!"

"I will return soon." I touched Sir Joscelin's hand once more and left.

More than one miracle happened that day. Just as I entered the main courtyard, Adar al-Mas'ūdī rode in along with a servant leading a heavily-laden pack mule. "How is my patient?" he asked without his usual courteous preamble. His brows were drawn together with worry. "I came as soon as I heard. There are … well, I see from your smile that Sir Joscelin must be mending, though you, Lady Sofia, look as weary as if you were the injured one."

I quickly told the hakim everything that had happened. "I will go to him at once. I brought wine to wash his wounds, the only thing it is good for!

"Oh, and Anna sends you gifts. My servant will take them to your infirmary."

"Gifts?"

"Some gowns. There is time for that later. Go now and get some rest."

I did as he said. I felt numb with weariness What would happen now? I knew only one thing: I must watch over my knight as constantly as I would my own child. If my love would heal his broken body—not my love but that vaster love that had once so filled me—I would gladly offer it all. And if I could no longer feel it around me, at least this miracle proved it was still here.

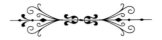

I never spoke to Sir Joscelin or Hugh of that answered prayer, though Hugh seemed a little overawed around me. All spring and summer my waking hours were mostly devoted to caring for my knight. One day he would feel so much better that he would get Hugh help him into the chapel for prayers. But the next day he would seem worse. This ebb and flow of health went on for the rest of the year, though the flows eventually began to be stronger and more frequent and the ebbs to be weaker each time. Once he had regained enough strength, he began training again. I was reminded of another injured warrior who had done the same, but Qabul was safely dead.

When I was not with my beloved, I was either asleep, worn out with caring for or about him, visiting the people in the village, or spending time with Anna. Whenever Adar al-Mas'ūdī and his servants returned home from visiting Sir Joscelin, he took me with him. He was very careful about all proprieties, more so than any Frank would have been. He also showed me his surroundings through his eyes, pointing out the names and properties of the plants that we passed, many of medicinal use. Once we saw a herd of gazelles grazing. When they heard us, they lifted their heads as if they were one creature and bounded off. The hakim laughed with joy. Sharing such times, not only did I grow very fond of him and his gentle, precise ways, but his love for the world began to melt that icy fear I felt every time I went out into it.

Anna was so excited about her upcoming nuptials that she forgot our ranks and was not always respectful to me. Her talk was too often about her new family and how they loved her; about some new bauble Adar al-Mas'ūdī had brought her; and, not so surprising when I thought about it, about her new-found friendliness toward Islam.

"Did you know," she once said, "that Muhammad had to flee his home in Mecca or be killed by rivals who envied him?"

"Yes, I did." I paused. "You seem to be learning much about Islam these days."

"So I am," she answered dreamily, fingering a filmy veil of turquoise silk. A large ruby adorned her finger, a gold collar of interlinked chains glimmered at her throat. Her old amulet was gone. "Much in it speaks to my heart … and what has Christ ever done for me?"

I paled, but she rushed on, "Not that I would consider changing my religion! But at least they do honor Christ, right?" She looked uneasy. "Adar says he was a great prophet and that Muhammad's revelations completed His, that Muhammad is the Seal of the Prophets."

"Yes, that is my understanding of Islam, too—"

I'd have said more, but she nodded as if I had eased her mind and exclaimed, "Do you not enjoy this lovely weather? Adar says he will bring me a nightingale soon and show me how to train it to sit on my finger and sing. Will that not be lovely?"

And the moment to speak further was lost.

Another time, she announced, "Did you know that in Iran we stayed among heretics? Alamut is a nest of murderers who are trying to overthrow the proper order of things! Adar calls them Hashishiya—rabble, you know—and says they must be destroyed. No wonder Selim and his family were killed! But Adar's elder brother said that Christians are Islam's true enemy, and he and Adar had a terrible quarrel. Adar told me his brother hates my mother-in-law for her religion."

"Yes?" It was all I could do to stop my tongue from giving her a good word lashing after all Selim and his family had done for us! And then a horrible thought struck me. How much had she told her fiancé about our stay in Iran—or among the Mongols?

Seeing my discomfort, Anna blushed and said, "It is of no moment." Silence fell between us and stretched out until I thought I must break. How could I ask her to keep secrets about our life—about my life—from her own husband?

"Well, if you must know, it was also about me," she burst out. "Mustafa feels Adar betrays Islam by marrying me. But my dear hakim says he stood up for me, and now when the family gathers, his brother no longer acts as if I'm some corpse in the corner."

"I am glad to hear that." I took a deep breath. "Anna, did you tell Adar al-Mas'ūdī about my … marriages?"

"Heavens no! Why should he care what you did? He never asks about you, and I never say a thing. I only told him we were forced to stay with

Selim's family and that you were so unhappy that you could never sit still and then we got stuck in a castle where I met Maryam. And that you wanted to leave and were so angry with Selim for leaving us there. And then when he wanted to know why, I told him about those Nizari. He knew who they were, and he said you and I were most fortunate to escape them. And that was that. But Sofia, he wouldn't mind about your marriages anyway. After all, Muslim men can take up to four wives, and you are now a widow free to remarry, so how can he mind?"

I suddenly felt unsure of anything, especially of Anna, who saw too much and yet read it so differently. "It's not your good man whose opinion worries me. It is Sir Joscelin's. He is Christian, and I might be seen as having deserted my faith. Please, never tell your husband about Selim or Kerim, and most especially about Argamon or Batu Khan."

Anna shuddered. "I never speak about that time! It was too horrible, and you were the only good thing about it." She reached out and touched my hand, to my surprise. "Your secrets are safe with me. I would never betray you. I learned well how to stay silent."

We parted with an embrace, but I felt as if I had fallen into a bottomless sea.

I began to visit less frequently. Instead, I often joined Sir Foucald in visiting the small village to bring Brother Dominic's medicines to the sick and especially to look in on one-legged Jean. He was too often in a hazy state of mind, and Sir Foucald had been right: hashish was the cause. But Jean was clear-headed enough to warn me one day that talk was growing about Sir Joscelin and me. He had heard garbled rumors, and I will only repeat the general drift of them, as they were both untrue and unkind: not only did I visit Sir Joscelin too often for decorum's sake, so I surely was up to mischief, but also I was consorting with Muslims, even to wearing the colorful gowns that Anna had sent me as a gift but which had come from Adar al-Mas'ūdī's hands. But the worst was, ironically, Sir Joscelin's amazing retreat from death. Some credited me with miracle-working, but others thought me a witch.

Yet when I asked him who had said these things, he refused to answer. "I should not have spoken at all. I never meant to hurt you, my lady."

I was so silent on the way back to the convent that even chatty Sir Foucald noticed. I finally told him a little of what Jean had said.

"Yes, I hear such nonsense from time to time. No one who truly knows you gives it a second thought. After all, wicked words always return to haunt those who speak them."

But without knowing who was speaking them, I found myself looking at everyone in the convent with suspicion. Well, there could be only one source. I stopped Hugh the very next morning as he was leaving the sickroom and I was about to enter it.

"Did you tell anyone about the morning that Sir Joscelin drew back from death?"

He looked abashed. "Only another squire. I thought he was my friend. He scoffed at me when I told him about your miracle, and I got angry. Then I told him about how humble you were, saying you were no saint, and he twisted my words around to mean … so I hit him. But I learned to say no more, even when others came to me asking about you."

"Well, now there is serious gossip about me."

Sir Joscelin sat up in bed and called to us. "Gossip? What are you two gossiping about? I want to hear, too." He smiled dreamily, no doubt from Adar al-Mas'ūdī's painkilling draft.

"It is nothing, just a little misunderstanding."

Hugh ducked his head, his cheeks aflame, and fled down the corridor while I went to my beloved's side and kissed him lightly on the lips, adding, "Alas, the gossip is about me. I have breached the convent's decorum, it seems, and now I must stop coming to you so often. No more kisses, my lord; no more embraces, either. That was the last one until…."

"Until what?"

"Until you are healed." I had almost said, 'until we are married,' but he had never spoken about marriage. And as an invalid, why would he? "I will sit with you until Hugh returns, and then I must go. Is your arm recovered enough for a game of chess?"

Sir Joscelin looked so strange for a moment; then his face became a mask.

"Yes, my set is over there. I will gladly play with you."

Play with me? My mind seized on the words. Too often I had been a man's toy, and now when I hoped for so much more, the thought that he might never intend marriage fell on me like a sharp-edged rock. Yes, he loved me, but given his past, that might mean only carnal love.

Needless to say, neither of us did well at our game; and when Hugh returned, I conceded and left. I could scarcely bear being trapped in the castle. After wandering about the courtyard for a little while, no doubt adding to the rumors about me, on a mad whim I climbed up the narrow stairs that led to the top of the ramparts. A walkway encircled it, protected by a crenellated wall. I took a deep breath and stepped up to it, carefully placing each hand on a crenellation for balance. For too long my world had been hemmed in by fear. Summoning all my willpower, I forced myself to look into the distance. Streaks and patches of green and brown, a few orange groves, olive trees swaying in the breeze, the blue of the far hills: all were at peace, in contrast to my frenzied heart.

Suddenly tears came, in great heaving sobs. There was nothing here for me, and once again I had tricked myself into hope. A guard came up the stairs behind me and began pacing along the walls. He greeted me courteously, forcing me to look at him, but I could see nothing but his eyes gleaming from beneath his helmet. Now I was probably adding fuel to gossip's flames! Flushing, I swept the tears from my face and ran down the stairs.

Where could I go? There were travelers in the women's sickroom, along with Old Agathe, who nowadays acted as if I should have left long ago. And the garden no doubt had the usual people hobbling about in it. Perhaps the chapel would hide me best; at least no one would accost me there if I seemed to be at prayer.

It was empty. Its one stained glass window cast fragments of color onto the flagstones, mirroring my fractured wits. I knelt among the shards of light and tried to think clearly. Sa'amar castle was turning into a prison instead of a refuge, but how could I leave it with Sir Joscelin still unwell and Anna still unwed? To whom could I turn for advice?

There were really only two people: Brother Dominic and Sir Foucald. I hesitated before deciding to approach the monk first. Although I had never confided in him before, he seemed likelier to know what to do about gossip. Sir Foucald, on the other hand, might be better at giving me practical advice once I was free to leave. For leave I must, with or without Sir Joscelin. I would not stay in a place where I felt so unwelcome.

The first step was obvious, though: I must write to my uncle Vasily. I had thought of doing so before, but there were so many reasons to put it off, even to believing that no letter would ever reach him. But if Maryam could write to her son, who lived so very far away, then it must be possible to find him somehow. After all, how many Rus' merchants could there be in Constantinople?

With a newfound sense of purpose—how had I simply drifted for so long?—I sought out Brother Dominic. He was in his little herb room, grinding dried roots from the looks of the scraggly things sitting next to his mortar, but he stopped for me.

"Ah, Lady Sofia, how does our—or should I say your—patient progress?"

"Well enough, good Brother." He nodded and kept grinding. But his body seemed to carry as much of a message as his words.

I began slowly. "I am at a loss for words, I fear … It is of my patient that I wish to speak, and of myself, if you are willing to listen."

He turned and faced me, his square jaw taut—or was that my imagination? "Let me finish my work here, and then we can talk together. This is not a confession—or is it?" I shook my head. "Good, since I am not a priest. Let us sit in the garden together where I can rest my bones for awhile."

At last after some delay, we were seated across from one another in the early morning cool of the garden. And I now I knew what I wished to say. I told him everything: my love for Sir Joscelin, the miracle that had happened on his deathbed, our few chaste kisses and nothing more. And about the gossip that had arisen around me from attending my beloved and from visiting the Muslim castle.

"So I seek your advice, Brother Dominic," I concluded. "I could go to Antioch, I suppose, and return for Anna's wedding, but I cannot leave Sir Joscelin until he is better. I know he loves me too, but he is still too ill to declare his intentions. Before today I always took it for granted that we would marry, but he has never said a word about it. I only know I cannot stay where I feel so unwelcome. I trust almost no one."

The monk nodded, scratching his tonsured head thoughtfully. "I have heard the gossip myself, Lady Sofia, and since I know you, I dismissed it to those who spoke to me. But it does linger on. You did well to tell me everything. First, I think you should go to confession. Our chaplain is among those who believe the gossip, and his absolving you will go far toward silencing wagging tongues."

"But how can I? Would he even hear my confession? I am of the Orthodox faith, not the Catholic."

He paused for several heartbeats. "Well, you might consider convert-ing. It would solve several problems at once if you plan to stay here, or even if you go to Antioch."

That took me aback. As grateful as I was for refuge among these Hospitallers, I had never considered changing my religion. But then, had it not already changed beyond recognition?

"I would indeed need to consider, for this strikes at the root of my faith. I could not do such a thing simply to quell gossip."

He nodded. "I know. But in essence, you have been a practicing Catholic for almost a year now. Other than crossing yourself wrong and not confessing your sins now and then, you take part in the life of Holy Mother Church in every way. Outward forms carry great meaning to some, but I know that when you cross yourself, Lady, you worship in the same spirit as a Catholic. Take a few days, pray for guidance, and then you might want to go to Father Boniface."

I thanked him and offered to help with his herbals. Back inside, we worked together in silence, each with our own thoughts until the chapel bells called him away, but I kept on, grinding away at his roots while my mind ground away at the idea of converting to Catholicism. Would I be behaving like that bride King Solomon had forced into his tent? I finally put my mangled thoughts aside and went out to sit in the garden again.

Sir Foucald arrived after prayers. He sat down beside me, only saying, "This is where Anna and I spent many happy hours together." He looked forlorn for a moment. "Well, I have lost loved ones before. Let us enjoy the beautiful day while we have it."

It was good advice, and I heeded it.

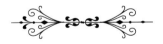

The next morning I asked advice on getting a letter to Constantinople from a woman staying overnight who was heading at least in that general direction. To my delight she offered to pass it on to a cousin in Antioch who could arrange for it to make the journey by ship. And with luck my missive might travel to Constantinople and pass from hand to hand until it reached my uncle. So I took out paper and ink—another gift from Anna—and wrote to him.

My next step, after a brief and unsatisfying visit with Sir Joscelin, was to ask Brother Dominic if I could read something about the Roman faith.

He looked surprised. "You can read?"

I nodded. "Latin and Greek."

"In that case I can find one or two manuscripts for you, mostly sermons by Church Fathers, and a penitential. And I believe we have a Church history, though our order was never devoted to learning like the Dominicans are. Oh, and a breviary that once belonged to an old woman who departed from this world."

Thus I embarked on yet another period of study, this time of the faith that we Rus' had mocked as madness. I found some differences in form that mattered much to the educated, like whether to use leavened or unleavened bread for the host. But the main block to me was the way the Catholics seemed to dwell on sin, especially sexual, rather than on seeking out God. Despite my own priest's fierce ways, even he seemed gentle by comparison with this constant harping on the temptations of the flesh and the terrors of damnation. He at least had also spoken about God's love and desire for us to find our way to him in everything we did. It certainly explained why Father Boniface was so ready to believe the worst of me.

Another difference, and this came from a sermon preached against the so-called Orthodox heresy, was that Catholics believe that the Holy Spirit comes not only from God the Father but from Christ His Son. Over this there has been much bad feeling. Since I could not take a stand on such a subtle point of doctrine, it was no obstacle to me.

The idea of Purgatory seemed strange to me, though. How can any of us know about the afterlife until after this life is over? But I decided not to worry about that, either.

The greatest hindrances to me were that the Pope is seen as the chief representative of Christ on earth, over all other churches, and that Latin must be the language of the Bible and none other. Odd since it was first written in Greek—this I knew from my long-dead tutor Alexander. And we Rus' had always looked to the Patriarch of Constantinople as the highest example of Christendom, even though he was not in Constantinople anymore. The so-called Christian armies that had seized the city decades ago had driven him out.

But Rus' had always had her own independent church, the Scriptures were written out for us in our own language, and the Mass was held in our native speech. As far as I understood it, this was true for every Orthodox kingdom, which made the Scriptures available to everyone. Clearly in this Roman faith, only the educated would know what the priest was even saying, much less be able to read the Scriptures for themselves. Of course few in Rus' knew how to read, but at least they could follow the spoken words.

I also neither understood indulgences nor knew how to pray with paternoster beads. But the monks at the Monastery of the Caves had used their chotki to keep their minds on their prayers, and since the paternoster beads prayer was to my patron, Holy Mary, I liked that very much.

I even approached Brother Dominic once again to ask him all my questions, but he knew nothing about the finer points of Church doctrine. "As I said before, Sofia, these things I take on faith with no need to question. I am here to serve, not to quarrel with anyone over doctrine." And the old monk's devotion to his patients and guests, some of them quite trying, was tireless. If this was what it meant to be a good Catholic, then my other questions seemed minor by comparison. After all, I thought, the Pope and these doctrinal disputes would have little influence on my life. I still had my own good mind and heart, and I trusted them to guide me along the path of goodness. And the rest was, as the monk had said, simple faith. I was not to learn my error until many years had passed.

During those two weeks, I only saw Sir Joscelin once a day and always in the company of Hugh, in hopes that my circumspection might be noted. He knew it was to quell the gossip about us, so he reluctantly agreed that what I was doing was for the best. I never told my beloved what I was considering, as I knew he would want me to convert, but he did notice my pensive mood.

"When I get better," he announced, "I will challenge these evil-tongued gossips to come forward and fight me!"

"What? Why?"

"To prove your—our—innocence! I know the full measure of this gossip now. God will hold up my arm and acquit you once and for all. He has shown me such grace in bringing you into my life—you saved me." He tried to sit up and winced in pain. "But I may have to wait awhile yet."

We both laughed, but in truth his words brought me no joy, for they seemed overwrought. And indeed when I felt his forehead, it was hot. That glitter in his eyes came less from zeal than from another bout of fever.

"I must go now, for you need to sleep. I will see you tomorrow, my love. Please get better soon, and not because I want you to fight for me."

But that was what decided me. Straightaway, I sought and was granted an audience with Father Boniface. The elderly priest met me in the chapel. "Come kneel before me in the confessional corner." I did as he said, only glancing up to see him staring at me with piercing blue eyes that seemed to radiate harsh judgment.

I had been in such a rush to see him that I had to pause to gather my thoughts. After a deep breath, I began. "Father, I seek guidance and forgiveness from you. These many months that I have lived here, I have been praying to find the best way to live in God's light. Brother Dominic gave me a breviary and some other readings that aided me in my search. Now, after further prayer and reflection, I wish to commit myself to the Catholic faith."

"Look at me, Lady Sofia." His stern visage, dry and sun-baked, had softened. His eyes were those of an old man, with little red veins snaking across them. How many years had he spent in this desert tending to the needs of fighting men who often had little idea what their faith even was? Pity took hold of my heart. What did points of doctrine really matter if one could rest in kindness? He must have seen the softness in my face, for the priest smiled.

"I always prayed you would come to the one true faith."

I quickly lowered my eyes, fearing he would see how his words chilled me. "Please teach me and show me what I must do."

He took my hands in his and said, "First, let us pray together."

And so that summer I became a Roman Catholic. I will not dwell on details. I was baptized and confirmed the following Sunday before his entire flock. Father Boniface deemed the second ceremony necessary to cement me into my new faith, sweeping aside the fact that I had received both these sacraments as an infant: "It was not in the true Church; now you are reborn." Again I kept my eyes downcast, for I could not abandon my past entirely, especially my beloved saints.

And I finally received what he somewhat ponderously called the Sacrament of Reconciliation wherein I confessed my many sins to him and was given a penance: because I was newborn into the Catholic faith, my past was wiped out, and I was only to count many repetitions of the prayer to Mother Mary on new paternoster beads that Sir Joscelin had given me.

In truth, both confession and penance turned out to be great consolations. I had wanted to be freed of the burdens of the past for so long, and I told the priest much that I had never told Sir Joscelin. Indeed, I think that the scandal of my love for him began to pale in comparison to having been raped and enslaved by Argamon and forced for my safety to marry not one but two Muslims. Yet at the end of confession, I still had secrets, especially about not entirely abandoning my Orthodox saints.

The morning of my baptism, as a sign of good faith I did, with much regret, put away the ikon I had always kept on the cord around my neck. After my baptism, Father Boniface gave me a small golden crucifix on a chain as a special gift. I strung it on the cord with the cross Q'ing-ling had given me—I silently insisted on keeping that, at least. And I think, having heard me speak of her goodness to me, he understood.

Some might say that I acted with base motives, but I do not feel so. How many people were converted by force over the centuries? My conversion was at least by my own will, and it kept my beloved from fighting needlessly. And I have behaved as a good Catholic ever since.

Sir Joscelin spoke only once of my conversion, just before I was baptized. I had told him of my decision, and he was delighted. But after making much of my new life in the true faith, he stopped as suddenly as if hit by a rock. "Did you convert for my sake?"

"No, I answered," knowing I was not telling the exact truth, "I did it for mine."

Sir Joscelin let out a deep breath. "That is good. Saving your soul should come uppermost. Yes, that makes it...."

After a silence of several moments where he seemed lost in thought, I suggested another game of chess, though I wished he would share what he had been thinking. On the other hand, I had no intention of sharing my reasons for converting.

Certainly the gossip seemed to stop. Many people witnessed my spiritual rebirth, and perhaps they felt humbled. I also stopped wearing the colorful Oriental gowns Anna had sent me; they seemed out of place and likely had added to my bad reputation. Thus I was able to stay on at the convent throughout Sir Joscelin's slow recovery and until Anna's wedding. Perhaps there were rumblings about my visiting her, especially since I did dress well then, but I went to the hours of prayer more often than anyone else and made a point of visiting the village once a week to help the old and needy. No one could fault that.

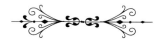

Late autumn: the wedding day was finally upon us. In an unusual gesture of friendship, Adar al-Mas'ūdī invited both Sir Joscelin and me. Before the final ceremony there had been a ritual where she and her hakim had exchanged rings, as well as a family celebration to which we were not privy. She had awaited her wedding with such impatience, gone over so many plans, shared so many happy dreams, all without saying anything new, that I had tired of hearing about it. But now I could rejoice for her freely.

We went early in the day, accompanied by Hugh and a pair of other knights' borrowed squires and laden with little gifts I had managed to have one of the Hospitallers bring me from Antioch—someone was always escorting pilgrims in one direction or the other. I was sorrier not to be happier that day, but Anna's wedding only reminded me of my own solitary state. Now that my knight was better, why had he not said anything? Despite his love for me, which he showed in many small ways, he clearly had no thoughts of marriage. And I would be gone soon.

We arrived and I was led to the women's quarters where Anna awaited me. Her hands and feet were hennaed, and she wore a silk garment trimmed with bands of elaborate embroidery as well as a cherry-red veil, also heavily embroidered. She clapped her hands when she saw me and drew me into an embrace. She smelled of sandalwood.

"Oh, Sofia, I am so glad you are here. I wish you could have been here for the other ceremonies. They anointed me with a special paste, and Adar and I gave each other rings, and there has been so much feasting I thought I might burst! And we signed the marriage contract already, but with no family of my own I kept wishing you were there. At least for today's religious ceremony, I have gotten Adar to agree that you should sit with Mother Jena and everyone as part of the family party, and Sir Joscelin will be like my older brother. No doubt Adar's elder brother Mustafa will act sour again, but I couldn't care less!"

On and on she bubbled, like a little spring waterfall, while Jena and her daughter moved about, stroked Anna's hair or lovingly touched her gown, laughed, sent servants for refreshments, smiled vaguely at me, and generally filled the room with flutter.

Drums boomed, cymbals clashed, and a stringed instrument began a melody. Jena took Anna's hand, gesturing to me to take her other hand, and led her to the wedding room, a largish hall that reminded me of the Great Hall back in my long-lost palace in Rus', perhaps because it was clearly used by a family. I shook my head. This was not at all the same: these were stone walls, not wood. Thick carpets covered every inch of floor. There was no stove, nor were there isinglass windows. Instead, morning sunshine poured in through lovely arched windows whose wooden beaded shutters were open, lighting up the colorful space.

A family group had gathered, including another group of women, perhaps more wives or daughters. This was clearly not a wedding for all the cousins and uncles and aunts and so forth, but an intimate affair, perhaps because it would be both Christian and Muslim. Something in the air made me wonder how welcome this marriage really was even to them. Did they think it a mad whim of Adar al-Mas'ūdī's? Well, at least Anna's new mother and sister had clearly taken her into their hearts.

Jena led Anna and me to a group of women sitting on one side of the room. I was given a cushion near Anna, who sat in front of us all. To my surprise, several men sat on the other side. Sir Joscelin, almost in front, was placed behind a stern-looking, straight-backed old man with a white beard who took pride of place and who must be the patriarch of the family. He sat still as stone. Next to him was Adar's brother Mustafa, looking sour indeed. He caught me looking over, and instead of averting his eyes he stared boldly back, a sneer forming on his lips. I hastily turned away.

When Adar al-Mas'ūdī arrived, clad in white silken robe and payjamas, the musicians played their loudest. But he did not straightaway sit on the cushion awaiting him. Instead, he came to me and, bowing, handed me a beautiful box inlaid with mother-of-pearl. "It is a gift for my beloved Anna's almost-mother," he whispered before moving to his cushion. I nodded dumb thanks and clutched it in my hands for the rest of the ceremony, about which I confess I remember very little. I do recall that it got quiet after Anna joined him. At some point mirrors were placed before the couple so that they could see each other's reflection, much as at little Banu's wedding, and the mullah read a passage from the Quran. I remember only part of one line, for it made me feel so alone:

The Almighty did create spouses for you faithful
so that you may dwell in harmony with each other, and He did sow
love and mercy between you ....

The rest of the ceremony must have been like Banu's, but I cannot say, and this is why: at one point, the Quran was placed between the couple and a scarf draped over them both, and it was then that I realized what had been before my eyes all this time. Now I understood Anna's questions about faith: this was an entirely Muslim ceremony.

I stared at her in disbelief, but her head was veiled and she seemed wrapped in happiness as well. How could she embrace the religion she had always hated? Again, the answer lay before my eyes. Every event in her life had led her to her hakim. Given her love for him, her shaky relationship to Christianity, and the difficulties her faith was causing him, of course she would convert. I spent the rest of the wedding with my head bowed, weighed down by how utterly strange and unexpected life was, by an equally utter sense of loss and, sadly, of fear both for Anna's soul and mine. What was the only true faith, or was there such a thing? Had I led her astray? Had I gone astray, too?

My mind spun ever-thicker webs of doubt around me until I remembered Q'ing-ling and Dorje. I could never doubt their goodness or the truths they had taught me. For once the Mongols seemed wiser than anyone else, for they say that each religion is like a finger on the hand of God, each rooted in His truth. In the same spirit, I could not take a stand for or against what Anna had done. Besides, she had never said she was converting. Should I not ask her instead of speculating and worrying?

After the ceremony was over, there was of course much feasting and jollity, the men of the family in the main hall and the women in the haram, each enjoying themselves in their own ways. I sat quietly at Anna's side while the revelry swirled around us. Servants plied me with treats, from tender lamb kebabs to flaky, sticky pastries, and Anna repeatedly urged me to eat my fill. I ate better than I had since leaving Selim's home, yet I tasted nothing.

At one point I summoned my courage and touched my young friend's hand. "Anna, are you now Muslim?" She stared at me for some time, then smiled and nodded. The smile contained such a mixture of shyness, defiance, and yet joy. I tried to smile back. "I wish you every good thing, even as you go where I can never follow."

Anna turned to me fully then and embraced me. "You will always be with me in my heart, Sofia. Without you, none of this happiness would have come to me. Thank you for … for everything." And then she whispered in my ear, "And I will always keep Christ in my heart." So if I kept my Orthodox loyalties to myself, was it not the same for her?

We might have said more, but another woman came up and took Anna by the hand to dance with her, while the others sang and clapped their wishes to her for many healthy sons and a long life to see them all become fathers of healthy sons in turn.

The song reminded me of an obstacle that might sow discord between Anna and her hakim. The next time I got a chance to whisper in her ear, I asked her, as tactfully as I could, whether he knew about the rape. "Well," she answered, "luckily he never need know about it, since I am still a virgin in the eyes of the world."

"What do you mean?"

"Argamon did not take me as a man should take a woman. He committed the sin of the men of Sodom on me." Seeing me blanch, she added, "Yes, it was horrible then, but I can only be grateful now. And Argamon never touched me again, thanks to you and how you shielded me from him." I squeezed her hand, and she leaned over to embrace me again.

The celebration stretched into the afternoon and showed no signs of ending when the sun began to stream sideways into the lovely, colorful, abundance-filled room. It must seem like Paradise to a peasant girl. But I must go before the sun set. So, having sent a servant to ask Sir Joscelin to meet me and having kissed Anna on the cheek, I slipped away, as it felt to me, out of her life. Anna called goodbye, but when I turned at the door of the haram, she was already happily singing, watching her new family dance, and nibbling on a sweetmeat.

The trip home was mostly silent. The sun fell so low that the world was divided into streaks and patches of gold and bluish gray. She touched the highest mountain peak, her shape changing from a red round to a half-dome to a sliver to a brief afterglow. Tonight I had forgotten to see her handmaidens; were they even there? Had they ever been?

I looked up at the stars as they came out one by one and wondered whether there truly was a dome of sky. It seemed so unfathomable, and a rush of fear came at me, the worst attack ever. Something must lie beyond it—God? Or perhaps more sky. What if it simply went on forever? I remembered a childhood argument over numbers I had once had with Pavel and Hlib, my long-lost servant boys. Pavel had learned to count to fifty and was so proud of himself. I had scoffed and said that I could count much higher than that.

Hlib had retorted, "Well, what is the biggest number in the world, then?" And I had answered, "A million million million." And Hlib had said, "What about a million million million million?"

Pavel added, "Or a million million million million and one?" They both laughed.

Feeling that my superior knowledge was at stake, I had denied that any such number could exist; there had to be a limit. And I had stalked off. But the doubt had been planted, and here it was again in a different form. All the verities I had ever believed in had vanished, so why not that one, too? But thinking of a world beyond the sky I knew, other than Heaven, was too much. I shivered and sighed.

Sir Joscelin turned to me. "Are you chilled?"

"No, I am just pondering my life and my fate. Nothing is as it seems."

"No," he answered somewhat sadly. We continued for some time in silence.

Finally I burst out, "Anna has become a Muslim. I asked her to make sure and, well, there it is."

"Does that shock you so much? She is so young, and Adar al-Mas'ūdī no doubt led her to it; it was bound to happen."

"I ... I worry about her soul."

Sir Joscelin looked at me keenly. "Yes. But God alone knows what will become of her soul. That was never in your hands."

A long silence stretched between us.

"Well, with Anna married, I suppose I should seek my uncle in

Constantinople."

Sir Joscelin seemed to catch his breath. "You would leave me, then?" What could I say? I looked over at my knight, wondering what he wanted from me. "Hugh, you and the others fall behind a little. I would speak with Lady Sofia alone."

A little thrill of hope raced through my body.

"My lady, I … I understand why you must leave." My heart dropped into darkness, and hope drained away.

"I would do everything in my power to keep you here," he went on, "but I have none. If it were my choice, I'd have taken you in marriage the day I met you. But I am not free to ask for your hand, not yet. I am bound to marry the woman my king approves. Months ago, when I was well enough to write again, I sent a plea to King Louis that he consent to my marrying you. I still await his answer before I can ask you for your hand.

"I suppose I should have said something to you before now, but there always seemed to be time. First I must heal, first Anna must be married, and surely by then I would have heard from him. Please, wait a little longer before leaving. Perhaps you could only go as far as Antioch; I know it chafes you to be trapped in the convent. I love you so. I hope you return that love. Please, do not leave me entirely. Give me hope."

My empty heart now flooded to overflowing with joy, with love, with a deep ache of happiness. I reached for his hand. "Of course I will wait. For you I would wait a lifetime."

He pulled his horse close to mine. Taking my hand, he kissed it, then leaned over and kissed me full on the mouth, then pulled me into a full embrace. Luckily the horses had the sense to stop or I'd have fallen off mine! I swear he might have taken me right then and there, and I would not have resisted. Such passion flowed between us that I thought I might burst into flame and be consumed utterly.

But the moment passed when Hugh almost rode over us in the dark. We both laughed and pulled away. At that moment, the almost-full moon rose over the far hills, flooding the valley with soft light. We happily wound our way home, both of us too full of emotion, and for my part, too inflamed with lust, to speak. We parted at the gates of the Hospitaller convent.

I was glad no one was in the infirmary that night, for I would have disturbed the other pilgrims with my endless tossing and turning. My mind overflowed with thoughts and plans. As for my body: well, it never stopped burning, even when I arose the next day. By my bedside sat the little box Adar al-Mas'ūdī had given me, still unopened, surely another gift of gold. But when I looked inside, it contained not coins but gems. I believe they must have been the last of the jewels Anna had taken from Batu Khan's ger before we fled. She had made me an exceedingly rich woman. And I felt rich: rich in love, in possibilities, in renewed life.

I arose, my sense of purpose restored, and sought out Brother Dominic. "Good brother, my time here draws to a close. Now that Anna is married, I have decided I will go to Antioch. Can you advise me?"

"You do not feel unwelcome, I hope?" He looked at me keenly.

"No, you always made me feel not only welcome but useful. It is just that the only way to completely quell the gossip about me and Sir Joscelin is for me to leave. He wants us to marry, but he must await permission from his king. He wrote him months ago, and it may take more months before he hears back—I am certain King Louis has other more pressing duties."

Brother Dominic smiled ruefully. "Yes, our king plans a great holy war to retake and rebuild Jerusalem, even to paying for it himself. He will be coming to the Holy Land soon. We just received a message that the knights here in our convent will be called to service. Your knight will likely be drawn into the king's war, too."

He saw my face freeze. "But you have time. Perhaps the message will arrive and you will be happily married before King Louis even reaches the Holy Land. After all, everything, even worldly love, is in God's hands."

"Yes. I must not lose hope...."

"As for the move to Antioch, can you help me?"

And we plunged into plans for my removal to this unknown city. Despite some unease over King Louis' war plans, I felt the thrill of a new beginning, of a happy future laid out before me. Happily, Brother Dominic knew much about the city, as he was on the convent council. The Hospitallers owned several properties there, houses and such, from which they drew rents. He thought he might be able to find suitable quarters for me in one of them if I could wait a few weeks, and I could stay at one of their hostels if nothing else was available right away. And he thought that old Sir Foucald might be glad to accompany me there. I rejected his offer to arrange a special journey just for me, as that would be a burden on the convent. Instead, we decided I would travel when its knights were escorting pilgrims.

I was not ready to leave that quickly anyway, and there were some small preparations I must make: to pay Anna and Adar al-Mas'ūdī a farewell visit and to give a parting gift to the convent. And I wished to give it directly to the chaplain or the convent master. I wanted them to look me in the eye and see a woman of virtue who was still generous despite the ugly rumors. I must even find an apt parting gift for Old Agathe. Yes, there was so much to think of and do. Fresh life blossomed in me like tender spring buds on a tree that winter had almost killed.

But when I next met Sir Joscelin and eagerly laid out my plans, his face fell.

"You will truly leave here, then? I never seriously meant you to go to Antioch. I merely wanted you not to fly to Constantinople. And how will you live without an income?"

"I have the gold that Adar al-Mas'ūdī gave me, and a gift of gems from Anna. I can grow my wealth if I meet merchants or...." I felt like a child.

But Sir Joscelin was rushing on. "No, no, when I think on it, you are right to leave here. It is like a prison to you, and I still can see you whenever I escort pilgrims there. Be of good heart, my love. You have done as well as any man in setting this all in motion, and Brother Dominic is so kind to help you. I am certain it will turn out for the best. My king's answer will arrive soon, and then I will be the happiest of men. I ... I wonder if you might stay here until after Christmas. And then we can begin to plan our wedding."

And he daringly took my hand and drew it to his lips, despite the possibility that someone might be watching us. I blushed and would have drawn it back, but he held it tightly. "There is no shame in our betrothal, my lady. I have already spoken of it to some of my fellows, and they claim that your beauty would tempt even a monk."

I laughed softly, but my eyes were casting about to see who might be observing and misunderstanding our conversation. No one seemed to be taking any notice, so I relented and let him kiss my hand twice more. Even that much inflamed my entire body. "Yes, of course I will stay."

When we left the garden, I glimpsed Old Agathe just inside the entrance to the convent, peering out at me. I caught such a look of—for lack of a better word—spite on her face before she turned away and began sweeping that I thought I had imagined it. I even stopped as I passed her and greeted her with attempted graciousness.

"Have you heard the good news, Agathe? Sir Joscelin and I are to be wed soon."

"If it happens, lady. If it happens." She bowed halfheartedly and went back to her sweeping, muttering something under her breath.

The following weeks saw me lost in arrangements and visits, first of all to Anna to thank her for the gems.

"It was nothing. I should have given them all to you long ago, but I was afraid of … of starving one day. But Adar says he will never let anything bad happen to me again." Her hand, however, went to a new little amulet that hung from a gold neck chain: the Hand of Fatima, Muslim Queen of Blessings. And my heart, too, did a little leap of fear at such bold hopes. But who knew, I told myself? Sometimes things did work out well.

I told Anna about Sir Joscelin and Antioch and all our hopes for the future. She clapped her hands and threw her arms around me, and all my annoyance and envy toward her melted away. Then she wept a little, with both sorrow and joy, "for you will be even farther away than you are now … but I am so happy for you!"

For the rest of that afternoon, we were no longer mistress and servant, nor even friend and friend, but sister and sister.

I bade farewell to Anna's hakim, too, for he came to the women's quarters after arriving home from some visit to a sick person. Evidently he was often away, caring for the ill and injured of all classes. From what I have read of Islam, I think he may have been the truest Muslim I ever met. Certainly he was the best of men.

I also paid several visits to the little hamlet below the convent. Brother Dominic had given me some small coins in exchange for one of the gold pieces from Adar al-Mas'ūdī's bride price, and most of these I gave to several people there. When I came to one-legged Jean, his housekeeper, squint-eyed Mary, was there. And on hearing I was leaving soon, she almost threw herself at my feet.

"Please take me with you! I so want to leave here and see the big world. No one wants me, and I will be the best servant anyone could ask for." And so on. Jean looked as surprised and alarmed as I felt, as memories arose of a similar scene with Anna. He looked ill-pleased at the thought of losing his cleaning girl, too, but even he softened at her tears of joy when I said, after some hesitation, that I would speak to her mother. And I assured him I could ask Old Agathe to come clean for him instead.

Both of which I did. To Mary's surprise and mine, her mother agreed with something like relief. There were likely feelings between them that I never learned about. Thus did I end up with a new servant, who, I must admit, never gave me as much trouble or did me as much good as my dear Anna.

I returned to the convent, ready in every way possible. Agathe was there, cleaning in her haphazard way, and even she seemed agreeable that day. Yes, she would care for Jean, whom she knew. "Perhaps I can even save him from his filthy habits," she said. I supposed the small gold coin I gave her had something to do with her graciousness.

Now there was nothing more to do but wait for the holy days to pass and to be with Sir Joscelin as much as possible until I left. Those times with him were brief, though, and not altogether satisfactory. I do not know what I had hoped for, perhaps some loving words, a few tender kisses, a parting full of hope. Instead, too often he seemed removed, as though an invisible burden had dropped upon him and was weighing him down.

Toward the middle of December, I decided to donate something to the convent. I wanted to offer something truly splendid, and I had my choice, thanks to Anna. I approached Brother Dominic about seeing the master of the convent, and he said he could arrange it within the day. And then I went to my casket for the best jewel in my little collection: a diamond that had been cut to perfection, with every facet casting rainbows when you looked at it.

It was not there.

And, I realized, a ruby that I had valued and a fair-sized pearl were also missing. In a panic, I searched my bedding and the floor. And then I realized the truth. If only one jewel were missing, I'd have thought I was careless, that Agathe had swept it up and thrown it away. But three? No, this was theft. I sat on my cot and thought back over the past week. I knew that all three gems had been there in that time, for I had taken everything out to choose one, and I had counted them and put them away carefully. And no pilgrims had been there. That left only one possibility, since Brother Dominic could not be suspected: Old Agathe.

Trembling inside and out, I found the monk next door busy amongst his herbs and happily singing a song of devotion. He stopped and smiled when I knocked and entered.

"Dear Brother, I feel as if I am about to spoil your joy. But I need your help."

He stopped and gave me his entire attention. Haltingly and with great self-doubt, I explained to him what had happened and why I suspected Old Agathe. His reaction at first was unease, which I took for disbelief. I stumbled on my words, came to a halt mid-sentence, and, hands spread hopelessly, said, "I cannot imagine anyone else even knowing about my casket, for I never told anyone but Sir Joscelin about it."

"This is grave news indeed. I thought she had been cured of her wickedness. Well, no harm done yet, for she cannot take them anywhere without bringing attention to herself. She is like a magpie, loves glittery things. She means no harm by it."

I was shocked, of course. Who knew how many women she had pilfered from without them knowing until they were well away? But I tried to match the mildness of my words to his. "Well, she may mean no harm, but she must return my gems. One of them I meant to give to this convent to show my gratitude. I suppose I should have known better than to leave the casket under my cot instead of hiding it, but when I lived among—" not wanting him to know about my captivity among the Mongols, I hastily changed course, "—with the family that took me in, no one ever thought of stealing from each other. But Agathe is not family, is she?"

"No," the monk sighed, his jaw jutting out a little more than usual, "she is a lost old woman with nothing more to do than spread tales—" He stopped short.

"Agathe spread tales about me? Why?"

He shrugged. "When we get your gems back, you can ask her yourself. She is somewhere here in the convent, doing her best to do very little." He smiled ruefully and hurried off to find an officer to bring the old woman to him.

When they arrived, she looking puzzled, the monk accused her straight-away. But instead of claiming wounded innocence, Agathe glared at me and cried, "You noticed, did you? You who have so much could surely spare something for me who has so little!"

"But I did—" Or had I?

She almost pounced on me, eyes glittering with hatred. "You have everything! Youth, beauty, strength to heal. Wealth falls on you like rain, you marry your servant off to a rich man, you find a handsome lover and now you will marry him! I have suffered nothing but disappointment and loss, but never once did you look my way or take an interest in me! And why would you, the great lady? I hate the way you mince about, acting like you are so noble. I know you for what you really are, you—"

"That is enough, Agathe. You have been given too many chances, and this is hardly the first time you have stolen from our guests. And your attacks on Lady Sofia are most unfair. I will have to take up with the council whether we should even keep you on anymore. Go now, and get what you stole from her. Brother Francis will go with you." Brother Francis, being more martial than brotherly, marched her off while she raged on against her lot in life.

I was shaking both with outrage and shame. Just as when Batu Khan had dealt so leniently with Qabul over Asetai's death, I felt as if justice had somehow slipped away and left me entrapped in a fire of emotions that I could not quench. Brother Dominic was looking at me curiously.

"Well, if I'd had any doubts about leaving the convent, Agathe certainly resolved them," I finally said.

The monk nodded sadly. "She is a lost old woman. But her story is sad. She followed her husband and son on pilgrimage to the Holy Land years ago and they both died in a raid. She was badly injured and left for dead, somewhat like you, but she lost everything. Now she must serve those who were once her equals. You see, she came of noble blood herself, but even after we sent word to her relatives in France, no one came for her. She has been slowly losing her wits for years."

"Well, I lost everything more than once. It never turned me bitter or into a thief."

He shook his head slightly and pressed his lips together. "You are still very young. But at least you will get your jewels back."

As if enough hadn't happened, a messenger appeared from the convent Master, saying he would meet with me right then. Still aflame with anger and a hazy sense of shame for all the good things that had indeed come to me, I followed him to a room in a part of the castle I had never visited before. If anything, this room was even more austere than Brother Dominic's little herb-adorned domain, for it contained only a simple lectern, a branched standing candelabrum in which only three tapers burned, a single bench, and a crucifix on one wall. The Master sat bent over the slanted desk looking at some documents, his tonsured head shining in the candlelight. His remaining hair was streaky gray; a scar ran over his forehead. He dipped his quill into a little bowl of ink and signed one of the documents before looking up at me.

I tried a modest bow, and then I realized that I no longer had the diamond with me and would not get it back until Old Agathe returned it. "I fear my visit is ill-timed, my lord. I intended to bring you a valuable diamond in gratitude for your generous hospitality in letting me stay so long, but it was stolen from me. It will be given back, but for now I stand before you empty-handed."

"Someone stole from you here in the castle? None of my knights would do such a thing!" Even in the gloom I could see his face change color.

"No, it was a servant."

"Who? He—or was it a woman?" His features darkened even more, and he looked ready to leap up and beat whoever the culprit was.

"Yes, but she will return it." And suddenly I too wanted to protect Old Agathe, who might lose her livelihood over this. "I do not want to cause any trouble. I have forgiven her."

He looked at me keenly. "You have?" I ducked my head, since in truth I had not, but I feared the Master might punish her far too severely.

"I will leave the jewel with Brother Dominic to pass to you. But at least I can thank you for your most Christian welcome to me. And I ask your good wishes for my betrothal to Sir Joscelin of Braissac, who has written to his king for permission for us to wed."

The Master, whose name I never ever knew, raised one eyebrow and sat silent for several moments. Finally, he nodded gravely. There was nothing more to say, so I bowed and left. I returned to the women's ward feeling as if a whirlwind had picked me up and dropped me. Indeed, now that I thought on it, Agathe's theft had given me a chance to practice Christian charity of my own, thus clearly establishing my virtue! I almost laughed aloud. Of course something would have to be done with her, but Brother Dominic would take care of that. Perhaps I would even give her another gold coin to show my forgiveness. Yes, I would! And I felt a rush of gladness that out of her petty evil had come good. Still, her theft gave me pause: among the Mongols, despite a host of other worries, I had never feared theft. I must learn caution.

SPRING ANNO DOMINI 1247
INTO SPRING, ANNO DOMINI 1248

Another penitential Advent and celebratory Christmas passed; again I helped Brother Dominic decorate the chapel. This time, though, I was a full participant not only in the Masses but also in the twelve days of festivity that followed. I had missed them last year, scarcely known there were any. But this year Sir Joscelin took me down to the village on the first day of January, where there was quite a display: a parody of the Mass called the Feast of Fools, with a Lord of Misrule, men dressed as women, and other follies!

With the festivities over, all that remained was for a band of pilgrims to pass this way, and I would finally be gone to Antioch. Waiting at the convent was a strange interlude of neither there nor gone. Finally a group of pilgrims arrived, and in a day or two I would leave. Sir Joscelin sought me out, and we strolled a little while in the garden and played a game of chess that neither of us put our hearts into. There was so little to say, not because we had nothing to tell each other but because we had too much. We spoke with our eyes instead.

At last he said, "I will see you in Antioch as soon as I can, my love. I begin to doubt that my letter ever reached my king, so I wrote him another, and this one goes with a ship's master I have known for some time and who just arrived in Antioch. He has carried important documents for King Louis and other dignitaries before. This time we will surely have success. Be of good heart, dearest. God holds us all in his hands." I could not answer. Sometimes God gripped us tightly and took us to places where we never wanted to go.

"One more thing, Sofia. You were most generous to Old Agathe. Now that she works in the kitchen, she can do little harm beyond stealing heels of bread. And the diamond you gave the convent will do much for us right now, too. We may be seeing many a battle in the not-distant future, for there are rumblings about a new holy war."

All I could answer was, "Yes, led by your king, I hear."

"So you know. This is another reason I may not have heard anything from him."

"Does ... do you think it bodes ill for us?"

"I cannot say. We must put our trust in God."

"Well, you can soon ask your king in person," I said lightly, but I was inwardly atremble.

The next day I left for Antioch. Sir Joscelin rode with us part of the way, but for form's sake he turned back after assuring me that we would not be parted for long. Instead, dear old Sir Foucald was my particular escort among our guides. And my new servant Mary, riding an ass behind me, was clearly delighted to be leaving. I was still surprised that I had taken her on. What kind of servant would she make?

Antioch was surprisingly close to Castle Sa'amar, only a few hours distant, and I was glad. I still did not like having to be out in the open for very long. I thought I saw bandits behind every pale, rocky hill, yet this land was not as empty or as dangerous as it seemed. We passed several castles that seemed to have grown out of the hillsides, with tiny villages and fields crouching below amidst patches of green. When I asked about them, Sir Foucald assured me that they were all held by Christian barons.

We arrived safely that afternoon, having ridden to the north end of spring-kissed, tree-clothed hills that swooped up from the flat terrain. Now we turned west and then south, and there was Antioch before us. We were soon crossing through a heavily guarded arched outer wall that led past the flanks of the largest mountain, with fortifications snaking up its sides and a strong citadel astride its peak. Inside and above this protected area, among green woods, I glimpsed what must be large country estates surrounded by their own walls.

Up close the tall, massive, turreted inner city walls looked as if they had survived some disfiguring disease, or at least many a battle. We passed through a broad gateway under a wide arch bordered by elegant carving, beyond which ran a straight street paved with great blocks of stone. It was the widest avenue I had ever seen, and it was teeming with people: soldiers; merchants with imamahs; finely dressed ladies with faces boldly exposed, mincing along with their servants and bodyguards; peasants pushing carts piled with vegetables or skinned lambs, or leading asses laden with grain sacks; and knights or perhaps nobles on horseback, their horses as gaudily attired as they were, followed sometimes by large retinues; a few ebony-skinned men dressed in flowing striped robes, often wearing heavy golden jewelry and crowned with unusually-wrapped imamahs, and followed by equally dark-skinned, strong-armed bodyguards; barefoot tonsured monks, some of them as filthy as Selim had said; and splendidly clad clergyman astride mules or borne in litters, surrounded by guards.

Yet that broad street held them all with ease. It seemed to go on forever, lined on either side with occasional pillared porches, most of them shabby and worn or half-fallen. Under them rested gaudy colored booths where men called out to passersby to see their wares. We pressed through the throng, past piles of lemons and baskets of olives or figs, braids of onions and stacks of peppers, great jars of oil, baskets large and small, lustrous pottery, and bright silks almost spilling off tables. The scent of pepper and other, more exotic spices tickled my nose. One man weighed salt on his scales, another weighed gold nuggets. Carpets as supple as cloth were unfurled before critical-eyed customers, and horses snorted and tried to rear as their handlers pried open their mouths to show wary buyers. I saw a slave market, too: naked children being offered up just like horses. Shouts and curses, bleats and whinnies, song and laughter filled the air.

Sir Foucald rode beside me, eager to point out and name all we saw. We turned off the great thoroughfare onto a side street that led to a smelly, slow-moving river he called the Orontes where passenger boats vied for space with barges carrying wood, sheep, chickens, and more. Half-naked children tossed bundles from shore to boat; boatmen cursed each other.

I grew faint with the closeness of so many bodies, such noise, such commotion. And then we were in the courtyard of an inn, dismounting, entering a large common room filled with cooking smells, trestle tables, and benches. One knight carrying our baggage led Mary and me up a flight of stairs. At the top was a hallway lined with doors. The other pilgrims were entering the room below and being greeted by an invisible host. Our guide unlocked a door at the end of the hall and waved us into a tiny room. Behind us came the pilgrims, led by a plump monk wearing an apron over his cassock. He and I looked at each other curiously in passing.

The knight set our goods on the floor. "Here is the key to your room. It is the best, kept for guests of the Master of the Convent. He offers it to you until you move to your new quarters. It is simple but clean." He bowed out.

I looked around at a tiny room scarcely large enough for a narrow bed, a chair and a table. A crucifix hung on the wall. It was, I reminded myself, simply a place for a monk knight to sleep. The castle had seemed welcoming by contrast, though the Master was being most generous to me.

Mary seemed happy, though. She began unpacking our things as though born to her new role. She stood a bedroll beside the door. "I will sleep by it tonight, my lady, and right now you can go out if you wish. I will make this place seem welcome. At least it is big." Mary seemed to feel more at home than I did. And as for big!

But I took her advice and went back downstairs. The common room was empty. I supposed my fellow travelers were still upstairs settling into even smaller rooms. I wandered outside, feeling utterly alone, to find my escorts lolling on benches in the courtyard, basking in the late-day sunshine and sharing some mild jest. They stood up with grave courtesy when they saw me, however, and Sir Foucald took my hand and, having led me to a bench away from the men, handed me a crude goblet of watered wine.

"Please take your ease, Lady Sofia. I have decided that I would like to show you some of the holy sites in the morning." He turned to his fellow knights. "We all wish to go, yes?" They nodded or grunted assent.

I felt as if I had gotten stuck in a dream where everyone else knew what was happening and I was a doll being moved here and there—surely I should be searching for a house—but I was too overwhelmed by this busy new world to protest. But then I decided perhaps it would be wise to explore the city while performing this pilgrimage and form a plan afterwards. I thanked him for his generosity.

The knight who had led me to my room was now lolling on a bench, too. He smiled and said, "We are grateful to you, too, Lady, for caring for Sir Joscelin so well. He would have been hard-missed by us all had he died. Although I hear we will miss him soon enough. I speak of your betrothal."

I blushed and nodded, glad to hear the bell summoning us into supper.

I awoke the next dawn to the pealing of hundreds of church bells. After breakfast, Sir Foucald, as eager as a boy with a new whistle, said, "We go on pilgrimage today."

So I went on my first-ever pilgrimage with him and his fellow knights, trailed by an eager Mary. I am glad that I went, for Antioch is a rare and wondrous star in the Christian firmament. It was there that the word Christian arose, I think when Saint Peter and Barnabas preached and assembled their first flock of faithful, who were no longer only Jews but also former pagans. It was there that Saint Paul and Saint Peter quarreled over those same Gentiles. And it was there that I ceased to feel afraid outside, for after awhile, all the noise and color and sheer numbers of people benumbed me!

I saw many holy relics that day that had reposed in Antioch from earliest times, including, they say, the very spear that pierced Christ's side. It was discovered by a man called Peter the Hermit just when the Frankish armies, trapped in Antioch after capturing it, needed a miracle. That tarnished the story in my eyes. In Rus', frauds were forever selling false relics. Besides, after my capture by the Mongols I no longer put faith in objects, even holy ones, to shield anyone.

But my heart would be ice not to be moved by the grotto Church of Saint Peter, built, according to tradition, right into the mountain by the saint himself. It was discovered and given a new facade by the same knights who took heart from the spear. The facade is adorned with arches and pierced with two great star windows and a square cross set aslant. Inside you can see fading frescoes on the cave walls, and a most ancient mosaic tile floor underfoot. The first fathers of the Church may have worshipped there once.

And high above the church is another kind of relic called the Charonion, carved right onto the side of the mountain: a massive bust of some cloaked being, beside it a smaller figure with a basket on its head, both of them ancient and worn.

"How odd," I commented.

One knight spoke up. "It is claimed that they were carved to appease the Roman gods during a plague. For all Antioch's vaunted wealth and beauty, it has suffered not only from repeated plagues but from wars and floods—and earthquakes, one of which killed over a quarter of a million people centuries ago." We all crossed ourselves, and I for one prayed that no such disasters afflict the city anymore.

We visited a few other holy sites and saw the relics of a Saint Simeon Stylites, who had lived for many years standing atop a pillar, praying, while his body wasted away and his feet rotted under him. We also had to visit the southern walls of the city, probably as holy to a fighting monk as were saint's relics. Surprisingly, the fortifications were lavishly decorated with beautiful bands of brickwork, even around each turret's arched window.

I arrived back at the inn too weary to think about what to do next. But I could not postpone my life forever, and the next day I arose determined to find a place to live. Fighting off dread, I broached the subject with Sir Foucald at breakfast, who looked surprised.

"Was that not settled between you and our Master?" I must have looked my confusion. "He arranged for you to rent a house owned by our order. I will take you there today. First, of course, you must find a cook and other servants besides Mary. And will you need to go to a money house? I do not wish to pry, but if you do need help with...."

I blushed and shook my head. "I had no idea which way to turn, and now it seems that all has been done for me. And thank you for your kind offer, my friend, but thanks to the hakim and Anna I have enough to be comfortable until Sir Joscelin and I are wed.

"But if I may, I would ask one favor: I have thought on this for some time. I wish to invest in some kind of trading venture." Sir Foucald looked unsure, and I rushed on, "Not directly, of course, but surely women are allowed to profit from the lively commerce I see going on all around me."

"Well, I'll see what I can find out for you. We Hospitallers have trade connections, certainly. Perhaps you can join in some venture as an invisible partner."

We visited so many offices and markets that day that I remember little but crowds, smells, colors, and one particular stall. We had hired trustworthy servants, found a few lengths of bright silk for me, and were buying things the cook at the Hospitaller inn wanted when a small, dirt-encrusted, dark-haired urchin appeared out of the corner of my eye. He darted between us, his hand already cupping a fruit, but the next thing I knew, there was a screech and the boy was dangling in the air by his arm, the merchant was shouting terrible threats, and I was seizing the boy's other arm.

"He is my servant; he was trying to help! He means no harm," I cried on impulse, hoping the boy was a stranger to him. "Let my boy go." The merchant looked disbelieving, but he released the child, who clung to my waist, howling.

"Stop that right now, Alexander," I said sternly, and took his hand as if we truly did know each other. "If you wish to learn how to serve me properly, you must stand quietly by my side while I finish my business here. You must never reach for things like that again."

"Alexander" was shrewd enough to go along with my pretense, but after we had left the market behind, he cried, "How did you know my name?"

"I didn't. And you are free to go now."

"But don't you see: I must serve you now! Fate says so. I will truly be your servant, and I will be your best boy in the world!"

Sir Foucald, meanwhile, who had been sending Alexander dark looks— and fuming at me, I suspect—burst out, "Now you stop bothering the lady. You were lucky today, but another time you will end up with your hand cut off for theft! Get on, now! Go home!"

"But I have no home." And the child burst into tears.

That settled it. "I must take him in, Sir Foucald. It is the Christian thing to do."

The old knight looked aghast and would likely have argued with me on both counts, but I added, "If you think me in error, perhaps he can find a place as a servant at the convent. When you return there, you can ask. Meanwhile I will care for the boy."

So with that quarrel averted, Sir Foucald finally led the way to my new lodgings. It was quite a parade: Mary, my new servants—a cook, a man-of-all-work, and Alexander—and an ass laden with my purchases, some basic provisions, and a few delicacies I could not resist. While we climbed a steep, roundabout road through thin woods, I got to know my new "best boy."

"Why do you have no home?"

"My mother and father died of plague." This he said as if he was merely stating that the sky was blue.

"When?"

"A year ago. I was nine, and my older sister's husband did not want me. He beat me, so I ran away and learned to beg. Better than beatings!"

"Beatings are wrong, but so is stealing. It is not begging, and you must not do it again. If you are caught, you might lose your hand and you will certainly lose my protection."

"Oh, lady, I will be so good, you will not remember the old me!"

At that, I looked squarely at the child. Under the dirt was a wise-innocent face with dark eyes, a grinning mouth that held more rotten teeth than good, and an expression of such mischievous sincerity that I had to smile, too. "When we get to my new home, you must bathe, and we will find you something besides rags to wear." Now Alexander looked aghast.

By late afternoon we had arrived at a compound, the red-tile roofed house surrounding a cool courtyard with an outdoor cooking area; had looked into the four spacious rooms; spoken many grateful farewells to Sir Foucald; and begun to unpack. My new home looked out over the city, and while my new cook Jonah sent wonderful aromas floating across the yard, I strolled to the edge of the property and watched the stars come out. Behind me Mary quarreled cheerfully with Alexander, insisting that she would be a better sister than his was and that he must wash all of himself or she would do it for him. His body held no surprises for her. She knew all there was to know about men.

My other new servant, a Greek named Efrem, was already at work repairing a disused outbuilding he planned to sleep in. And I had plans, too. Soon my beloved would join me, letter of permission in hand. Meanwhile, with the introductions to a few merchants Foucald had found for me, I would grow my wealth into a proper dowry. I spent a few more delicious moments bathed in soft evening air before going happily to bed.

The next morning, eager to put my plans into action, I set Alexander to work planting a garden with Jonah the cook while I took Maria and Efrem down to the shipyards. It turned out that finding a merchant willing to allow a woman to invest her money with him was not easy. Of those who even gave me an audience, most scoffed at me. But finally I found one who would listen. We wrote up a contract, had it witnessed by a notary, and I was suddenly the owner of shares in olive oil and silks bound for a city called Marseilles. It was thrilling to be part of the trading world again, though my new partner, Matthew of Edessa as he styled himself, warned me that if the ship foundered, there was no redress for my monies unless I bought some form of insurance. So I did, though some-how, after enduring so much doubt for so many years, that day I felt held up by God. I knew all would go well.

When I returned home with simple new garments for Alexander, he was almost beside himself and put them on right away. He preened about like a peacock until I brought him to order and sent him off to help Efrem. Mary and I finished unpacking our things, and by day's end she had swept and scrubbed floors while I set out carpets and arranged two old chairs and a table in different ways, pushed my bed into a better place, and gen-erally made the house into a home.

Over the next few days, I felt like a rosebud unfurling its petals in the sun. I found the nearest church and diligently went to Mass twice, taking all my servants with me. Alexander was not well pleased, but he submitted nonetheless. My servants and I explored the many markets, where Efrem held court. A youngish man, heavily bearded, evidently to hide a scar, for part of it crossed his nose, he was both pleasant-mannered and dignified. He seemed to know almost everyone; certainly he had come well recom-mended to Sir Foucald, who had hired him for me. Mary, I think, fell straight in love with Efrem, and he soon had Alexander following him about like a puppy. He showed us all around the city, explaining bits of history he had picked up or even picking up tiles off the ground, lost from some ancient mosaic wall or floor. Antioch is truly a city of marvels, both sacred and profane. Its past includes everything: self-denying saints and vicious chariot races, Roman ruins and Greek cathedrals, fabulous wealth and desperate poverty, and more kinds of people and faiths than I had seen since the Mongol camps.

By the following Sunday, I felt settled in and ready to greet my beloved. Nor was I disappointed. Sir Joscelin was awaiting me at my house after Mass, taking his ease with a cup of wine and some leftover bread.

Indeed, it was Hugh's voice I heard first, shouting to his master as he came out of Efrem's hut. "It's a carpenter's workshop, Sir Joscelin! A good one, just like at home—Oh, my lady, I beg your pardon!"

I was laughing, Sir Joscelin was smiling broadly as he strode forward to take my hands and give me a chaste kiss on the cheek, and even my new servants seemed pleased for me. That entire afternoon seemed golden with happiness, for he stayed almost too late to find his way back to the Hospitaller inn in the dark. Yet I remember not a single word that passed between us, only that every glance was filled with promise, every smile was a door into further gladness.

Sir Joscelin took me riding the next day; he had found a mild mare for me as a gift. I tried to decline, but he insisted, saying that it would be mine soon enough, anyway.

"Does that mean you have news?"

"Not exactly. A royal ship arrived last night, though, and I hope to find a letter from my king awaiting me. In fact if you wish it, we could go into town together and see for ourselves. I go back to the convent the day after tomorrow, though, and I would spend all of today with you if I could." I could not refuse him.

That afternoon, leaving Hugh demonstrating swordplay to Alexander, we explored the woods surrounding my house, following animal trails and getting delightfully lost. We found a shady dell where water poured from a rocky fissure, and my knight helped me dismount. He led me by the hand to sit on a soft sward of grass near it, where we sat side by side, no words needed.

Then I was in his arms. His kisses alone would have inflamed me, but his hands gently touching me here and there made me drunk with passion. He could have done anything with me he wanted. I moaned with pleasure.

And he stopped.

Pulling away, he cried, "Forgive me, my heart's treasure!"

"What?"

"Dear God, I would never hurt you. We must wait. We both know it, you better than I. I almost forgot the harm that came to Yolande through me!"

I could not speak, had to turn my head away to hide my despair, I wanted him and hated her so much right then. But I think he took my gesture to mean something else.

Without another word, we got up and returned to my house. Only when he was leaving did I find my voice. "There is nothing to forgive, my love. I am no saint, either."

Sir Joscelin smiled dimly and kissed my hand. "I will be back tomorrow morning, hopefully with the best of news. In the meantime, think kindly of me, dearest."

Sleep was no comfort that night. A dream came to me. I was on a windy beach awaiting a ship, but it was not mine. Someone was on it, though, with an important message for me. Out to sea, dark clouds were blotting out the sky. Suddenly a torrent of rain swept toward me, churning the waves, carrying them forward, pulling them into the sky, until I was facing a wall of deep blue-green water, the ship a blur in its depths. I tried to run, but the water was faster. It picked me up and tossed me like a leaf, and I awoke, drenched in sweat.

I waited for Sir Joscelin all morning. Just before noon, Hugh appeared alone, with a message for me to come to the city. He would say nothing more to me, nor did his bearing offer any clues. I followed him straightaway, my heart in my throat. Something must have happened. Once in Antioch, he led me to the dockyard where a ship was taking on cargo as well as a few knights with their horses and servants. There stood my knight, directing workmen and looking stern. Taking my hands and kissing them, without a word he handed me a thick-papered letter. I opened it.

"You must read it to me; I cannot make out such ornate writing."

Sir Joscelin nodded and began:

> *Louis by the grace of God King of the French,*
>
> *Greetings to my right worthy subject, Sir Joscelin of Braissac.*
>
> *You are commanded to wait upon me in Paris so soon as you receive this letter. My ship will bring you hither. Be thou righteous and loyal to me.*
>
> *Your most royal sovereign,*
>
> *King Louis IX'"*

"What does it mean?"

"I am as mystified as you are. It arrived by courier this morning. He surely summons me because he will use my knowledge in aid of his war plans. But it makes me doubt that he received my letters. At least when I see him, I can present our pleas directly. I leave tonight." My eyes welled with tears and he hastened on, "But I have been thinking while awaiting you. Perhaps you could accompany me."

This seemed a splendid idea to me, but when he approached the ship's captain, the man flatly refused. "This is not a passenger ship, and I have no room for women! You'll have to leave your pretty little piece here and hope she doesn't desert you while you're gone."

"She is my betrothed!"

I thought Sir Joscelin might strike him, but I drew him away and spoke quietly. "Just promise you'll be back as soon as you can. Never fear; I will wait for you."

"Every moment will be an eternity. Do you need or want anything before I go?"

"No, only the comfort of your arms and heart. Someday we will have both cleanly. But as Saint Paul said, 'It is better to marry than to burn, so hurry back to me!'"

We both laughed wanly.

We spent the rest of the day together aimlessly wandering about the busy city, saying little. At one point Sir Joscelin bought me a filigreed necklace and golden earrings, "To wear on our wedding day."

And then he had to leave. Though I tried to keep up a brave face, after many tender farewells at the ship, I made my way home, alone, cold despair slowly seeping into my heart. Who knew when he would return, if ever?

SUMMER INTO AUTUMN
ANNO DOMINI 1248

Spring passed in a blur, summer unfolded, and Jonah's garden flourished, as did my little establishment. Toward midsummer I received a too-brief letter from Sir Joscelin, containing many endearments and the news that he had arrived in Paris and was awaiting his first audience with the king. I spent my time quietly, often going to Mass with my servants or practicing peace in the dell that I now regarded as my special retreat.

My ship returned and made me, if not wealthy, at least well-off. I invested most of these gains with Matthew of Edessa again, this time in spices and dyes, as the profits promised to be even greater. But that was just the merchant in me, for what use had I for profits if I did not have my beloved?

That fall my birthday came and went, and I even knew its date. I went to Mass that day, but the Holy Mother's feast day is different in the Roman faith, so I simply made a large offering to the church, requesting that the priest pray for the souls of my parents, my nursemaid Baba Liubyna, Lady Q'ing-ling, and my lost friend and the kindest Mongol I had ever known: Asetai. I didn't tell him that my family was Orthodox, one friend was a heretic, and the other was a pagan.

Alexander, when I was not tutoring him in both manners and letters, was always in the kitchen or in Efrem's workshop. Jonah and Efrem began teaching him a little of their respective trades—I think they even competed a little over him. And Mary was fond of him, too, despite the silly tricks he often played on her. But one morning he disappeared, and no manner of our calling or searching for him turned him up.

Finally Mary said, "We may as well leave it for now, mistress. He knows how to handle himself, and if he has gotten up to mischief, it is a boy's nature. There is no real harm in him. He knows where we are."

Sure enough, late that afternoon he reappeared, escorting a pair of children as ragged and dirty as he had been, both with wildly tangled, curly dark hair that reminded me of my lost tutor's curls. "I brought you more servants," he said. "We used to st—beg together, and I thought to myself that they could work for you, too." I was taken aback at first, but then a memory of Derbent came to me: all those lost, unloved beggar children I hadn't been able to help.

"Well, then, what are your names and ages, and where are you from?"

The children seemed surprised that I hadn't simply turned them out, but the boy spoke up readily enough. "I am Fotis and this is my sister Irene. I am eleven, I think, and she is two years younger than me. We are from a village in the country. We came here with our parents last summer, they left our older brothers and sisters behind. Father said we would get to see the big city. He told us to wait in a market square while they went on an errand, but they never came back. Maybe they just wanted to be rid of two more mouths to feed or maybe something happened to them. We met Alexander that night. We were so cold and hungry and scared. He shared his food with us and taught us how to beg and st—. He is our good friend."

"Well, I will take you in on two conditions: first, you must never steal or even beg again. Next, you must obey me in all things. If you ever break our agreement, I will turn you out." I spoke rather fiercely, I suppose, but it had the desired effect.

Both children cried, in a mismatched chorus, "Oh yes, we will! We are good, really we are! We can work hard!" And so on.

I laughed. "I believe you. Now, the first thing is, as Alexander will tell you …"

"A bath," Alexander crowed, "and clean clothes!"

And so began a new chapter in my life. Alexander, though not the eldest, was clearly the leader of the three. Over the summer they settled in. I gave them lessons, my servants gave them work, and on the rare times when we had no use for them, they were off in the wood playing games of chase or war. Once Irene came back crying that she had been left out, so I began teaching her sewing. And the boys seemed to select a skill naturally: Alexander became Efrem's apprentice in the workshop and Fotis helped Jonah. With so many children around, I began to feel almost like a mother myself.

And then the idea came to me. There must be untold numbers of beggar children in Antioch. Why not make a home for them? The longer I thought on it, the more I liked the idea. I was comfortably well off, and I could use part of the profits from my ship ventures to buy a suitable house with enough rooms to hold at least a dozen children. I would need a reliable steward and a woman, not just to keep house but to mother them. And while Efrem and Jonah taught them their skills, I could teach them reading and writing and mathematics! By the end of these reflections, my imagination had filled the house with happy children learning to lead useful lives.

Charged with a new sense of purpose, I decided that the best place to start would be with Efrem, who knew his way around Antioch so well. He was not keen on the idea at first and came up with many reasons against it. "After all, you were lucky with the first three imps you brought home, but not all street children are so good. You may be asking for trouble."

"Well, let us see what we can find out, and then find the children. Indeed, when I think on it, I wonder about the slave market, too."

I began looking for a suitable town house right away. After a day of searching with Efrem's help, I realized that to lodge my future wards in the heart of the city would not work. Antioch is a place designed to tempt the wayward of all ages and ranks. But with so many outbuildings on my property, why not use it? I straightaway wrote to the Master of Sa'amar castle asking him to help by either donating the building or selling it to me; and I got Efrem and Mary to make rooms ready in the abandoned buildings.

But then I thought, why wait for his answer? I summoned Alexander and asked if he could find other likely beggar children. His eyes lit up. "Oh yes! And I will watch out for the bad ones that go in gangs. They would slit your throat as soon as look at you!"

"Then be very careful who you bring me."

I also went to the slave market, which was almost too painful. I thought myself well off, but not enough to buy more than two children among the dozens for sale. I did find two sweet-faced girls, one dark-skinned and one pale as the moon, both about ten, both almost frighteningly pliant. The dark girl, whose black hair was like little coils of filigree, was named Banjuu; the pale girl, even to her hair, was Marguerite.

The two could not have come from more different worlds, but their stories were just the same. Banjuu was from somewhere called Mali, a place so distant, she said in halting Arabic, that even she could not imagine it. Marguerite was Frankish and knew nothing but her native language. Luckily I had learned enough French from my knight to speak with her.

I drew out their stories as I led them back home. Each had been captured in raids, their parents had been killed; both had been terrorized and sold to the slave merchant I had dealt with. I suspect that his plan had been to sell them to wealthy men or, failing that, to whorehouses, as both were still virgins from what I could glean. They were pitiably grateful to be set free and given a home, and each clung to one of my hands as we wound up the mountain path.

On arriving home and presenting them to the other children, though, I began to see what a challenge I had set myself. The boys gaped at Banjuu in wonder, while Irene was all frowns at both girls. Well, I had learned from Anna what that meant, so I straightaway sat them all down before me.

"Boys, Irene, these are my rules. These girls are like your little sisters. They need your help. It would be best if you can make friends, but I will not demand that. What I do expect is that you will teach them what you have learned from me. There will be many more children living here soon, and each time I bring someone home, you and now Banjuu and Marguerite will need to pass on what you are learning. If you cannot do that, then you no longer belong here. Is that understood?" I looked at each child in turn, who nodded solemnly, looking a little afraid.

I softened. "You know I treat you all gently, and that is because there is room in my heart to love you all, but part of my love is these rules. Now, Irene, show Banjuu and Marguerite where they will sleep."

And so began my little orphanage. Giving the children lessons, seeing them learn from my other servants, listening to them at play, witnessing their steps toward self-control, I realized I had not been so deeply satisfied with life in years. And when I received a courteous if puzzled reply from the Master that allowed me to use the buildings as I had planned—they would remain Hospitaller property, but I would pay no rent—I knew in my bones that my plan would succeed.

Many events flowed from those first days: finding a different place to live, hiring people to run the orphanage, seeing to supplies, and so on. They filled my days with so much activity that I had no time to worry about Sir Joscelin and brood about our future, except at nights when I dreamed of him. I wrote to Anna and Maryam and they replied; all was well with both. My third ship came in, and I decided to invest twice as much as before: in two ships, one carrying spices, hemp cloth and rope, and dried fruit; the other lumber and silks. Those ships returned safely, too, carrying elegantly wrought gold and glass items from Venice that I had ordered to sell in Antioch. With profits pouring or perhaps sailing in, I was able to rescue even more children.

And I realized I also had a personal reason to amass wealth: to grow my dowry.

I moved into the heart of Antioch. It was hard to find a suitable place to live in that busy city, but after much searching, I finally found a town house bare of everything but dirt, set around a little courtyard with a stove. Leaving Efrem and Jonah behind was hard, but they loved the children too much for me to ask them to come with me, and they were such good teachers. But squint-eye Mary came with me. She was heartbroken. She cleaned the place thoroughly, tears dripping off her nose; but then she pulled herself together and hired a boy for menial work, while I bought and arranged simple furnishings.

My street was noisy day and night, and there were rogues aplenty in that city, of every age and color. I soon realized how lucky I had been coming and going alone after a man tried to lift my wallet. I fought him off with screams and a strong punch that knocked him off balance when he grabbed not only at my money but at my breasts! But after that I always hired extra guards whenever I went out, which thenceforth was in a hired litter. Mary's boy took to sleeping in front of my bedroom door with a knife after the night when a fight among drunken sailors down the street led to murder. So I hired a burly man with a perpetual scowl and a heart of gold to be both manservant and guardian: Bardas. He hailed from Cyprus, though his family roots were in a country just north of Antioch, called Cilicia, which he told me was Armenian and Christian.

After settling in, I spent my time teaching my wards, visiting the slave markets to find new children, and introducing new charges to the orphanage. Sometimes I wrote Sir Joscelin or Maryam or Anna, and I always enjoyed hearing from my lady friends. No word came from my beloved, but he was so far away that I felt lucky to have received his first letter. Truth be told, though, all three seemed so far away. And had I not been so busy, I might have been very lonely, for I knew no one else in Antioch.

However, that was about to change. At Christmas after Mass, a heavyset young woman, richly clad in the Oriental style, approached me and asked if I might be Lady Sofia. "My name is Lady Helene of Belmont, and Sir Joscelin of Braissac recently sent me a message by way of my husband asking me to befriend you and make you welcome. Lord Gilles is come home from Paris to prepare for King Louis' arrival, and I think he bears a letter for you from him."

"You know Sir Joscelin?" I asked eagerly.

"Only slightly myself, but Lord Gilles served a noble close to Amaury de Montfort back in Paris and became friendly with Sir Joscelin then. He is some years older than Joscelin, but I think he took him under his wing when he was a squire and Gilles was already a knight. They renewed their friendship after Lord Gilles came out to Antioch on his own lord's business. That was also when my husband and I met." She blushed.

As we walked down the church steps, she took my arm in the most natural way, causing me a pang of memory. Where was Perijam now? I did not want to revisit those memories, especially right then!

"And how did you meet Sir Joscelin?"

"Here in Antioch when he sometimes visited us after bringing pilgrims here. We both think him a brave and courteous knight. Lord Gilles was recalled to Paris for some months, but he just returned. He says Sir Joscelin will soon join him in Antioch, which news I imagine will gladden your heart. But until then, if you wish, we will gladly present you to others of our rank. Many of them already know of you: the widow who saves orphans. We would be honored if you would join us after the Feast of Circumcision Mass for our own celebration."

I readily accepted, glad not only to make friends but grateful that my beloved was keeping watch over me even at a distance. I could scarcely wait for that letter, but happily Lady Helene sent it over to me right away. It contained all the same news she had given me, but with many loving thoughts added that made me fairly float with joy.

When I arrived on the appointed day with Bardas close behind me, I was impressed by the superior location of my new friend's home on a quiet street on a hill overlooking the busy city. I felt a pang of envy and wondered how one found such fine lodgings. I would not mind moving!

The door opened, and a servant bowed me into the fine house before directing Bardas around back to the kitchen to take his place with the other servants. Lady Helene came forward and took my hands, and her husband, a hearty man as big as an aurochs, with massive moustaches, introduced me to a group of friendly and curious people. At first I felt shy, fearing I might let something slip about my past, but they were more interested in their witty exchanges and gay laughter than in prying secrets from me. I finally let down my guard and joined their merry games, though when the floor was cleared and the music began, I would not dance with any of the men who asked me.

Soon Helene and her friends were visiting back and forth with me and including me in their outings. Their companionship was my first easy friendship with women in years. Several of them also offered clothing and alms for the children, most welcome.

Winter turned into spring. I observed Lent, celebrated Easter. The more I saw of the city, the more I realized that it was a place full of temptation, and not only for lost children. Helene was constantly trying to widen my circle of acquaintance, which of course included eligible men of high degree, some of whom seemed to think that as a widow I might welcome their flirtations and, perhaps, more. Yet none of the men I met could compare with my own dear knight, and none tempted me.

My temptations were material. I was prone to buy some pretty trinket on a whim and then to buy several more to give to my little girls. And my wardrobe became quite lavish, if rather Oriental, though that was common in Antioch among man and woman alike.

Helene also took me to everything from religious festivals to jousts, always surrounded by many guards to fend off thief and beggar alike. I did not care for the jousting, though.

I liked the horse races better, evidently a legacy of a time when Romans raced chariots in a great building called a hippodrome, a pile of rubble now, which had been freely pirated for other buildings.

And of course there were always my children to visit and letters to write to Sir Joscelin and my friends. I heard from him once more, though evidently he had written one letter that I never received. That was one of many letters that went astray over the years. However, he had received my last letter. His read thus:

Beloved Sofia,

Greetings from Paris, where I am now one of many in the king's war council. He seems to trust my judgment about battle strategy if not my morals, and I have been able to suggest a few changes to his plans that should prevent a long war. But I feel thwarted at every turn by his brother, Prince Robert of Artois. The man has never seen real battle, and he not only glorifies war in the vainest way, he proposes foolish tactics that I try to turn aside, not always with success!

From your last letter, I realized that my most recent missive did not find its goal, that is to say, your fairest of all hands. But I want to say how amazed I am at all you have done, and how proud of you.

I wish I could give you firm word about our betrothal. I have tried to raise the question with King Louis, but he will speak to me only of the upcoming war as I am valued strictly for my experience in the Holy Land. I fear the days of personal friendship are over. Nonetheless, I will not rest until I have got his permission!

Meanwhile think kindly of me, your errant but worshipful knight.

Adieu, my dearest,

Sir Joscelin of Braissac

This letter was something of a blow to me, although in my hopeful dreams, all would soon be happily resolved. King Louis had to see how devoted his subject was to him, and surely that would lead to his not only restoring my sweet knight to his favor but also allowing him to marry me. After all, I was not only now a wealthy woman but was descended from royalty, including the royal family of Francia itself, so neither riches nor lineage could be any obstacle to our union!

Another missive that I received soon after was a delightful surprise: it was from my uncle. When I had written him, I'd had no idea whether my letter would ever reach him, but the traffic between Antioch and Constantinople is constant and mostly reliable. His letter was short but full of news:

Dear niece,

I cannot express my delight over receiving your letter. It was a miracle sent straight from God! I wept when I read it, just as I wept many tears over the loss of my family when I heard of the fall of Kyiv. I am of course amazed that you somehow survived.

I am now married to a noblewoman from Venice, Caterina Falieri, and we have three children and expect another soon. I also have done well for myself as a merchant—Kyiv's legacy lives on in my blood—and I have a hand in the thriving trade with the kingdom of Nicaea. In case you don't know, it's the most powerful of the survivor states that arose after Constantinople fell.

Sofia, you are welcome to come to me any time. I will take you into the bosom of my family, and this can be your home from then on.

With love and blessings,

Your uncle Vasily, now known as Basil the Rus'

How ironic that my long-cherished dream was now in reach just when a new one had been born!

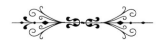

The news I had yearned for came:. Sir Joscelin wrote that he was returning to Antioch and to me by midsummer. When the time neared, I hired a boy to keep watch for my knight's ship at the docks.

When he brought word that a ship carrying knights from Francia was docking, it was a cloudless morning promising heat; thankfully, a soft breeze blew away some of the city's stench. I hurriedly collected the first five children I had adopted, and we went to the quay with high hopes. They made a pretty sight among the gritty laborers and sailors who thronged the docks. All too slowly, the passengers left the ship—lines of armed men with squires and pages and horses and arms. I had begun to despair when Sir Joscelin appeared. Abandoning all pretense of dignity, I began waving to him wildly until I caught his eye. He broke into a huge smile and, with a word to Hugh behind him, strode straight down the ramp. At my signal, my girls stepped forward with flowers in their hands and my boys bowed courteously. I could not have been more proud of them.

I had never seen Joscelin look so happy. Hugh and another squire behind him led down two heavily-laden horses, one a monster of a war-horse. Ignoring stares of passersby and a few lewd calls from some wharf men, Sir Joscelin swept me into his arms and kissed me on both cheeks. My children cheered, and so did a few onlookers.

After we had stared into each other's eyes as if to enter each other's souls, Sir Joscelin finally pulled back and looked around. "So these are your new wards."

"Only the first five," I laughed. "Another thirty now live in my home for children."

After presenting each of the children to him, we strolled over to the Hospitaller inn, sharing morsels of news as they arose in our minds. There he left all but one of his many bundles, a bulky package that one of the children asked him about. He just smiled secretively.

"You will see later. Come, Sofia, we can leave Hugh and Philippe, my new squire there, to unpack." The handsome dark-haired youth bowed courteously.

"I want to see your home for children," Joscelin added, resting his hands briefly on Fotis and Irene's shoulders. They looked as if they might swoon with delight. As we walked into the city and up the hill to the home, Irene slipped her hand into his, and he smiled down at her. Once again I was reminded of my Papa, and my heart almost stood still.

What an afternoon that was, too full to recount half of its joys. A feast awaited us at the end of our long walk, and two of the children had even woven wreaths for Sir Joscelin and me. I cannot say how they knew so much about us, as I certainly had said nothing, but child and adult alike were determined to make this a happy reunion. And in turn my beloved gladdened every child's heart when he opened his package to reveal small wooden toys and sweets for them all.

He had a gift for me, too: a new journal. "I seem to recall that you lost at least one in that Bedouin raid, yes? I thought you might like to try writing again now that you have some good memories to put in this one," he smiled. I had written nothing since filling and then losing the book Batu Khan had given me. I had not even thought of replacing it, but I could scarcely contain my delight, could only thank him with a voice choked with emotion. Indeed, now I did have good memories.

We returned to Antioch as the sun touched the back of the mountain top, and by the time we had reached my house, it was almost dark. We kissed good night, a long kiss that hinted of pleasures to come, and it was not until he had left that I realized we had not once spoken about his interview with his king. Well, that could wait until tomorrow, I thought happily as I drifted into sweet sleep.

Early the next morning, someone began pounding on the front door. Surprised but certain it was Sir Joscelin, I sent Bardas to answer it while I put on my best gown. But when I came downstairs, two bearded strangers stood in my small main room, glaring at each other. Then they turned the same fierce faces on me.

"Bardas, stay with me, please. And who, sirs, might you be?"

One of the men, whose imamah resembled Adar al-Mas'ūdī's, stepped forward. "As I arrived first, I will speak first." The second man looked offended but merely crossed his arms. "You are the Lady Sofia and you have a home for children, yes?"

"I am and I do. Again, who are you and what is your business with me, to enter my home so rudely and with no introduction?"

"I am Mullah Mustapha ibn al-Auda. I serve those few of True Faith allowed in the city. And you are kidnapping Muslim children and forcing them to convert to Christianity!"

"And Jewish children, too!" the other man added. "I am Rabbi Benjamin of Antioch, and I am here to protest this outrage!"

I stared at both men in confusion. "I hardly know what to say. I never thought to ask my children about religion. They do all go to Mass on Sundays, but none ever objected—"

"Of course not. Doubtless they are terrified to let anyone know what their faith is, and it was only by All-Merciful Allah's grace that I even learned of this. You house a girl named Banjuu, do you not? And a boy named Yaqub."

"Why, yes, but as I say, it never occurred to me. Nor do I know of any Jewish children among my wards." I turned to the rabbi, whose head covering I now noted, was not an imamah after all. Some kind of small box was also bound to his head, just above his forehead, and black straps were wrapped in a pattern around his left hand before winding up his arm. "What are their names?"

"One only; his name is Isaac. Not a Christian name at all," the man said scornfully.

"Well, let me think a moment. Please, be seated." Luckily, I had indulged myself by buying two chairs with my table. The men looked at me suspiciously but sat down, each pulling his chair as far from the other as he could manage in that small space. I told Mary, who was peering in, round-eyed, from the courtyard, to bring in refreshments for my unwished-for guests. Bardas, meanwhile, had taken root in one corner with his arms crossed and a protective scowl on his face.

At that moment I heard another, gentler knock on the front door, and Bardas strode over and opened it, glaring until he saw who it was. Sir Joscelin strode in smiling, followed by Hugh. He came forward to take my hands and before he saw the two men, said, "Greetings, beloved. I am here to take you riding."

My guests stood once more, looking flustered and angry, as though I might somehow have summoned help. Nor did Sir Joscelin look well pleased when he saw who was there. I quickly presented them to each other and explained their business.

He said, "I am glad I came when I did," and placed himself firmly and somewhat challengingly by my side. The other men slowly sat back down. How glad I was to have him there! The men sat in silence while Mary brought around fruit, which they refused, and I explained why they were there. I had no idea how to respond to these angry men.

"All I can say is that I was so intent on saving my children from the street and from slavery that I never thought about religion. But do you have homes for them? And are you willing to let them choose whether they wish to leave with you? If they do not, and if I promise not to send them to Mass anymore and to protect them from harm from the other children and my servants, are you willing to let them stay with me?"

Both men looked utterly surprised. Sir Joscelin spoke up. "I think you had better answer thoughtfully. You are lucky: Lady Sofia is not one to hold a man's religion or his ill will against him. You came here knowing she was alone and possibly helpless, but she has many friends who will not be so tolerant of your behavior."

"If you wish," I added, "you can come with us now to see where they are lodged."

Benjamin of Antioch, clearly daunted, spoke quickly. "I agree."

"And I, too," said the mullah, who still looked more angry than afraid. And so we went.

By the end of the morning, having seen all there was to see and spoken to the children, the two men were about to leave. The boy Isaac, who was new to the home, was glad to go to a Jewish family and was waiting nearby. There was a bruise on his cheek, and I had to wonder if it came from more than the hard the play boys favored. The Muslim boy, also a newcomer, was eager to go, too. But Banjuu had hidden her head in my skirt and wept when given her choice. And I was ready to fight for her—not, as it turned out, that I needed to.

"You can have the girl. Just see to it that she is never forced to convert and that she is allowed to pray as she should," said the mullah. "It is more important that I rescued the boy."

I turned red at the man's rudeness and might have spoken harshly, but I held my tongue and merely replied, "I only care that all three of them are safe! I am glad this was resolved so easily, and when I adopt other children I will ask them about their religion. So," as I glanced at each man in turn, "if I find a Muslim or Jewish child, should I let you know?"

Both spoke in unison, "Of course." And cutting in on each other, they gave me to understand that there was no need for an orphanage in their respective worlds, that families in their communities would take in any child, educate him, and give him a living. They seemed to feel contempt for a Christian society that did not do the same.

I cannot say we parted with much mutual goodwill, as I thought both men ungrateful. But from that day forward, I fulfilled my promise. Whenever I—and later Efrem and Mary—found children for them, they found them families. That at least was a happy arrangement.

After everyone had left, though, I felt as wrung out as a scrubbing rag. My knight looked at me and said, "I am still taking you riding. Hugh has awaited us for some time." And, soon astride our mounts, we hastened to my special dell to find a cold repast spread out on a cloth, but no squire. I was so happy!

His lips brushed my hand as he helped me to sit, and a thrill ran through me. But I was too wrought up to eat more than a few bites, for I only wanted news from this Frankish king who had so much power over my future.

Sir Joscelin would have eaten more heartily, I think, but he caught my mood and only swallowed a few bites before taking my hand and saying, "Do you want me to tell you now what my king said?" I nodded, looking up into his grave gray eyes. "I was finally able to present my request to him, so that is going forward, but I came away without a definite yes to give you. He tells me he will think on it and give me his answer when we meet again on the island of Cyprus this fall. I am to bring you with me and present you to him. I take that as a most promising sign."

A little chill went up my back, and I shuddered and sat back up.

"Are you cold? Here, take my cloak. It is cool here."

"No, I'm fine, but I had hoped that after a year our wait would be at an end."

"And I as well, my love. But a few more months are nothing. As I must prepare for my king's arrival, I'll mostly be in Cyprus—I hope to take you there at least once before he arrives—but I will come to Antioch often to see you."

We both sighed, each knowing what the other felt. After a long silence, he drew me into his arms and kissed me long and deeply. As we rode back toward the city, I decided to set aside my worries and simply enjoy our time together. After all, none of us know how long we have on this earth, and it was best to make the most of what I did have.

I cannot recall much else of note from that time, as later events are so heavily imprinted on my mind. With Efrem and Jonah teaching the young ones skills and the other caretakers following my directives to be both kind and firm, my home for children was blossoming. One day Sir Joscelin brought me a boy and girl of about ten who looked better fed than some of my wards, but he said that they too were orphans, having recently lost their families.

"Since they are children of people who served me once, I hoped you could find room for them, too."

"Of course," I smiled.

Rotrou and Agnes were soon quite at home, but then there was no more room. It was most unsatisfactory because I wanted to bring even more children in; there were so many more in need. Finally Jonah began to mutter under his breath about too many mouths to feed, and I realized I could lose him. So after much searching, I bought a house of my own: a half-ruined villa in the forested mountains some two hours away, near a lovely village called Daphne. It took some work to repair the old building, which wrapped around a courtyard that also had to be put back in order. Several of the older orphans helped. The verdant surroundings and high walls made it worth the trouble, since above all I needed distance from Antioch.

As Efrem had warned, some of my wards were inclined to repeat their violent or dishonest past, and this new home would be for them. I also hired extra people to see to them, partly necessary because Daphne is full of wealthy people, both Frankish and Greek, who were suspicious of us at first. Only with time were we able to prove that my children would not scale their walls, kill them in their beds, and rob them.

Of course not all went perfectly in either home, but I do think my approach worked well. Over the years as my children grew up, they left with an education and a trade, and some of them even stayed on to teach new arrivals.

Sir Joscelin was often away seeing to the preparations for his king's arrival on Cyprus, but we still saw as much of each other as we could. And in late summer, Mary and Bardas and I sailed with him down the Orontes and boarded a fine new ship in the bustling port of Saint Symeon, which I had once called by its old name from an old map: Seleucia Pieria. It was my first voyage on a true sea, and I was enchanted by the silence, the green water, the blue sky, our fellow ships gliding silently through the creaming waters, the lookouts on the warships that guarded our convoy keenly watching in every direction—something I appreciated more than most passengers. But then, so many of them fell ill from the boat's rocking. I found the sensation delightful.

And then there was Cyprus, a fair island with sweetness in the air, full of vineyards, grain, sugar cane fields and mills, and with mountains rising from its center. As in Syria, it seems to be another layered world, though here it was not Muslims but Orthodox Greek peasants chafing under the control of a handful of Frankish lords who kept mostly to their cities and fortified castles. A heavy guard always accompanied us into the countryside, which was dotted here and there with small churches, clearly Orthodox. I secretly wished I could visit one for the sake of memory.

In Limassol, a small fortified city with a citadel inside a small castle where the king lived, and which swarmed bee-like with workmen, Sir Joscelin proudly took me from one strong-house to another where everything from grain to arms was stored. Clearly his duty was simply to see to the final arrangements, for all these things could not have been gathered in only one summer. Indeed, he told me that for many months, King Louis had been sending stores ahead to be guarded by King Henri of Cyprus until the French army arrived. There were piles of wine casks on one field as tall as buildings, and Sir Joscelin showed me hills all sprouted with wheat or barley, which he told me were merely crusts that would be removed to get at good grain underneath, quite a wonder to me. I also saw the meadows where King Louis would post his troops as they arrived, the site where the many royals would be housed in great tents, with more tents for the various important visitors he expected, from the masters of the Templars and the Hospitallers to various lords and kings throughout Palestine.

Cyprus was ruled by a fat, jovial man, King Henri, and his frail wife, Queen Stephanie. We attended a feast that he held, and I had never before seen such a fabulous display, from his square, vaulted feasting hall bright with banners and resounding with music to the jongleurs who acted out stories or performed tricks. And that banquet put Batu Khan's to shame: meats of every description, fish, birds, pies, jellies, soups, sallats, sauces, all fancifully prepared. King Henri must have welcomed the flow of wealth that was coming his way from King Louis for his great holy war, for he did everything else in lavish style, too, even to riding down the main street of Limassol to distribute largesse to its citizens, many of them merchants who were gathering to supply the needs of the enormous army that was expected.

But while I found all this fascinating, there was so little time to be alone with my beloved, who was often so busy that I felt in the way. When I returned to my own pursuits back in Antioch—my children, my friendships, even my investments—life seemed simple by contrast.

Then it struck me that if I must meet the king, I might need to move to Cyprus for some time. It might well be where Sir Joscelin and I would wed. He had written that many nobles and knights would be bringing their wives, so I could even join him on what promised to be a short and almost bloodless military expedition! I spent the last summer days readying myself for those possibilities, making certain that my two homes were well-endowed with monies—Matthew of Edessa, who now invested my profits for me, was a godsend, for he knew how to do all this and had proven himself utterly trustworthy—and finding a new maidservant to take with me. I had entirely missed how far the romance between Efrem and Mary had progressed. While her love for him had always been obvious, I had not realized that he returned it. I only found out when I made the mistake of assuming that she would move with me to Cyprus.

"Oh no," she cried. "I cannot leave him!" And then it all came out: the rare, secret meetings, the promises and plans made. I could only rejoice for them both and be witness to their marriage and Mary's removal back up the mountain to Efrem's little house.

Happily, I quickly found not one but two new servants: Banjuu and Marguerite, who begged to go with me when they heard about my plans. Irene, whom I also invited, wanted only to stay with her brother where she felt safe.

And I was right to prepare. Sir Joscelin arrived in Antioch in late August to announce the imminent arrival of his king and that it was time for him to take me to Cyprus. We had but a week, but just before we left he escorted me to bid farewell to Anna and Adar al-Mas'ūdī. It was a poignant time for us all. The men went off to the castle's main room, while we women sat in the garden and recalled our adventures together and anticipated those to come. To my great surprise, Anna announced she was with child.

"I am so happy. He is such a gentle lover, he has made me forget the ugly times," she confided. "I so want to give him a son, and besides, it is too hard in this world for us women." I said nothing; men seemed to have their own hard times.

"And when will you exchange vows with Sir Joscelin?"

I could give her no satisfactory answer. "I only know that I want to leave all the waiting behind me and that I pray this war is over quickly and without much bloodshed!"

"It will happen. Allah wills it, and he is truly All-Merciful. Just look at me."

The day came to bid farewell to Antioch and to my women friends, servants, and my dear children. Helene, who had kept up my spirits while I awaited my beloved, embraced both Joscelin and me with special warmth. Even Matthew of Edessa was there. For once my parting was not sad at all. How glad I was not to be fleeing from anything!

With a fair wind at our backs, my beloved and I went to sleep knowing the other was close by. Our convoy reached Cyprus by morning, where Sir Joscelin had already found furnished quarters for me, though he had to return to his duties right away. And there was much to do. My girls vied with each other to unpack and make the rooms presentable, giggling and whispering together like sisters. Bardas had also accompanied us from Antioch; as he had been born in Limassol, he was glad to be home again. After disappearing for half the morning, he returned with bounty from farm markets, along with his sturdy, cheerful brother, introduced as Leo, who straightaway installed himself as my cook!

I was actually well pleased, since with Mary gone I lacked a cook in Antioch, and Leo claimed that when I left Cyprus he was willing to follow me back.

By the time my knight came to me in my new apartments that evening, all was in order. We supped together and then wandered along the harbor. It might have been ill-bred of me, but when he led me to the beach I could not resist slipping off my sandals and walking along the gray sand in bare feet. It was still warm. What a lovely night, with the moon rising over the water and spilling light over the sea and the city, more lights glowing from the high castle windows, palm trees scissoring the sky with black fronds. Although Hugh, Bardas, and the children followed us at a discreet distance, it was the first time in many days that Sir Joscelin and I had been even somewhat alone together. Part of me wanted to melt in his arms, and I think he felt the same way. We walked so close to each other that I could feel the heat of his body enfold me.

He finally said, "How I long to take you in my arms right now, to hold you close, dearest. It is so hard to wait until we marry. Soon...."

But then he added, dispelling the magic of the moment, "Ships carrying troops have begun to arrive, and tomorrow I will take you to see the camps if you wish. I fear it will be my last free day before my king lands. There is so much to do."

"I will go anywhere with you," I answered, suppressing a sigh.

After that first morning of touring what seemed like miles of campgrounds filled with knights, squires, horses, soldiers, and noise, I spent the rest of the week mostly alone, wandering through the town with my girls and Bardas. Fair and dark and holding hands, my little maidservants caused quite a pleasant stir, so I hastily sewed them matching gowns of deep green with tunics of pale blue, which added to the drama and to their delight.

Sir Joscelin did find time to take me to King Henri's castle twice, where I found I mingled easily with the fine lords and ladies. I secretly thanked Lady Helene, who had been subtly teaching me how to behave without my being aware of it. I wondered whether I might see her in Limassol soon, as Lord Gilles was already there working side by side with my beloved. Indeed, people were arriving daily, so far mostly merchants who hoped to enrich themselves.

And I gained an unexpected friend. I was invited to attend Queen Stephanie, a wan, dark-haired woman, no older than thirty. A few noblewomen were with her in her chambre des femmes, which was also her bedroom, but most seemed interested only in their embroidery and whispered gossip. She often coughed, and her cheeks would burn with fever. Once I saw her cough up blood into a napkin that she quickly gave to a maidservant to remove. But she and I liked each other straightaway, though it quickly became clear that the inspiration for her hospitality was her tender regard for Sir Joscelin. I dare not say she felt love for him, for that would disrespect a queen, but I could see why. Her good husband King Henri was twice her size—he had nearly starved to death as a child during a civil war on Cyprus and was clearly making up for it—and half as handsome as my knight.

Over the next weeks, she and I developed a deep mutual sympathy, followed by an equal trust. We each spoke of our childhoods, the first time

I had spoken of mine since leaving Kyiv. Hers was spent in the kingdom of Cilicia. A warm and welcoming land, according to her, which she still missed, and the last refuge of the Christian Armenians who had been forced to flee west by Seljuk Muslims. Her half-brother, Hetoum, was its king. And to my surprise, I learned that King Hetoum had recently submitted to the Mongols!

"He and my other brother Sempad made such a brave journey through unknown lands, danger on every side, all to meet and form an alliance with someone important called Baiju Khan. But that was not good enough, so King Hetoum traveled on to Karakorum itself just last year, and he was gifted with a Mongol bride. Such a mark of honor!"

I had to bite my tongue. I was certain that no Mongol was to be trusted. But she had her own proofs of their good intentions. "And there is more. The king of the Mongols sent us a friendly letter that King Henri then sent on to King Louis. This letter gives us hope that we Christians might ally with the Mongols and crush the Saracens forever! And it could well happen, you know. Nearer to hand and most important to my homeland, the Mongols recently conquered Cilicia's bitter enemy, Rum. It was once Armenian until those terrible Seljuk tribes overran it. Those Seljuks have oppressed our good Christian people in Rum for too long, and they deserve whatever the Mongols do to them!" she exclaimed.

I said nothing, tried to look interested if not sympathetic, for I knew who usually suffered the most, and it was rarely the rulers or the rich.

"Did you know," she added rather sadly, "that Rum was once proudly Roman? Only its name remains."

I shook my head. "How odd is it not, that traces of other times linger all around us, sometimes entirely forgotten. I have seen such places in my travels."

That was a slip I instantly regretted! But the queen did not pry. "You know, you are something of a mystery to us all," she said pensively. "You were once a princess, and even without knowing that, anyone can tell that you are of noble blood. But you have journeyed so far from home, my good servant Sir Joscelin knows so little about your past, and now you hope to gain King Louis' favor. I must give you some frank advice."

I blushed and bowed.

"Tell Sir Joscelin everything. He must be able to speak to his king with authority, for though I can offer you my patronage, which lends some support to your cause, you are simply not known to his king. No ruler worth his throne will give up an important marital alliance for love, not even one who has found love in his own marriage. But I will make you one of my ladies in waiting, which at least gives you a position at court."

I could only thank her deeply for her advice while secretly determining never ever to tell Sir Joscelin about some things, for they would surely destroy his good opinion of me!

Not that there was a chance of saying anything yet, as he worked day and night all the rest of the summer and we rarely saw each other. Happily, I was not lonely, for Lady Helene soon arrived and joined me as one of the queen's attendants. In the following weeks, we did almost everything together, sharing much laughter and good cheer and even dining with our men on rare occasion. She also presented me to even more of the nobility and gentry who were arriving daily from around the Latin States. I had always wanted to have just this sort of adventure, and now I had finally gotten my wish. It was pointless to count the years I had lost. The past was gone, and I was determined to enjoy my present.

AUTUMN INTO WINTER
ANNO DOMINI 1248-1249

On the seventeenth of September, the Year of Our Lord 1248, a day of glorious sunshine, King Louis arrived. Dressed in my finest—a pale green gown of samite shot with silver, cut in the latest style known to Antioch, and a sheer green veil trimmed with a silver border—I stood behind Queen Stephanie and King Henri with Lady Helene and several other noble attendants. The king and queen of Cyprus wore fur-trimmed gowns of blue and red, their hair crimped most royally under their crowns. As King Louis and his queen embarked from his ship onto a gaudily-trimmed small-boat, horns blared, drums rolled, and a nearby choir began a loud song of holy war. My eyes strayed not once from the man in the boat, for he held my fate in his hands.

Cypriot noblemen in gay silks waded out to pull the boat ashore, and King Louis stepped out onto a red carpet, the first of many that lined the path all the way to the castle. He was tall, much taller than most of his knights, and thin but muscular-looking. His gown of red silk brocade fairly glowed, and his blue velvet mantle was trimmed with ermine. A golden crown of fleurs-de-lis sat on his head. Strands of his flaxen hair shone like gold in the bright sun as the sea breeze lifted and tossed them. Although his face was so thin as to seem ascetic, overall he seemed solemn without sourness, both stern and kind. My heart rose in hope, for here was a just man. I could feel it in my bones. He turned and helped Queen Marguerite ashore, a lovely, sweet-faced woman of noble bearing, clothed in blue damask to match her eyes. A secret smile passed between them that bespoke love, so perhaps they both would favor Sir Joscelin and me.

The king's brothers and their ladies disembarked. It almost seemed as if he had brought every one of them and their households along. As it turned out, not only was that mostly true, but many nobles and barons and even common soldiers had indeed brought their wives. I wondered which one of these noblemen was Robert of Artois. Behind them came various high-ranking men of the Church, as well as monks and priests, each in their distinctive garb. And then there were the hundred great knights with their retinues who came as mercenaries. After all the armies of God and man had disembarked, the landing area was fairly clogged with Franks of all walks of life.

By then King Henri and Queen Stephanie had come forward to welcome the royal pair and exchange words of friendship, after which they had all mounted gaily caparisoned, perfectly matched white horses. The assembled princes, dukes, barons, knights, courtiers, attendants, wives, and more followed them on foot as they slowly rode up Limassol's winding streets, where every window seemed adorned with a flag and filled with cheering citizens. More cheers came from the people crammed along the streets. Some threw flowers. Such noise, such gaiety, such proud men and women, such a display for the less-well-off! King Louis threw coins into the crowd, to everyone's delight.

I glimpsed Sir Joscelin ahead of us walking with Lord Gilles a few rows behind their king, his entire being radiating attention and devotion to his sovereign. Lord Gilles spoke in his ear, and they slipped away up a side street, clearly intent on reaching the castle before our massive parade of majesty and pomp arrived. Up we went into the castle, where a great feast awaited us. By the time we reached it, poor Lady Helene was out of breath and leaning on my arm; for the first time, I noticed that she was growing even heavier.

This welcome feast staggered the imagination. Seated halfway down one of the two long tables that extended into the room from each end of the royal dais, and honored to be among the queen's favored attendants, I watched in awe as dish after dish was brought in: roast peacock re-covered with its feathers and fire shooting from its beak, spicy herb sallats, great roasts, meat pies—including a huge one that was filled with live birds that flew out when its top crust was removed—sugared almonds, poached fruit, fine wines. Great noblemen served the kings and queens, but only King Henri ate heartily. King Louis especially scarcely touched his delicacies. Lesser nobility made certain that we ladies were given dainty slices of meat, and not on the usual bread trenchers but on pewter plates. With Helene by my side making silly jests, with so much to see, and with my beloved seated across from me sending looks of love, looks that this time I could safely return, my happiness was complete.

Several days passed without Sir Joscelin, but I knew he was attending his king and dealing with who knew what details or problems. As well, King Henri and his guests, including King Baldwin II of Constantinople, a dark man I could almost pity when I saw the desperation in his eyes, came and went between Limassol and the capital, a city called Nicosia. Limassol was filling up as more and more ships full of soldiers arrived, everyone cramming into all the hostels and inns and houses that were to be had or spilling out into nearby villages or camps, where gaily bedecked tents flew the flags of many far-flung duchies and baronies. I was glad Joscelin had found me good apartments! The sights and smells and noises of knight, merchant, soldier, peasant, and beasts of all kinds were almost overpowering; yet the fresh marine air could never quite be banished, and the sea always sparkled.

Lady Helene and I continued to attend Queen Stephanie, as the queen's ill health kept her from moving about much. Queen Marguerite and her equally lovely sister Beatrice were often there, and it was a pleasure to witness their regal bearing, although Countess Beatrice seemed somehow discontented. Perhaps it was because she was heavy with child. Their ladies in waiting attended them, making for quite a full room, though I much enjoyed their singing and lute playing while we sewed or embroidered or whispered together.

There was one maiden among the French queen's attendants, though, who from the first would stare over at me whenever she raised her eyes from her stitching. Her pale hair was wound in a circle over each ear and bound by a chin band in the latest style, her pale blue eyes were ringed with almost white eyelashes, her breasts were just forming. I guessed her age at no more than thirteen. After a day or so of this, I leaned over to Helene and asked if she knew who the girl was.

"No," she whispered back, "but I see how rudely she stares at us. Perhaps she has never seen women from the Holy Land before. We do dress somewhat differently."

I wondered if the stares were at both of us or only me. "Would it be courteous of us to befriend her? I fear committing some blunder among these strangers."

But before Helene could answer, Queen Stephanie summoned me to her side. "Show us the piece you are embroidering."

I had been working on matching linen wallets for my two girls, done much as I had learned in Iran, but a little like what I'd have done in Rus', with geometric vines and running stitches that did not fill the leaves but left little dots. After examining my work, Queen Marguerite spoke. "It differs from anything I have ever seen before. Is this for church use?"

I blushed. "No, my Lady, it is for one of my children—one of my adopted—I mean one of my servants." She looked at me curiously as I stammered to a halt.

"Yes, Queen Stephanie has told me about your good works. And I imagine they stem from a deep piety, even though your embroidery is not for sacred use."

I could only nod, hoping that my frivolous pursuit had not destroyed her goodwill.

The maiden who had been staring at me moved to her queen's side. "Curious, and so foreign-looking: there are no people in it, no saints. Would you care to see my work, Lady … Sofia, I believe? I am Lady Ysabel of Biancet. "Mine is for a church altar." She looked at me slyly as she handed me a long piece, which she was heavily working in silks and gold thread.

"Very lovely," I answered with what I hoped was a friendly voice. In truth the work seemed crude and shapeless to me after the exacting style I had mastered in childhood.

"I am making it for my private chapel," Lady Ysabel replied. "I mean," she glanced over at her queen, "my king's." Queen Marguerite raised an eyebrow at her but said nothing. I returned the altar cloth and received a glare in return. Why Lady Ysabel would take such a dislike to me I could not understand, but I was quickly beginning to feel the same toward her.

I withdrew with a bow to the two queens and sat back down with Helene, who promptly whispered, "What was that about?"

"I wish I knew, but I seem to have made an enemy for no reason that I can see."

That was sometime around the beginning of October. Shortly thereafter I visited Antioch briefly to see to my orphanages and my shipping ventures, as there was little to do in Limassol but wait for glimpses of my beloved. The seas had grown rough and chill, and I was glad to arrive back on solid ground. Having overheard another passenger, very seasick, claim that it would only get worse as winter deepened, and having seen that everything was well with my children, I returned to the island just ahead of a great storm. And glad I was that I had gotten safely inside: water poured from the sky and ran in rivers down the streets to the bay. I could just see the shore from my window, where rows of great waves crashed on the shore, reminding me of my nightmare. I shuddered and turned away to see Banjuu and Marguerite, arms carelessly draped over each other's shoulders, murmuring together, and my heart warmed again.

As fall deepened into winter, more and more troops arrived and spread out around the city. I saw my beloved rarely, but every visit was like a bright flower planted in my heart. I fell even deeper in love with him. He was forever bringing me little gifts, and one evening he also brought me some gladdening news. He had just settled himself by the table where I was embroidering an altar cloth. Queen Stephanie had suggested it in Queen Marguerite's presence, saying she would use it on her private altar as I did the prettiest embroidery she had ever seen. I could only be grateful, as Lady Ysabel was expanding her private war with me—asking me why I could not sing or play the lute, for instance, which were highly valuable skills that she of course possessed. Queen Marguerite had even rebuked her once for her pertness—I'd have called it something harsher.

"My king and his trusted counselors—and he counts me among them again—have decided to wait until next spring to launch his expedition," Sir Joscelin began. "All we would need is one winter storm to lose half his army to the sea, so we will stay here and train the soldiers further. Without something to do, they will turn unruly. They are fifteen thousand strong already, but the king expects more to join him from England and the German and Italian states. King Henri has even vowed to take up the cross.

"And now that King Louis has settled on his strategy—there is more, but I must not reveal state secrets!—he will grant me two boons. The first is that on last Holy Day he will personally knight my squire Hugh, who certainly deserves such an honor!"

I clapped my hands in delight. "But what about Philippe?"

"He is still too young. But that reminds me: what would you think of my taking on Alexander and Fotis as grooms? You could bring Fotis and his sister Irene here and place her as a servant with a noble family, perhaps even with Lord Gilles and Lady Helene."

"What a brilliant idea! Do you think I could place other children in the same way?"

"Indeed I do. But I drift from my purpose: my king's second boon. After the Christmas Holy Days, he will meet you in person to make his final decision on our marriage. I believe he looks on it favorably, as otherwise he'd have denied my request by now."

A thrill of hope and then another of fear ran through me. "Then I must do my utmost to please him."

"You already do; Queen Marguerite has spoken well of you to him."

He paused. "Rumor says that you have found a 'Lord Amaury' of your own in Lady Ysabel. She has been King Louis' ward since her parents died—wealthy, highborn, convent bred for some years, and thinks far too well of herself. The king will soon send her back to Francia, to whatever nobleman he has chosen as her husband, so you'll be rid of her." We both laughed, I with relief.

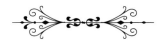

One day soon thereafter, while attending the two Queens, my ears pricked at the word 'Mongol'. "Come to my side, Lady Sofia. You will be interested to learn that, thanks to my brother Sempad, two Christian Mongol envoys are on their way to meet King Louis in Nicosia. I will return there myself in a few days, and you must come with me."

"You are most kind, my Lady." Although in truth, I'd have preferred to avoid them.

So I went, shutting up my house for the winter. Limassol was now crowded with soldiers, as rough as are soldiers anywhere, so I was at least glad to remove my two girls to safety. It was a short journey through countryside beautiful even in winter, with snow-dusted hills, drab olive trees, bare fields and sleeping vineyards. And rooms in the city awaited us ladies.

Advent was observed most strictly that year, as King Louis was so pious. We prayed several times every day in a newly built cathedral, Saint Sophia, which was elegant and brightly decorated but not at all like the Saint Sofia of my childhood, now probably in ruins. Lady Ysabel made a great show of offering her newly completed altar piece to Queen Stephanie for use in the cathedral, which made me like the place less, I must confess.

I saw far too little of Sir Joscelin, who seemed ever more burdened by care, but we had an unspoken agreement to speak only of light things when we were together.

A few days before Christmas, the Mongol envoys arrived with their servants. One of King Louis' advisers, André de Longjumeau, a middle-aged, thin-cheeked Dominican friar who always wore a white habit and black cloak, spoke their language. Their names were Dawud—David— and Marc, and they were indeed Christian; at least they made a great show of going to the cathedral to pray every day before they were granted an audience with the king. Since they spoke no French, the friar translated when King Louis met them in King Henri's throne room, surrounded by nobles. He had modestly declined sitting in Henri's throne, and sat on another one placed at Henri's right. King Louis was surrounded by his brothers, including the haughty, handsome Prince Robert, and the room was crowded with curious people, all wanting to see their first barbarian Mongol.

I was there as one of Queen Stephanie's attendants, and when the two men, dressed in rich Mongol-style robes and hats, came forward and genuflected as to a khan, I tried to slip well behind the queen. Lady Ysabel, also in attendance on Queen Marguerite, noticed my retreat and stared most boldly, as usual.

But they were both strangers to me, come from the area of Tabriz. They bore a letter from a Noyan Eljigidei that, had it been properly translated, would have shown King Louis the true nature of their visit. David read it aloud in Mongol speech. What he said was, as best I can recall it: "By the Force of Tengri, Kuyuk, Supreme Ruler of the entire World, sends word by his faithful Noyan Eljigidei, who acts in his name, to Khan Louis,

Great King of many provinces, Sword of Christianity, Upholder of Sacred Law who brings Victory to his Faith." After that came various wishes for King Louis to triumph over his enemies and to free all Christians from bondage; but that according to the Laws of Tengri, he must treat all Christians alike, whether Nestorian, Orthodox, or any other persuasion of Christian faith. There was also a promise that Christians would be well treated, their churches be rebuilt and their bells resound if they submitted to Kuyuk and his Mongols, which made me grimace. While it was true that priests and other holy men would be handled gently enough, ordinary Christians would be treated according to the whims of their local basqaq or governor or whatever noyan happened to be nearby.

That is enough to give the tone of the letter. But what a surprise when the priest translated, if you could call it that, what David had said: "By the blessings of Almighty God, Kuyuk, Supreme Ruler of many kingdoms of the world, greets you, King Louis of the great nation of the Franks, through my loyal general Eljigidei." Close enough, but highly softened— it sounded to me as he was unwilling to reveal how superior the Mongols felt themselves to be. And the rest of the letter was couched in equally moderated speech. When Friar André translated the section about treating all Christians alike, and knowing that heretics were being burned at the stake across King Louis' fiefdoms, I looked to see how the king was responding. I saw a shadow cross his face, but he managed not to show how this demand might affect him. I decided that he must have a great stake in this visit.

But there was more, for David and Marc had been entrusted with a proposal. This they told directly, while the friar translated. I could see him struggling to find words to replace their often blunt and arrogant speech, but I knew what they were saying, and I knew it for what it was: a poisoned carrot held out to one they considered to be a stupid donkey that would believe anything. Basically they proposed that the Mongols and the Franks ally against the Arabs, with possession of Jerusalem held out as the carrot to King Louis, while Baghdad was to become a Mongol possession. They even spoke of Prester John as if he had some kinship with Kuyuk, and of Kuyuk's mother, whom they claimed was Christian—I didn't know about the mother, had thought she was either Muslim or the follower of some Oriental religion—but I knew for certain that everything they said about Prester John was a string of lies! And who was Noyan Eljigidei, and what had happened to Baiju Khan? Well, I cared little as long as they never came near me.

At any rate King Louis trusted the friar completely, and I was in no position to gainsay what the man told him. Even beyond my own secrecy about my past, it had been years since I had lived among the Mongols, so things might have changed. This Eljigidei might be sincere in wanting to work side by side with the king. So I kept my own counsels, and history unfolded in its own way.

And Kuyuk had finally been elected Great Khan—how had Batu Khan reacted to that? I doubted I would ever find out, but I suspected that, as my old friend Dorje had once predicted, those two rivals would be the first sticks to fall from the Mongol bundle of unity.

While attending Queen Stephanie later, I sat meekly while she happily shared her certainty with Queen Marguerite that Cilicia had brought two worlds together. I worried a little about her. She seemed thinner than ever, she coughed more, and her cheeks were often far too flushed. But all she cared about was that the Franks and all the Christian states would soon have the powerful Mongols at their backs if only they would go through the motions of submitting to them. I secretly thought that the Franks and the all the Christian princes would do well to watch their backs with the Mongols, no matter what else they did!

And I had other things to think on, as a letter from Adar al-Mas'ūdī had just arrived, joy and pride in every word. Anna had given birth to a son, both were doing well, and the child was to be called Hasan ibn Adar. What a happy occasion for gifts: when freed for the day, I bought many little tokens both for her and the baby and even found a book of herbal remedies to send him. Soon I too would be married and perhaps bearing a son for my own beloved!

Another letter from my uncle had arrived in the same packet, although it had been sent much earlier. Again he invited me to come live with him. He was worried about me with no male relative to protect me, and he was suspicious of all Franks, having seen what they had done to Constantinople. I wrote back that I was grateful but that I did have a protector, one who loved me deeply and to whom I would soon be wed, and I asked for his blessing.

Then a third letter arrived, not to me but to Sir Joscelin, and I truly believe it was on the day of Hugh's knighting, which was held on the last of the Christmas Holy Days. I did notice that my own knight looked surprisingly grave while Hugh and several other young men went through the solemn ceremony. They would have stayed up all night in the cathedral, performing a vigil, which explained Hugh's strained face.

Afterwards there was no chance to speak to him, as a huge feast and celebration followed, again hosted by King Henri with his love of grandeur and abundance. There must have been thirty dishes for each course, each dish served to people of appropriate rank. Lady Helene, who had continued to gain weight, ate most heartily and kept demanding that more be placed on my plate, too, for, she said, "You are much too thin these days." I laughed thinly, so to speak, recalling a long ago and much less pleasant feast held near the ruins of Kyiv when a Mongol noblewoman had said almost the same thing to me.

After jongleurs and minstrels and various short enactments, the feast ended with a 'subtlety'. This one was a castle of pastry being stormed by marzipan knights, with little marzipan Saracen soldiers posed along the battlements, tiny arrows or spears thrust through their chests and much red coloring around their 'wounds'. Everyone thought it a marvel of ingenuity and realism, whooping and clapping as gaily clad servants carried it around the tables for all to see. I cast a wry and loving glance at Sir Joscelin, but the king was calling him to his side. They spoke, and my beloved left on, I assumed, some errand.

A week later, King Louis summoned me. I had hoped Sir Joscelin would be with me, but I had heard nothing from him since the night of the feast. I was led alone into a tower room decorated with tapestries and laid with fresh rushes, where a stool sat at a lectern. There was no other furniture. King Louis was sitting and writing, and, surprisingly, dressed in what looked like a monk's cassock, but he looked up and smiled sadly as I entered and made obeisance. I dared not look straight at him, but I could feel him examining me closely.

Formal greetings having been exchanged, he began. "Lady Sofia, you have been with us for some time now, and I have heard many good reports of you. Long have I considered Sir Joscelin's request that I allow you to wed, and please know that I looked favorably on your cause from the beginning. But two objections held me back. I wish I could find a more delicate way to put this, but I cannot. The first is that you are a foreigner from a kingdom that has fallen into ruins. Your noble bearing and goodness won me past that point, but the second objection is more serious. For several months I had been receiving reports that Sir Joscelin's elder brother was in failing health. He having been widowed a year ago without issue, I had thought to send him a bride to ensure his line. But I knew that if Sir Anchetil were to die, I would then confirm Sir Joscelin in his possession of his brother's holdings. In such a case, I could not then marry him to someone who holds no lands and is known to engage in trade." He paused.

"I received word on New Year's Day that Lord Anchetil died a month ago. But Sir Joscelin already knew this and did not tell me. I asked him directly after the knighting ceremony, and he did not deny it. For now, he is banished from my sight. And despite my desire to honor the bond that lies between you, I must refuse his request. He must marry for his king and for Francia, not for love.

"Lady, this is a cause of deep regret to me, as I know what love between two united souls is like. But I must protect my kingdom first, and love must never come before the needs of my domains. But I am not without heart. I propose that I endow your orphanages and also give you an allowance that will free you from the necessity for engaging in further vulgar trading adventures."

I had stood listening to all this, struck dumb, trying to see beyond my own need. My heart had at first soared with joy, but now it crashed like a bird shot down by an arrow from nowhere. I almost swooned, and the king started up and took my arm to steady me. He even tried to give me his stool, but I shook my head. I looked up into his eyes and saw only pity.

Finally, after a long silence, I replied, my throat growing tight from holding back the tears. "Sir King, I know I must accept your judgment, and if Sir Joscelin failed to tell you in a timely fashion, I am certain it was not out of disrespect for you. He said nothing to me, either, so perhaps there is some explanation that we both have yet to hear. He is the best man I have ever known, and he loves you as his king and his friend. I entreat you to forgive him. I will accept your offer to endow my children's homes. There are always more children in need, and I can only be grateful for your help.

"But as to rank, I come from the royal line of Yaroslav of Kyiv, whose daughter Anna married one of your ancestors. You and I are therefore distant cousins. Yaroslav's royal line never looked down on trade, nor do I. I am proud of my ability to take care of myself. And so, it seems, I must." And, before tears flooded my cheeks, "May I go?"

"Yes, and may God bless you, my poor child. I wish it could be otherwise for you and your gallant knight. Seeing your good heart, I can only forgive him absolutely."

I was almost out the door when I turned. "May I ask: have you found him a bride?"

"Yes, the maiden I'd have sent to his brother, Lady Ysabel of Biancet."

I could not even answer, just bowed my head and left. Of course this marriage was a great honor for Sir Joscelin. Lady Ysabel's title and all her holdings would make it highly desirable—she had spoken of them with pride. But all I could think was: 'As though land means wealth, when the very delicacies kings enjoy at table come from merchants risking their lives in far-flung travel!' And so, insensibly, my grief turned into rage.

Outside on the street, I began to race toward my lodgings. Where was Sir Joscelin? I must find him; we must decide what to do. No, to see him again would be further torture. But I must do something! I could not stay on Cyprus anymore, possibly to witness his marriage to that....

Had she known something all along and seen me as her natural enemy? By the time I reached home, my servant Bardas fairly running after me asking what had happened, I was resolved to quit Cyprus as soon as possible. First I would hold the king to his promise, and then I would go to Antioch, set my affairs in order, and remove to Constantinople.

A shocking surprise awaited me, though. The two Mongols, as well as Friar André de Longjumeau, were standing stolidly in my front room. I hastily collected myself to present a neutral if not welcoming face to my unexpected guests. The friar stepped forward, making the sign of blessing, and spoke. "I am sorry to come unannounced, Lady Sofia, but my two guests wished to meet you before we leave bearing important messages for Noyan Eljigidei. They heard that you speak fair Mongol, and their curiosity was aroused."

"Well, I do speak simple greetings and the like." Behind André the one called David was eyeing me closely. "It helps me in my trading ventures to know a little of several languages. But I do not understand why he and his fellow envoy would be interested in that."

David broke in sharply, "Speak in Mongol; I do not understand this

Frankish babble."

"This is a lady of high degree," retorted the priest. "She will be offended by rough ways, and what is gained by that?"

The Mongol shrugged and stared at me again, though it was André he addressed. "It is rumored that a woman translator, a slave from Rus', fled Batu Khan's ordu some years ago. She disappeared, some say eaten by wolves. But others are not so certain. And there is still a reward offered for her return. Indeed, Khakan Kuyuk would be most interested in finding one who has caused his enemy so much trouble."

I pretended not to fully understand and let the priest translate, then drew myself up haughtily and glared at David. "And?"

The friar, who had turned red, translated with as much grace as he could, but I knew what the man had really said: "And you, Lady Sofia, may well be that same woman, for that was her name."

I retorted in French, "Tell him this: You know little of Frankish customs if you think you can come into my home and accuse me of being an escaped slave! Now, good Brother, I must ask you all to leave, for my ship departs on the next tide. I have been deeply insulted, and I have half a mind to take my grievance to the king and queen!" In truth I meant King Henri through Queen Stephanie, but I hoped he would think I meant King Louis and Queen Marguerite.

"Oh dear, I had no idea this was why they wanted to see you! I deeply regret this. Please say nothing about it to anyone. The future of many souls hangs in the balance, for I have great hopes of converting the Great Khan as well as the entire Mongol nation to Christianity!"

"I wish you only good fortune in your mission, but it has nothing to do with me! And frankly, Brother André, most Mongols I have met are not trustworthy when it comes to politics, and I think you should be more cautious in your dealings with them."

His face grew redder, and he cried, "You speak as though you know more than I do, but I say to you that I have traveled across western Asia and seen how Christianity flourishes! Not only that, the Great Khan offers to ally himself with our king in this Holy War and will deliver Jerusalem herself into our hands!"

I was about to argue that he had not actually lived among the Mongols when I realized the trap I'd have set for myself. Besides, his mind was already set. Retreating into courtesy, I begged his pardon and sent them all on their way.

Once they were gone, though, I called all my servants together, no longer out of mere grief but also out of panic. "I must get back to Antioch straightaway. Bardas, go to Limassol and see if you can find a suitable ship leaving soon. Leo, if you are still willing, I want you to go back with me and continue serving me. And girls, begin packing at once!"

"But what about your wedding?" Marguerite burst out.

"There will be no wedding, and there is no reason for me to linger here witnessing—" I could not go on. I almost fell onto a bench, sobbing. Banjuu and Marguerite rushed to me, stroking my hands and weeping with me. Bardas and Leo faded away, driven off by tears.

We were well along in our packing by the next afternoon. I had settled up with the landlord and sent a message for King Louis giving him notice of my plans before Bardas returned with news that he had found a ship leaving for Antioch in three days. Soon enough, but it did not seem so to me, who now wished only to vanish without a trace! Then I realized I must bid Queen Stephanie and Lady Helene farewell. Perhaps I could even find safe haven with Helene until I departed.

Of course part of me kept hoping Sir Joscelin would appear at my door, sweep me into his arms, and tell me it was all in error and that we would never be parted again. And part of me was profoundly disappointed— and worried—when he did not. It was possible that he was in Limassol or was meeting in some council or was even in private audience with the king, being forgiven. But what purpose would be served even to ask? I must never again dwell on airy possibilities.

I hastened to Lady Helene's house, Bardas close behind, feeling as if those Mongols or one of their servants might be following me or lurking behind some alleyway. When I was admitted, she rushed up to me and embraced me. Her cheeks were marked with tears.

"What has happened?" I asked, wishing only to weep out my sad story to her.

"What happened is to you, my friend. Sir Joscelin and Lord Gilles just arrived with the news, and Sir Joscelin was on his way to see you. He is crushed, and it is a sorry sight to behold. For that matter, I have never seen you so pale and shaken. Come in, take some drink to restore yourself. You must be shattered."

I just wanted to turn and run, but Sir Joscelin had heard my voice and the men were already with me before I could make my escape. My knight took my hands and kissed them, tears welling from his eyes. Helene hastened away, shooing her husband before her.

"I was just on my way to find you. Oh, dear God," Joscelin moaned, "this is the worst of fates for us both! How can I... what can I...."

"What can either of us do," I answered, suddenly so glad to see him that I wanted only to rest in his arms. "When did you learn about the king's plans?"

"Not half an hour ago. He had banished me to the camps, but I returned early this morning with Lord Gilles to plead for an audience and to explain what had happened. I learned of my brother's death the same day as King Louis, but he misunderstood my grieving silence and thought I had withheld the fact from him. My tongue was tied in knots, for I grieved not only for my brother but for its import. I knew what would come next.

"But today I had to wait all afternoon to see him. I just left him ... and that little piece of trouble he commands me to marry. I stopped here just for a moment on my way to see you, hoping my friends could somehow help, and then you came to me! My dearest love, I am desolated for us both."

So we stood together by the door, sometimes weeping, sometimes talking together as the day faded as surely into night as had our dreams. But truly there was nothing to be done. We finally went to Lord Gilles and Lady Helene and asked if I might stay there until I returned to Limassol to take ship. It seemed natural to ask, but in truth my reasons and Sir Joscelin's were not the same. Of course they welcomed me.

Now came the hardest part. I asked my knight to take me to the cathedral to pray together. Wrapped in cloaks against the winter wind, we walked through thinning streets and found the cathedral doors open. And pray we did, as other pilgrims came and went, lighting candles for the dead or praying for some boon from God or Christ or the Holy Virgin.

At the end, I finally did what I must. I led him into a small side chapel and bared my entire past to him. It seemed fitting, since my story had virtually begun in Saint Sofia, and now it would end in Saint Sophia. Lady Ysabel's altar cloth added an ironic touch.

He was clearly shocked, and I felt sure I had given him enough cause to dislike me that we could part cleanly. But after listening to everything, from Argamon to Kerim, from Batu Khan to the Grand Master, and having learned about my frightening encounter with David and Marc, he sat utterly still for what seemed like forever to me.

I finally added, "I only pray you will be able to think better of me someday, and that you will wish me well in the meantime. I tell you this now because I no longer have any claim on you, and I always regretted keeping secrets when you were so open with me. Now I can face the future with a clean heart, at least, and if it helps pave the way for your future with your new wife—" I could say no more.

"I can never stop loving you, though I now have not one but two knives in my heart!" He paused again. "It will take time for me to make sense of all you told me, and to see how your silence … I do not yet know what to, how to.…

"But," his voice took on a neutral tone, "how did these Mongols know about you?"

I could guess, but I did not want to make further difficulties in his marriage. Lady Ysabel knew I spoke Mongol, and she had noted my fear of David and Marc when I first saw them. A brief conversation with the friar and the damage would be done. She would not have known what trouble she was stirring up, but she would likely be glad. So I simply shrugged and said, "Several people know I speak Mongol."

And, glad to find another subject, I added, "Now that my secrets are laid bare, I must warn you that André de Longjumeau did not translate the letter from those envoys truly, for Kuyuk Khan's message was actually insulting. It was a demand that King Louis go to the Mongol capital to submit to him. I would have you warn your king, too."

"Well, the embassy is gone this very night, Friar André with them, so there is nothing to be done at present. He plans to go to Karakorum on the king's behalf, where he thinks to convert the Great Khan. He is full of hopes and plans, and he claims that our True Faith has already spread across Asia—but I see you nodding your head, so you already know about that part.

"But now I must take you back to Lord Gilles' house. The hour has grown late."

We returned in silence. Once I was inside, he kissed my hand with dreadful finality, turned, and left with no endearments or words of farewell, much less an embrace.

The next morning Lady Helene and I went to Queen Stephanie's chambers. I was never so glad to have a friend beside me. As it happened we arrived at the same time as Queen Marguerite and her attendants, so we stepped back for them all to pass. Lady Ysabel managed to be the last in line, and as she went by, she sneered, "Ah, my betrothed's whore!"

"Liar bitch!" Lady Helene hissed back, but I was speechless. Was this what everyone thought of me, or was this viciousness born from the mind of a selfish child?

It took all my strength to enter and offer graceful farewells to the two queens. Queen Stephanie, whose eyes seemed more sunken than ever, took my hands in hers and looked long into my eyes. Tears formed in hers. "I always feared it would come to this. But you will ever have a friend in me. Both Queen Marguerite and I have parting gifts for you, as I knew you would not want to stay," and she called one of her ladies to bring her a beautifully inlaid casket. "In here you will find enough to endow another home for forsaken children, a worthy cause to which we all know you have devoted much of your life and wealth." Before handing it to me, she pierced Lady Ysabel with her gaze. The girl had the grace to flush and look down.

Meanwhile, one of Queen Marguerite's attendants had brought forth a slightly larger and even more ornate casket. The queen gave it to me, saying, "And this is from my king and husband and from me. We both wish you well."

I bowed deeply and thanked them, my voice almost choking, and asked to be allowed to go. No one had mentioned my loss directly, but it hung in the air like a ghostly wound.

"And may I leave, as well? Lady Sofia needs help carrying your generous gifts," asked Lady Helene, looking at me with concern.

So, with last farewells—many good ladies joined in them—I left, certain I would never see any of them again. At least I was glad to be parted from one of them.

Helene accompanied me back to her house, where my girls and men awaited me. I would not have called her close in my counsels before this, but she had proven her steadfast heart to me, and I could not begin to express my gratitude to her.

"Think nothing of it. Soon you and I will be together often in Antioch after the armies go to war, since I for one will not go with my husband.

And remember: none of us knows how long we have on this earth, or what may yet come to be! Perhaps our men's children will play together at our feet one day."

"That would take another Immaculate Conception," I said rather tartly.

"So the rumors are total falsehoods, then," she replied without rancor.

I sighed. "If only I had at least tasted the joys of the sins I am accused of."

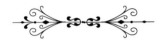

On the next day, Helene and I parted with tears and embraces, and in short order my servants and I were once again on our way to take ship in a little fleet sailing under protection of a warship. It took a full week to reach Antioch, as such a bad storm blew up that we were forced to seek safe harbor off a small island. It gave me someone else to think about, for Banjuu and Marguerite were terrified, but I'd not have cared if I had fallen overboard and drowned. And it was hard to rouse myself once I arrived in my house, for there was nothing to look forward to. Indeed, for several days I did little but stare at nothing, barely sleeping or eating. I did attend Mass once, although I scarcely paid attention.

But my girls, who did their best to cheer me up, were a reminder that I had other obligations: to my young wards. And my new wealth would indeed buy another home and pay for its caretakers. After visiting my orphans, Alexander foremost among them, and seeing that overall they were thriving—and learning that Mary was already pregnant—I took Efrem with me to find a third house.

We found a rundown villa for sale not far from the Hospitaller home. And after some hard bargaining, which Matthew of Edessa handled, it was mine. With Efrem as overseer, several of the older children came over and put it into shape, and I was ready to find my next set of foster parents and the children they would raise. In a little more than a month, all these tasks were nearly completed. I had found good people and freed over a dozen children. I gave Efrem the responsibility for all three homes, for my mind was already turned toward Constantinople. I had written my uncle Vasily accepting his invitation, since very soon there would be nothing to keep me in Antioch.

I had also written Lady Helene and received not one but two replies. She would take Irene and Fotis both as servants, since they refused to be separated. But if Sir Joscelin still wanted other boys to train as squires, she would help me see to that as well. And she would gladly find other noble homes to place more children as servants, for there would be a great need for extra hands once all the men went to war. She also added that Countess Beatrice, sister to the French queen, had borne a son.

But her biggest news was that plague had struck King Louis' troops, and soldiers were dying like chaff thrown into the wind. She had written her will in case she succumbed, too, and she planned to return to Antioch as soon as she could safely leave. And, she added, most tactfully, all marriages were postponed. I had assumed that Sir Joscelin's to Lady Ysabel had already occurred, so my heart went to my mouth, both in fear for him and, I admit, in brief hope that she somehow would—well, I could not say the word 'die' to myself, but I knew it in my heart, even though I felt obliged to pray for everyone's safety.

Happily, the second letter, which had been written a few days later, contained good news. King Louis himself had gone among his troops, tending some men personally and praying for them all, and the plague had died down. Bringing in fresh water and cleaning out the latrines had helped, too, Helene noted wryly. She said nothing about marriages.

One morning shortly after Lent had begun, Matthew of Edessa sent word to me that all my ships had arrived safely once again and what would I like to do next? He knew that I would be leaving soon, and he seemed to think I would no longer use him once I was in Constantinople. But I could imagine no one more capable or loyal, so I went to him in person and assured him that I trusted him to invest my profits as he saw fit. We wrote up another contract, and now that he was certain of my business, he also offered to introduce me to his trading partners in Constantinople if I wanted to extend my interests into new areas beyond his reach. One partner, he added, was a merchant from faraway Rus'!

"Would his name be Vasily Andreevitch?" I asked eagerly.

His eyes widened in surprise. "Why, yes. Do you know of him?"

"He is my uncle! I suppose I never told you about him before." We both laughed.

"Well, you are in good hands, then, Lady Sofia, for I never met a tougher or craftier merchant, though he is also an honest man. He protects what is his with an iron fist!"

I left feeling such a lifting of spirits as I had not imagined possible. In another month or two I would be back with my family, able to go forward with my life. I had thought little about what it might be like to be even farther away from my beloved. Well, I already felt like a widow, so perhaps I would keep the same identity in Constantinople. I had bared my past to the only person who needed to know it, and from now on it would lie buried forever, for I was no longer a child or a slave or a prisoner or even a virtuous lady of Antioch. I would turn twenty-two this year. I would never forget the man I loved, but having found a calling among the forsaken of the world, I would pursue it in my new home, as well.

I was so lost in this train of thought that I was inside my house before I saw two men waiting in my public room: one was young Philippe, the other Sir Joscelin. I gasped and stepped back, scarcely able to believe he was flesh and bone and not a ghost.

"Yes, it is I, dearest." He strode forward and took my hands.

"How ... why are you here?" My mind leapt to that forbidden hope—had plague in the camps freed him?

"King Louis sent me on a mission to purchase our final supplies, as we leave in mere weeks. He surely knew I would come to see you, and this was his kindness to us. I am also to collect Fotis and Irene for Helene, and three other boys to train as grooms. Now that I have completed my duty, I have this one afternoon to spend with you before I return to Cyprus."

"But ... what about ...."

"Philippe, wait for me outside." The dark-haired youth bowed and left, me looking after him curiously. Who was this handsome boy?

I looked a question, which my beloved read in my eyes. "I never said before: young Philippe was sent to me by his father to finish his training and be knighted. Their barony lies near Braissac."

I turned to Bardas and my girls. "All of you go with Leo to the market for fresh fish, bread, and a good wine, and take Philippe with you. And here is extra for a sweet. Then get Alexander, Fotis, and Irene and the other boys. Have them pack, and bring them here."

Once they had all gone, I led Joscelin out to my little courtyard, which contained only a bench, a few pots of flowers, and an outdoor stove. "Come sit with me," I said. "My knees are weak."

"I know this is a surprise, and perhaps an unwelcome one, but I had to see you again. Our last time together has haunted me ever since. Though you must have expected my shock, I was less than gallant at our parting, and I beg you to forgive me. I see now that you were trying to free me to marry Lady Ysabel without regret, but that was not possible. Sofia, I love only you, and if I must love you from afar, so be it. I wish I could say otherwise, but I am now wed to that little ogress, at least in the eyes of the Church."

It was the end of all hope for me. "Why, then, do you come to haunt me here?"

"Because our marriage never was and never will be consummated. Ysabel heard about Yolande's death from someone, and now she is terrified of the marriage bed. Just as well, as I have no desire to lie in it with her, and unlike some husbands, I would never force myself upon her in the name of duty. I have begged my king to release us from each other, and he now seriously considers granting me permission both to seek an annulment and to wed you once I return from this war—if you will still have me." He paused. "In my eyes, Sofia, you have always been the true wife of my heart."

I leaned forward and took his face in my hands. "And you have always been my husband in my heart."

We kissed, long and sweetly, and then he rose, picked me up in his arms, and carried me back inside and up to my bedroom. Gently he laid me onto my bed. Slowly he undressed me and then himself, all the while looking at me with such love that I could not turn my eyes away. What a strong body, scarred from battle yet strengthened and perfected by his travails. He lay down beside me. "Do you truly want this, or should I wait for another eon to pass?"

"I want this."

And he enfolded me in his arms, slowly and gently kissing and caressing and praising my entire body. And, finally, I gave myself to him with my whole being—I felt like a flower unfolding in the sun. This was not mere lust, I swear it. It was the joining of two souls into one and, as Aristotle might have said, the birth of one soul in two bodies. And I will never regret that afternoon, nor forget one moment of it.

Afterwards as we lay entwined with each other, spent, he spoke. "I must leave soon. But Sofia, I want you to remember this: you are my only love and my true bride, my wife for all eternity. I make this a binding vow before God. And I give you this as its token." He removed the chain carrying the king's ring and placed it around my neck. "With this I do plight my troth to belong to you alone and to be true to you always, nor will I forsake you ever again."

I took the ring and kissed it. "And before God I do vow the same to you, nor will I forsake you or hold back anything from you again."

We shared a last brief embrace, dressed, and went downstairs. I doubt three hours had passed, and soon our servants returned, but without Alexander. He had refused to leave the orphanage, claiming he would never desert me. Sir Joscelin and I supped together in haste, as he must leave before dark. When I told him about wanting to move to Constantinople, he paused thoughtfully. "I agree that you should seek out your uncle Vasily. He is your only living relative, and he can offer you protection while I am away. I think you should even stay with him for awhile. But I hope you will return to Antioch to await me as soon as this war ends. It will not be long. How I look forward to our formal church wedding."

Now it was my time to be thoughtful. I had set my heart on leaving Antioch and settling with my uncle before Joscelin had appeared. "I would indeed like to stay with my uncle, and for some time, my love. It would be hard to part with him soon after such a long separation. As long as I can write you and let you know where I am, will that not do? I hate living on this noisy street, but knowing I'd be leaving soon, I didn't want to move yet again. Returning here soon means finding another place to stay, not an easy task. As for our wedding, as far as we are concerned, are we not already married? We will find each other easily enough after the war is over, what with all the traffic between Constantinople and here."

Joscelin smiled and squeezed my hand. "You must do as seems best to you. I'll find you here or there, no matter. Just send me word when you are settled, and if you move, you'll let me know."

I accompanied my beloved to his ship, his young squire marching proudly behind him, where Sir Hugh awaited him. He bowed to me, and we smiled. And I watched my beloved sail away. In another month, I would be in a new world, but I would wait for him forever if necessary.

But it was well after Easter before I was finally able to finish all my business and leave. In that time I did pine for Sir Joscelin, but I also felt wholly embraced in his love. I almost felt him by my side, invisibly holding me up as I went about my day. His kisses lingered on my skin, and my entire being stayed aflame in response.

The reason for the delay was Lady Helene, who returned to Antioch with Fotis and Irene just as I was about to leave—the children were now seasoned sailors! I received a message asking me to call on her and saying that she had letters from Sir Joscelin for me. I found her abed, her belly amazingly swollen. "I am with child again and have been these past eight months, she announced." I looked at her in surprise. I knew of no other children, and how had I missed the signs of her pregnancy? Well, she was heavy, and she always dressed in loose clothing, unlike the Frankish ladies with their gowns laced tightly to reveal tiny waists and full bosoms.

"Why did you say nothing to me before?"

"Twice I lost babies after three months, the first time when I was fourteen, so at first I said nothing to anyone, not even my husband. Now I know with certainty that I will carry this one to full term, but I wanted to come home, away from the possibility of another plague, so Lord Gilles let me go with many warnings to take care of myself. I told him that I would ask you to care for me, and so here I am, at your mercy. Will you stay in Antioch and look in on me until I give birth?"

Of course I could not refuse her.

That evening back at home, I read and reread my beloved's letters, mostly full of endearments and plans for our future. But the last one burned with outrage: he had discovered that it was Lady Ysabel who had betrayed my presence to the Mongol envoys, and he had moved out of the chambers assigned to them. The entire court, now in Limassol with their departure for Egypt imminent and the plague over, had been in an uproar when Lady Ysabel's perfidy had been discovered. The letter ended with, "She is a human plague, and I look forward to war just to be rid of her!"

I was a little shocked at his harshness, but I could not deny that I agreed. Pushing that thought away, I crossed myself and prayed that he be safe not only from plague but from further wounds of war.

Two weeks passed, far too slowly. I was with Lady Helene during the birthing, which was in the hands of a most competent midwife. Despite her earlier failures, Helene was built for having babies, and after several hours of gasps and shrieks, terrifying to us both, she was delivered of a red, screaming, angry boy. I had never seen a woman so tired and so happy.

"He will make a fine lord and knight someday," she rejoiced, all misery forgotten. "I will name him after his father." She held the tiny screaming creature briefly before handing him to his wet nurse and pulling me close to whisper in my ear. "The nurse looks to be a good woman, does she not? Her build and temper are like mine. I would not want her milk to make the baby take on the wrong character." I was surprised, even thought Helene might be a bit delirious, but I reassured her about the woman.

I spent another week with my friend, but with growing impatience. It seemed as though everyone but me was either pregnant or giving birth to sons. Besides, I had begun to waken each day feeling unwell and wanted to be away as soon as possible in case some illness was tainting Antioch's air. So I finally bade her farewell, with many promises to write and even to visit Antioch sometimes. All had been in readiness for so long that my servants and I were soon aboard a ship that would take us straight to Constantinople. I was carrying a last precious letter that had just arrived from Sir Joscelin, full of news both happy and sad. I reread it as the oarsmen put their backs into rowing the galley out to sea, where its sails would soon unfurl and billow into life:

Dearest,

The manifest failure of this marriage is apparent to all, and King Louis has granted me permission to seek an annulment on the grounds of consanguinity. He considers it a great blessing that I never consummated the marriage, which would have been a further sin. Lady Ysabel and I are related in the third degree, something he had not realized. Otherwise we might have had to wait for years for an annulment, so this is a great boon for us all, even for Ysabel, who has announced she will take the veil. My king's great-grandfather Louis VII divorced his wife Eleanor of Aquitaine on these same grounds, she being related to him in the third degree, but truth be told, we nobles are all so intermarried that our bloodlines are hopelessly entangled. So in a few weeks I will be a free man.

Alas that there will be no time for me to take you to church before I leave, but we expect an easy victory and I will be by your side soon, never again to be parted. I regret this so much, as King Louis would have allowed you to come with me as my wife had there been time to arrange everything.

And I have sorry news. Queen Stephanie is dead, carried away by the same plague that swept the camps, we think. King Henri mourns her most pitifully, but she is in God's hands now. She was never strong, and I hear that she was glad to leave this life and passed away peacefully ...

The letter had ended with many endearments and was accompanied by the gift of a silver ring small enough for my finger, a symbol of our betrothal. The day it had arrived had been a strange day for me: already preparing to leave, happy for his news about us, equally saddened by the news about the good queen. I had shed tears and gone to the nearest church to light candles in her memory. Now I shed a few more.

And then I turned my mind, if not my heart, toward my new life. I was finally on my way to Constantinople, my beacon for so many years, while my beloved was to sail in the opposite direction. I would devote every day to prayers for his safe return to me. And I would amass such a dowry that not even King Louis could object to me anymore—perhaps I would even send agents to this Occitaine to find land I could purchase, if that was so important to these Franks.

I took Bardas, Leo, Banjuu, Marguerite, and Alexander with me. The boy had pled with me to take him, so I did, and to this day I am glad for it. The journey took but a couple of weeks, with no storm in sight, no pirates, and easy sailing among lovely islands. Our convoy sometimes stopped at them overnight, which allowed us to disembark and walk along white sandy beaches. I had been looking forward to the clean air—I had been so certain it was the dirty city that was making me feel a little sick every morning, so it was both shocking and astonishing that I, who had always prided myself on my lack of seasickness, felt more and more ill. Toward the end of the journey, I actually had to vomit overboard several times, to the delight of the captain and crew. And how my breasts hurt!

So I was doubly glad when the lookout shouted that the walls of Constantinople were in sight. We all crowded to the rails of our little ship, eager to see the Mother of All Cities. It began as a thin line of white that slowly resolved itself into the tallest walls and battlements I had ever seen. White and banded with red brick, and rising up almost directly from the water in many places, they were several stories high and apparently encircled the entire city, grim and beautiful, challenging all invaders to crash and dissolve upon their mighty sides like the sea's waves on rock. I could not imagine how anyone had ever gotten past them or how we were to land. A lighthouse rose over the westernmost side of the walls, where they began to curve northwest, and I noted a few small bays where small boats might come ashore.

But we continued northeast. At one point the captain told us passengers to look to the left, where the enormous domes of a mighty church soared so far above the line of the walls that it dwarfed them: Hagia Sofia herself! Many of us crossed ourselves, for this was a most ancient and holy cathedral. Further along we glimpsed a high hill where a cluster of buildings stood, surrounded by a wall.

On and on we sailed past those endless astounding walls, which curved as if around a giant toe into a great water passage, before we dropped anchor in a little bay. After the captain had shown his papers and paid either a tax or a bribe, we were allowed to come ashore and pass through a formidable set of heavily guarded gates. I had thought that Antioch would seem like a backwater by comparison, but there were surprisingly few people on the streets.

After some searching, Bardas and Leo found porters to carry my belongings and lead us to my uncle's house, and they hired a litter for me and the girls. But this litter allowed me to see everything, for while it was canopied, its sides were open! At first I felt as though I had reentered a nearly-empty Antioch built on a grander scale. We did pass through a few markets frequented by men and women of every age, shape, color and dress. Wealthy Franks and their armed attendants brushed the shoulders of equally wealthy Greeks and their attendants, all of them on guard for pickpockets and other scoundrels. How I could tell them apart I did not know: perhaps the swagger of the Franks or the greater elegance of the Greeks.

Once a tall, gray-haired man with the face of a young angel passed me, limbs strangely elongated and with the gait of a woman. He was accompanied by the oddest assortment of men, all well-dressed, armed, yet oddly womanish. He caught my stare and smiled wryly back. A pair of ladies, heavily painted—or were they whores?—swept by him with their armed retinues; peasants pushed carts heaped with skinned lambs or colorful produce; beggars cried out their misery from street corners while displaying great sores, empty eye sockets, or missing limbs.

But though the thoroughfare we followed was fairly well-kept, I could see down side streets where garbage and empty shells of houses stood; two rats boldly raced along one street; two thin dogs and a cat followed close behind. One district had burned to the ground and never been rebuilt; other areas seemed old, shabby, and thinly populated.

We passed through a better neighborhood where some buildings stood over three stories high, with gated windowless walls on the ground floor and windows only on the ones above, each arched and holding little round panes of glass embedded in stucco. Their iron-railed, bulging-bellied balconies overhung the streets. Most houses were square-fronted with iron doors, some clearly of great age and much-patched, others of recent and indifferent build. A few were large, well kept villas with high walls and studded iron doors, heavily guarded. We passed an empty, half-burned chapel that seemed out of place with the fine villas, and then we crossed a square with a fountain in its midst. Around its base lay the shattered remains of some huge statue that might have dated back to ancient times. Our litter bearers simply flowed around the mess as if around rocks in a stream.

How long ago had those so-called Christian knights taken and wantonly sacked Constantinople? It must be forty-five years, yet still signs remained of their three days of greedy, bloody, mad mayhem, and there was almost no sign of rebuilding. And now, ironically, I was betrothed to a descendant of those misguided warriors.

Finally we turned into a wealthy quarter composed of thick-walled two- and three-storied houses, all fine and all heavily guarded. The porters led us up to the iron-clad gates of one of the largest of these, where two guards stood up from their posts to stare at us curiously. One of them turned and disappeared inside. Having dismissed our guides and litter bearers after further haggling over payment, Bardas proudly escorted me to the gates.

As the second guard swung open the gates, he bowed low in the old way I remembered and said in Rus', "We have been awaiting you these many weeks, Lady Sofia." My own language, here, brought tears to my eyes.

"And long have I awaited this moment."

Beyond him was a courtyard compound that brought to mind Selim's home, but smaller. Stables and outbuildings lay along the outer wall, screened by trees. A broad, short path led straight to a house with a heavily carved door. A richly dressed, heavy set man with fading red hair was hastening toward me. "Uncle Vasily?" He nodded and held his arms wide for an embrace.

"Holy Mother, I would know you anywhere, my dear. You have fulfilled the promise of beauty you made as a child: you look just like your mother!"

We walked slowly across the yard to the door opposite the gate, and I discovered that my impression was right. The house was built around a lovely, mosaic-floored courtyard that contained pots of sweet-scented roses and a young olive tree. It looked so much like the villas of Antioch or even, sadly, Selim's beautiful lost gardens. Awaiting us was a thin woman of perhaps thirty with dark circles under her eyes. She was dressed in a fashion I had not seen before: the sleeves of her wine-colored gown almost reached the ground, while the filmiest of veils almost floated above her. Although not a beauty, she had a strong nose, finely arched brows, and an elegant way of holding herself. She wore a polite smile, but her sharp eyes were critically surveying our little group.

"This is my wife, the Lady Caterina. And here come our children, Antonio, Nicolo, Paolo, and Cecilia," as children aged between about ten and three tumbled past her to run, laughing, up to us. The eldest, Antonio, stopped and performed a little bow, and then asked to be presented to his aunt and her friends.

"And is there not a fourth child? You wrote me …"

My uncle put a finger to his lips. "Died at birth," he whispered. "My wife is still recovering."

After leading us inside where Caterina turned and gave me another critical look, Uncle Vasily turned a curious eye on my retinue. "Oh, these are my servants: my loyal Bardas and his brother Leo, my excellent cook; Banjuu is the dark girl and Marguerite is the fair, and they serve me; and Alexander is the first boy I took in and also my faithful servant." My girls and Alexander bowed courteously, ignoring the other children's stares, while Bardas and Leo lowered their heads sheepishly.

"Well," Caterina stepped forward after a moment's hesitation, holding her hands out to me, "we welcome you all. My husband has grieved for many years over his lost family, and it is a miracle to find you here at last."

"A miracle indeed," I agreed, "and one whose outlines I would share with you." She waved me into the main hall, where I was led to a large cushioned chair with a round seat and a back shaped somewhat like a barrel, one of several, which bespoke great wealth and ease. Little Cecilia climbed into my lap as if we had known each other forever. I looked down and smiled at the pink-cheeked child, her blond ringlets carefully curled and her little mouth as sweet as a rosebud. That old yearning arose in my heart: oh, for such a child of my own! Refreshments were offered while my menservants were shown to lodgings in the servants' quarters behind the building. My girls hovered about me, serving me fruit or olives or other dainties, and looking a little suspiciously at the boys and especially at my little girl cousin, who had soon fallen asleep.

Share my story I did, but only the outlines. And Uncle Vasily had much to tell me, too. It took most of the afternoon for us to recount our stories, as one of us would stop for the other. The picture I formed of his marriage, much of it gleaned from what was not said, was of a merchant alliance that had served him well. His wife was of noble Venetian ancestry, hence the children's names, for Uncle Vasily, now known as Basil of Kyiv, had allied himself with Venetian interests.

Venice might once have been a daughter to Constantinople, but, I pieced together, it had been behind its mother's overthrow into the arms of the Franks and now enjoyed exclusive trading privileges with the occupied city. As well, both Venice and Uncle Basil enjoyed a brisk trade with the kingdoms that were the remnants of Byzantium. All had made him a very wealthy man.

I was also able to allay any doubts his wife might have had about my kinship with her husband when he and I recalled early memories of Papa, our country palace, Baba Liubyna, Grand Prince Mikhail of Chernigov, and more. I almost heard her sigh with relief when it became clear that I was also wealthy and that I thought I might use part of my capital for joint ventures with my uncle.

"And when do you marry?" Caterina asked after one of our rare pauses.

"Oh, I am already married," I said, regretting the words as soon as they slipped from my mouth. But our solemn betrothal was as good as a marriage vow and just as binding, and Ysabel might already no longer be Sir Joscelin's wife—and I did have a ring. I slipped the chain off my neck and removed the little silver ring from it. "He will soon leave on King Louis' expedition against the Sultan of Egypt. I was afraid of wearing my ring until I reached the safety of your home."

"And what is that other one?"

"A gift from King Louis of Francia himself, which he gave to my beloved, and which my beloved gave to me in turn."

"Well, it would seem you have some powerful friends. It is good to have a protector."

"Yes," I replied, "that is what both he and Uncle Vasily say," and I looked at my uncle gratefully.

"Uncle Basil," he corrected with a smile.

That night I went to bed in an upstairs room, my own room in the home of my last living Rus' relative, with my girls on pallets at the end of my bed and Alexander outside my door. I felt both sad and grateful, for I had accomplished a dream held for so many years, yet so much had been lost in the meantime. And then I thought of Sir Joscelin, soon to join me, and the sadness fled. I fell asleep with his image before me, his love warming my heart.

Alas, the next day I awoke feeling deathly ill again. Marguerite hastily brought me a basin, and I vomited until I was wrung out. Meanwhile, Banjuu, who spoke little Greek, had fled to find help. Lady Caterina soon appeared looking most alarmed, with Uncle Vasily right behind her look-ing concerned.

"Go away, Basil. This is a woman's matter. What is it, Sofia? You are so pale. I have already sent for my physician, but meanwhile you must go straight back to bed. Oh dear, there are so many terrible ailments one can catch when traveling! We must find a cure for you as soon as may be. It would be the worst were we to lose you almost as soon as we found you!"

She sat by my bedside and stroked my forehead, called for clean water and a cloth, and wiped my face while we waited for the physician to arrive. How long it had been since anyone had acted as a mother to me. At one point I took her hand in both of mine and thanked her, tears in my eyes, and she smiled back in the kindest way.

The physician reminded me a little of Ben Hasan, as gentle as the Jew had been and as well-versed in medical matters. He too felt my pulse, took a sample of my urine, and looked at my tongue. "How long ago did your last menses occur?" he finally asked.

"Heavens, perhaps three months ago? It has never been regular, and I never think much about it."

"And when did your husband and you last lie with each other?"

Until that moment, I had not understood where his questions were leading. I turned fiery red. "About seven weeks ago."

"Well, I think you are carrying his child. I will confirm my opinion in a week or so, but already I see the glow of the pregnant woman."

I lay back, stunned, yet glad I had uttered that little falsehood about marriage. And thus began my journey across a sea of lies.

Look for volume three of The Tiger and the Dove:

CONSOLAMENTUM

A sea of lies. I was soon awash in them, beginning with my own, and not only to my uncle and aunt but to myself. When Caterina's physician first told me he thought I was carrying a child, I was startled but not convinced. I had always believed I was barren. But when after a week he had confirmed the truth, I was stunned at first and then gladder than ever that I had not told the strict truth.

Once I had accustomed myself to this strange turn of events, I was surprised at how elated I felt: I was carrying my beloved's child! Nor did I feel I had done anything wrong in lying with Sir Joscelin. According to what I had gleaned from the Frankish court ladies on Cyprus, a betrothal as lengthy and public as ours should have been as sacred and binding as a marriage. I simply wished away the fact that I did not know yet whether his Church marriage had been annulled. After all, I told myself, it could not count anyway since it had never been consummated. Still, while I felt I had not strayed too far in saying that I was already wed, the untruth hung between me and my new family.

At first I was too sick each morning and too sleepy during the day to care much about anything anyway, but when after a few weeks I was feeling better, I realized that things were somehow not right. Certainly Caterina was kind to me and most attentive to my health, and Uncle Basil, as I was learning to call him, was concerned and affectionate on the rare times he was home. I wrote several letters to my beloved, which my uncle promised to send to Cyprus with a reliable captain.

And once I felt better, I was so enjoying getting to know my niece and nephews that I did not notice that Basil and Caterina seemed in no hurry to take me around Constantinople or even to make my presence known to anyone else. I saw not a soul beyond the physician and my servants, and my world was as bounded by the four walls of their villa as it had been in Selim's andarun or the Nizari and Hospitaller castles. I could only hope that with better health, everything would change and I would be free to explore Constantinople and, after my visit, to return to my own home to await the return of my beloved Sir Joscelin.

Then my cook, Leo, who had been preparing special delicacies and sending them to me by way of my faithful young servant Alexander, disappeared. As I was feeling better, I thought nothing of it. However, when I asked burly Bardas how his brother was doing, he looked at me a little strangely. "He is doing well now. He is employed at an inn in the city."

"He left my service? Why? And why do you say 'now'?" I asked.

"She," he tilted his head toward an imaginary Lady Caterina, "turned him out, said the household didn't need two cooks, that he would have no trouble finding work elsewhere. Lucky he had saved a little working for you, because it wasn't easy at all. This is a city of ghosts, and he was finally forced to find work under Franks at a pittance. I wondered if you knew, Lady, but you were so unwell that I could not bother you. But we both are furious. She is not our mistress; you are! And so I told her when she tried to dismiss me at the same time. But Leo left anyway. He was too insulted to stay—he said he's a better cook than hers is and if she can't tell the difference between an artist and a peasant, he won't waste his breath arguing."

I was distressed, of course, but I supposed Caterina's logic made sense—after all, when would she have tasted Leo's superior fare, and why keep two cooks? And with me so ill, she might have decided to act on my behalf and then forgotten to tell me. So as her guest and feeling beholden to her and my uncle, I made no protest to her. I did send Leo a couple of old silver coins of original Byzantine mint—Latin coins being terribly debased—and a message that I hoped he would return to me when I set up my own household. And then I tried not to resent Caterina's interference.

Until the day she slapped my servant Banjuu, who came weeping to me. That I could not tolerate!

But when I confronted Caterina, sitting embroidering in the shady courtyard, she smoothed her crimson silk gown and looked up at me with shockingly cold eyes. "She refused to obey me when I ordered her to do a small task for me."

"Well, first of all, she is my servant, not yours, and secondly, she is but a child from a faraway land and is still learning how to serve!"

Caterina's eyes narrowed and she leapt from her seat, her work spilling to the paving stones unheeded. "What monstrous ingratitude! We take you in, nurture you, protect you from your wrongdoings, and this is what I get?" She stormed inside.

Wrongdoings? I could understand her feeling a little piqued about Banjuu, but rage and accusation were not called for. I followed her inside where she was busily straightening her barrel-shaped chairs, which were already in strict order.

"Caterina," I said in my most contrite tone, "I never meant to offend you. But you confuse me utterly. What wrongdoings have I committed that you protect me from?"

"That child you carry is a bastard! And worse, its father is a known se-ducer and liar! We have been at a loss over what to do ever since we found out, for surely you believed this Sir Joscelin's falsehoods or you'd never have lain with him—I can only hope so, at least. But you endangered my entire family's reputation with your heedless conduct. While you were so ill, your uncle Basil took steps to protect you, even established himself as your guardian. But we still have no idea how to untangle you from the web this man wove around you."

By the time she had finished speaking, she had calmed down consider-ably, but her words were hammer blows on my heart. I sat down on one of her chairs to gather my thoughts. When I finally spoke, I could not hide the quaver in my voice. "Where did you hear such things?"

"Basil has many connections in Antioch and beyond. It took only a month to discover the truth from his agent in Cyprus. He had to quell the terrible slanders he heard about you, for he would not believe his dear niece was anyone's concubine—and that is the kindest word he heard used about you! But the more Basil heard, the more alarmed he became. When he told me all this, he first thought to take you to our country estate as soon as you were fit to travel. But I urged him to wait, to put about more enquiries into your holdings and so forth, and to set about protecting you in case your seducer might have seized anything through some trick."

"Good God, these slanders, I assure you, are utterly unjust. Both of us behaved with the greatest restraint for over a year, always considering ourselves betrothed to each other. But then that terrible girl was thrust upon him in marriage, which was a disaster for us all, even for her. Their marriage was never consummated, and Sir Joscelin has probably already completed the process of annulment with the blessings of King Louis himself! He has behaved with complete virtue toward me, and we are truly betrothed, which is as good and binding as marriage. Indeed, we are married in the eyes of God if not the Church.

"And if he lied to me, why give me not one but two rings, one of the utmost value to him? I am certain the evil rumors you heard about him stem from the death of his first wife, for which he utterly blames himself, and from naught else. He has been paying for that terrible death ever since. He even went to the Holy Land hoping to die in battle, a death I am so glad our Merciful Lord refused him!"

Caterina looked at me as if I had grown another head. "You are sadly mistaken, Sofia. It was bad enough at first when I learned of your previous marriage. No one who has been widowed should remarry—and you already told us you were widowed—but I thought this last marriage had already taken place and that there was no more to be said about it!" I paled, afraid of what would come next. Why had I ever tried to cover my tracks by mentioning that?

I had not even told the exact truth about the so-called marriage, just that I'd been married to a merchant who had died on our journey west. They'd have been far more horrified had they known I had married not one but two Muslims, Selim and then his son Kerim after Selim was murdered. Ironically, both marriages had been temporary, which took advantage of a custom among the Shi'a and was merely a way for me to belong to Selim's family and then to escape Alamut with Kerim. Neither had been consummated, though a little guilt flitted through my heart. Had Kerim not been murdered, too, I might have relented one day and lain with him. I had been celibate for so long and was so ruined already that the sin of it would not have stopped me.

Caterina was continuing relentlessly, "But worse, in the eyes of God you committed fornication and this Sir Joscelin committed adultery, no matter what lies he told you about betrothal. And only confession and penance will wipe out that stain on your soul! I will send my confessor to you; that at least I can do for you.

"But now I agree with your uncle that it would be best for you—and your precious servants—to remove to our country villa. There you can bring your bastard into the world and then give it away in secret. After that, out of respect for my husband—do not think I feel the same for you, but you are family—I will bring you back into society and even find you a real husband if you wish. Not that I would force anyone upon you, of course." She smiled in what I supposed was meant to be a friendly way.

I was reeling by the time she had finished, and so upset that I had overlooked a vital fact that she had let drop. Trying to keep the rage out of my voice I merely replied, "If my presence is a hindrance to your welfare, I will go at once. I am wealthy enough to find my own way, and I have business interests that make me independent. And I can find my own confessor."

She smiled again, this time with no pretense of friendliness. "You are under your uncle's guardianship now, Sofia. You will have to go through him for monies or permission to go anywhere. And neither of us wants you to leave. You are, as I have already said, family." She did not wait to hear my response, as her little daughter Cecelia ran into the room at that moment, pursued by her nursemaid and crying that her brother Paolo had hit her. Without a word, Caterina turned and left.

I stayed, though, my mind a blank, my heart beating out of my chest, and every fiber of my body screaming protest. After many deep breaths to calm myself, I faced the reality of my new life. I had walked into yet another trap, this time of my own making. I disbelieved anything Caterina said about Sir Joscelin. I knew his heart. But I had put myself at the mercy of people I thought I could trust before I even knew them.

Now I saw how I had misinterpreted my welcome. Caterina's solicitude for my welfare had hidden a mercenary mind. Worse, either my uncle was under her influence or was just as mercenary. And I had been trying for a good ten years to reach these very people! It made me sick that all those years as a slave among the Mongols and then as a virtual prisoner in haram and in Alamut, my one happy goal had been to find my uncle, the last of my family and my last link with my beloved Kyiv, and to make a happy home with him.

Rage and disappointment gave way to dark fears: did they hope I would die in childbirth, or having removed me to the country, would they keep me prisoner while using my wealth to their own ends? There was only one way to learn my uncle's intentions, to confront him and read his signals, a skill I had learned as a translator among the Mongols and had happily abandoned after reaching what I thought was safety. That was another mistake I would never make again!

I needn't have sought an occasion to speak with him. That evening, after a silent supper—neither Caterina nor I would look at each other— Uncle Basil said, "Sofia, it is time that you and I talk alone." A significant look passed between him and his wife.

"Indeed yes!" I glared at Caterina, but she was carefully avoiding my gaze.

He led me to his room of business, crowded with a lectern desk and stool, a barrel-backed chair across from it, and cupboards and shelves stacked with documents.

"Please sit here, my dear," he began, waving me to the chair and placing a cushion at my back, all most courteously. Instead of seating himself, he stood before me, a troubled expression on his face. "I understand you and Caterina had a misunderstanding today."

"You might call it that, but I think my understanding was quite clarified!"

He held out his hands in a mollifying gesture. "My lady wife can have quite a spicy temper sometimes, and I fear you tasted it today. She is ashamed now and only wishes for your forgiveness."

"Why does she not come to me herself?"

"Alas, her other besetting sin is pride. She wants me to prepare the way for her."

"Well, I am happy to accept her regrets once she offers them, but that does not touch on the matters we quarreled over, and those will not go away!" This time, it was I who held up my hands to show I would stand for no interruption—a trick I had learned from more than one man.

"First of all, and I may have been wrong to do so, I lay with my beloved on the clear understanding that our betrothal, of much longer standing than his unconsummated marriage, was as good as a real marriage. I know he believed it so, for he called on God Himself as his witness.

"Sir Joscelin may have committed many sins in Occitaine, but he confessed all those twice over long ago—both to his priest and to me—and he has done penance to atone for them! He has led a chaste life for many years, and he went to the Holy Land to die for God in reparation for his sins. He never meant to hurt me. And when he returns, God willing, we will be church-married straightaway. It is most likely that he is no longer even married, since before he left on crusade he and his so-called wife sought an annulment with the full consent of King Louis! So let me be clear: in my eyes, we are already wed, and if that offends Caterina, there is nothing for it.

"Furthermore, I intend to write my will now, and I will leave all my wealth to him and our child; the only other provisions will be for my servants and my orphans. I want to make that clear because Caterina let slip that you think you have taken on a guardianship over both me and my possessions that I neither asked for nor want! I am of age, and I have been handling my own affairs for years.

"Besides, I am beyond angry. If there is anything I signed when ill, which I do not remember doing, I will seek court redress for it. I do not know the laws here in Constantinople, but I have powerful friends in Antioch who will support me in my suit! Think well before you answer, Uncle, for I am a woman of the world and a good businesswoman, too!"

A storm of successive emotions had swept across Uncle Basil's face: dismay, outrage, and even, briefly, shame. "It seems not so to me, Sofia, for you were taken in by a sly fox. This whoreson's by-blows are scattered across the Holy Land. Ours is too small a world for gossip not to spread, and whatever lies he told you, I ferreted out the truth soon enough. I am only protecting your interests and those of your unborn child, for I feared some such folly on your part. You may go to court if you wish, but my authority comes straight from the king himself; and until you are safely wed to a proper husband, I am your guardian whether you will it or no!"

"King Louis would never do that!"

"I speak of my king, King Baldwin of Constantinople. Here is his document—" He started sorting through a sheaf of official-looking papers as if to show me, but I stayed to hear no more. Fleeing to my room, I found Alexander loitering about laughing with the girls, tossing his dark hair back and looking somehow much older. My heart almost stopped with love for my three dearest orphans, all so happy together: him, Banjuu, so dark-skinned and lovely; and fair Marguerite, whose hair was still as pale as wheat. Who knew what fate awaited us all? Straightaway, I orderedBan-juu and Marguerite to start packing. "And Alexander, go to Bardas and tell him we leave for Antioch straightaway, then return here to help us."

Alexander, looking worried for a change, hurried off.

"What has happened, Lady?" Banjuu answered.

"I will tell you later. Do you still have the little chest I entrusted to you, the one with the gold coins?"

"Yes, I kept it safe and secret for you."

"Good, we'll need it! I think my uncle has robbed me. At the very least he may control a good deal of my wealth, and we must escape here and return to Antioch before he does more damage." At that, tears of rage and disappointment insisted on flowing, though I wiped my eyes and set to with a will. I was weary of tears.

It was not until we had finished packing everything that I stopped to think how I would escape. "Girls, they must not see that I plan to leave late tonight. In case someone with prying eyes comes by, store everything under my bed and arrange things to look as they did before. Marguerite, we may have to climb down over the balcony from the outside window. Go to Bardas and tell him that he and Alexander must await us outside. And why hasn't Alexander returned, anyway?"

We found out when she tried to open the door: it was locked from the outside. And when I looked out the window, a guard stood below. Tears gave way to simple rage. I had had enough of being kept in thrall like some slave!

Rebecca Hazell is both author and artist. Her award-winning non-fiction books for older children have been purchased for distribution by MercyCorps and Scholastic Inc., and been published in Greek and Korean. She is passionate about history, both for its romance and for its value in understanding how we are always connected to and driven by the past—unless we understand it! She has also written educational materials for high schools on such far-flung topics as Islam and Russian serfdom, produced award winning needlepoint designs, created science kits for children, and was a tailor and dressmaker/clothing designer in her youth. As well, she is a senior teacher in Shambhala International, a worldwide Buddhist organization. She has been married for over 40 years and has two grown children. For more information on Rebecca and her other works, both literary and artistic, please visit her website: www.rebeccahazell.com.

Manufactured by Amazon.ca
Acheson, AB

16086134R00224